THE
TOTEMS
OF
ABYDOS

THE TOTEMS OF ABYDOS

JOHN NORMAN

OPEN ROAD

INTEGRATED MEDIA

NEW YORK

978-1-4976-4878-4

This edition published in 2014 by Open Road Integrated Media, Inc.
345 Hudson Street
New York, NY 10014
www.openroadmedia.com

THE
TOTEMS
OF
ABYDOS

CHAPTER 1

It was near sunset when Horemheb left the village. He had
with him his staff, a small sack of meal, and the parchment,
from the raised impressions of which, beneath his fingers,
might be traced the sayings. The brethren took look little
note of him as this journey was not unprecedented with
Horemheb, even at this fearful time of day.

In a short time, Horemheb had found the string stretched
amongst the trees, it tied from tree to tree, at a height
convenient to his hand, it marking the trail he would follow.
He touched the string and, sometimes, when there would
be a stirring in the brush near him, the sound of a body
moving in the darkness through the undergrowth, the
sound of a branch moving overhead, perhaps tossed by the
wind, perhaps depressed by the tread of a small foot, he
would stop and clutch the string. It was the string, it seemed,
that protected him from the night of the world, a tiny string
tied between trees in the darkness, but in Horemheb there
was a darkness within a darkness, and within the interior
darkness he had groped for a string, but had never found it.

Horemheb continued his journey, not leaving hold of the
string.

He did not fear that he would be followed, nor did it
much matter to him if he might be. Rather we may suppose
he would have pitied any who might have been tempted to
follow him, and, indeed, had he been younger, he might

have remonstrated with them, not for his sake, for he was lonely, but for theirs, to return to the safety of their walls, to the hearths of the village. When he was younger he had been tempted to call others after him, of course, not only for the comfort which they might afford, or, more selfishly, for the dangers they might share, but in the hope that they, if not he, might discover what lay at the end of the string, that they might come with him to the place where the sting ended, where the rocks were, and the platform, and that they might tell him what they had seen.

It was no secret to the brethren, of course, as it seemed to be to Horemheb, what lay at the end of the string. Many was the time in the bright daylight hours, when all is warm and cheerful, that they had followed out its length, and come to the place where the platform was, a place not much different from other places, and seen how empty it was, and how meaningless, with only the wind there, and stirring leaves, and small, soft sounds from amongst the rocks.

To be sure, the brethren would never follow Horemheb from the village at night. In the darkness were many shapes, and not all benign, and, often enough, of a moist, dewy morning, had the evidence been clear that even near the string had prowled stealthy, hungry ones, the sort which were reluctant to traverse the cleared area outside the fence.

Horemheb stopped.

There had been a stirring near him, a shifting, like a sudden swirl or eddy in dry water, and then a rippling of branches. It was not likely to have been a stealthy one. Of such a one Horemheb, nor even the younger and more acute of perception, would have been likely to detect the approach, until its closure, which would have taken but the fraction of an instant, but scarcely, it was said, half the beat of a heart. It was said one would not even have time to be afraid. That was supposed to be comforting, one supposed. But that thought frightened Horemheb, not having time enough to be afraid. He would not have liked that. It was better to have had time enough to be afraid, for that, too, was, like the string, something to understand, and grasp. But

Horemheb took comfort in the thought that even within the grasp of a stealthy one, helpless within its embrace, one would surely have an instant, or part of an instant, of understanding, if only so fleeting an understanding, of what had occurred. That was important. Horemheb would want to understand. Surely that would be most terrible, not to know, not to understand, what had occurred. How terrible to perish like a flower or a blade of grass, to have been so beautiful, and so alive, and not to have known it, and then to perish, unaware even of the oblivions between whose margins it throve. That was what Horemheb most feared, not knowing. Surely he feared that more than death. Otherwise he would not have made the journey. Indeed, life seemed a small enough, and a reasonable enough, gift to exchange for knowing, or understanding, or truth. To be sure, you must not misunderstand me here. Horemheb was not a vainglorious man, nor even a very proud one. He did wish to understand, but not really a great deal, and only in a small, modest way, and in a way suitable to himself, to his own lights and limitations. That would have been enough. It need not be significant from your point of view, for example. He just wanted, you see, to catch a glimpse of a part of the world, so to speak. To come to grips, truly, so to speak, with a particle of rock, a pebble, a grain of sand, a drop of water, perhaps a branch, such small things, that would have been enough for him. He did not seek to penetrate the mysteries of matter, say, that there should be such, or those of stars, and time, and worlds, and space. Nothing significant, you understand. Indeed, his ambitions did not even extend, really, to the pebble or the branch, so to speak. Rather he wanted to understand the brethren, and himself, and, if it must be anticipated, the beast, that which he knew, and the others did not, lay at the end of the string. That was the quest of his life, its purpose. Indeed, that was the meaning of the journey. Too, it was not that Horemheb had really chosen to make the journey. People seldom choose to make such journeys. Rather such journeys choose them. In a sense, one might even think of him as having been condemned to the journey, or destined for it, much as a stone is condemned to be subject to the law of gravity, or destined to abide beneath its sway, much as fire, without its choice or collusion, is condemned to be beautiful and savage, and water the medium of life's nutrients and yet, at the same time, the most frightening of all substances, in whose suffocating depths it would be, for such as Horemheb, impossible. And so Horemheb left the village, and at night. He did not begrudge the others the walls, or the fence, or the cordiality and warmth of their hearths. Sometimes he envied them. But the journey had called him. He had been chosen by the journey. Perhaps that was why the stealthy ones had not claimed him, why he, of all the brethren, seemed invulnerable to their clasp. Or rather, perhaps more sensibly, it was because they knew he clung to the string, and that the string led to the platform. The stealthy ones, too, had their fears, and they were seldom found in the vicinity of the platform. They feared to go there. The string led to the platform. Perhaps that was why Horemheb had, for many times, over many tens of revolutions of his world, returned from this journey. Surely the brethren did not, as a folk, possess such invulnerability, such immunity from the stealthy ones. And indeed, sometimes the brethren, about their hearths, puzzled, and speculated, and wondered how it was that the stealthy ones did not claim him, as they had others, sometimes even in the brightness of the sun, in the heat of the day, in the summer, not only in the winters when the lantern fruits were shriveled on the frozen branches and their prints could be found in the snow, about the edges of the clearing, sometimes near the fence itself. The brethren knew about the string, but they did not understand it. Too, they knew about the platform, but they did not understand it, either. To understand the platform one must have, like Horemheb, come there at night. Then they might have understood.

Midway in his journey, near the string, Horemheb stopped and put his staff to one side. He sat down there, on the ground, prey to what might choose to have him, what he could not, in any case, have evaded, not crouching like the younger ones, ready to dart at the snapping of a twig, the crinkling of a leaf, to safety. He sat there, in the weariness and patience of age, too old for the journey and himself knowing it, yet having begun it once again, now not really with that peculiar resignation appropriate enough, one supposes, for those who carry the weight of many winters in their bones, for there was little that was resigned in the bright, ancient spirit of Horemheb, but with a carelessness of, or insensitivity to, what might terrify or threaten another, sitting there with the insouciance of those who feel they have little left to protect of life, and little left to lose, rich only in rags and dust, and questions, and dreams, content in the security of this poverty, this unenvied affluence, vulnerable to the forest, to the darkness, and what might lurk within it, and partook of some of the meal from his small sack, no more than a handful, wetting it with his own saliva and, grain by grain, swallowing it. He did not eat all the grain, however, as it was in its way a fruit of the field, and was to be placed on the platform.

As he fed, and afterwards rested, Horemheb pondered again on a not uncommon theme of his meditations, the brethren. He was not, in his simple way, an untutored man, or unlearned man. Surely in his youth, long before he had found the platform, he had been no stranger to the parchments, those whose surfaces needed no irregularities to communicate their wisdom, or its counterfeits. Too, he had six times traveled from the village, not merely to the platform whence he had often gone, but on the legs of youth, even to the place, far off, beyond the forest, beyond the darkness, where there were steel ships that sailed vertically into the skies, with smoke and fire, then seeming to fade away, like stars in the morning. He had even in that place, far, far away, encountered those who were not of the brethren, men who came and went in such ships, and tended them, and fed them, rough, stormy folk, giants of foul aspect and voice who stank and thundered when they spoke. But even they would not come back into the forests, not even following

the clearly marked trails of white stones, which glowed in
the darkness, retaining the light of day almost until dawn.
There was little in the forests that interested them, or
intrigued them. And there were the stealthy ones, of diverse
genera, whom they feared, even as the brethren themselves
did. Horemheb thought that of interest, that the giants
should fear the stealthy ones, in spite of their loud voices,
and their bragging, in spite of their lights, and their wires,
and the tubes which seemed to have envesseled lightning
itself. Sometimes they turned these tubes on one another and
Horemheb had once seen this, that the light, with its swift
blaze dispelling darkness, had left behind little but ashes and
body fluid, bubbling and smoking. Horemheb had fled from
the place of the giants, and had returned to the forest. The
brethren need not fear the giants in the forest. In the forest
the giants, too, were small, and were afraid. The brethren
did not have such tubes. They had little, and by their own
choice, but sharpened sticks, and weighted cords, and the
scarps, the tiny gouges, small, sharp, and hooklike, which
served so many purposes, even, on one's hands and knees,
the cultivation of the soil. How was it then that the brethren
had survived in the forest, Horemheb wondered. They had, it
seemed, for generations and generations, Horemheb did not
believe anyone knew how many, eked out their living in this
difficult place, petitioning year in and year out the selfish,
begrudging soil for an uncertain, meager harvest, and all
the time there were, in the forest, and outside the fence, the
stealthy, hungry ones. Horemheb knew of extinction and
was of such a mind that he did not decide that his people, any
more than thousands of other forms of life, or, indeed, more
than many a larger, stronger, handsomer, finer people, was
somehow immune to its twilight and unending night. But
they had survived. They had continued to live in the forest.
Perhaps some of the brethren understood this. Horemheb
thought that might be possible. He himself, known from
youth as different, had never been permitted in the secret
places, or taught the oldest lore. Some of the brethren, and,
indeed, many far younger than Horemheb, might know

these things, but they had never told him, or many others. Gradually over the years Horemheb had begun to sense certain things, not really to understand them, but to sense them, to tiptoe, as it were, on the edge of understanding them. He did know that the most profound truths are sometimes those most seldom spoken, and indeed often those whose utterance was, as though by some secret compact, forbidden, even denied with vehemence. Indeed, those who knew them might be the first to claim ignorance, or to deny them. This undoubtedly gave them power, great power, to know these truths, and act in terms of them, and yet to pretend they did not exist, or must not be believed. But sometimes truths are embodied in traditions, in customs, in ways of life. They are silent, so to speak, but real in the lives of a people. Traditions carry them on, invisibly. Perhaps it was so with the brethren. Perhaps, like unseen companions, with them truths walked on soft feet. These could be like shadows always behind them, never seen, or like furies, come from some remote hell, or angels with swords, guarding gateways through which they could never return. Or they might be memories too deep for recollection, of deeds antedating by eons not only the most ancient of annals, and not only the most ancient fragments of the histories drawn on rocks, and not only the most ancient fragments of the winter songs, taught at hearths since the capture of fire, but speech itself. Yet these memories too deep for recollection, these thoughts too deep for thinking, in any normal sense, which may have antedated the invention of the meaningful sound, might remain active in the people, forming them, giving them shape. Horemheb considered how such a memory, or traces indicative of such a memory, recreating its surrogate and image, its fidelity, or indeed its recurrent actuality, through genetic selections, through innatenesses, might be transmitted from generation to generation. Such a thing would be possible Horemheb knew, but, if it were actual, surely profound and subtle. Let us suppose that a natural memory consists of, or is caused by, or is invariably correlated with, a certain alignment of fibers, or certain patterns of electrochemical activity, or interactions, or certain states of the brain, or with some such complex and mysterious thing, or arrangements, or patterns. If these same alignments, so to speak, can occur in more than one way then it seems one might speak of a memory, or of something perhaps even deeper, which lay beneath both memory and invention. In this sense one might, in a sense, without recourse to a putative preexistence of individuals, or the transmigrations of souls, or such, be said, even in a frail, doomed, mortal frame, to remember events, and deeds, and thoughts which antedated one's birth, deeds which, so to speak, might have occurred thousands of years before the birth of one's oldest known ancestors. To be sure, if one wishes to restrict discourse narrowly, one might say that such is impossible, because of the meanings assigned words, to remember what one has never personally experienced, but that is, in a sense, to beg a question. For example, it would be easy enough to use words differently, so that one might, in a new sense, be said to remember what one has never personally experienced except, of course, in its memory. But more importantly, if the alignments, so to speak, however produced, whether by some genetic transmission, perhaps eccentric to a species, perhaps favored by selection, or by the subtle, unspoken transmissions within generations, through simple but subtle enculturations, by those ways in which we learn, and are unaware that we have learned, what most deeply shapes us and moves us, are indistinguishable from those of the natural memory, it seems one might speak of "memory." But these thoughts, Horemheb told himself, are absurd, and what have they to do with the journey, and the string, and the platform? But then who knows what are the deepest and most secret motivations of the heart? It is known they cannot be what they are commonly claimed to be, and are frenziedly and hysterically insisted upon, but what are they?

Who, Horemheb wondered, are the brethren? And, too, Horemheb wondered upon himself, for he did not know who he was, but only that he, too, was of the brethren. He had never denied that, and never would. He was of the brethren. Without the brethren, outside of the brethren, he was nothing. But, too, he was different. He wanted to know who they were, and who he was, who was one of them. That was not too much, surely. And so it was in search of knowledge, called by the journey, summoned by it, enticed by it, driven, tormented, and lashed by it, eager to seek and fearing what might be found, that Horemheb had once again left the village at sunset, that he had once again sought the string which would take him to the platform.

Horemheb drew shut the strings on his small sack of meal and, with difficulty, aided by the staff, rose to his feet. He looked up into the moonless sky. On his ancient visage was reflected the dim, yellowish light of the lantern fruit, retaining its recollection of the day's sun, but Horemheb did not see it, of course, as he was blind. He had not always been blind. Once he had been as sharp-sighted, as quick, as any of the brethren. But long ago, so long ago that there were none amongst the brethren alive now who could remember it, he had sought the platform, the first time that he had done so after sunset. At such a time, of course, not even the string had been tied between the trees. Long before that first nocturnal journey Horemheb, of course, had undertaken his travels, sat at the feet of elders, read his parchments, sought others, conducted his researches, and pondered on the puzzles which had, even from his early youth, intrigued him, and then, as his wisdom increased, begun to frighten him. He was already old, and shivering in his hut, when the images, like furtive presences in the night, like rodents in the darkness, had begun to haunt him, had begun, so to speak, to prowl about his ears, and scamper over his old body at night, as though scornful of any longer concealing their presence from one so weak, from one from whom they had nothing to fear. It was difficult to catch these images in the darkness, for they were quick and elusive, but Horemheb thought they were the shadows of truths, not some blazing, triumphant truth that would vindicate the brethren and himself, that would dispel darkness with light and trumpets, with sunlight and processions, but small truths, not really important in the vastness of the universe, truths more like shadows, more like rodents in the darkness. And these truths, if such they were, for he did not care to welcome them as such, hinted at the greater thing behind them, at the darker thing behind them, the thing which was more vast and terrible than they, at the forces in the heart, at the memory. One night Horemheb had awakened and thought that he had screamed a scream, though it must have been a silent scream for it aroused none of the brethren. Something had come to him in his sleep which had terrified him. This was not, he knew, one of the small truths, which spoke of the diminutiveness of the brethren and himself, so tiny in the framework of things, but a truth which was not of the brethren, but was in its way the brethren, much as one might have a truth which was not about the pebble or the branch, but which was, in some mysterious cognitive alchemy, the being of the pebble or the branch, or its explanation, or its code or key, what told what it was and why it was so.

That very night, still shuddering from the dream, drenched with sweat, shivering in his blanket, Horemheb rose up and, heedless of the stealthy ones, hastened to the platform. He had realized that the secret he sought lay not in the bright court of the village, to be found in the light of day, within the fence, but outside the village, beyond those frail palings, through the forest, away from the village, in the darkness. That was the first time he had gone to the platform at night. He had come back alone in the morning from the platform. He had been noticeably different then from what he been the day before. He sat alone in his hut for three days, seeing no one and not eating. On the third day he taken his scarp and gouged out his own eyes. This, as I have indicated, occurred long ago. Indeed, as I have indicated, there are none alive today who remember it, other than Horemheb himself. He did not explain why he had done what he did, nor was he asked. The brethren are a tactful folk and the endemic courtesy which is custom, if not law, with them mitigates against the impropriety of inquiring too deeply into matters which might prove sensitive. They assumed, doubtless, that Horemheb had had his reasons for his act, reasons which must be, in his own mind at least, sufficient for its accomplishment, reasons it might not be wise to inquire into. They did determine that he had gone to the platform at night, however, which is not customary, though it is not unlawful, for the brethren. Perhaps he should not have done that. Who knew what he had seen there? It was conjectured it must have been unpleasant. The brethren were content to let Horemheb bear the weight of this secret, if it were one. Better he than they. Now, of course, all accepted the fact that Horemheb was blind, and old, and foolish. Still he had seen something that they had not seen. But perhaps it was better that it not have been seen.

Horemheb, of course, never told anyone what he had seen. From this one might have supposed that perhaps he had learned the secret, or that he had apprehended the truth, or that he had discovered the memory, or the thing like a memory, which lay like a stone and a fountain within the brethren. But this was not so. If he had learned these things, or recollected them, or whatever, he would not have returned later to the platform. You see, to the contrary, at the platform that night, he had not really learned the secret; he had not there, before the platform, understood the memory, the half-suspected memory, which might not even exist; no, he had not there, at the platform, perceived the truth at last, something which might have redeemed himself and the brethren, which might have made it all worthwhile, or, if not that, at least intelligible; no, no coin was obtained there of inestimable worth, or even one of paltry value, nor even a truth which might in its glory or hideousness have blasted him. Rather it was something else he saw there, something which he had not expected and which frightened him. It was only after he had returned home and thought and thought, and twice dreamed, that he suspected the meaning of what he saw, not that he knew that meaning, or understood it, but only that he suspected it. What he had seen there, he became certain, although it was not in itself the secret, not in itself the truth, or the

memory, was something which nonetheless appertained
to the secret, something which was not the truth or the
memory but which might not be entirely unrelated to the
truth, or to the memory, something which had something to
do with all three, or one, as the case might be, or else it was
something which might, in some terrible way, itself know
the secret, the truth, the memory. After Horemheb had
inflicted such indignity and pain upon himself, he did not
return for revolutions to the platform. Then, one evening,
ten revolutions, and a hundred mournings and festivals,
after he had inflicted his cruel injuries upon himself, that he
might not again see what he saw, that his eyes should never
show him such a thing again, he returned to the platform.
We do not really know why he returned to that fateful place.
Perhaps, in the beginning, he was curious to know if he had
been mistaken on that distant night, if he had really seen
what he thought he had seen, or if it were an illusion of the
senses, or a dream. Perhaps, on the other hand, he was mad
or labored in the grip of some monstrous compulsion. In
any event he had had the string tied by the brethren during
the brightness of the day and then, one evening, when the
sun was sinking behind the trees and the shadows of the
fence were long and jagged on the clearing, and the fruit
of the lantern trees was becoming visible in the gloom, he
returned to the platform. Since that time he had made the
journey several times, many, many times, a great number of
times, taking with him his staff and his small sack of meal.
The string which was now again dried and thin, worn by
the winter and the weather, pelted by the rain, sometimes
sheathed with ice, chilled by snow, swaying beneath the
trees, had been replaced a number of times. But it was, in a
sense, you see, the same string; it was always the same string,
as it always marked the same trail; it always traced the same
journey. It is in that sense it was the same string. It always
led to the platform. Why then did Horemheb return to the
platform? We do not really know. I think it was because
he suspected that in its vicinity was the secret, the memory,
the truth. I think he came back to the platform because he

wanted to know, because even in his age and pain, and his fear, and given the terror of what he suspected, he wanted to know, or perhaps because it was merely he had not yet been satisfied, or because he was insatiably restless, or because he was inveterately curious, that perhaps as a consequence of some ineradicable affliction inherited from some remote unknown ancestry, an ancestry he might in an earlier day have despised or found laughable had it suddenly, from a depth of bushes, peered out at him, or perhaps because he still hoped to unravel the riddles of his distant youth, that youth like an unfinished dream, so lost, yet so constantly present, so far away, yet so near. On the other hand, he may have come back to the platform because he had no choice really, because the journey called him. Perhaps the truth is as simple as that. Let those to whom journeys call speculate on the possibility of that. For myself I do not know, and I do not think others do either. Perhaps he was merely the sort who cannot refrain from digging with sticks into the sores on his own body. That is possible. The species are rare in the universe, but they exist, those which torture themselves.

Now Horemheb continued his journey. Then, after less than one of the twenty-five segments of a rotation, the divisions of a lightness from a lightness, he felt beneath his feet not the softness of the forest trail, the crushed leaves and the dust, that curious mixture of particles wounded to powder by long treading, but the flat stones. It was there that the string ended. With his staff Horemheb tapped ahead of himself, scratching now and then at the stones to determine their setting, and the directions of the cracks between them. It was still night. Had he been able to see them the stars were full and, behind, in the forest, the lantern fruits hung like lamps from the branches of the trees. He supposed the platform looked much the same as always. No one knew its age, but it was known that there had been an innumerable number of platforms before this one, built on this same spot. That was testified to by records as old as those the brethren possessed. No one, at least as far as Horemheb knew, knew why the first one had been built here, or what the point of the platform was.

In a little time, for the area of the flat stones was not really large, the tip of Horemheb's staff, moving gently before him, inquisitive, like something alive, sniffing, groping, alert, an extension of his spirit, an emblem of his quest, touched the first stair. There were three of these, if one counts the level of the dais on which the platform had been erected. Horemheb climbed the steps and, because he conjectured he was early, he sat down, cross-legged, before the platform. The platform itself was not high, once one had ascended to the dais on which it was erected. Horemheb, who was not large, not even amongst the brethren, could have put out his hand, had he been standing, and placed his full palm upon it. But he did not stand before the platform, as he was surely early. Rather he sat there, cross-legged, before the platform, with the sack of meal and his staff beside him, took out the parchments, and, from the irregular surfaces, traced the sayings. He did not fear the stealthy ones in this place, for they did not come here.

After a division of a revolution Horemheb rolled the parchments and tied them shut.

He then rose slowly to his feet. He did not use his staff this time to help him rise. He did hold the sack of meal.

He had heard it ascend to the platform, with one movement, from the back. It had been quiet but Horemheb did not think that it had been concerned to conceal its presence. Rather that was the way it moved.

"Speak," said Horemheb, after a time. "Speak!"

Horemheb knew it was close to him. He knew its presence, especially here, in this place. Sometimes it was so close to him he could have put out its his hand and touched it. Once he had done so, on a rainy night. The fur had been wet and matted. There had been a strong smell upon it.

"You know why I have come," said Horemheb. "Speak."

The thing moved about, twice, turning, on the platform, and bit at its fur, doubtless to rid itself of vermin.

"Speak," said Horemheb.

But the thing did not speak.

Horemheb had read the parchments, but they had been

silent. In his distant youth he had sat before the elders, but they had not told him, if they knew. He had made long journeys, even to the place of smoke and ships, but had not found what he sought. Now, again, he had come to the platform.

"Speak," begged Horemheb.

But Horemheb heard only the wind, and the soft sounds from amongst the rocks.

"I have come through the forest," said Horemheb. "I have braved the darkness. I have stood before the platform. A thousand times I have brought my body and my staff, and my question, to this place, and have not been heeded. A thousand times I have returned to the village empty-handed."

"Speak!" said Horemheb.

But it did not speak.

Horemheb then put the sack of meal on the platform, as his small offering, small in value to many, but a gift of considerable price to Horemheb.

Horemheb then bent down and picked up his staff. He descended from the dais and found the string once more, which he would follow back to the village.

Behind him the beast looked down at the sack of meal between its paws. It was not such stuff that the beast ate.

CHAPTER 2

"So you are at the beginning of your career?" said Emilio Rodriguez.

"Or perhaps at the end of it," smiled Allan Brenner.

"For you are on your way with old Rodriguez to Abydos?" smiled the other.

"Something like that," said Brenner. He was not certain, really, how to address Rodriguez. Should it be as "Mister," as "Professor," as "Doctor"?

"Didn't they teach you grantsmanship?" inquired Rodriguez. "Is this the best you could land?"

"I was assigned," said Brenner.

"To keep an eye on me?"

"I don't think so," said Brenner. He didn't.

"What time is it?" asked Rodriguez.

Brenner smiled. That was an odd question. Did he want a body-time, indexed to some recent port, perhaps one where they had had a layover for bioadjustment; did he want a local time, and if so, indexed to what world, and to what coordinates on what world; would he like a solar time, a sidereal time, or one indexed to the half-life of a specified element, or what? The ship functioned on commercial time, of course, indexed to the prime meridian on Commonworld, a neutral wilderness of little note or interest in the galaxy other than the fact that its imaginary gridwork of coordinates provided more than four thousand worlds with a common frame of reference.

Rodriguez answered his own question. "It's late," he said. That seemed an odd answer to an odd question. "It's late," he repeated. Brenner assumed he meant that he was tired. That was probably what he meant.

"You have kept much to your cabin," said Brenner.

"Surely you have no objection to that," said Rodriguez.

"No," said Brenner. "But if we are to be colleagues—"

"There are strong worlds and weak worlds," said Rodriguez.

"What?" said Brenner.

"We come from a weak world," said Rodriguez.

"You shouldn't smoke those things," said Brenner, "and drink that stuff."

"It will make my heart like the hoof of a four-horned korf," said Rodriguez, perhaps quoting some authority, and this stuff," said he, raising his closed mug, the slurp hole closed, "is a bladder irritant, a disaster to the liver, a poisoner of the bloodstream, and a destroyer of brain cells."

"That is about it," granted Brenner.

Rodriguez sat back in the webbing. He puffed on a roll of Bertinian leaf. It was outlawed on many worlds, but could be obtained, as one might expect, in various black markets, to which the digital purses of various officials owed remarkable economic latencies, available upon the punching of special numbers, putatively not on file with the state.

An odious cloud, like some noxious fog or lethal gas, drifted toward Brenner but never reached him, being caught up in the intake of the filtering system. In one hand, Rodriguez, his large, slovenly frame back in the webbing, grasped the zero-gravity mug, a stein of Velasian Heimat. "I take a modest pride in being a man of many vices." he said.

Brenner wondered why Rodriguez didn't partake of the various lozenges and wafers, the candies, or medications, available on many worlds, and even from the small commissary on the freighter, which provided relatively innocuous intoxicants and controllers, stimulants, euphoriants, anesthetics, depressors, inhibitors and such. But Rodriguez, it seemed, preferred the naivety and violence of more primitive poisons, poisons of a sort which on many worlds had not been known for millennia.

"I have, until now," said Rodriguez, idly, "courted death."

"And it seems you are still at it," said Brenner.

Rodriguez looked up at him.

"With weed and brew," smiled Brenner.

"I have sought her on mountains, and in the depths of gaseous seas, on fields of war stretched between stars, in the bistros of subterranean worlds, amongst thieves and assassins, in jungles and ice deserts where my footstep was the first from the beginning of time."

Brenner was silent.

"Do you know why these things are outlawed?" asked Rodriguez.

"Certainly," said Brenner, "they are poisonous substances."

"Because," said Rodriguez, a little wildly, "they are the counterfeits of life, and that it what is fearful about them.

They are false images which call to mind a reality, a reality which is secret."

"You are drunk," said Brenner.

"In their pernicious way they point to life," said Rodriguez, "like a lie points to the truth."

Brenner was quiet.

"Life, and truth, are illegal, like reality," said Rodriguez. "The small people, the mice, the insects, the flowers, are afraid of them. They do not even recognize the battlefields in their cellars, the jungles beneath their porches."

"No one is small," said Brenner.

"True," said Rodriguez. "All are the same size, by fiat. No one is small, no one is weak, no one is stupid, no one is petty, no one is futile, no one is failed, all are marvelous, and wonderful, and precious and, a statistical anomaly, all are the same size, except that the smallest are the best, the noblest, and the largest."

"Do not be bitter," said Brenner. Difficulties of the sort to which Rodriguez might be alluding had been resolved on certain worlds by court rulings long ago, in particular, those having to do with the oneness and brotherhood of life, in which all life forms on a planet, without discrimination with respect to arbitrary placement on a phylogenetic scale, became citizens of the planet, their votes, in many cases, being cast by proxies. Needless to say, severe political conflicts had occurred over the control of these proxies.

"Do you realize that most of the people you meet are dead?" asked Rodriquez.

"Come now," said Brenner.

"Yes!" said Rodriguez.

"I never noticed," Brenner admitted.

"They have never been alive," said Rodriguez, wiping his face. An escaped droplet of Heimat, like a small, luminescent world floated toward the steel ceiling of the lounge. "And that is the same thing. Then, eventually, their bodies will cease to function and they will never even find out they were never alive. They will never have discovered they were never alive!"

"They are alive," said Brenner, moodily.

"Yes, I suppose so, in a way," said Rodriguez.

"Certainly," said Brenner.

"Chemically," said Rodriguez.

"More than that," said Brenner.

"You are a humanist," said Rodriguez.

"A lifest," said Brenner. The current conditioning programs instituted in most school systems had rendered the term 'humanist' odious, because of its ethnocentric connotations.

"Yes," said Rodriguez, thoughtfully. "They have their small glow."

"Certainly," said Brenner.

"Like the grub, and the flea," he said.

"Not at all," said Brenner.

"At one time," said Brenner, "I courted death, for I thought to find her hand in hand with life. But I do so no longer now, for I am come to Abydos."

Brenner, who was young and blond, and innocent, and perhaps bright, regarded Rodriguez, puzzled.

"In the end," said Rodriguez, "do we not all come to Abydos?"

"I have read your writings," said Brenner.

At this point in their conversation one of the panels in the lounge, some feet from the floor, slid back, it opening to the network of access spaces outside, leading even to the vast hold spaces, some of which were closed, and some open, with the cargo floating in its nets, and the engines, and the captain entered, unblinking, the long digits of his appendages spread, open, climbing across, adhering to it with a secretory fluid, what was to Rodriguez and Brenner, relative to their position and the placement of their webbing, the ceiling, and then down one wall until he rather squatted before them, his hind legs outstretched, only their nails in contact with the floor, the nails of the forward appendages, the digits widely spread, hovering in space. He exchanged pleasantries with the two passengers, who were his only passengers. He seldom had passengers and his ship, a medium-class freighter of the R-series, registry Noton II, with barges in tow, was designed neither for the accommodation or comfort of such and its route was one not likely be taken except by those who did so in the line of business. To be sure, these were not his first passengers. He had occasionally had Ellits, Bellarians, and the tiny Zevets aboard, generally prospectors and mining engineers. Also, he had sometimes had organisms of the sort of Rodriguez and Brenner. It was for such as these that four cabins had been welded onto the girderwork abutting certain closed holds and the small lounge, with its now-closed, shielded port, installed. The conversation, brief and polite, for the captain was a shy, reticent sort, was accomplished by means of a nearby cabinet, of a not very sophisticated design, for it was an old freighter, which translated certain hissing sounds into visual displays, and responsive auditory vibrations, of a sort naturally produced by Rodriguez and Brenner, into variant displays, unintelligible to them but apparently meaningful to the captain. As all were visually oriented organisms all went smoothly, and they felt a certain bond, to some extent, unworthy though it might be, between them, predicated as it was on so arbitrary a basis. With the tiny Zevets the captain had never managed to feel at ease, with their detestation of light and the swift, snapping movements of their tiny wings, so sudden that they had more than once provoked the darting forth of the captain's tongue, to the embarrassment of all.

"I have a heard a noise," said Rodriguez, addressing the captain, though speaking toward the cabinet.

The captain's head lifted politely, peering at the cabinet. Such things, thought Brenner, have long necks.

"It comes from somewhere in one of the holds," said Rodriguez.

The captain's head turned toward Rodriguez.

Brenner had heard the noise, too, usually in the sleeping period, late at night, so to speak. He had heard it several times. He, too, was curious about it. On the other hand, in his occasional meetings with the captain, or one of the small crew, for the ship was largely automated, there had been no cabinet at hand.

Brenner noted that the captain was looking at Rodriguez, almost as though he could understand him without the cabinet. Its neck is long, thought Brenner.

The captain then turned to the machine. A soft stream of sound, carefully modulated, almost thoughtfully, as though steam escaping from a valve might become a medium of communication, impinged on the receptors of the cabinet. "It is an animal," flashed on the display panel.

"It must be a very large animal," said Rodriguez.

"Yes," said the captain.

Brenner, whose cabin was closer to the sound than was that of Rodriguez, though the cabins of neither directly abutted its presumed holding area, presumably as a tactful gesture on the part of the captain, or of the officialdom of the company whose vessel this was, had often heard it.

"What sort of animal is it?" asked Rodriguez.

"I do not know its code, or its classification," said the captain.

"Do you know its common name?" asked Rodriguez.

"No," said the captain.

"It is probably enroute to the games at Megara," said Rodriguez to Brenner.

Brenner shivered. He did not doubt that Rodriguez, who had seen so much, had looked upon the games of Megara, or games similar to them. Onlookers, tourists, thrill-seekers, gamblers, the jaded of a thousand worlds, the gourmets of the spirit, tasters of exquisite refinements, came from the remote corners of the galaxy to witness such games.

"Perhaps to the preserves on Habitat," said Brenner, "or to the field laboratories of Freeworld." These, in effect, were planetwide zoological gardens, with restricted areas for scientists and naturalists.

"It is mammalian, or mammalianlike, and carnivorous," said Rodriguez.

"Yes," said the captain.

Brenner, too, had surmised that, from the sounds of the animal. He had often heard it, and was much more aware of it, really, than Rodriguez, as his cabin was much closer to its holding area. Indeed, he sometimes fancied, during the quiet watches, when he was lying buckled in his webbing, trying to sleep, the ship and its barges drifting with their momentum in the loneliness and stillness of space, their path occasionally altered by as little as a finger's breadth by the brief whisper of a vernier in the night, attended by its vigilant guidance system, that he could detect its pacing, a restless, energetic, relentless, seemingly unceasing pacing. Too, sometimes he heard, with no mistake about it, the scratching of claws on steel, and the hurling of a body with its mass and weight against bolted plates. It did this again and again, but, of course the plates held. It could only hurt itself by doing this, but it did not stop. But there would be no mistaking, either in Rodriguez' cabin, or elsewhere on that ship, containing more than three cubic acres of interior space, the screams of the animal, or its howlings, or those thunderous roars, those challenges to steel, those protests against a fate not understood but resented, those utterances which came angrily, unresigned, unforgiving, unreconciled, from its dark beast's heart. Brenner was pleased that there were no pacifiers about, to release the beast, pledged to be the first to die that it might be free. Such things would dominate most food chains. It was for that reason he suspected that the beast was not bound for the gardens of Habitat or Freeworld. He did not think that even the zoologists would care to share their world with it. Only in more natural places, in darker, crueler jungles, could such a thing find its throne.

"In the morning, at ten, we will enter orbit at Abydos," said the captain. This would be ship time, in this case, commercial time, indexed to Commonworld. The ship would not dock at Abydos, of course, but would, so to speak, lie off the reefs, and be served by lighters. Abydos was not an outpost planet, not one lying at the fringes of known life forms, but a backward planet, in its way. It had, in effect, been noted, charted, cataloged, and then left behind in the march of a thousand life forms across the galaxy, with whom folk such as Rodriguez and Brenner had come along, more as passengers than explorers or frontiersmen. Their own world, long ago, had turned inward on itself. It had, as a world, long ago, forgotten to look at the stars. It had turned rather toward comfort, obedience, law, sameness. It was now one of the homogenized worlds which prided itself on its superiority to more ambitious, curious, aggressive worlds, habitats to more ambitious, curious, aggressive species. The promise of the world of Rodriguez and Brenner had never been fulfilled. After all, the stars are far away, and not everyone could reach them. And the long, painful climb toward the stars requires not only strength, but sternness, and will, and hardness, and power, vices of a troubled youth now happily outgrown in the maturity of a species. And so the promise of the world of Rodriguez and Brenner, were it ever truly a promise, had never been fulfilled. Their world had made its decision, cloaked as all such decisions are, and must be, else their pathetic horror might be more easily detected, in moral fervor, and a righteous vocabulary: It had become not great, but nice, not hot and needful, but tame and warm.

"At ten," repeated the captain.

Rodriguez nodded.

There was little of interest on Abydos to the rest of the galaxy other than its fueling station, one of the several such between certain mining worlds, the charters to which were held by various corporations. To be sure, beyond this, at least in the area of the depot, there were some company dormitories, a parts warehouse, a few muddy streets, some bars, a few small businesses, a barber shop, such things. It did have an atmosphere which might be breathed by both the captain, and his sort, and Rodriguez, and his sort. It was not one of those worlds to which one must take oneself in a bottle, so to speak, enclosing oneself in a surrogate of one's home world, without which appurtenances an unpleasant death would promptly ensue. If there were difficulties to be met with on Abydos they were not such as to require the encapsulation of visitors in friendly gases and temperatures. Rodriguez and Brenner could walk on Abydos without fear. Its atmosphere was benign, its surface temperatures were within tolerable limits, its water was drinkable, its soil, though thin, was not poisonous, its rain was not lethal, its gravity was not crushing, and its invisible life forms were such that they could be dealt with by the natural defenses of most organic systems. Moreover, its diurnal and annual cycles were similar to those of many comparable worlds, a fact which to many species is morally and psychologically, and even biologically, important. In a sense no species is satisfied until it has come home. Had its soil been more fertile, its mineral resources more remarkable, its vegetation more appealing, its scenery less tenebrous, its mountains less bleak and forbidding, or even if its location had been more propitious, Abydos might have been better known. But as it was, it was not even strictly analogous to a small town, overlooked by progress, on a more favored planet, far off the beaten pathways between more interesting places. Rather it was more, or at least in the vicinity of the depot and yards, a company camp, a merely dirty, unpleasant place, where rough men of ill-favored visage spent brief tours of duty, little more than a convenience to a corporation, to most of whose officers, of those who knew of it, it was no more than an entry on records. Even the captain of the vessel, for example, though he was surely not important in the corporation, had never been on its surface. His first officer, however, had. Still it was not a likely place to put ashore. As you may be interested in knowing what might be the interest of Rodriguez and Brenner in Abydos it had to do with the Pons.

"At ten, then," said Rodriguez.

The captain then lifted an appendage and Rodriguez, clamping the smoking Bertinian leaf between his teeth, and transferring his stein of Heimat to his left hand, shook one of the extended claws. Brenner, in turn, did the same, leaning forward in the webbing. The claw was dry and well polished. The captain then clapped together his jaws twice, a gesture of contentment and warmth amongst his kind, for even their gods are said to do so, and, with a tiny pressure from his back feet, rose up, turned about, rather like a balloon, in the zero-gravity field, and took his departure.

"Damned reptile," said Rodriguez.

"He is a nice enough fellow," said Brenner.

"I like him," admitted Rodriguez. "At least he can look at you."

He then swirled the stein about, mixing the remainder, popped open the slurp hole on the mug and sucked up some of the fermented poison within.

The captain, of course, was not really a reptile. It was only such things as the skin, the tail, the appendages, the neck, the long tongue, and such things, which suggested that. To be sure, perhaps the captain's species, in some sense, at some time in the past, might have evolved from reptiles, or something like reptiles, but then, so, too, if it must be known, had that of Rodriguez and Brenner, and from other things before that, which were not even reptiles.

"You are pleased that I called him a reptile," said Rodriguez, looking narrowly at Brenner.

Brenner blushed. "Was it a test?" he asked.

"No," said Rodriguez.

Brenner felt ashamed. Although he himself was pleased to hear things said which he himself found amusing, or true, or both, but would not have dared to say himself, he did tend to suffer for it. This was an effect of his conditioning program. But perhaps it had not been totally efficient, or had not fully "taken," so to speak, for he was not sickened at the vulgarity of Rodriguez, his offensiveness, his abusive honesty, or at least his attempt to speak and say the world as he saw it, as accurate or awry as his perceptions might be. Rodriguez was more free, and more terrible, and more abominable, and more glorious than any human being Brenner had ever known. He did not know how it was that such a man, who in his time it was said, had been a wastrel, a gambler, a freebooter, a smuggler, a soldier, had become involved in his own field.

"Are you afraid the machine is recording?" asked Rodriguez.

"Do you think it is?" asked Brenner.

"No," said Rodriguez.

"Oh," said Brenner.

"What if it is?" asked Rodriguez.

"Nothing, I suppose," said Brenner.

"I don't think it is," said Rodriguez. "If I thought it was I would have been more outspoken. There are a few things about the company I would have said."

This worried Brenner. He did not wish to be stranded on Abydos for an extra three or four of its revolutions, if not indefinitely.

"The politeness titles are not in force out here," said Rodriguez.

This was good news to Brenner. The politeness titles, some two hundred and six, or so, of them, with their numerous subsections, specified in some detail various behaviors, thoughts and actions which might be construed as impolite. For example, Rodriguez's referring to the captain as a reptile, regardless of the accuracy or inaccuracy of this reference to the captain's ancestry, or his own satisfaction with it, or even his own rightful pride in such a line of descent, or his indifference or insensitivity to it, could be, in various places, subject to various sanctions, ranging from nuisance demands for hypocritical apologies to the removal of a means of livelihood. The politeness titles were usually monitored by bureaucrats, and involved processings which were both lengthy and expensive. These things, interestingly, had usually emerged in putatively democratic societies, much to the surprise of the great majority of the putatively free individuals in such societies, who did not understand how they could have come about. Political scientists still spoke of the "plural-elite" model of governance in which law and policy emerged from the conflicts and compromises of lobbies and power groups, to which groups the putatively freely elected representatives of the putatively free electorate, were beholden, functioning, if they would survive and maintain their own places, positions, and powers, such as they were, as overt or covert agents. Some poets, in underground writings, had likened the politeness titles to the webs of spiders and the bureaucrats to the spiders. The analogy, of course, was not perfect, for a natural spider would eventually in the way of nature, in its directness and cleanliness, devour its prey. With the politeness titles, however, it was more as if a spider's webbing was hung everywhere, and nothing, not even the zealous bureaucrats themselves, so self-righteous, so eagerly, and narrow-liddedly watchful, so jealous of their modicum of power, could move. And there was nothing to eat the victims. They would just be left in the webbing, unable to fly, unable to move, left there immobile, helpless and tangled, not even to be eaten, just to be left trapped and helpless until they died, with other thousands, just additional nodules in that black, dry carpet of death, over which new insects could scarcely crawl.

"Do you want me to unplug it?" asked Rodriguez.

Brenner looked at him.

Rodriguez stretched out his foot and carefully wound the cable twice about his foot, soberly, and then jerked the cable out of the machine. With a swirl of his foot, rather neatly done, he freed the cable and it floated away like a buoyant snake until it stopped and waved about, as though it had its tail stuck in the wall. Such crude mechanical connections, cords and cables, and such, were inexpensive, and tended on the whole, to be more reliable in the long run than the contrivances responsible for more subtle connections. Similarly many folk preferred, even today, to wrap packages with tape and string, and, similarly, staples, rubber bands and paper clips were still known, as they had been in medieval times.

"You don't think the captain would really care, do you?" asked Rodriguez.

"No, not the captain," said Brenner.

"He is a good fellow," said Rodriguez. "To be sure, he is a bit formal, but his species tends to be reticent."

Brenner nodded. That was true. Members of the captain's species had sometimes squatted before emissaries, and even one another, when time permitted, for several divisions, as though absorbing one another' presence, and the warmth of a benign sun, before, subject to the imperatives of, say, business or diplomacy, eventually breaking the thitherto sustained purity of silence, muchly prized amongst them, with an almost apologetic courtesy. The entire crew of the ship, incidentally, was of the captain's species. Very few ships maintained mixed crews. There were a number of excellent reasons for this, having to do with several matters, such as optimum atmospheres and temperatures, difficulties of communication, particularly in emergency situations, diverse chemical requirements, diverse parameters pertinent to comfort and accommodation, numerous diverse methods-engineering factors, such as colors most easily discriminated and odors most easily detected, suitable placement of instrumentation, and numerous diverse devices, designed for convenience, depending on the prehensile appendages in question, for controlling the ship's systems. There were senses in which many species did not even see, feel, hear, smell, or taste the same world, so to speak, that is, that their experiences would have been exotic and perhaps even unintelligible to those of other species. To be sure, these numerous experiences would presumably be related in some topological manner to an independent reality, or, at least, that seemed the most economical hypothesis to explain how two different species, say, Zatans and Ellits, could get different ships to the same place by prearrangement at the same time. Without some such accommodations interstellar commerce, warfare and such, would have been almost impossible. Certain of the manufacturing worlds did design ships for diverse species. There were even ships in the galaxy which were designed for, and had been purchased by, and were flown by, representatives of Brenner's and Rodriguez' species, to be sure, those of colonial worlds, that is, of individuals whose ancestors had purchased passage on alien vessels to other worlds, often individuals who had been uncomfortable, inefficient, or unsuccessful on the home world. Indeed, some such individuals had been deported, that their ideas could remain in quarantine, so to speak, in remote asylums, unlikely to contaminate the ideal tepidities, or, more kindly, the serenities, of the home world, achieved at such cost over many centuries. To be sure, this was now seldom done, because of advances in neurological engineering achieved over the past two centuries, in virtue which triumphs many notable successes had been achieved in reforming the eccentricities of such deviants. Indeed, some of these individuals had climbed to unusual heights in the bureaucracy, and even, it was rumored, in the metaparty, the existence of which was often denied. The convert, after all, is the most zealous of adherents, as he must, before his own stern tribunals, before his own doubts and remorse, suspecting himself, not certain of his true motivations, defend and justify his decision, or betrayal. Another technique was that of the postnatal abortion, in which a mother's oversight, forgivable given her ignorance, her lack of foresight, was rectified by court order and the state at a later time. The state, after all, and the metaparty, with which it was in effect identical, if such a party existed, surely in its collective wisdom, knew better than any particular individual. Indeed, Rodriguez had fled more than one world to escape such a termination, not of his person, of course, which would have been heinously immoral, but, retroactively, of his judicially decided nonperson. Postnatal abortion had replaced capital punishment, the immorality of which was notoriously transparent. On some worlds populations had been subjected to such abortion. An additional argument of great force in favor of such merciful termination, done with all kindness, and all possible avoidance of pain, was that the state, the people, the community, or whatever putative entity might be involved, or the metaparty, if there were such an organization, was asserted to be the truest "Mother," and accordingly, at her discretion and convenience, had inalienable death rights over whatever might be temporarily housed within her.

"We can get away with a great deal," said Rodriguez to Brenner, "as we are known as slovenly creatures in the galaxy, and little is expected of us. For example, if a Narnian were to have said what I said, there might have been something of a flap."

"I see," said Brenner.

"Our species is despised throughout the galaxy," said Rodriguez.

"Absurd," said Brenner.

"And quite rightfully so, in my opinion," said Rodriguez, "in spite of the titles of politeness. They change nothing of importance, you know, at least when we consider the interstellar expanses, the multiplicity of worlds, and such. Only people like you take them seriously."

"Surely that's not true," said Brenner.

"So don't worry," said Rodriguez, blearily.

Sometimes Brenner did not care to talk with Rodriguez, though, to be sure, he had really not often done so, not to a great extent at any rate. It was not as though they were cronies or confidants, in spite of the months they had spent, even at hyperlight velocities, making their way from one port of call to another, from one system to another, sometimes on commercial lines, of one grade or another, sometimes on military vessels, patrol ships, and others, sometimes on research ships, most often, on one or another of the out-the-way routes, on one freighter or another. Rodriguez, except when drunk, tended to keep his own counsels, and if Brenner belonged to a species Rodriguez felt was rightfully despised throughout the universe, he had little doubt but what his own particular portion of that species, in the lofty criticality of Rodriguez, within the scope of which he undoubtedly, with magnanimous consistency, included himself, was not likely to be much more exempt, if that, than any other. Talking with Rodriguez was a bit unnerving at times, much like handling an unfamiliar piece of charged apparatus, not wholly understood, which occasionally, for no clear or obvious reason, reciprocated the attentions bestowed upon it with a series of unpleasant shocks. Brenner did know, of course, that his species was not generally regarded as one of the serious life forms of the galaxy, which discovery by the species, which had stood at the top of its own food chain for centuries, had come as a disillusioning surprise. A great deal of literature, poetry, and philosophy had come, almost immediately, to be seen in a quite different perspective. But then his species had encountered such surprises before. It did disturb Brenner to know that his species, a backward one, except in its own view, a view adjusted in such a way as to define progress in its own terms, commanded so little respect in the galaxy. It was generally regarded as a set of weak, uninteresting, self-righteous mediocrities. It was not a species with a project, not a species with a dream, to accomplish which it was willing to work and sacrifice. It was not, many said, a species which belonged amongst the stars. It would stain the stars or demean them. There was some agitation to keep it isolated, and treat it as unwholesome vegetable matter, not to be brought across stellar borders. It was better left, some said, to crawl on the surface of its own world, like worms, looking for small comforts. They were not giants, whose hands might pull them upward, from planet to planet, scaling the cliffs of space, giants whose brows might crash against stars, in whose hair would race the stellar winds. It did not strive, it did not care, except for itself; it did not think in terms of millenniums, but in terms of the day. Take one day at a time, it said. And that is how many of its members managed it. They took one day at a time, until one day came along on which they died. So, asked Brenner to himself, are we really no more than the clowns and cabin boys we are taken for, no more than tiny riders clinging in the fur of more venturesome, nomadic animals, in effect, parasites surviving in the chinks permitted to us by higher forms of life? How something deep in Brenner rebelled at this thought, yet, how quickly, he censured himself for his unworthiness, his envy, and rebellion, his defiance, and ambition, such atavistic temptations belonging to violent, archaic eras. "If you cannot kick, you cannot run," had sung a poet of such a violent time. "If you cannot form a fist, you cannot grasp." Brenner shuddered. Rodriguez was looking off, across the lounge, lost in his own thoughts, and the smoke, and the Heimat. No, thought Brenner, there are few mixed crews. How different it turned out from the crude fantasies of the early medieval period, days when it had been conjectured that his species would set the pace to the stars, joining in joyous brotherhood with other life forms. Indeed, such fantasies, until a century ago, had still been popular on the home world, where the real truth was not generally known, or, at any rate, much publicized. The naivety of such fantasies, their neglect of thousands of practical factors, had not militated against their popularity. And, indeed, they had even been used as devices to propagate the very values which would preclude their accomplishment in reality. On the other hand, they were now outlawed because they did call attention to the stars, and to what the species was not. They directed attention, you see, upwards and outwards, rather than downwards and within. They spoke, even in their beautiful, childlike simplicity, of unfavored ends, and of action, and of ardor and achievement, not of tranquility; too, they challenged the imagination; they issued, in their way, a rallying cry in a world weary of rallies, a world which suspected them, and feared them, and perhaps for good reasons; and they suggested a goal, a project, an adventure, and projects and adventures are always dangerous, even in the imagination. The stars, you see, may lure and summon, much as mountains did once, and then later, the sky; and there might be those who would hear this call, really hear it, and actually, completely misunderstanding the matter, place their feet upon such trails. Rejecting the values, and the absurd means, they might accept the end, the goal, the adventure. This would be dangerous, and jeopardize the hard-won victories of centuries. And so such things, innocent as they might seem, were outlawed. Yet, their outlawry was probably not essential, for in a leveled world, where even the tallest, their backs aching, must bend down and pretend to be little, in a world in which elites, whether they existed or not, were illegal, a world which would by statute subvert, squander, and repudiate its occasional gifts won in the genetic lottery, its own pathfinders, its own commanders, its own aristocracy, as it might spring up here and there, like flowers and trees, the stars could not be achieved. How insignificant are the parameters of physics compared to the gravity of the mass. From that bulk what must be the accumulated force, the consolidated and directed power, that could achieve escape velocity? And so organisms such as Brenner and Rodriguez were, on the whole, little more than passengers, neglected and scorned, amongst the stars. Yet Brenner did not begrudge his fortunes. He would have come, really, even in spite of his being "assigned," for he could have challenged the assignment, with anyone to the stars, even such as the captain, even such as Rodriguez. He was there, and this was enough for him. He would have been happy, could he have afforded it, to have purchased passage in steerage; he would, like many others, if he had received the opportunity, have been delighted to work his passage from system to system; he would have cheerfully kept cabins and polished brass; he would cheerfully have carved strange vegetables in the galleys; he would cheerfully have cleaned the cages of transported animals, even those of the blue-skinned Serian slave girls, bred for beauty and passion over generations, as loving as dogs, as incapable of rebellion as cattle and sheep; or even the slaves taken from his own planet, many of them, in their cages and chains, as lovely and as needful as the Serian sluts, women who had been homeless on a world shut against them and their deepest, loving nature. They would find worlds on which they were prized, worlds on which they brought high prices.

"I was saying," said Brenner, returning to what had been on his mind before the visit of the captain, a visit a consequence perforce perhaps of etiquette, or perhaps even of his own innate politeness, as landfall, so to speak, at Abydos was to occur in a few divisions, ship time, or, to be more precise, a.s.t., adjusted ship time, her governing chronometer having been set, as was typically the case, and has been suggested, to commercial time, indexed to Commonworld, "that I have read your writings."

"No, you haven't," said Rodriguez.

"I beg your pardon?" said Brenner. To be sure, he had probably not read everything which Rodriguez had written, but he had done his best to find what he could, shortly after learning the identity of his projected senior colleague. For the most part he had secured monographs in the library of his base university, to the faculty of which he was attached as an adjunct researcher, certain sections of which he had extracted for personal notes.

"What did you read?" asked Rodriguez.

"*Congenital Heraldic Design: An Analysis of the Shells of Holarians*," said Brenner. "*The Phratries of Chios, Ritual Meiosis: An Essay on Segmentation in Tunnel Societies, Avoidance Behaviors amongst the Milesian Amphibians, Asymmetrical Endogamy amongst Four-Spined Creodonts: A Study in Genetic Randomization, Aquatic Clans, Rites of Passage in Seven Societies*, such things."

"*Rites of Passage?*" asked Rodriguez, looking up.

"I found it in paper," said Brenner.

"And you weren't afraid to read it?"

"No," said Brenner.

"Good," said Rodriguez. "That was the first book I wrote which was banned."

"I do not see why," said Brenner. "It did little more than collect and record indisputable observations."

Rodriguez laughed, a not pleasant laugh. Then he said, "My real writings are all in paper."

"In books—with pages?" asked Brenner.

"That sort," he said, moodily, "not the sort on spheres, not the sorts on cubes and plates. You can't broadcast selective magnetic erasure signals, coded to the sphere, the plate, or cube, and destroy the manuscript, simultaneously, wherever it might exist, on an entire world."

"'Book burning'?" said Brenner.

"One match does for the entire pile," said Rodriguez.

Brenner nodded.

"But with pages, with books with pages," said Rodriguez, with a sort of grim satisfaction, apparently considering the labors set authorities, "you have to hunt down each one, each one, slowly, painfully, expensively. And how can you be sure you have them all, even if you have? There might be one in hiding, one you do not know of. What do you think of that? Does that not worry you? That is how a book with pages can survive, by hiding. By hiding, and by being copied, often by hand, and passed from one reader to another. Such manuscripts are precious. They are carried from place to place, in knapsacks and boots, like contraband." He slurped some more Heimat, a word which, incidentally, in a once subtle, expressive, beautiful language, now muchly improved, simplified, and functionalized, had meant "Home" or "Homeland." Indeed, several such languages had been similarly improved by grammar engineers, until their loftiest flights, those incipient twitches in the wing muscles, were now well within the reach of, could now be easily understood by, the most elementary, or most occupied, or most casual or careless mind. Prose inaccessible to, or not easily comprehended by, the mass violated basic principles of egalitarianism. Its discriminatory nature had been proven in various courts of law, in various historic decisions, by suitable, clear-thinking, humane political appointments. Dissenting judges had occasionally been removed from the

bench on the basis of judicial incompetence. On the other
hand, the important matter was always the majority, and
a token opposition, futile and ineffectual, was desirable,
guaranteeing, as it did, the openness and objectivity of
the judicial process. To be sure, on some worlds collectors
of incunabula, of antique manuscripts, were permitted to
pursue their eccentric hobby, and in this way, if no other,
certain fragments of a pernicious, superseded literature,
putatively valued for its historical value, survived. One
manuscript, a tattered hand-copied manuscript of a book
called *Pride and Prejudice* by a J. Austen had brought seven
thousand, two hundred and twenty-one Commonworld
Credits, a standardized economic unit, interestingly indexed
to an imaginary economic system on the wilderness of
Commonworld, that system itself representing a correlation
of more than four hundred common currencies, at a
small auction on Naxos. To be sure, at the same auction,
a beverage can dating from more than eight centuries
ago, had brought more than nine thousand. Interstellar
commerce, incidentally, was founded largely on barter,
involving a great deal of compromising and bargaining.
More than one world's currency had been subverted through
sudden unilateral revisions of its worth, based against the
Commonworld Credit. Also, wholesale unilateral abolitions
of debts, contract cancellations, expropriations and such,
based on perceived internal need or newly discovered
moral principles, tended to make interstellar transactions
a matter of serious economic risk. It was easier to decide
on the value of a weapon-system powerpack or a sack of
Bellarian flour, from one's point of view, as compared to a
quantity of ore or a bushel of Velasian grain than on any
one of these to a given number of credits, even those of the
Commonworld. Speculators in currencies, of course, throve.
So, too, did various forms of insurance companies, the
professed objective of which was to provide some measure
of protection against statistically predictable fluctuations
and disasters.

"I would like to read some of your other works," said Brenner.

"You are better off not knowing about them" said Rodriguez.

"Thank you," said Brenner.

"They might confuse you," said Rodriguez. "They might make you think."

"Thank you," said Brenner.

"That is a kindness on my part toward you," said Rodriguez, "indicating I have some concern for your future. Why should I risk you, as I saw fit to risk myself? Too, it is a compliment, as it suggests that I regard you as being capable of thought."

Brenner was silent.

"Yes," growled Rodriguez. "You are still young. You are still naive. You are still prizing the rhetoric of inquiry and truth. And you have not yet learned that it is just that, the rhetoric which is to be prized, not the realities, which can be embarrassing, and dangerous."

Brenner did not understand this.

"I suspect you have not yet learned to dismiss canyons and mountains where none appear on the maps you have been given," said Rodriguez, looking off toward the end of the room. "I suspect you would be actually troubled to give the map priority over the canyon, to award it precedence over the mountain. You do not yet realize that it is not the canyon and the mountain which are important, but the map. And the map is important not as a representation of reality, which it is not, but as a putative representation of reality, which it is; it is important not because it is true, which it is not, but because it is useful, because of its social utility, its political value. You have not yet learned to dismiss these unmapped canyons, these unrecorded mountains, to keep them to yourself, to publicly deny them. They are there, of course, in all their formidable height, in all their quantitative massiveness, however ignored, and in all their terrifying widths and depths, dark and unsounded, however denied, however neglected, Perhaps it is as though, in a sense, they are really on the maps, but in invisible ink, and have been for centuries, at least in the works of some cartographers, some explorers, and that they await only the proper social reagent to suddenly emerge, then appearing openly on the map, as they have in the reality. To be sure, some of these mountains lie in remote regions, in the mind; some of these canyons are in dark places, in the heart. But perhaps this will never occur. Surely reality is more hazardous than the map. How many have been injured falling off a map, or tumbling into one? We can control the map; it can be done with a formula, a compass, a straight edge, a little care; the reality is more recalcitrant."

"I have understood nothing of what you have been saying," said Brenner.

"Good," said Rodriguez, blowing out a dark cloud of smoke.

Brenner watched the smoke disappear through the filtering system. He was pleased that the lounge was equipped with this device.

"Do you have any of your other works with you?" asked Brenner.

"No," said Rodriguez. "I am not stupid."

Brenner nodded. It might have been difficult to bring certain materials through customs.

"They have been published here and there?" asked Brenner.

"Yes," said Rodriguez, "here and there."

"Anonymously?" asked Brenner.

"Sometimes," said Rodriguez.

"And under various pseudonyms?" asked Brenner.

"Sometimes," said Rodriguez.

"And under your own name?"

"But not number," said Rodriguez.

"I see," said Brenner.

"It depends on the world," said Rodriguez.

"Of course$_r$," said Brenner. Here and there, of course, there were open worlds, quite different from most worlds, which had almost uniformly discovered the perils of openness. To be sure, almost every world claimed to be an open world. But there were in the galaxy few Hollands, so to speak.

"The sheep," said Rodriguez, "are told they are gods

and with tears in their eyes they yield themselves up to be sheared by their own kind."

"What?" asked Brenner.

"Nothing," said Rodriguez.

Brenner was silent.

"Better they were sheared without apology," said Rodriguez, "as what they are, as what they were born to be, as what they should be, as what more than which they can never be, should never be, and will never be. Better not to lie to them. That truly demeans them. Let them joyously yield up their wool without lies. The hypocrisy is what I most object to. Rather let them joyously yield up their wool as what they are, the givers of wool."

"You are quite drunk," said Brenner.

"On so many worlds there are the shearers and the shorn," said Rodriguez.

"And which are you?" asked Brenner.

"Neither," said Rodriguez, gloomily. "I am one who stands outside the fence, one who observes, one who laughs, and cries."

"I see," said Brenner.

"And there are masters and slaves," said Rodriguez.

Brenner was silent. Too often had he himself been troubled by such thoughts.

"Should those who should be servants not be servants?" asked Rodriguez. "Should those who should be slaves not be slaves?"

"All are the same," said Brenner.

"It is not so on the strong worlds," said Rodriguez, moodily.

"The strong worlds?" said Brenner. Rodriguez had used that expression before, he recalled.

"Yes," said Rodriguez.

"Openly stratified worlds?" asked Brenner.

"For the most part," said Rodriguez.

Brenner shuddered. He had little doubt that Rodriguez had in mind, at least for the most part, the numerous worlds, tending muchly to keep to themselves, in which social structures were explicitly stratified, as opposed to being implicitly, or covertly, stratified. Rodriguez would like that. He would like the honesty of that. He was the sort of fellow who found intellectual dishonesty distasteful, however expedient. He might even regard it as undignified. Such worlds tended to be characterized by rank, distance, and hierarchy, expressed in a variety of forms, or structures. There were, for example, familial structures, clan and subclan structures, class structures, merit structures, hereditary structures, feudal structures, caste structures, and such. In such worlds, in one fashion or another, the aristocracy of nature tended to be revealed in civilization, rather than distorted and concealed, or, as the case might be, subverted by those whose talents and self-interest lay largely in the corridors of subterfuge, prevarication, and manipulation.

"I refer, of course," said Rodriguez, "to stratification within the same species."

"Of course," said Brenner. He knew, of course, that even on the artificial worlds, or worlds of convention, or most of them, even on those worlds which pretended to the homogenized sameness of the dominant life form, for political reasons, despite all evidence to the contrary, other species, such as his and Rodriguez', might not be accorded similar dignities. On some such worlds certain species, such as their own, were not permitted except in specified zones, and only at certain times or seasons, could not openly and freely obtain food or rest space in all hostels, required papers or licenses for debarkation, business, and travel, could not obtain citizenship, were not permitted to maintain a permanent residence, and such. Indeed, sometimes ambassadors of one species or another, in early contacts with newly discovered civilizations, a situation in which those of Brenner and Rodriguez's species were seldom involved, found themselves incarcerated in zoological gardens, or being presented, as exotic fauna, or pets, by one potentate to another. And indeed more than one member of Brenner's and Rodriguez' own species, given by one alien life form to another, had served in similar capacities. Moreover, it was not unknown for them, on dark streets, in lonely areas, unwary in a bar, to be seized for diverse purposes, usually as simple as serving in some menial capacity in a passing vessel.

"Are these various writings of yours known?" asked Brenner.

"Some," said Rodriguez.

"And others must be suspected," suggested Brenner.

"Doubtless," said Rodriguez.

"Is this why you have been sent to Abydos?" asked Brenner.

"To get me out of the way?" smiled Rodriguez. "Maybe. But I could have wrangled other assignments. They would have served, as well."

"The work of yours which I have read, the *Phratries of Chios*, and such," said Brenner, "was edited, was it not?" There had been certain roughnesses and gaps in it, not so much in the prose, where transitions had been supplied by a editor apparently concerned to conceal his work, but in the thought. It is hard for an editor to clip thoughts smoothly. The hole in the thought remains, suggested by a subtle cognitive incoherence, alerting the reader, perhaps intriguing him.

"Yes," said Rodriguez. "That is why it is still on the cubes and such. But unedited versions are available elsewhere, not on the home world, unless they have found their way back there, but elsewhere, in separate books."

"I have one objection to your work, what I have read of it," said Brenner.

"What?" asked Rodriguez.

"It does not seem scientific," said Brenner.

"You mean in not agreeing with the official science?" asked Rodriguez.

"No," said Brenner. "Rather it does not seem value-free."

"Like the official science?" asked Rodriguez, interested.

"No, obviously the "official science," as you call it, has its own values, its own ends to subserve."

"You recognize that?" asked Rodriguez.

"Yes," said Brenner.

"Good," said Rodriguez. His Bertinian leaf was now no

more than a stub. He put it out, scraping it in a black sooty smear, on the webbing.

We are slovenly creatures, indeed, thought Brenner. This conjecture was further confirmed when Rodriguez crumbled the stub into a confetti of flakes and, with one hand, tossed them into the air, to be attended to by the filtering system.

"You think science should be value-free?" asked Rodriguez, intrigued. "That is interesting. How could anything we care about be value-free?"

"Oh, I accept the metavalues," said Brenner, "the value of the enterprise itself, the values of honest inquiry, of testing, of subjection of one's results to public scrutiny, such things. It is rather that value seems to enter directly into your work, into your reporting, so to speak."

"It does!" said Rodriguez.

"Your approval and disapproval shows," said Brenner.

"Should I have attempted to conceal them?" asked Rodriguez.

"At least," said Brenner.

"A form of unspoken lie?" said Rodriguez.

"Better, of course, not to have values, feelings, and such," said Brenner.

"But what of the love, joy and brotherhood of all life, and such," asked Rodriguez, "the embracing of the cockroach, the admiration of the worm, the camaraderie of the viper, and such?"

"I am not speaking of the prescribed values recognized by all right-thinking moral agents," said Brenner, "but those of science."

"I think that my researches have been conducted carefully, and my results arrived at in an objective, verifiable manner," said Rodriguez.

"I cannot fault you there," admitted Brenner. Indeed, the work of Rodriguez, or at least his observations and compilations of data, were occasionally cited, by politically naive, or careless, colleagues, as a model of scrupulous exactitude.

"Indeed," said Rodriguez, "most of it is quite low level,

almost at the level of reportage. We are still theoretically primitive in our science. Indeed, I often envy the fellows who only have to worry about what molecules do, and not what they meant by it, what they had in mind, whether or not it makes sense, what was the point of it, how it came to be done in the first place, whether it should have been done in the first place, how it should best be interpreted, and such."

"Be serious," said Brenner.

"Do you have something particular in mind?" asked Rodriguez.

"It was clear in your work, in the *Aquatic Clans* book, that you disapproved of the sacrifice lotteries of the Zenic crustaceans."

"They were rigged," said Rodriguez.

"And that was the foundation of your objection?" asked Brenner.

"I did not think highly of them, independently," admitted Rodriguez.

"More deplorable was your reference, in the *Phratries* book, to the feces-tasting ceremony of the feather-gilled Humblers of Lesser Carthage as disgusting."

"I would not have wanted to do it," said Rodriguez.

"A great many people on the home world regard that particular ceremony as being very meaningful and beautiful, finding in it a veritable celebration in its way of oneness and love, an emblem of joy and humility, a way in which one life form, with gracious delicacy, acknowledges its own small place in the palace of life."

"That sounds to me like a value judgment," said Rodriguez.

"It is not claiming to be science," pointed out Brenner.

At the time I wrote that," said Rodriguez, "I had not realized that Humbler missionaries had made so many converts on the home world, but, even so, I would have written it." A great Humbler prophet, incidentally, over a century ago, had taught the proud, vainglorious Humblers that one did not have to have feather gills to be a Humbler. From his time on, this lesson having been absorbed with due repentance and guilt, Humbleism had been preached even to the diverse assortments of gentiles, so to speak, available in the galaxy. There were many Humbler martyrs.

"We are not supposed to make judgments," said Brenner. "We are not supposed to prescribe, but to *describe*. It is not the business of science to change things, or to reform the galaxy, but to explain things, to give accounts of them."

"Did you have any difficulty telling the facts from the values?" asked Rodriguez.

"Of course not," said Brenner, irritatedly.

"It is possible to understand something," said Rodriguez, "and still not like it."

"Perhaps," said Brenner.

"Indeed," said Rodriguez, "it is sometimes difficult to understand things without finding oneself feeling one way or another about them, without coming to like them or dislike them, so to speak."

"Perhaps," said Brenner.

"And what better grounds on which to form a liking or a disliking than on an understanding?"

"But anyone could do that sort of thing," said Brenner.

"Of course," said Rodriguez.

"Where is your frame of reference?" asked Brenner.

"I carry it with me," said Rodriguez.

"And so, too, does every Narnian and crocodile in the galaxy."

"Not mine," said Rodriguez.

"It is your own gauge," said Brenner.

"Why then should I throw it away?" asked Rodriguez.

"At best it is relativized to a species," said Brenner.

"To my species," said Rodriguez. "That is important."

"Galactically, that is unimportant," said Brenner.

"But then I am not a galaxy," he said.

"I am a modernist, and a lifest," said Brenner.

"You are a traitor to your species," said Rodriguez, "or are trying to be, but I suspect you will not manage it."

Brenner smoldered in fury.

"Others, too, may have suspected it," said Rodriguez.

"What?" said Brenner.

"That may be why you have been sent to Abydos," said Rodriguez.

"Nonsense," said Brenner.

"We are more alike than you know," said Rodriguez. "But others know it."

"I am not like you," said Brenner.

"No species chauvinist?" smiled Rodriguez.

"No," said Brenner.

"Yet you have come to Abydos," mused Rodriguez.

"The assignment seemed interesting," said Brenner. "I did not challenge it."

"I see," said Rodriguez.

"What do you think to find on Abydos?" asked Brenner.

"I do not know what I will find," said Rodriguez. "But I know for what I am searching."

"What is that?" asked Brenner.

"The beginning," said Rodriguez.

For those of you to whom this might not be clear Rodriguez and Brenner are anthropologists. To be sure, this designation had become something of an anachronistic misnomer, suggesting, as it does, in its root, that it had to do with a particular species. At present, of course, its meaning was no longer limited in such a provincial and circumscribed fashion. Earlier its scope, in virtue of certain interdisciplinary connections, had been extended to certain organisms on a given home world which were not always of the same species as that of Rodriguez and Brenner. After this, of course, there was not the least difficulty in extending it to numerous life forms in various systems, life forms which had little in common but the possession of some form of what we might think of as a cultural complexus. To be certain, the boundaries of the discipline were quite unclear, and the relationships with numerous kindred sciences, collateral or contained, as might be argued, such as sociology, political science, ethology, ecology, and genetics, were still a matter of disputed demarcations. Some individuals preferred to think not so much of separate countries of inquiry, each jealousy guarding its own borders, so to speak, as of inquiries themselves into which light might be shed from various directions. To be sure, the matter was complex. There was a sense, of course, in which some still thought of "anthropology" as being the "science of Man," and that was the sense in which many now used the expression 'man' to refer to many sorts of creatures which would not have originally been regarded as "men" or, say, "human," in the archaic sense of the word. For example, the captain of the star freighter, who had paid his respects earlier to Rodriguez and Brenner, might, in that extended sense, have been regarded as a "man." You have probably been assuming, incidentally, that Rodriguez and Brenner are men. I shall not challenge this assumption, but, given the broad sense of the term, as it is now used, I think it only fair to point out that it is, on your part, an assumption. For example, you have not really seen Rodriguez and Brenner. If you were to see them, of course, you might more easily then decide whether or not you felt comfortable in calling them men, and, if so, in what sense.

At this point Rodriguez finished his Heimat with a noise for which even Brenner would have been hard put to find an epithet more accurate than 'disgusting'. Rodriguez then thrust the emptied stein, which was his own, into which earlier in the commissary, open between certain ship hours, had been drawn a specified quantity of Heimat, into a pack at his belt, unbuckled his webbing, and, leaning forward, and with a small push away from the webbing stocks, moved toward the wall. There, arresting his progress with his finger tips, he reached for, and grasped, a wall bar and, with his other hand, his feet a few inches off the floor, pressed in sequence two buttons, both recessed in the plating, in response to the signal of the first of which the illumination in the lounge was extinguished, and in response to the signal of the second of which the shielding of the observation port slid to one side.

Brenner eagerly unbuckled his own webbing and, in a moment, had joined Rodriguez at the port.

Some said it was the only way to see the stars, from such a perspective, within deep space, outside the distorting effects of an atmosphere, preferably at a sublight velocity. They were now at such a velocity, of course, having been decelerating for more than three Commonworld rotations, or Commonworld days. They were on their approach to Abydos.

"There it is," said Rodriguez, pointing.

"Abydos?" asked Brenner.

"Her sun," said Rodriguez, patiently.

Of course," said Brenner.

It was natural for Rodriguez to have spoken of the star whose satellite was Abydos as "her sun." Both Rodriguez and Brenner, and many of their kind, particularly those who had undertaken long voyages on dark, empty seas, tended to think of worlds in the feminine gender. Even some of their species whose archaic languages might have prescribed differently in this respect, as they had entered space, had adopted this custom. The world, far off, gleaming, beckoning, was the hearth against cold, the shelter against storms and loneliness, the haven, the home, the harbor, the precious thing, the womb of life, the platform of her strivings or ineffectualities, of her choices, of histories, and of refusals of history. It was in this sense then, as the light in the window, as the harbor, as the home, arrival at which betokened the end of long journeys, as the vast mysterious matrix from which consciousness and curiosity, and meaningfulness, had emerged, that one might think of the world in the feminine gender, or, more simply, as the mother. To those who might think of worlds as mineralogical curiosities, consequent upon remote condensations, living upon their familiar surfaces, but not really seeing them, they might continue to be "it." To those who viewed them from space, however, they would remain "she."

"It is on Abydos," said Rodriguez, "that I hope to find out something."

Brenner looked into the night.

"It is not much, of course," said Rodriguez. "It is not the key to the universe, or anything. It is only a little something that I have been curious about, for a long time."

"The beginning?" asked Brenner, recollecting something from earlier, not clearly grasped.

"Yes," said Rodriguez. "How it started, what it all means, what it is all about, so to speak."

"You should have gone into cosmology," said Brenner.

"Oh, no," said Rodriguez. "I am not talking about those walls, against which so many heads have been bloodied, about the worlds, the metaworlds, the metatimes, and, at the end, the mystery met with once more, concealed beneath yet another mask. No, no. I am talking about a small problem, about something which may well have an answer, even a discoverable one."

"Perhaps in the end there is no answer," said Brenner. "Perhaps in the end there is nothing."

"I will not accept that," said Rodriguez.

"You have considered the possibility, I trust," said Brenner, not pleasantly, "that reality may not be much concerned about what you are or are not willing to accept."

"I only want to know a little thing," said Rodriguez. "I am not an ambitious man."

"And what is that?"

"I would like to understand myself," said Rodriguez, "who I am, who we are, how we came to be as we are, what my species is, how it came to be as it is, what it is all about."

Brenner thought it possible that there might an answer to that question, at least if it were subjected to certain clarifications. It was another question, of course, as to whether such an answer could be found. It was, he speculated, much like trying to discover the origin of a custom, or a practice, what it meant, or what it used to mean, or what it might mean now. Certainly anthropologists could speculate on such matters, and might, indeed, hit upon correct answers, even if they would never be able to demonstrate their correctness. To be sure, it seemed as if Rodriguez might have something in mind which was more primitive, more fundamental, than a given custom or practice, or even a constellation of such.

"Hitherto," said Rodriguez, "as it is said, we have only been picking up shells on the beach."

"That is worthwhile," said Brenner.

"But where have the shells come from?" asked Rodriguez. "Surely you have wondered about that. What lies behind them?"

"You wish to see the sea?" smiled Brenner.

"Yes," said Rodriguez. "I wish to see the sea."

"Perhaps the origin is not the sea," said Brenner, "but an artifact, or a deed."

"The first firebrand, snatched from a flaming forest, the stone knife, the social compact?" said Rodriguez.

"Let us be content to pick up shells, and describe them," said Brenner.

Rodriguez was silent.

"Surely you do not think to find what you seek on Abydos," said Brenner.

"What I seek lies everywhere, I think, but it is feared, and lies well hidden," said Rodriguez.

"And you hope to find it on Abydos?"

"Yes," said Rodriguez. "I hope to find it on Abydos."

"It would be less hidden there?" asked Brenner.

"I think so," said Rodriguez.

"That seems a strange place to search for a secret local to our species," said Brenner.

"I am interested in this, of course, for its pertinence to our species," said Rodriguez. "That is my personal motivation, self-regarding as you might expect. But I think it lies at the root not only of our species, but perhaps at the root of a billion others, perhaps, in one form or another, at the root of all."

"All?" asked Brenner.

"Those of interest to our science," said Rodriguez.

"Those who have attained some form of culture?" said Brenner.

"Yes," said Rodriguez, "those capable of standing at crossroads, those who have sundered the bonds of elementary circuitries, those who are no longer simple, who are no longer like rain and wind, those who have put behind them the innocence of the barracuda, those who have discovered choice, and questions."

"There is nothing important on Abydos," said Brenner.

"Why did you come?" asked Rodriguez. "Why did you not protest your assignment? Surely you had not expended your set of refusal rights."

"It gave me an opportunity to step off the porch," said Brenner, "to see the stars."

"You should not have come," said Rodriguez. "There is nothing for you on Abydos."

"I might find a shell or two," said Brenner.

"I am intrigued by Abydos," said Rodriguez. "On Abydos is to be found one of the few remaining, and perhaps the most pure, of the totemic cultures."

"It is known only by a footnote in old texts," said Brenner. He had, of course, as far as he could, in the university retrieval system, researched the matter.

"Also in company records, of course," said Rodriguez.

Brenner's visage clouded. Such records, of course, would not be in the university's library. Indeed, most of the corporations were rather secretive about records, or at least their personal records, as opposed to their official records, readily available for public review.

"The totemic cultures," said Rodriguez, "are the oldest known to our species. They lie not only before civilizations as we know them today, but even before earlier civilizations. They are older even than the gods and the heroes. They may be at the beginning itself."

The theme here, of course, was a common one to anthropology, the thesis that the earlier stages of more complex civilizations may be discovered in more primitive cultures. In the examination of such cultures, for example, in a consideration of their customs and beliefs, their monuments and tools, their works, ways, and traditions, their stories, their songs, their drawings, their legends and myths, their religions and sciences, their feelings, there might be found, in such rubble, so to speak, the origins and meanings, perhaps elaborated or distorted, of more complex modern forms. And, to be sure, there seemed little doubt that many such remnants, or relics, of one sort or another, sometimes primitive, if not actually embarrassing, lingered into more enlightened eras. To be frank, of course, much of this was controversial, for a number of reasons, and it must be pointed out, as well, that it was not always clear as to whether a culture was truly primitive or not. For example, a culture which had achieved no technology other than what might be attained with a hammer and a blade might be as old in its way, and have a history, however quiescent, behind it as ancient as that of the most advanced star world, routinely exploiting triumphs in hyperspace navigation. Too, of course, even totemic institutions might develop, undergoing various refinements and elaborations. Accordingly, one might even distinguish between, say, primitive totemisms and, so to speak, developed, or advanced, totemisms.

Brenner did not respond to Rodriguez. He was familiar with such matters, and speculations, of course. Rather he was enrapt with the vistas before him, and reminded himself that he was, in a sense, looking backward into the past, and that many of the lights which he saw, as those which he had seen from the surface of the home world, had begun their journeys thousands upon thousands of years ago. The light of the sun of Abydos, on the other hand, had begun its journey but a moment past. Astronomically, on standardized star charts, the sun of Abydos was identified by its catalog number, and the identificatory numbers of Abydos and its satellites, if it had had them, would have been indexed to this same number. For example, although the number of the sun of Abydos had several digits, let us suppose that its number was as simple as 17. The number of Abydos, then, would have been 17.3. You would then know that Abydos was the third planet from its star. If Abydos had had satellites, say, three of them, and we wished to refer to the second of them, figuring outward from the parent body, in this case Abydos herself, it would have been identified as

17.3.2. Abydos, on the other hand, as we have mentioned, had no satellites. It had once, incidentally, had a satellite but it, a long time ago, had been fragmented and removed from its orbit, in connection with a mining operation conducted by an advanced star world, which had need of its materials. The operation was a legitimate one, unlike certain shadowy operations conducted here and there in the galaxy, having been cleared with, and approved by, appropriate authorities.

"How glorious are the suns, and worlds!" exclaimed Rodriguez.

"Yes," said Brenner.

There was something awesome, and beautiful, and terrible, about the universe, about space, the stars, the worlds, the grandness of it, the mystery of it.

In this portion of the galaxy, with the naked eye, from the perspective of the port, one could see several thousand stars.

The night of space blazed with the light of these myriads of far-flung mornings.

Some sixty-two percent, or so, statistically, of the visible stars in this portion of the galaxy controlled the orbit of one or more habitable worlds, on most of which, given customary interactions, life had actually developed, expressing itself in one set of forms or another. And Abydos, it might be added, did not lie near the populous center of the galaxy. Its location, rather, was somewhat more toward the periphery.

"What do you know about the Pons?" asked Rodriguez.

"Very little is known about them, as far as I have been able to determine," said Brenner. "They are extremely simple, extremely primitive. They lack even pottery. They are small, timid, furtive, isolated, few in number, and given to secrecy. We may expect, of course, the usual features of a totemic complexus, in particular, the reverencing of the totemic animal and exogamy."

"Company records provide further information," said Rodriguez, "but nothing much of scientific interest. Pons occasionally, individually, or in small delegations, have in the past, at certain intervals, made contact with company employees, usually at Company Station, for purposes of trade, exchanging gathered forest products, commonly pods of various sorts, for diverse manufactured articles, in particular, a small metallic tool manufactured to their specifications, called a scarp, used for a variety of purposes."

"They do not have any native metallurgical capability?" asked Brenner.

"One gathers not," said Rodriguez.

"They live near Company Station?" said Brenner.

"No," said Rodriguez. "They live somewhere back in the forests."

Brenner looked at him, startled.

Rodriguez nodded, and returned his attention to the stars.

"You are familiar with the eco-profiles of the forests?" said Brenner.

"Of course," said Rodriguez.

Even surveying crews from Company Station, it seems, had seldom penetrated far into the adjacent forests. To be sure, parts of them had been flown over in various cars, rovers, vans and such. And they had been extensively surveyed from orbit. The probes however had revealed little of mineralogical interest. The temperate latitudes of Abydos, in both hemispheres, were heavily forested, usually with varieties of deeply rooted, seasonally foliaged trees. Brenner's surprise was occasioned primarily by his recollection of the eco-profiles of the forested areas, which suggested a rich variety of fauna, several of which, given their natural camouflage and predatory habits, might be supposed to be distinctly unpleasant.

"And," added Rodriguez, "the Pons eschew weapons."

"I find that hard to believe," said Brenner.

"You will like them," said Rodriguez. "They are your sort of people. They are amongst the most innocent, kindly, humble, harmless, and inoffensive creatures in the galaxy."

"How do they live in the forest?" asked Brenner.

"They have apparently done so for thousands of years," said Rodriguez.

"Apparently there is something to totemism," said Brenner.

"One gathers so," laughed Rodriguez.

As this was a joke which is likely to be obscure to those not of Rodriguez' and Brenner's field, I shall, with your permission, explain it. The relation between the totem and the totemic group is complex but it is usually understood that the totemic animal, perhaps in exchange for certain considerations, such as veneration and honor, and in the light of the special relation in which it stands to the group, understood as that of father and ancestor, will provide certain services to the totemic group, its children, for example, that it will look after their welfare, that it may be inform them of the future, and so on.

"What is the totemic animal of the Pons?" asked Brenner.

"A very fitting one," said Rodriguez. "The Abydian mouse."

"That?" asked Brenner. We may think of the Abydian ground git, or as it sometimes referred to, the Abydian mouse, as a small, stub-tailed rodent. That seems reasonable, given its habits and the nature of its incisors, which continue to grow during its lifetime, necessitating their reduction by gnawing. The git is primarily herbivorous, but is not above scavenging, and often cleans the bones of prey abandoned by larger animals, bones which it can climb, and cling to, with its tiny, clawed feet; the ground git, incidentally, is not to be confused with the tree git, a similar sort of animal, but one which has skin stretched between the front and hind legs on each side, which enables it to glide from tree to tree, and swoop down on food sites; sometimes there is an sudden, small, dry sound, like a tiny, firm clack, and one turns about and finds one clinging to, say, the exposed rib of a fallen animal; the tree gits usually nest in dead trees, and the ground gits usually nest in burrows; both are almost always black in color, which coloration blends in with the dark "greenery" of Abydos, so efficient in light-energy absorption. They are small creatures, both the ground and tree git, and might be held in one of Rodriguez' or Brenner's hands, usually weighing between one hundred and one hundred and fifty grams.

"Have you kept up with your exercises?" asked Rodriguez.

"Yes," said Brenner. The ship did not, like some of the more impressive ships, sphere, wheel and cylinder ships, provide an artificial gravity in virtue of rotation. At certain points on such ships, for example, on the equatorial deck of a simple sphere ship, or at the circumference of a simple wheel or cylinder ship, one might think oneself, in a careless moment, on one's native world. The force of the artificial gravity, of course, by means of controlling the rotational speed, could be indexed to a diversity of home-world masses. On this ship, however, Brenner had attempted to resist the deconditioning which was such a natural concomitant of long-term exposure to low-gravity conditions by more direct and mechanical means, by recourse to special apparatus integral to his cabin, an apparatus consisting of harnesses, hand grips, pedals and such, attached to resistant springs. The captain, and his crew, in their own quarters, incidentally, had similar devices, adapted to their particular physiques. Even so, an adjustment was almost always required after debarkation.

"I am puzzled to know how this contact came about," said Brenner. "That was never explained to me."

"That is an excellent question," said Rodriguez. "I shall tell you what I know. We, of the home world, you understand, have known obscurely of the Pons for hundreds of years. They were often thought extinct. Company Station, built on the sites of previous camps, exploration base camps, navigational beacons, outposts for early-warning systems, neutral trading points agreed upon by diverse systems not wishing to risk contamination of their own worlds, and such, is itself, as you know, more than four hundred years old. Indeed, the Pons are well hidden in their forest. The agents at Company Station did not even learn of their existence until more than a hundred years after the founding of the town. The second contact occurred some one hundred years later. In the meantime it had been conjectured the Pons had perished. Recently, however, in the last hundred years, there have been more recent contacts, perhaps as many as two dozen in that time."

"What of scientific and cultural contacts?" asked Brenner.

"The first was made, apparently, or the first we know of, given the records of Naxos, when they became available to us, more than two thousand years ago. And then, following the records of Eos, another was made something like a thousand years later."

This was interesting, thought Brenner, as his own species was common on both Naxos and Eos.

"You are speaking in very general terms, of course," said Brenner.

"Not really," said Rodriguez. "If we adjust for the revolutionary period of Abydos herself, the time she takes to complete her orbit about her star, these two contacts occurred exactly one thousand revolutions, or years apart, in Abydian time, so to speak."

"These were both contacts invited by the Pons?" asked Brenner.

"It seems so," said Rodriguez.

"And now," said Brenner, "it is a thousand Abydian years later?"

"Precisely," said Rodriguez. "In about two Commonworld months."

"You accept this as an unusual coincidence, of course," said Brenner.

"Consider the probabilities," said Rodriguez.

"I do not care to," said Brenner.

"There is a cycle here," said Rodriguez. "It is not necessary that there is a cycle here, of course, but I think there is one. I really do."

"The Pons are primitive," said Brenner. "They do not even have kings, or chieftains."

"Many primitive peoples are sophisticated with respect to calendars," said Rodriguez, "particularly peoples who depend on agriculture. It is only necessary to mark out the exact point of the rising of a given star on a given day. One can even use the mother star for this purpose, but it is better not to do so, because of its apparent dimension at the horizon. When the star, preferably not the mother star, rises in exactly the same place a second time a year, or a revolution, has occurred. One may mark this place with a portal, an altar, an obelisk. One may count the days between the risings, and divide the year into smaller or larger units, say, weeks and months, or whatever units will serve. Leftover units, say, days, or hours, may be intercalated. From the thousand-years cycle I think we may conjecture the Pons have a base-ten mathematics."

"And a five-digited hand," said Brenner.

"We know they have that," said Rodriguez.

"They do not even have pottery," said Brenner.

"If I am right," said Rodriguez, "they can at least count to a thousand. That is not so complicated. It is a convenient multiple of ten digits. Ten digits times ten digits, two hands times two hands, so to speak, is one hundred digits, and then if one again multiplies this by the base, by two hands, or, better, by ten digits, one arrives at a thousand. This can also be done by addition, of course. The whole calculation might well, to a primitive mind, seem to have a certain naturalness, or mystic rightness, about it."

"One thousand is a nice round number," said Brenner.

"More so than two hundred and sixteen, or one thousand, seven hundred and twenty-eight, or two thousand, seven hundred and forty-four?" asked Rodriguez.

Brenner regarded him.

"You have a five-digited hand," said Rodriguez, "not one with three digits, or six digits, or seven digits."

"And I am a primitive mind?" inquired Brenner.

"Possibly," said Rodriguez. "On the other hand, you are probably capable of making a distinction, at least intellectually, between a felt aptness, one particular to a given species, and a key to the universe."

"One thousand is a nice, round number," said Brenner.

"I agree," said Rodriguez, "but I do not know if the captain would. He might prefer five hundred and twelve." The captain, it might be mentioned, had four digits on the forward appendages. The six-digited rear appendages were not used for precision gripping. "The Pons, of course, would presumably side with us,"

"You are doing these calculations in your head?" asked Brenner.

"Of course," said Rodriguez. "They are simple multiples."

Brenner then began to understand why Rodriguez was so unpopular with many of his colleagues, why they scrutinized his works for the tiniest of errors, why they pounced like Chian zibits on sentences which did not seek to conceal their power, their significance, and passion, why they disdained his affection for the odd, the real, the ancient, and the beautiful, as though orchards and roses, and old clocks, might be less perfect than subway stations and plastic cups, why they were eager to disparage what they could not equal, why they were eager to denounce as execrable insights of which they were incapable. To be sure, Brenner was well aware that these casual calculations were little more than parlor tricks, such things, and many more of their sort, far more complex, being well within the reach of many idiot savants.

"They are indeed beautiful," said Rodriguez, regarding the vast lamplit night, "the suns, and the worlds."

Rodriguez had spoken of strong worlds and weak worlds. Brenner had attempted to twist this distinction into one of diversities of stratification, which was a perspective adequate in its way, but yet perhaps slightly awry. Certainly one might have explicitly stratified worlds which might not be aptly characterized as "strong"; they might be rigid, degenerate, fossilized, brittle, arrested, frozen into obsolescent social crystallizations, worlds dominated by perpetuated but failed aristocracies, worlds closed to the fresh blood of the more knowing, the higher and the more meaningful, those capable of the greatest pain, the most profound agonies, and the ecstasies of the most unspeakable joys. Once, Brenner recalled, long ago, in ancient times, on some worlds, the word 'democracy' had meant horizons, and the opening of a thousand doors; it had constituted not a denial of the aristocracy of nature, but had projected a path to its achievement. To be sure that would be a path which few, even of those capable of the ascent, would care to climb. The trail is narrow and steep, and dangerous. The mountains do not issue their call to all alike. There are some musics which can be heard only by the ear that is born to hear them. One might have spoken, as well, Brenner supposed, of natural worlds as opposed to artificial worlds, of reality worlds as opposed to convention worlds, or even of harmonious worlds, worlds which were harmonious wholes, worlds with social ecosystems, the parts fitting one to the other, in a whole grander than any part in itself. A democracy of opportunity is one thing, thought Brenner. A democracy of fictionalized sameness, of hypocritical pretense, was something different. One was an interesting, if precarious, possibly dangerous, social experiment, dangerous for many reasons, because of its likelihood to lead to instability, to conflict, to the subordination of the best interests of the whole to those of certain more determined, or better organized, or less scrupulous parts of the whole, to the eventual compromise with quality, to the undermining of difference and meaning, to the putative obliteration of distinctions, to the subtle control of a manipulated mass, regulated by secret Caesars, to the world of the hive. The other was a lie. But then, thought Brenner, perhaps it is better to be lied to than told the truth. Surely there was no particular reason to suppose that the truth must be in the best interest of a species. What would be the likelihood of such a coincidence? Perhaps the ideal was to proclaim one's allegiance to truth while avoiding it at all costs. Surely Brenner's species, on the whole, had tended to live from one lie to another. Brenner wondered what it might be for a society to live in terms of truth. He wondered if it would be possible. He wondered if somewhere societies might live in terms of truth. Perhaps on some of the "strong worlds," he thought.

"Never old, always new,
Crowned with clouds,
Enrobed in blue,"
quoted Rodriguez.
Brenner completed the poem:
"I shall not seek another.

You are my world, my mother."

"But rather we approach Abydos," said Rodriguez.

"How is it that you are here?" asked Brenner. It was one thing that Rodriguez might have wished to come to Abydos, for one reason or another. It was quite another that one such as he, presumably out of favor, would have been permitted to do so.

"The directress," said Rodriguez, "wanted me out of the way, off the home world, of course, somewhere else, probably as a result of some pressure from some quarter."

"Anywhere would have done?" asked Brenner. Brenner could imagine several quarters from which such a pressure might have emanated.

"Provided it was sufficiently obscure, and sufficiently far away," said Rodriguez.

"But you wrangled Abydos?"

"Yes," said Rodriguez, chuckling. "I wanted Abydos. I have always been curious about her."

"It is surprising, from what I know of the directress," said Brenner, "that you were permitted to come here, supposing she knew that that was what you wished to do." The directress was a young woman, but vain and petty. She regarded herself as being of unusual importance, and, as if this importance required it, or merited it, enjoyed exploiting, and nursing, the crumb of power to which she had access, often using it to surprise and frustrate colleagues. Perhaps her sense of self-importance, and her consciousness of her own power, required its unexpected, arbitrary or capricious exercise, else it might have seemed that circumstances, criteria, and such, regulated its activity, and not her personal will. Too, she was the sort of woman who enjoyed censoring, censuring, obstructing, thwarting, and ruining, where possible, men such as Rodriguez. Perhaps she felt that the artificiality of her position, and the sensed political fragility of it, sustaining it, required such.

"She didn't know it, of course," said Rodriguez. "Indeed, I even let her think it was the least interesting and most distasteful of the possibilities at her disposal. This was touchy, of course, as she did not even realize the alternative of Abydos at the time, though she pretended to, after I had mentioned it."

"She loathes your work," said Brenner.

"Yes," said Rodriguez. "On the other hand, as you might expect, she has never read it. But this is not unusual. Most form their opinions, and with great firmness, on the basis of the reports of others who, also, may not be acquainted with the original texts. Most opinion, even the most fanatic, is founded on hearsay. There is something to be said for this approach, as it saves time. To be sure, if she had' read it, I do not doubt but what she would have loathed it, as she would understand that that is what, in her particular personality network, her particular power structure, would be expected of her. Very few individuals have the intelligence for private judgment, and of those who do, very few will dare to differ. With respect to the latter point, the matter has been made clear by numerous psychological experiments."

"She did not know about the thousand-year cycle?" asked Brenner.

"No, did you?"

"No," said Brenner.

"I did not care to mention it to her, as she might have found it of interest."

"Nor to me, it seems," said Brenner.

"You don't have to disembark," said Rodriguez.

"You did not trust me?" said Brenner.

"Why should I have trusted you?" asked Rodriguez. "I do not even know you."

Brenner was forced to concede the point, which he did, in silence.

"It might be only a coincidence," said Brenner.

"Of course," said Rodriguez.

"So how did you obtain your grant?" asked Brenner.

"My exile credits?" said Rodriguez.

"If you like," said Brenner.

"The clincher," said Rodriguez, chuckling, "was when I

let it drop that the Pons trace lineage through matrilineal descent.

That decided it."

"But that is almost universal amongst totemic groups," said Brenner.

"She does not know that," said Rodriguez.

"I thought her background was in anthropology," said Brenner.

"No," said Rodriguez.

"But she is directress of the anthropology division of the consortium," said Brenner.

"She is a political appointment," said Rodriguez.

"But not one with her background in anthropology?"

"No," said Rodriguez. "Indeed, she wanted to be the directress of the division of physics."

"Her background is in physics," said Brenner.

"No," said Rodriguez. "But that division is thought to have greater prestige. Besides you do not have to know anything about anthropology to be directress in the anthropology division or anything about physics to be directress in the physics division. The posts are primarily administrative. If one wants some help, one can always ask a question or two, or take an opinion or two, and then make some decision or another. In these fields it doesn't much matter, as all that is sacrificed is knowledge, which, in effect, was given up long ago. Besides, anyone can do anything. All are the same, and so on."

"I see," said Brenner. Sometimes Brenner did not care for Rodriguez' mocking his politics. Surely Rodriguez had been exposed to the same conditioning programs as himself, conditioning programs which inculcated suitable values, opinions, and attitudes, reviewed and approved by appropriate authorities. Had Rodriguez grown up in a social vacuum, or was he one of those aberrant types who made up his own mind, who, in effect, dared to form his own opinions on matters? Did he put himself above the people, the community, the local interspecific consortium, the authorities, the metaparty, if it existed?

"Her background is in interspecific group relations," said Rodriguez. "Her work was characterized by duplicativeness, triviality, unimaginativeness, and mediocrity. In addition, and of even greater importance, it was consistently and unquestioningly politically orthodox. It was natural then that she should have petitioned for, and been granted, a more lucrative post, one in administration."

"I see," said Brenner.

"To be sure," he said, "even that would probably not have been enough. She owes her position to being the niece of an individual in the metaparty."

"There is such a thing?" asked Brenner.

"Of course," said Rodriguez.

"She is a member of it?"

"I do not know," said Rodriguez. "Somehow I regard it as unlikely. I think she lacks the intelligence, the ultimate ruthlessness, for that."

"I see," said Brenner.

"She should be on her knees, scrubbing floors, in chains," said Rodriguez.

Brenner looked at him, horrified.

"Stripped," said Rodriguez.

"Rodriguez!" protested Brenner.

"Surely you found her curves of interest," said Rodriguez.

Brenner gasped.

"Wouldn't you like to have her at your feet, in a collar?" he asked.

"Stop!" said Brenner.

"There are worlds where that is where such as she would be," said Rodriguez. "I have seen such worlds."

"You're joking," said Brenner.

"No," said Rodriguez.

Brenner regarded him, horror-stricken.

"Not every world is like the home world," said Rodriguez.

"There are mediocrities in all fields, male and female," said Brenner.

"True," said Rodriguez, affably. "But she would still look well in a collar."

"But what if she were not as she is, not merely attractive, if she is, not that I would notice such a thing, but was exquisitely beautiful, sensitive, even brilliant?"

"She would still belong in a collar," said Rodriguez.

"A collar?" asked Brenner.

"An animal collar, a pet, or a slave collar, such things, in any case, owned."

"I do not understand," said Brenner.

"She is a woman," explained Rodriguez.

"I do not understand," said Brenner.

"That is what they need, what they want," said Rodriguez.

"I do not understand," said Brenner.

"One must own, or be owned," said Rodriguez. "In their hearts they know that it is they who are to be owned. Not owned, freed by men too weak to own them, it is natural that they lash out in frustration. Denied their identities, they attempt to usurp spurious identities, turning their lives into pretenses; too, in their frustration and pain, they will attempt to punish men, as they can, for their weakness, for denying them to themselves."

"What of the previous expeditions, the scientific and cultural expeditions, to the Pons," asked Brenner, "that from Naxos, that from Eos?" Brenner thought it well to change the subject.

"I suppose they were completed," said Rodriguez. "But in interlink I could do little more than pull their departure dates."

"Their reports were not filed, their studies?" asked Brenner.

"I do not know," said Rodriguez. "Perhaps they were destroyed, or lost."

"When did the expeditions return?" asked Brenner.

"I do not know," said Rodriguez.

"Is it known that they returned?" asked Brenner.

"Why would they not have returned?" asked Rodriguez.

"I do not know," said Brenner.

"Surely we may presume they returned safely," said Rodriguez, puzzled.

"You have consulted records, of course?" said Brenner.

"Of course," said Rodriguez.

"What did you learn?" asked Brenner.

"The records are silent on the matter," said Rodriguez.

"They could have been lost," said Brenner.

"That is possible," said Rodriguez. "There are surely dangers in space, technological failure, miscalculation, meteor storms, mutiny on long voyages, war, piracy, any number of possibilities." Indeed, we might note, there might have been any number of possibilities. It was not, you see, even in these modern times, the case that the rational species had conquered space. At best, they seemed to have won a certain, perhaps begrudged, toleration.

"Those expeditions were presumably fully fledged expeditions, properly staffed, suitably equipped, and provisioned, and such," speculated Brenner.

"Presumably so," smiled Rodriguez.

"With their own ship, or ships," said Brenner.

"Ships which might have a considerable value, if obtained in a relatively undamaged condition."

Brenner swallowed, hard.

A state-of-the-art starship, if taken in salvage, was a trove of equipment and fuel elements.

"But I do not think that we have to worry much about that," said Rodriguez. "Besides, this is a company ship." The great companies, of course, maintained their own police, their private armies, and such. Their ships, broadcasting their identificatory signals, commonly negotiated the silent seas of space with impunity. The annual budgets of some of these companies, it might be noted, in passing, exceeded the gross estimated wealth of many worlds.

"But we do have information on the Pons," said Brenner.

"Certainly," he said, "but from surveyors and traders, and, in the last century or so, largely from contacts at Company Station."

"I do not like it," said Brenner.

"In all likelihood," said Rodriguez, "the expeditions returned in good order and, in time, filed their reports, their studies and such, and then these documents were later destroyed, or lost, perhaps in one politically mandated revision of knowledge or another."

"You think then there might be something of interest on Abydos?"

"I think it is possible," said Rodriguez.

Brenner looked out the port. Perhaps he imagined it, but it seemed to him that the star of Abydos, a yellow star, might appear to a bit larger now than it had earlier.

"We will conduct our researches at Company Station?" said Brenner.

"No," said Rodriguez. "We are going back, into the forests."

"That could be dangerous," said Brenner.

"You won't find out anything of interest at a trading point," said Rodriguez. "Besides, we have been invited in, by the Pons themselves."

"That seems surprising," said Brenner.

"Yes," said Rodriguez.

"Perhaps they want to open themselves to cultural contacts," said Brenner.

"Undoubtedly," said Rodriguez.

"If we discover anything uncongenial to the home world," said Brenner, "presumably it, too, in its turn, would be suppressed."

"Doubtless," said Rodriguez. "But we will have known it, for a moment at least."

Brenner shuddered, understanding then a little better the nature of his senior colleague.

"You think there may be something about the "beginning" on Abydos?" said Brenner.

"I think that is possible," said Rodriguez.

"Totemic societies are unimportant," said Brenner. "They are an anthropological dead end."

"That is the official position," said Rodriguez. "Indeed, if the Pons were thought to be of any serious interest, the sort which might improve a scholar's credentials, earn him a promotion, secure future fellowships and grants, win prizes, bring recognition and honor to the consortium, and such, it is not we who would be here now, but others, the highly placed sycophants of the metaparty."

"I am not eager to go back in the forests," said Brenner.

"You can stay on board," said Rodriguez. "I can punch enough credits for your return, on the back loop, to some port or another, from which your own credits should suffice for passage back to the home world. Indeed, I suspect that the captain, who seems a good fellow, would be willing to overlook your presence on board, at least to Chios."

Brenner was silent.

"I'll speak to the captain in the morning," said Rodriguez.

"No," said Brenner.

Rodriguez turned away from the port and stars, to look at Brenner, the adjunct's face pale in the light from without the port.

"I'll come with you," said Brenner.

"Why?" asked Rodriguez.

"It is a voyage of months back to the home world," said Brenner. "Besides, I accepted the assignment."

Rodriguez did not free Brenner of his gaze.

"I, too, from what I have heard, am curious about Abydos," said Brenner.

Rodriguez returned his attention to the vistas beyond the port.

"You were assigned?" asked Rodriguez.

"Yes," said Brenner.

"I wonder why," mused Rodriguez.

"I suppose I was suitably unimportant," said Brenner.

"You are not politically suspect?" asked Rodriguez.

"No," said Brenner.

"You have not expressed unapproved opinions, or been lax in your overt and frequently reiterated subscription to approved opinions, have you?" asked Rodriguez.

"Certainly not," said Brenner.

"You have adequately guarded your expressions, and your behaviors, even subtle ones?"

"It is not necessary for me to be on my guard in such matters," said Brenner.

"You have not betrayed atavistic tendencies?" asked Rodriguez.

"I would think not," smiled Brenner.

"You have not alienated the directress, have you?"

"Not to my knowledge," said Brenner.

"She may have sensed something in you that she feared," said Rodriguez.

"Preposterous," said Brenner.

"Something that makes her uneasy," said Rodriguez, "something that even you yourself are unaware of."

"That seems to me preposterous," said Brenner.

"I did consult your records," said Rodriguez, "your origins."

Brenner stiffened.

"Then you realize that I am unimportant," said Brenner. To be sure, Brenner was, in effect, without connections, relationships, and family. He was, at any rate, not integrated in one of the major matriarchally traced kinship networks.

"You never knew your father or mother?" asked Rodriguez.

"Of course not," said Brenner.

Brenner was, in his way, rather the result of an experiment. He was what was known, somewhat disparagingly, even in a time which disparaged disparagements, as a "vat brat," the result of a fertilization of stored gametes, the development of which was brought to term *in vitro*. The Brenners of Home World tended to be embarrassments, in their way, lingering holdovers from earlier times, from more benighted eras. Most of these materials had been disposed of.

"I am a modernist, and a lifest," Brenner reminded Rodriguez.

Rodriguez nodded. "I understand," he said. It would be particularly important to Brenner to fit in, he supposed, to repudiate a dubious, obsolescent genetic heritage which had, in effect, through an eccentric byway of science, found itself precipitated into a time not its own. Perhaps that is why he was given this assignment, Rodriguez speculated to himself, because his genes were feared. On various worlds Rodriguez' own genetic heritage, and that of those like him, and of other sorts, as well, in the name of the good of the community, had been outlawed.

His was a genotype the community was not eager to see perpetuated. No longer did it fit in. The time of the captains, the commanders, the explorers, on such worlds, was gone. There had been agitation on more than one world for Rodriguez to be "smoothed," or anatomically perfected, that his energies, his passion, his drives, the cutting edge of his intellect, be dulled into conformity. It was not easy, however, to pick up Rodriguez, as it was a more inconspicuous victim and remand him for therapeutic surgery. He was known and, in some circles, seemed to have power. It was even speculated he had connections with various hypothesized underground organizations whose interests might not be identical with those of the community as a whole. Two police who had called for him had been found dead. No further police called for him. It would be enough then to deport him, and deny him future entrance visas to such worlds.

"I knew my father and mother," said Rodriguez, "when I was little."

"That is nice," said Brenner.

"I was about ten," said Rodriguez, "in Commonworld revolutions," looking out absently into the stars, at the sun of Abydos, in the distance. "I caught my father abusing my mother. I killed him."

Brenner was startled, and felt the hair rise on the back of his neck.

"I was her champion, you see," he said.

"You didn't know what you were doing," said Brenner.

"No, I didn't," said Rodriguez, "but in a sense more profound than you realize."

"What happened?" asked Brenner.

"My mother cast me out of the house," he said. "I lived in the streets. I was alone. I survived."

"What of your mother?" asked Brenner.

"Shortly after she had cast me out," he said, "she committed suicide."

Rodriguez then pressed the first of the recessed buttons at the side of the port, and then the second. The illumination in the lounge was restored, and the plating of the port closed. "Until tomorrow at ten," said Rodriguez.

"What is wrong?" asked Rodriguez.

"Nothing," said Brenner.

Rodriguez, with a small motion, pushing off, floated back to the webbing he had occupied. There, steadied by a hand on it, he turned back to regard Brenner.

"Are you afraid?" asked Rodriguez.

"Yes," said Brenner.

"Of me?" asked Rodriguez.

"No," said Brenner, after a moment.

"Of the Pons?" asked Rodriguez, skeptically.

"No," said Brenner. "They are innocent, simple, and inoffensive."

"Of the forest?" asked Rodriguez.

"From what I have heard of it, yes," said Brenner.

Rodriguez hooked one arm in the webbing. "Don't be," he said. "Come here. Look."

Brenner, with some skill, that which he had developed in the past weeks, joined Rodriguez at the webbing, and clung to the straps.

Rodriguez opened his small pack, which he seemed never without, that into which the emptied stein had been placed.

"What is it?" asked Brenner.

"It appears to be a telescope, collapsed, does it not?"

"Yes," said Brenner.

Rodriguez then removed the object from the pack, rotated it 180 degrees and extended it. He also slid a panel back, revealing a breech. Following another adjustment, a trigger, housed in its guard, dropped into view below. "It is a Naxian rifle," said Rodriguez.

"That is a forbidden weapon," whispered Brenner, with an eye to the translating equipment, that by means of which they had communicated with the captain. "How did you get it through customs?"

"I picked it up on Chios," he said. "Things are less tight out here. Too, I did punch out a bribe to a private number twice."

"It is illegal to have it," said Brenner.

"Not everywhere," said Rodriguez.

"Certainly on a company ship, without authorization," said Brenner.

"And at Company Station, without authorization," said Rodriguez.

"I would suppose so," said Brenner.

"Certainly," said Rodriguez.

In order that this matter may be more clear I might mention that on many worlds weapons were not permitted to citizenries. The result of these ordinances, naturally, was that the citizenries of these worlds, for the most part, found themselves at the mercy of two groups which were somewhat diverse, but were in fact occasionally allied, to speak briefly, authorities and criminals. The means for their own protection was removed from them for their own protection. Interestingly enough, private transportation on various worlds was usually responsible for hundreds of times the deaths that had been wrought by the use of certain classes of weapons in the past, but such transportation was seldom removed from citizenries for their own protection. It might also be noted that private citizens who wished, for one reason or another, to do away with other private citizens, now denied the use of certain classes of weapons, did find themselves forced to new recourses, such as piercing with pointed tools, striking with heavy objects, and administering toxic substances.

"The Naxian rifle is a powerful weapon," said Brenner.

"This model is," said Rodriguez.

Brenner looked at the object, alarmed.

"With three charges from this," said Rodriguez, confidingly, "I could open the side of the ship. One charge would be enough to cut a bull of Sybaris in two."

"How many charges do you have?" asked Brenner. This was not a simple beam weapon, of the sort with which one might etch patient laceries in steel. The power of this weapon was discharged in concentrated bursts.

"Several," said Rodriguez.

Brenner looked at him.

"Concealed in rolls of Bertinian leaf," he said.

"Be careful what you smoke," said Brenner.

"The charge is armed only in the breech," grinned Rodriguez.

Brenner nodded. Heat, then, was not the precipitating agent. In that case, one could presumably hold a lighter to one of the cartridges, or charge casings, without getting more than a bad smell.

"What about impact?" asked Brenner.

"Hardly," said Rodriguez.

"Of course," said Brenner. Impact-activated charges, connected with firing pins, and such, were seldom found on civilized worlds. To be sure, they were still found here and there, in certain systems. But so, too, here and there, were pointed and edged weapons. Indeed, there were certain interesting worlds which had adopted sophisticated techniques, vehicles, and weapons for interplanetary aggression or planetary self-defense but which, on their own surfaces, had achieved carefully constructed neoprimitivisms, by means of which they sought to exercise ecological caution and liberate the processes of natural selection. On such worlds, by a sort of progress in reverse, were the rights, the ranks, and the glories of nature restored. Some of these worlds were of the sort which Rodriguez would presumably have characterized as "strong." To be sure, there were features of such worlds which Brenner would doubtless have found deplorable. On them, for example, martial arts were practiced; and on them might be found warring camps, and not infrequently, it must be admitted, slave markets.

So do not fear the forest," said Rodriguez, closing the weapon, which action restored it to the appearance of a simple telescope.

"I do not want anything killed," said Brenner.

Some brief indications of Brenner's concerns are in order. On his home world, long ago, the horrors of killing anything had become clear. This was no longer viewed as the way of life. Life had been improved upon, succeeded by certain moral postures. It had begun in particular with the illegalization of utilizing certain privileged sets of life forms as food. One popular expression was that it was wrong to "enslave animals for food purposes" which slogan indicated a confusion of slavery with animal husbandry, two quite disparate institutions, and was not regarded as requiring any plausible explanation, defense, or justification. Shortly thereafter it was pointed out by botanically sensitive individuals that vegetable matter, too, was alive, and might well have some dim sort of consciousness. Various bills intended to outlaw the enslavement of vegetables, fruit trees, and such, for food purposes just failed of enactment in certain areas, after lengthy expert testimony was taken from the scientific community on the minimalistic, if that, nature of the mentality of these various plants, and such, as though the mere minimality of the mentality were at all germane to the question. Where the bills were enacted they tended to be popularly ignored, though some individuals, as a moral duty, starved to death, attended by widespread publicity in the press, rousing general sympathy but in the end accomplishing little with respect to altering the ultimate fate of most vegetables. It had also been observed that the meaning of the command, "Thou shalt not kill," had only recently been discovered, after several thousand years. It was noted that the original community to which this directive had been issued and which, presumably, would have been in an ideal position to understand it, had failed to grasp its import. Several members of that community, for example, had been shepherds, and others had been farmers and vintagers, and such. Too, one supposes that some amongst them would not have been above angling. Also, they seem to have had few scruples about putting tribal enemies to the sword, and, indeed, in certain cases, seem to have undertaken it as a duty incumbent upon them in virtue of obedience to the will of the very entity which had issued the original injunction pertaining to killing, an anomaly, at best. The injunction against killing would apply, of course, not only to animals and plants which might be utilized for food, but, naturally, more generally. An obvious, even painfully so, life form, was the insect. Insecticides, of course, were banned. A number of other accommodations were also in order, such as screened bulbs to prevent injury to flying insects and special shoes designed both for comfort and support and reduction of the number of contact surfaces with the ground, the latter to minimize the danger to crawling insects. Children were warned to be specially watchful not to step on six-legged brothers, and so on. These were, of course, negative precautions. The next logical step was insect welfare, putting out food for them, encouraging their breeding, etc. In some communities of the more enlightened variety special walkways were designed to protect individuals from hovering swarms. Insect welfarists often tore down these screens, as artificial barriers. Some individuals would wander about with serene smiles upon their countenances, their bodies swarming with insects, providing the little fellows with harbors and refuges, and nourishing them even, depending upon the variety, with their own blood. Whereas the saintliness of these individuals was readily admitted by the community at large, it must be admitted that their example, however inspiring, seldom elicited, or was honored by, emulation. Whereas it was true that a certain amount of edible material could be synthesized from certain chemicals these processes tended to be complex and expensive. Aside from questions of the nutritional equivalence of this material, if this was thought important, which still remained controversial, there were additional problems connected with its palatability, which might be ignored, and its long-term side effects which did not yet seem to be fully understood. But this sort of thing was not practical economically for most individuals, and of those to whom it was economically practical, few seemed to be interested in it. Most would make do with some forms of mashes and pulps. It might be added, for what it is worth, that various species of animals which had hitherto been enslaved, if one may so speak, for certain values or products, such as eggs, fur, or meat, had now lapsed into extinction. Naturally the enslavement of animals such as dogs, cats, tropical fish, torgos, inwits, and canaries was also outlawed. On several worlds these animals, too, were now extinct. Happily they survived on others. A further natural development, earlier mentioned, was the extension of the franchise to these fellow citizens of worlds, to be exercised, of course, by proxies, the control of which was a matter of great political moment. On the other hand, it seemed these life forms should have a say, too, or that there should be a say on their behalf, in various parliaments, diets and congresses. Things, of course, were not quite as one might expect on Brenner's home world, given these axiological principles and commitments, because of the recrudescence of the "reality principle," so to speak. Many of the subscribed values were given little more attention than was required by deference to the militant minorities, suffused with righteous zeal, that championed them. Many an insect, guilty of no more than the attempt to exercise his natural rights, was doubtless done in the privacy of one's own compartments. There were, of course, certain individuals who committed suicide, overcome by guilt at the perpetuation of these secret murders, confessed to in notes left behind, and there were occasional mothers who, in view of the clearly stated utilitarian principles of the equivalence of all life forms, had sacrificed their child to save two cockroaches, but these were rare. The rational races tended to be saved, once again, by hypocrisy, the value of which is perhaps too little understood as a facilitator of social survival. Too, certain historic decisions, still controversial, emanating from high judiciaries, perhaps expressing the opinion of an alarmed metaparty, had made it clear that it was not morally incumbent upon the rational races, no more than other life forms, to surrender and depress the quality of their own life, or to seek their own extinction, no matter how moral the cause. To be sure, these matters remained legally and morally confused. It might be mentioned, lastly, that a black market thrived on most of the civilized worlds in which certain goods, foodstuffs, and such, for a price, remained available. To use a metaphor, many individuals who would not have enjoyed sticking a pig continued to relish pork chops. Too, the rich, and the powerful, as one might expect, had things much their own way. Even on the home world, it was rumored that they could buy anything, even women.

"I do not want anything killed," said Brenner, repeating himself, firmly.

"It is sometimes necessary to kill," said Rodriguez.

"Never," said Brenner.

"I suppose you are right, or at least generally," said Rodriguez. "One could just do nothing, or die, or let something else die."

"Of course," said Brenner.

"What of the bird that captures and eats an insect?" asked Rodriguez. "Has it committed murder?"

"I am not responsible for the bird," said Brenner.

"Do you regard it as guilty?" asked Rodriguez.

"No," said Brenner.

"Why not?" asked Rodriguez.

"That is just the way of life," said Brenner.

"And you do not regard yourself as part of the way of life?" asked Rodriguez. "You exempt yourself from its ways?"

Brenner was silent.

"Every time you take a breath, every time you move, every time you lie down, every time you step," said Rodriguez, "you kill, say, some tiny thing, some bacterium, some virus, some mite, such things. Your very body, with its natural defenses against disease, is designed by nature to survive, and to survive by killing."

Brenner said nothing, but was angry.

"You live," said Rodriguez, "because it is a killing machine."

Some individuals, incidentally, sensitive, unusually morally motivated individuals, aware of, and horrified by, these possibilities, and attempting to curtail, or minimize, breathing, to avoid movement, and such, had gone insane. Most, however, in virtue of the predictable reassertion of what might be spoken of as "the reality principle," as we have called it, in a disgusted spasm of health, rather reflexively, threw off these ideas, almost as one might vomit poison, no longer attending to them, rather getting on with the business of living, accepting themselves at last honestly as one animal amongst others in the kingdom of life, and one with its own nature, concerning which it need not be apologetic, and a nature with a potentiality for dominance, one with its place in the order of nature, one with a right to its place in the food chain.

"You are angry," said Rodriguez, closing the pack.

"No, I am not," said Brenner, heatedly.

"Answer me this, truthfully," said Rodriguez, looking at Brenner. "Let us suppose some predatory animal were intent upon devouring a child, and you could save the child by killing the animal. Would you do so?"

"Yes," said Brenner, angrily.

"You would give priority to your own life form?"

"Yes, said Brenner, in fury.

"Then you do not, truly, believe in the equivalence of life forms."

"It seems not," said Brenner.

"Then you are a species chauvinist," said Rodriguez.

Brenner said nothing, but was furious.

"And so perhaps it is appropriate that you, too, have been sent to Abydos," smiled Rodriguez.

"Perhaps," said Brenner.

"Have you never wondered what it would be like, to breathe freely, to walk free, to fulfill yourself, to be yourself, as what you really are, truly?"

"I do not understand," said Brenner.

"Good night," said Rodriguez.

"About the directress," said Brenner.

"Yes?" said Rodriguez.

"I think you owe me an apology, on her behalf," said Brenner, "for how you spoke of her."

"I do not understand," said Rodriguez.

"Having to do with your offensive remarks about "curves" and "collars" and such."

"Oh," said Rodriguez.

"I really feel you should apologize."

"Look there," said Rodriguez. "There on the plating at your feet, in that exact place."

"Yes?" said Brenner, puzzled, complying.

"Imagine her there now, in a slave collar, perhaps in chains, if you like, at your feet, stripped."

Brenner, startled, stared down at the plating.

"Is she in chains?" asked Rodriguez.

"Yes," said Brenner, hesitantly.

Rodriguez laughed.

Brenner reddened, angrily.

"Now," said Rodriguez, "she lies at your feet, docile, curled up, in her chains."

"Stop!" said Brenner.

"She is a woman," said Rodriguez. "Let them lie there, at your feet, in the shadow of your whip, knowing they must obey. They will lie there, and purr with contentment."

"Stop! Stop!" said Brenner.

"What is wrong?" asked Rodriguez.

"I will not have you uttering such words!"

"Are her lineaments, so soft and well turned, so luscious, not of interest to you?"

"I must not think such thoughts!" cried Brenner.

"Why?" asked Rodriguez. "Do they make you uncomfortable? Do they make you too conscious of your manhood?"

"I am not a man," cried Brenner, "or not in what I take to be your dreadful sense! I must not be a man, not in that terrible sense! No! I am a person! I must be a person! Manhood, in your sense, is an anachronism, belonging to more primitive times, less enlightened eras. It is now, in that sense, as you well know, outlawed."

"Yet in you, deny it as you will," said Rodriguez, "is a man."

"No," wept Brenner.

"And in the old sense, that which you find so frightening, that of pride and power."

"No!" said Brenner.

"Accept it, fulfill it, and relish it," said Rodriguez.

"No, no!" said Brenner.

"You find these things reprehensible, objectionable?" asked Rodriguez.

"Yes!" said Brenner.

"But the pupils of your eyes are dilated," said Rodriguez.

Brenner turned swiftly away, that Rodriguez could not see his face, or body.

"Well," said Rodriguez. "Dream of the directress, and as you would have her."

"No," said Brenner. "No!"

"Good night," said Rodriguez, and, releasing the webbing, moved lightly across the plating, toward the exit from the lounge.

"Doubtless you will dream of her!" cried Brenner, clinging to the webbing, like a rope in the sea.

Rodriguez turned about, at the exit, and, one hand on the handle of the panel, grinned. "Perhaps," he said, "but I think not. I have others in mind who I think would be even more interesting subjects of such dreams."

"Monster," said Brenner.

"And surely you, too, might do better than the directress," he suggested, "not that she is bad, in her essentials, you understand."

"Monster, monster!" said Brenner.

Rodriguez spun lightly about, preparing to leave.

"Rodriguez!" called Brenner.

Rodriguez, his feet a bit from the floor, turned back. "Have you had such women," asked Brenner, "women in such a way.

"Such women, women in such a way?" asked Rodriguez.

"You know what I mean!" said Brenner.

"Slaves, female slaves?" asked Rodriguez.

"Yes!" said Brenner.

"Of course," said Rodriguez. "They are common, on various worlds."

"But the women of Home World do not even know of such things, do they?"

"I would suppose that most do not," said Rodriguez.

Brenner regarded him.

"There are, of course," said Rodriguez, "some such, even on Home World."

"Impossible!" said Brenner.

"Kept secretly, of course," said Rodriguez.

"Impossible," insisted Brenner.

"Their chains are as real as those of the girls on Megara, kept as prizes, awarded in the games," said Rodriguez.

"Impossible," repeated Brenner.

"Not everything on the home world is on the surface," said Rodriguez.

"What are slaves like?" asked Brenner.

"Once you have tried one," said Rodriguez, "you will never be content with anything less."

Brenner swallowed, hard. He knew that the home world, and such worlds, were notorious for the low quality of their female companionship.

"And," said Rodriguez, "I have little doubt that even the directress, properly embonded, and brought under suitable discipline, might prove to be not without interest."

Brenner regarded him, aghast.

"It would certainly shake up her frigidity at any rate," he said.

"Please," protested Brenner.

"Consider her at your feet, begging, with tears of need in her eyes," he said.

"Stop!" said Brenner.

"Dream of the directress," smiled Rodriguez.

"No!" said Brenner.

"Or others," said Rodriguez.

"No, no!" said Brenner.

But then Rodriguez had left.

Brenner clung for a time to the webbing, and then, for no reason he clearly understood, made his way back to the far side of the lounge, where he extinguished the lights and retracted the port shielding. Then he hovered there, at the port, looking out into the night of space, at the stars, alone. It was clear now that the sun of Abydos, which he recognized, in spite of the slightly different orientation of the ship, was larger. By morning it would be painful to look at it, and some of its worlds, perhaps even Abydos, might be visible, like small disks basking in its light. Brenner was angry, and muchly agitated by his disturbing conversation with his senior colleague, so unlike typical colleagues, sheltered children of the universities, unfamiliar with dark streets and the night. How had such a person as Rodriguez, who had done many things, come to the academic world, to his own field, anthropology? He had wanted to understand reality, it seemed, but not by means of categories and classifications, important though they might be, but by handling it himself, by digging into it, with his own hands, so to speak. Perhaps that was the main difference between Rodriguez and so many other colleagues, thought Brenner. Rodriguez was ignorant. He was naive. He did not truly understand the ways of academia. He was not yet content to substitute concepts for the concrete. He had not yet learned to replace reality with abstractions. As for the ship, Abydos would be no more than a convenience, a depot at which to draw fuel, at best a mere way station on routes to points of greater importance. Brenner looked at the distant star. On one of the worlds of that star, on Abydos, back in the forests, were the Pons, one of the few remaining totemic groups known to the civilized worlds. The field, of course, was no longer interested in totemic groups. It regarded them as unimportant. Rodriguez, on the other hand, had been curious about them.

Indeed, it seemed he thought there might be something of interest to be discovered in the forests. He had even spoken, somewhat cryptically, of learning something about the "beginning." But there was nothing of importance on Abydos, not of serious importance. Brenner was sure of that. If there was anything of importance down there, it would not have been given to an over-the-hill, scarred, irascible, controversial, dissolute, politically suspect reprobate like Rodriguez, abetted by no more than himself, an inexperienced adjunct. Then, looking out upon the stars, and wondering about worlds, Brenner felt his agitations returning, and hastily slid shut the shielding for the port. In this fashion he did not have to look out upon stars which might shine upon worlds which he might have found objectionable, worlds of which he might have disapproved, deplorable worlds whose values might not be identical with his own. Interesting that the suns should shine with the same neutrality, the same equanimity, thought Brenner, on such diversities of worlds. And how difficult it was to tell, from far away, the differences amongst these worlds. The instruments of astronomy, it seemed, required refinement. How can one ascertain the distances, the rotations, and revolutions of meaningfulness, the patterns of values, the magnitudes of significance? But Brenner reminded himself, angrily, that he knew the good, the true, the beautiful, the meaningful, the correct. He had been taught them. Why then, Brenner asked himself, was there so much diversity amongst the worlds, even the civilized, or, better, the technologically advanced, worlds on such matters. Too, if his world were right in the ten thousand proprieties, and such, why was there so much misery, so much pain and unhappiness on it, not the misery and pain, the unhappiness, of basic negativities, such as inadequate shelter or food, or care, but the leaden miseries, the gray, dismal miseries, the seemingly hopeless miseries, the constraints, the inhibitions, the boredoms, the ennui, the pretences, the lies, the hypocrisies, the frustrating awarenesses, on the part of some, of dupery and manipulation, the special emptiness, and pain, that could remain, even in a warm, dry room, even after the receipt of certified nourishments? Could there be other nourishments, Brenner wondered, nourishments on which the heart, and the hope, and the cry for significance and meaning, might feed? Perhaps that is what is missing, he speculated. Then he put his hands on the plating. "No," he thought to himself. "No, no!" But his world was correct, he knew, for it had been arrived at by correct procedures, developed by behavioral and axiological engineers sensitive to, and responsive to, the most enlightened political imperatives and nuances. But then why the pain, the misery, the ennui, the frustration, the grief, the sorrow, he asked himself. But then he thought how foolish this was, for why, really, should there be some striking congruence between the "good" and what people might find to their liking, or between the right, or the correct, and that which might prove productive of fulfillment, satisfaction, or happiness? Perhaps the entire issue had been viewed askew, and actually it was good and right, or appropriate, or correct, that the members of his species be unhappy, that they suffer emptiness and misery, that they remain unfulfilled. But Brenner did not care for this possibility at all, perhaps as a consequence of some insistent, unreconciled deviation in an uncorrected genetic makeup. Besides, he asked himself, how then should matters be determined. If there were no necessity for the good and the right to conduce to satisfaction or happiness, then presumably there would be no necessity that they should conduce to dissatisfaction or unhappiness either. Would one not expect random correlations? But the correlations on the home world did not seem to be random. They seemed on the whole detrimental to human satisfaction, to human welfare, happiness, and meaningfulness, at least if these things were taken in an uncritical, primitive sense. Was it essential that civilization prove inimical to human fulfillment, Brenner wondered. Were these two values, if values they were, antithetical, mutually exclusive, incapable of accommodations, incapable of achieving simultaneous fruition. That did not seem likely. To be sure, certain modalities of civilization might require the rejection, the repudiation, of human fulfillment, but surely, amongst all the dazzling infinities of social possibility, such were not the only conceivable modalities. And, too, what then were the touchstones for good or right, or for the proper, or the correct, he wondered, if not just such things as happiness, satisfaction, and meaningfulness, things so often, and so grievously, impaired and thwarted, if not actually absent, from the world he knew. But perhaps there is no common will, he thought. Perhaps there is no common interest. In the end perhaps there is only the struggle, the conflict, and the

fraud, the victory of some announced as the victory of all.
What was his species, he wondered. Brenner then became
alarmed for he had lost touch with the plating. As he had
closed the port and not yet reillumined the lounge he had
been in the utter darkness. Suddenly he was no longer certain
of his orientation, or bearings. He did not now know where
he was, what was up or down, relative the webbings, or
what was left or right. He reached out, turning in the
darkness, out of touch with contact points as simple as the
grip near the port. Suddenly the lights went on in the lounge.
At the entrance panel, with a certain rather puzzled attitude
of head and neck, was one of the crew. Immediately Brenner
could obtain his bearings. Gratefully, when he could get a
hand on a solid object, in this case, the wall at the side of the
port, he pushed toward the webbing, and, in a moment, had
it in hand. The crew member with loping strides, and a
series of small clicks on the floor plating, as tiny magnetized
disks attached to the first clawed digits of its rear appendages
made their contact with the metal, went to the observation
port and checked its closure. It then turned about to regard
Brenner. It was making its rounds, clearly, and on these
rounds one of its duties was apparently to check the closure
of port shieldings. The port shielding, incidentally, when
opened, activated the lounge entrance lock, closing off the
lounge, except to authorized crew members. In this fashion
if the port should be shattered any attendant decompression
would be limited to the lounge. To be sure it would take a
considerable impact to threaten the quartz of the port, and
any object capable of injuring it would presumably have
been picked up long ago by the ship's sensors, their signals
feeding into the guidance system in such a way as to initiate
an evasive action, to be followed by a later return to course.
Brenner waved to the crew member, that it might understand
that all was well. It may have wondered what the point of
Brenner's floating about in the darkened lounge might have
been but, tactfully, it did not approach the vicinity of the
translation device and inquire. Besides, it was really none of
its business. It was only a second-class crew member and

Brenner was a passenger. Too, discovering Brenner in this unusual situation may have confirmed, or seemed to confirm, some preconception or other in its mind. It then loped to the exit with tiny clicks, where it turned, once again, to regard Brenner. It was difficult for Brenner to read expressions on that sort of face. The magnetic attachments at the rear claws were most often used when managing controls or monitoring panels, where one might wish to retain one's exact position and orientation without reliance on secretions, which were occasionally unreliable, or, more mechanically, by webbing. Also, of course, these devices, when in contact with metal, provided immediate leverage for movement. Brenner waved again. He would turn off the lights. The crew member lifted a claw, opened its mouth, clapped its jaws twice, and then left. Brenner felt foolish, having been discovered in such an embarrassing state, so helpless, so disoriented. But his race, he knew, to many in the galaxy, counted as little more than amusing caricatures of rational life, nonentities, mediocrities, interesting perhaps as pets or clowns. Brenner, an arm anchored in the webbing, looked down at the plating where Rodriguez had directed him to imagine the directress, and in a certain sort of fashion. It was well thought Brenner, angrily, that she was not there, and in such a fashion, else she might have been, for no fault whatsoever of her own, whipped, and merely because he had been discovered in an embarrassing situation by another life form, merely because he felt foolish, merely because he was angry with himself. He supposed that such women were occasionally subjected to such attentions, and for no better reasons, that it was in effect a part of the hazards of their condition, or of their lot, that they were subject to such things, that they might be abused, or kicked, as might be any other form of animal, say, a dog.

Brenner looked about the lounge. Things were now in place. The lights were on. The webbing floated about, attached to its stanchions. He could see the door. He could see the controls for the lights, both at the port and near the door. By listening carefully he could detect the soft hum of the filtering system, regulating the gases in the room. He was still agitated by his conversation with Rodriguez, but now his blood had ceased to churn, no longer was he drenched with sweat, no longer was he afraid, or angry. He now, once again, had his values in order. How absurd for him to have let Rodriguez disturb him. Brenner's tentative little odyssey of thought, stimulated by the hurricane of Rodriguez' monstrousness, had subsided. To be sure, there was a lingering uneasiness in him. Rodriguez could have that effect on people. He did glance down once at a certain place on the plating but quickly glanced away. He must control his thoughts. He must not let them rise in him like a sun in the morning, or spring up like flowers, like grass or mountains. He must not attend to them. Who knew where such thoughts, such things, emerging as though from lairs concealed beneath distant horizons, asserting themselves imperiously, naturally, as though springing from forgotten seeds, as though growing from deep soils, might lead? Rodriguez is a monster, thought Brenner. Then he made his way to the exit, turned off the lights, left the lounge, and, amongst the pipes and girderwork, made his way to his cabin. Shortly thereafter, he had hooked himself in his rest webbing, and retired.

He did not go to sleep immediately.

He thought of a number of things, and, in particular, his assignment, and the world, Abydos.

As he grew drowsy, he found it more and more difficult to keep his mind from drifting back to his conversation with Rodriguez.

He is an unregenerate monster, thought Brenner.

And, too, as he grew more and more drowsy, it was difficult not to remember what the directress had looked like, as he had imagined her, with such specificity, on the plating, in that exact place. Even her expression recurred to him, and how she had lifted her hands, in their linked bracelets. Then, too, she had looked well, lying on her side, looking up at him. And he thought, too, of other women he had seen, perhaps even casually on a conveyance or on a street, or known, from one place or another, and wondered what they, too, might have looked like in various situations, and attitudes, not in their mannish garbs designed to protect their personness, as though it would much need protection on the home world, of course, but in snatches of cotton or shreds of silk. And when they ascended the block, of course, they would be permitted not even so much. How well they served! And their glances, how soft, how shy, how timid. And that one, did she not dance? Brenner turned in the webbing, trying to force these thoughts from his mind. It seemed their whispers were about him, almost inaudible, tiny, plaintive whispers requesting attention. He scarcely dared to open his eyes lest he should seem to see them, shadowy in the darkness. Were they there? It almost seemed he might feel their touch. He turned in the webbing. He was in misery. He chastised himself mercilessly. How could he, a modernist and a lifest, have such thoughts? And had he not actually known some of these women, as fellow students, as colleagues, and such? How then could he conceive of them thusly, as though they might be naught but Naxian property girls, owned as much as a dog or a pig on Chios? But Rodriguez, he supposed, angrily, would have taken it all in his stride, and, indeed, got what he wanted from them, and more. Then doubtless he would have sold them, before returning to the home world. It would not do, of course, to bring in such merchandise, not to the home world. Then, failing to rid himself of these thoughts by various acts of will, requiring one degree or another of heroism, he hit upon another tack, and simply ordered the women from his presence. Clearly some were reluctant to leave, but none, it seemed, dared consider disobeying. Brenner found that of interest. Brenner now lay quietly in the webbing. He was on a company ship. He was alone in his cabin. Shortly thereafter he went to sleep. To be sure, the women returned in his sleep, to kneel, to serve, to be near him. The directress was amongst them, but her place was farther back. Brenner saw that one of the women, a brunette, in a bit of silk that did not more than scorn the pretense that she was a person and not a female, rose to her feet and approached him. She leaned over the webbing. In the darkness her body seemed pale. About her throat was a tiny, closely linked chain, with an attached plate, bearing her name, a single, simple name, and her number. Her lips were about to touch his. Then, suddenly, frightened, angrily, in a cold sweat, he awakened. Shortly thereafter he went back to sleep. He was awakened once more that night, but by the roar of a great savage beast. The roar echoed about the ship. He had heard it before, on other watches. It emanated from a cage, or containment, not far away.

Then Brenner went back to sleep.

CHAPTER 3

"I need a drink," said Rodriguez.

The mud in most places was more than ankle deep on the unpaved streets of Company Station. Here and there a few boards, wet and slick in the muck, were laid end to end, of which boards Brenner, as he could, took advantage. Rodriguez, wading from point to point, with Euclidean methodicality, availed himself of these boards only as they might be so fortunate as to lie in such a way as to be coincident with his independently elected path. This was perhaps not irrational as there were clearly limits to the amount of mud which could adhere to a single pair of boots and trousers. Brenner, who had fallen twice already, was covered with mud. So, too, was the valise he carried. Inside his boots, it was like wading within wading. Every time he put his foot down, it forced water to the sides and over his foot, which water, as he lifted his foot, eddied back to the insole. A light drizzle, having succeeded a harder rain, was still falling.

"Let's check in at Company Hostel," said Brenner, slipping, regaining his balance.

"That's not the sort of bar I'm looking for," said Rodriguez, looking about in the gloom, the soft rain.

Brenner was not enthusiastic about Company Station, even from the first moments after they had disembarked from the fueler. It was still hard to see in the gloom, with the drizzle, and the cloudiness of the day. Company Station seemed, for the most part, to be a depressive, dismal, squalid collection of low, unpainted, unimpressive buildings, many, in spite of their age, being of the sort which would normally have been regarded as temporary. Some might date back from the transitional period between a camp and the first days of a town. To be sure, here and there, back from the main buildings, were occasional small buildings, quite possibly residences, cottages and such, with white fences, with window boxes, with some hint of landscaping. Brenner squinted against the drizzle, squeezing water from between his eyelids. The bulk of their baggage, which was not much, was being held by the day agent at the fueling depot. It was to be delivered to Company Hostel in the early evening, by the porters of the night agent. The standard vehicle for such deliveries, at this time of year, was the mud sled, in the traces a quorn, a web-footed, salamandertype creature, wheeled vehicles tending to be impractical in the mire. The company, of course, also had at its disposal motorized mud sleds. Brenner did not care for the thought of the baggage being delivered in virtue of the exploitation of a beast of burden, doubtless enslaved for such a purpose, but, after all, he was not in charge of Company Station and also did not much care to his try his hand at drawing the sled himself. For one thing, the quorn was much better at such things than he would be, being much more powerful, much more sure-footed, and so on. On many worlds, incidentally, the use of beasts of burden was not unknown, and, in spite of its possible moral impropriety, was accorded some justification on the basis of various ecological considerations, such as avoiding poisoning the atmosphere. Indeed, on some worlds, the form of animal known as the horse, long extinct on the home world, continued to thrive in such a capacity, and several others, such as affording mounts. Indeed, on some of the openly stratified worlds, or "strong worlds," as Rodriguez might have called them, riders were common, sometimes with slaves at their stirrup. Too, on some worlds Brenner knew that his own species served in similar capacities, largely as beasts of burden, mounts, racing stock, and such, for more technologically advanced, if not superior, life forms. Unable to do anything about this, given the cumulative consequences of their own moral, technological, and cosmic choices, many members of his species praised this, claiming to see in it a form of compensatory justice, a putative compensation for wrongs perpetrated by their species in the past. To be sure, such members of Brenner's species seldom visited such worlds, in this perhaps manifesting some puzzling inconsistency, apparently being unwilling to risk being seized as stock, in spite of the fact that such a fate would clearly seem, at least from their own point of view, to contribute to the redressing of outrageous wrongs, to the righting of the hitherto skewed balances of justice. The population of Company Station was about two thousand individuals, most of whom were of Brenner's and Rodriguez' species. Most stations were manned, at least substantially, by members of a given species, for reasons earlier suggested. Most, but not all, of the individuals at Company Station were company employees. As would be expected, given the type of chartering involved, such as was granted by nations or worlds claiming sovereignty over various territories or worlds in virtue of discovery or exploration, the company controlled the land within specified limits, and was additionally entitled to the exploitation of certain rights, in particular mineral rights, beyond it; naturally, too, the company managed and maintained, to one degree or another, all permanent structures erected within the strict charter limits; lastly it might be noted that the company owned and managed most businesses within the same limits, in particular, businesses which had to do primarily with the supplying of goods, such as groceries, clothing, equipment, and numerous sundries, as opposed to services, such as barbering and laundering. This is not to deny, of course, that there were some services controlled by the company, such as medical and dental care, nor that there were various goods available on the shelves of small businessmen who were not company employees, businessmen, however, or business

creatures, if you like, for they were not all members of
Brenner's and Rodriguez' species, who leased their premises
from the company. The bars, for example, were on the whole
in the keeping of these independent fellows, or creatures, as
the case might be. The only official currency at Company
Station was company credits. Commonworld credits, and
others, however, might be transformed, for a fee, into
company credits at the current rate of exchange, and, of
course, subject to company approval, usually easily obtained,
company credits, for a fee, could be transformed into various
currencies, this for the convenience of individuals who
might be leaving the station. Naturally, as on many worlds
in this portion of the galaxy, most exchanges consisted
simply of shifting numbers amongst accounts, rather than
in the actual exchange of material tokens, such as pieces of
paper or metal. Barter, too, of course, as always, provided
an additional medium of exchange. It is interesting to note
that on several of the openly stratified, or "strong," worlds,
material tokens, in all their primitiveness, tended to remain
in use. Here the thought seemed to be that something real
would be exchanged for something real, for example, a coin
for a woman. On some of these worlds there was a coin in
circulation called the "slave." In this sense a slave might be
purchased for one or more "slaves." In these worlds where
realities were exchanged for realities some thought it was
regarded as incumbent on a female slave, regardless of the
price put on her, to strive to the best of her ability to vindicate
her purchaser's confidence in her, and his expectations,
testified to by his actual paying out real money, of whatever
amount, to obtain her. This, of course, is a misconception
as it is incumbent on the slave in any case, in virtue of the
very nature of her condition, and regardless of the modality
in virtue of which her ownership is acquired, even if it is
only in virtue of the shifting of numbers amongst accounts,
to be totally pleasing. It is also interesting to note that on
the strong worlds, as opposed to certain other worlds which
commonly make a meretricious pretense to moral posture,
sophisticated devices of correction or punishment are

seldom, if ever, used. Relatively primitive modalities, such as those of leather and iron, in keeping with the tendency of such worlds to maintain natural relationships, apparently well serve their needs.

There was a rolling, grinding sound from overhead, and Brenner looked up, startled, and almost slipped.

"Be careful," said Rodriguez.

Overhead, on the track system raised above the street, a small engine, controlled by a single trainman, was pulling a train of canisters strapped on hemispherical cars.

"The ship hasn't left yet," said Rodriguez.

The ice formed on the canisters suggested that they contained an oxidizer, probably for the freighter's auxiliary power systems.

Fuel, and such, as I have suggested, was conveyed between the freighter and the depot by smaller ships.

"The ship may not even be unloaded yet," added Rodriguez.

They had left the ship on the first return trip of the depot fueler.

Brenner speculated that what Rodriguez had said might be correct. Doubtless, at any rate, there would be supplies, and such, which the freighter would disembark, via fuelers, at Company Station. It needed its goods, as well as the freighter its fuel. No passengers from Company Station had come up from the surface to the freighter, nor had Brenner noted any in the vicinity of the agent's office. That, however, he supposed, was only to be expected. Aside from the occasional trips, and routings about, of company employees, their comings and goings on leaves, or upon the initiation or completion of their assignments, and such things, he supposed there would be very little passenger traffic at Company Station. "Company Station," incidentally, is identified in company records by a number, associated with that of Abydos herself on the charts. That number, in effect, is its real name. To certain elements of those in the middle executive ranks of the company, it was known as "Abydos Station." To those in the higher levels of the executive ranks of the company it was probably not known at all. Since those on Abydos were well aware they were on Abydos, and, it seems, did not wish to identify their location by a number, they spoke of it simply as we have, as "Company Station." And Brenner and Rodriguez, as you may assume, also adopted this policy. It is not germane to our account, but one may speculate that there were several way stations, fueling depots, and such, throughout the galaxy, to which diverse companies held charters, which were also identified, at least locally, as "Company Station." But this is not unusual; in many areas, even countries, there will be more than one town, or area, called by the same name. This normally works no hardship on anyone as long as the diverse locations of these towns, or polities, or areas, are clearly understood. Similarly, of course, numerous members of diverse species, rational and otherwise, bore similar names. We may assume, for example, that here and there in the galaxy there were several individuals who bore the names 'Allan Brenner' and 'Emilio Rodriguez'. They are not such strange or unusual names. Too, some of these entities might not even have been of the same species as our Brenner and Rodriguez. For example, given the missionary work of the Humblers, earlier referred to, several members of Brenner's and Rodriguez' species had taken Humbler names. Similarly perhaps, for one reason or another, perhaps in virtue of amity or, more unfortunately, in virtue of derogatory judicial discrimination against certain minorities on various worlds, certain members of other species may have been assigned names usually found more commonly amongst members of the species of Brenner and Rodriguez. One should not totally discount either the possibility of an independent origin. Too, many members of the species of Brenner and Rodriguez, particularly those living on certain worlds, had abandoned traditional names in favor of more modern appellations. For example, Brenner and Rodriguez doubtless did not have the same names as those of remote forebears, say, of the sort who might have occupied limestone caves and concerned themselves with the working of stone, wood, and bone.

"How will we make contact with the Pons?" asked Brenner.

"They will meet us outside the fence," said Rodriguez. The fence, incidentally, was a force fence. This could be important, given the proximity of Company Station to the forests. Indeed, it represented an enclave of civilization in the midst of such forests. One needed a pass from company officials, incidentally, to go outside the fence. It was not that there would normally be any difficulty in obtaining this permission, either to leave, or to come in. It was a more a matter of keeping track of things, or of an innocent security. On the other hand the company would not wish, for example, to have expensive equipment leave the station without authorization. Such equipment, surveying equipment, drilling equipment, samplers, mineralogical testing devices, and such, was valuable.

"When?" asked Brenner.

"Anytime," said Rodriguez. "I checked with the agent and he says a camp of them has been located outside the fence for a week now, to the south."

"In this weather?" asked Brenner. He had been given to understand at the agent's office that the weather had been much like this for the past several days. To be sure, that was not that unusual at this time of year, in the early fall, in this latitude on Abydos. The ship, incidentally, was some five Commonworld Revolutions behind its originally projected schedule, as a result of a rerouting mandated by the company some months before Brenner and Rodriguez, after making diverse connections and transfers, had embarked on her, on Eos. As this earlier rerouting is not altogether unrelated to our account I shall mention that it involved a side trip to a world which, not concerning ourselves with its number, was known in this portion of the galaxy as Persia.

"There should be a bar around here," said Rodriguez.

"They should let them inside the fence, give them shelter!" said Brenner.

"They probably don't want in," said Rodriguez. "They are a shy, secretive lot."

"Perhaps they will be offended," speculated Brenner, uneasily.

"Not at all," said Rodriguez, looking about. "They are a charitable, gentle, long-suffering, innocent, humble crew. Compared to them a Humbler saint would come off looking like a king lizard.

Brenner did not think the allusion apt as in his experience the Humblers tended to be amongst the most arrogant of rational species, tending, for example, to be rather proud of their humility. They did, of course, regard themselves as superior, particularly in virtue of their moralities and teachings, to all other life forms. That, in itself, even if they were humble about it, did not seem too humble. On the other hand, most life forms, it seemed, at least of those capable of doing so, regarded themselves as superior to all other life forms. That seemed to be almost a necessary condition for qualifying for a rational life form. Brenner supposed it was healthy. He knew members of his own species, for example, who regarded their species as the superior life form in the universe, not that it was the strongest, or most successful, or most intelligent, or most prolific, or the most widespread, or the fiercest, or the most innocuous, or the kindest, or whatever, only that it was the best. Brenner himself, in spite of all evidence to the contrary, and his commitments to modernism and lifism, tended to share this belief. So, too, he suspected, did Rodriguez, who even went so far as to identify himself, alarmingly enough, as a species chauvinist. Brenner did think there was something interesting, or nice, at least, about his species. To be sure, as we have noted, it was held in an unusually low regard generally in the galaxy, and doubtless for several excellent reasons.

"There must be a bar somewhere around here," said Rodriguez.

"Surely we must make contact!" said Brenner.

"Tomorrow morning will do," said Rodriguez, stopping, puffing in the rain, wiping his face.

Too many Bertinian weeds, too much Velasian Heimat, thought Brenner. But, he, too, was tired. It was not easy slogging through the mud. More important, doubtless, was the fact that neither of them, as yet, had recovered their "surface legs," so to speak. Both were still somewhat unsteady, despite the regime of shipboard exercises which Brenner, at least, had maintained. Indeed, this may help to explain why Brenner had occasionally lost his footing and slipped from the walking boards, those laid here and there across the mud. To be sure, several of the boards had not provided a secure footing, being slick with mud and water.

"Do you see a bar?" asked Rodriguez.

"Let's find the hostel," suggested Brenner, who was cold enough and miserable enough, to find Rodriguez' suggestion about tomorrow morning less objectionable, and less an affront to scientific enthusiasm, than he might have otherwise. And Rodriguez, after all, was the senior colleague.

"That's ahead," said Rodriguez.

The rain, a few moments ago, had begun to fall more heavily again. Brenner squinted into the gloom. He then saw the sign, not lit this early in the day.

He started out immediately, gratefully, but in doing so, obstructed the passage, producing a collision with, a small figure, one of the few individuals Rodriguez and he had seen on the streets, once they had left the vicinity of the agent's office. The small figure, clutching a cloak about itself, with a hood, cried out, angrily, and Brenner, slipping, stepped back, to apologize profusely. Briefly, within the folds of the wet hood, Brenner glimpsed a lovely, rounded face, almost exquisite, with an expression of anger, of petulance, with red lips and deep, dark eyes. And then the hood was pulled even more about the face, angrily, and she hurried on.

Brenner looked after her. He could see her bared, muddy calves within some circular garment, beneath the cloak. Beneath such a garment one might even, easily, put one's hand.

"What is that she is wearing?" asked Brenner.

"It is called a 'dress,'" said Rodriguez. As an anthropologist Brenner was familiar with this term, but he had never seen one on a person before, except, of course, in pictures, from distant worlds, and from the home world, going back to

benighted times. Brenner shuddered. Such garments so
debased and degraded a woman! Surely she would not, of
her own will, have donned such a garment. Perhaps she was
a whore, intent upon stimulating maleness. Such garments,
on many worlds, were outlawed, because of dreaded moral
and social consequences. But she did not seem to be a whore.

"That is what they give them to wear, outdoors," said
Rodriguez.

"'Them'?" asked Brenner. "'Give'?"

"Yes," he said.

"She is barefoot," said Brenner, looking after the small
figure, disappearing now in the gloom, beyond the hostel
entrance.

"It is easier to wash feet than clean boots," said Rodriguez.

"I do not understand," said Brenner.

"If it were colder, later in the year," said Rodriguez, "she
would have been given foot bindings, or boots, or something."

"'Given'?" asked Brenner.

"You do not think that women come of their own free
will to Company Station, do you?" asked Rodriguez.

"Of course," said Brenner.

"Oh, some do, I suppose," said Rodriguez, "the mates of
certain employees, or such."

Brenner was alarmed, standing there in the mud, the rain.
On the home world mating had been abolished, at least in
any official or recognized sense. It had been established
by suitable panels of experts, to which various judiciaries
deferred in certain decisions, that that institution constituted
an infringement of species freedom, at least in Brenner's and
Rodriguez' species, if not in that of others, such as those
of penguins, king lizards, sticklebacks, and inwits, that it
humiliated all partners involved, in whatever numbers or
arrangements, interfered with the indisputable role of the
state in guiding socialization into correct channels, and
was in clear violation of numerous rights which had been
recently discovered. Mating now, and, indeed, sexual
relations, and, in particular, heterosexual relations, with
their appendant dangers of populationalism, was regarded

on many worlds as either a crime, ranging from a felony to a misdemeanor, a civil wrong, or tort, or a vice, depending on the world. Breeding on several of these worlds, of course, tended to be supervised through various state boards. If the state had a right, for example, to require licenses for operating certain forms of equipment, for example, vehicles, or businesses, or to regulate the possession of, say, bladed weapons of more than two inches in length, surely it had the right, it seemed, to supervise the far more important matter of the number and nature of the constituents of the commonwealth itself. Advanced biological techniques, for example, for fertilization and storage, were helpful in these matters, as well as *in vitro* nourishment or, in most cases, recourse to host mothers. In some cases, gametes were so prepared and fused that the genetic endowments pertinent to a given organism could be traced to an indefinite number of "parents," so to speak. Emotional relationships, such as love, had long ago been seen for the cruel and heinous traps they were, the ingenious devices of insidious forebears, designed to exploit and suppress certain portions of the species. To be sure, love, directed toward its proper object, such as a movement, party, or state, was encouraged, depending, of course, on the particular movement, party, or state in question. Various companies, incidentally, it had been recognized, particularly within the companies, were also fit objects for the exercise of this devotion. To be sure, many of these principles, prescriptions, and such, were by certain portions of these populations more honored in the breach than not. Many members of a species tended to remain incorrigible. It was also speculated that numerous dissenters, or even nonconformists, or even recusants, might exist in secret. The business of reconstructing a species in its own best interest, of transforming it, in effect, into something different, remained, as always, difficult. But such work constituted a challenge to the behavioral engineers, and, indeed, this challenge encouraged many to enter the field, often idealistic youths willing to take upon themselves the responsibility for the amelioration of the species. The approach, as might be supposed, was often two pronged, psychological and biological, the psychological aspects having to do with the control of conditioning programs, for the most part, aside from affirmative and negative control of the media, administered through supervised, centralized school systems, proven to be the most efficient in producing reliable educational output, and the biological aspects having to do with selective breeding, politicized eugenics controlled through screening, replication licenses, abortions, prenatal and postnatal, and, of course, genetic engineering. It is interesting to note that on the home world of Brenner and Rodriguez aborting a member of their own species, particularly one of certain groups, was regarded as unobjectionable, especially when done under the direction of the state, which often bore the expense of the operation, whereas aborting a member of another species, rational or subrational, was not, but rather constituted a felony. The rationale for this seemed to be that the state had the right to control its own body, in effect, its body politic. In many cases, of course, it must be admitted that the state accorded the liberty of such terminations to the mother, whether the conceiving mother or the host mother, and whether the member of the species was within a body or in a nourishment vat. Postnatal abortions at the option of either the conceiving mother or the host mother could be performed during the first several years of the organism's life, the matter of being within or outside a body, or vat, being sensibly regarded as biologically irrelevant, given the gradualistic nature of organic development, which obviously continued from the first fusion of gametes at least until adulthood. Most states, on the other hand, retained abortion rights throughout the life of the organism, this provision making it possible to rectify any later-discovered oversight or to counter any irrational sentimentality on the part of a conceiving or host mother. On some worlds, in deference to biological facts, fathers were also given abortion rights over the member of the species, whether it was within the body of a mother or in a vat, these rights again extending to a certain point in the

life of the organism, coterminous with the point to which
the mother's rights, whether a conceiving or host mother,
extended. The exercise of these rights did not require
mutual agreement because that would, as various jurists
had pointed out, infringe the rights of the other partner.
None of this, of course, compromised the rights of the state,
which in all cases, as was proper, given its greater amount of
information, the longer, broader perspectives at its disposal,
and its wisdom, took priority. In speaking of incorrigibility,
and such, it might be mentioned that Brenner, whereas he
tended on the whole to be a. morally responsible citizen of
the home world, did not favor abortion. His view seemed
officially to be predicated on a suspected inconsistency
between the putative morality of aborting a member of
his own species and the putative immorality of aborting
a member of another species. This also seemed congruent,
at least in his mind, incidentally, with the thesis of the
equivalence of life forms, he supposing that a member of his
own species, such as it was, ought to be entitled to the same
rights as those accorded to, say, squirrels, rabbits, or terbits.
On the other hand, one suspects his views may also have
been influenced by the fact that he had discovered, at the
age of some twenty Commonworld years, that he himself
had narrowly escaped abortion. Indeed, a vat attendant
had refused to flush out the vat and place the fetus in the
garbage. And, as Brenner was pleased that he had not been
aborted, he tended to disapprove of abortion, in spite of its
putative convenience to one party or another. To be sure,
Brenner seldom expressed his reservations on these matters,
which was perhaps just as well.

"You do not think then," said Brenner, peering off through
the rain in the direction in which the young woman had
taken her way, picking her way through the mud with her
bare feet, "that she is a "mate."" He shuddered a little as he
said that word, with its disgusting aspects of salaciousness.

"I would not suppose so, not here," said Rodriguez.

For some reason Brenner was pleased with this
speculation on the part of Rodriguez. Upon considering this,

Brenner speculated that his relief must be due to the fact that the young woman was spared at least an implication in a relationship so carnal and deplorable, so antithetical to personness.

"But what then?" asked Brenner. He was dimly aware of an odd sense of expectation, or hopefulness, even an unworthy, excited hopefulness, in himself as he asked this question.

"Who knows?" asked Rodriguez.

"What do you think?" asked Brenner.

"She was barefoot," mused Rodriguez.

"Yes?" said Brenner.

"Did you get a look at her neck, or her left wrist?" asked Rodriguez.

"Not really," said Brenner.

"I didn't notice any chain or anklet on her left ankle," said Rodriguez.

"'Chain'? 'Anklet'?" said Brenner.

"To be sure," said Rodriguez, "such would have to be dried, and cleaned, very carefully, if it were worn in this weather, in the rain and mud. It could, of course, have been removed, before she was sent on her errand."

"An errand?" asked Brenner.

"One supposes so," said Rodriguez. "This is hardly the sort of weather in which one would be likely to make social calls."

"What is she?" asked Brenner.

"I don't know," said Rodriguez.

"Is she a—slave?" asked Brenner.

"Quite unlikely, for a number of reasons," said Rodriguez. "First, she was angry when you obstructed her passage, when you struck into one another, and even cried out in anger, or made some sort of angry noise. It is highly unlikely that a slave would have done that. A slave might rather have been terrified that she might have been found displeasing. A slave would have been down on her knees or belly in the mud, in an instant, contrite and fearful, begging your forgiveness, perhaps trying to placate you by licking the mud from your boots. She would not wish to be beaten."

"Men have such power over slaves?" asked Brenner, in awe.

"Of course," said Rodriguez. "They are slaves."

"But you do not think she is a slave?" asked Brenner.

"No," said Rodriguez. "Are you disappointed?"

"Of course not!" said Brenner.

"The second reason, or second main reason," said Rodriguez, "that I doubt that she is a slave is because this is Company Station, and it is highly unlikely that they would have slaves here. The company, you see, like many of the companies, at least in public matters, must maintain its image, on the home world and similar worlds."

"I see," said Brenner.

"It would scarcely do for the company to be discovered to be keeping slaves here," said Rodriguez. "Think of the political embarrassment, and the leverage this might provide competitive companies."

"I understand," said Brenner.

"The company, however, doubtless keeps slaves one place or another," he said, "in one out-of-the-way place or another, perhaps on vacation worlds, or resort worlds, such places, for their executives, or something along those lines. Too, of course, the company does have holdings on several worlds, even strong worlds, where there are slaves, and who is to say on such worlds to whom those slaves, in one holding or another, belong. Too, it is rumored that the company, and other companies as well, here and there, do dabble in the slave trade, that they capture or buy such merchandise, that they transport it, train it and sell it, such things."

Brenner was silent.

"The Serian girls, the little blue beauties, are mostly bred now, of course," he said.

"Like cattle?" asked Brenner.

"If you like," said Rodriguez. "But they are, of course, also educated and trained."

Brenner was silent.

"Some companies are doing this, here and there," said Rodriguez, "with women of our species."

Brenner looked at him, aghast.

"Yes," said Rodriguez.

"But what of the woman we just saw?" asked Brenner. "What is she?"

"I would guess," said Rodriguez. "That she is either a convict, or a delinquent assignee, or, more likely, a contract slut."

"What?" asked Brenner.

"A woman who is contracted," said Rodriguez. "This can come about in a number of ways. For example, she may have been subjected to contract in virtue of incurred debts, or she may have contracted herself for a certain fee, for a certain time, or this may have been done to her by a reformatory board, or a correctional board, many things. Her contract can be bought and sold and she, with the contract, passes from one hand to another."

"And what are her duties for the contract holder," asked Brenner.

"Whatever he wishes," he said. "He holds the contract."

"When does the contract expire?" asked Brenner.

"Normally when it is paid off," said Rodriguez, "but, as she is considered a free woman, and is usually charged for her board and such, things are usually arranged in such a way that she cannot pay it off."

"Then she is in effect a slave?" said Brenner.

"Her contract might be purchased by someone, who pays it off for her," said Rodriguez.

"Is that likely?" asked Brenner.

"Not at all," said Rodriguez.

"What is the usual outcome?" asked Brenner.

"The usual outcome?" he asked.

"Yes," said Brenner.

"Usually, on one world or another, sooner or later, they find themselves reduced to bondage."

"They become full slaves?"

"Exactly," said Rodriguez.

"I see," said Brenner.

"The hostel is ahead," said Rodriguez, who had by now caught his breath.

"I thought you were looking for a bar," said Brenner.

"I don't see one, do you?" said Rodriguez.

"No," said Brenner, making certain that he did not look too carefully.

"Let's check in, and change our clothes," said Rodriguez. "I want a shower. I want to be warm and dry. Then we can go out again."

You can go out again, thought Brenner. I will stay in the hostel. He did not find Company Station an inviting locus for ambulatory peregrinations.

"The bars are probably off the main street," said Rodriguez. "Are you all right?"

"Yes," said Brenner. To be sure, he still seemed short of breath. Too, his heart was pounding, and he was in a state of agitation, perhaps from his encounter with the young woman and his conversation with Rodriguez, or perhaps from the normal adjustments involved in adapting from the weightlessness, or comparative weightlessness, of the ship to the gravity of a world. In such a transition one recovers a sense of the cubic content, the weight, the reality, of one's body, which, of course, after a period of adjustment, is forgotten.

Brenner then, bag in hand, trying to keep his footing in the mud, squinting his eyes against the precipitation, now again a drizzle, followed Rodriguez toward the double doors of the hostel, some two hundred yards, or so, down the street. He looked up once at the overhead tracks, which were now unburdened by cargos. The ship, he assumed, would have left by now. They had come to Company Station, on Abydos. There would not be another ship for months. Through the glassed paneling of the hostel's doors shone a welcome illumination. Too, as they approached the building, the sign was lit. Doubtless this was a coincidence, and constituted no more than a belated concession to the misery and darkness of the day, but it cheered Brenner.

CHAPTER 4

"D o not be disturbed," said Rodriguez. "It is merely that you have not seen women of your species in this way before."

Brenner did not dare to look down at her, to where she knelt beside him, as he stood at the bar. Her hands were on his left leg. Her head was down, her cheek pressed against his thigh.

"Get away," he hissed to her.

The bartender, a zard from Damascus, a life form thought by many to be related to that of the captain of the freighter, though smaller and more upright in carriage, looked up from where, a few feet away, behind the bar, he was polishing glasses. The relationship of the zard to the species of the captain, incidentally, despite popular conjectures on the subject, is regarded as improbable by most zoologists, given the diversity of worlds and the timing of certain technological developments on these worlds, in particular, their attainments of interstellar flight capabilities. These zoologists tend to attribute the resemblance to the parameters of convergent evolution which, to be sure, has apparently produced numerous resembling species throughout the galaxy. The subject, however, remains open, even in learned circles, because of the unusual similarities of microscopic genetic structures between the two species. Too, it is obvious that a third species, which had, in the remote past, and perhaps even one now extinct and lapsed from notice in galactic records, which did possess interstellar capabilities, might have been involved, for example, in settling certain specimens of a primitive species on a different world, on which world, over periods of time, these specimens, wending their own ways, would develop into a new variety of the old species, or, if one likes, into a new species. Certain crossings between zards and others, for example, of the captain's species, had proven fertile. The problems, of course, had to do with probabilities in such matters. In spite of the fact that life forms on diverse worlds often bore remarkable similarities to one another, presumably because of resembling adaptations to frequently similar ecological niches, the chances of crossfertility between diverse species tended to be calculated in the millions to one. It is possible, of course, that that million, or millions, to one chance might obtain. Too, of course, a sufficiently advanced life form, might be able, through chemical and physical alterations in genetic materials, deletions, additions, and such, to produce hybrid forms. Much progress had been made, for example, in developing new agricultural products along these lines. Needless to say, animal husbandry had also profited. In general, in speaking of adaptations, and adaptational advantages, intelligence, or rationality, tended to be extremely common in the galaxy. It is difficult not to acknowledge the obvious value of this adaptational device. It is interesting to note, incidentally, that normally only one such form, one such rational form, tended to be found on undisturbed worlds, that form which, it seems, in one way or another, overcame its rivals. Rationality, you see, is not always conjoined with kindliness and tolerance; it may be as often conjoined with fanaticism and ruthlessness; rational species which did not, at least in some point in their development, practice the principles of priority and tyranny, tended on the whole to disappear or, at least, to have their numbers controlled by the dominant species. Only in current times, with a plurality of worlds, and available room for expansion, at this point in history, and the balances of power between certain species, and the advantages to be obtained from commercial and technological exchanges, it seems, did clearly diverse rational species set about the business of tolerating one another's existence. The zards, incidentally, were the dominant life form on Damascus, though other life forms, in diverse menial and servile capacities, were permitted amongst them. Their reputation in this portion of the galaxy was to the effect that they were shrewd businessmen, or creatures, that one must be wary of bargaining with them, and that their word was not to be overly trusted. They tended, on the whole, to be an aggressive, commercially active species. Whereas one could commonly count on them being civil and polite in the pursuit of business, and sometimes even ingratiating and obsequious with prospective clients or customers, they had a general reputation, it must be admitted, outside of interspecific transactions to their advantage, of being severe to inferior life forms.

"Easy," said Rodriguez to Brenner.

Brenner turned a bit away from the girl, to his right. He did not wish her to see the effect on his body of her proximity.

"If you do not want her there," said Rodriguez, "cuff her away. She will crawl back, but probably keeping out of your reach."

"This is a human female," whispered Brenner to Rodriguez.

"Do not demean her," said Rodriguez.

"How could she be more demeaned than she is?" asked Brenner.

"Drink your drink," said Rodriguez.

Brenner, unsteadily, almost tipping the glass, reached for the drink.

He glanced at the bartender, who then looked away, continuing to dry the glasses.

The young woman did not release his leg, and she kept her cheek pressed against his thigh. She seemed frightened.

Brenner also glanced to his right, and back, well beyond Rodriguez at the bar, to a counterlike desk near the rear of the room, behind which sat the proprietor of the establishment, like the bartender, a zard. This desk, near the rear of the room, not far from a beaded curtain to its right, as Brenner looked at it, was set well back from the main floor with the small tables, and, at one side, booths. Near some of these booths, and tables, rings were set in the floor. Rodriguez and Brenner, perhaps because of the hour and weather, were at this time the only customers in the establishment. The proprietor looked at Brenner, and then returned his attention to the papers before him. On the top of the desk, at hand, so to speak, lay a stout, two-foot-long leather quirt. The young woman who knelt beside him was the second woman who had been summoned forth, through the curtain, the first a blonde, to hasten to the bar, by two blows of that quirt on the top of the desk, loud, sharp, and resounding blows, almost like the reports of primitive firearms.

Then Brenner had his hand on the glass, and, slowly, deliberately, in misery, as steadily as he could, took a tiny sip. It was a cheap cooler, flavored with imported citarine extract. The bartender, if Brenner had not been mistaken, had served it with a certain contempt. Rodriguez was nursing a glass of Heimat, for which he had a taste.

"I cannot have this person in this position," said Brenner.

"She is a female," said Rodriguez. "If you would look at her, you might notice that."

"I cannot have this young woman in this position," said Brenner.

"Call her a "girl,"" said Rodriguez.

Brenner looked at him, angrily.

"She is a girl," said Rodriguez.

"Rodriguez," protested Brenner, half under his breath.

"She is pretty enough, and menial enough, to be a girl," said Rodriguez. "And considering her status, there is no doubt about it. She is a girl."

Brenner looked away, angrily. Too, he was worried. He recalled the first woman, the blonde. She had hurried forth from behind the curtain, in response to the signal, but then, for the merest instant, had stopped. She had regarded them. She had seemed startled, and then flushed, as though with sudden hope. Her hand had gone, seemingly inadvertently, to the narrow, silken sash of her garment, tight about her waist, but then she had jerked it away, frightened. She had looked to the proprietor, and the bartender. Neither, it seemed, was paying her attention. Of course, she had responded to the signal. Neither, too, then, would have observed her tiny, arrested, furtive movement, that of her hand near her sash. She then gathered herself together, and smoothed down the sides of her brief garment. On her left ankle was a small chain. Attached to it was a tiny disk. She had then approached them in a manner which might have made Brenner cry out in protest and desire, on all fours, had he had not detected something of falsity in it. Before Brenner and Rodriguez, Brenner surmised, she was, in effect, acting. This was to be a secret between the three of them, to be kept from the zards. Surely Rodriguez, too, with his perceptiveness, had noticed these things. "Sirs?" she had then asked, kneeling before Rodriguez, whom she naturally took to be first amongst them. He looked at her, and she looked puzzled, and then she smiled, knowingly, and spread her knees more widely. This, too, Brenner gathered was to be a part of the secret. He had to look away from her, as it disturbed him to see her as she was garmented, and in her current attitude. Such things made his blood scream with need. In a moment or two, he could look back, as the woman had withdrawn, Rodriguez having ordered, the food to be brought to one of the tables. Brenner was hungry, as they had not eaten since this morning on the ship. A few moments later the quirt had struck down twice again on the desk, suddenly, loudly, sharply, the sounds startling Brenner, and the second woman, a brunette, had come forth, and quickly. There had been no doubt whatsoever as to her prompt response to the signal. Then she, too, as had the other woman, had stopped. Then, angrily, she had dropped to her knees and, in a moment, as Brenner supposed she was expected to do, head down, approached them on all fours. Although she was angry, resentful, frustrated, she was not like the other woman. This one, before them, was truly on all fours.

Then she was before Brenner, and put her head down, and kissed his boots, first the left and then the right, and then knelt near him, holding to his leg, and putting her cheek close to, and then against, his leg. He had tried to draw back, but she had kept close to him. She seemed angry, but frightened, too. It was then that he ordered her away from him. She had not, of course, as we recall, surrendered her position. Brenner, putting down his drink, was in consternation. He had never seen women like this before, of course, or known they could be like this, except perhaps in his dreams. But it had not occurred to him that the substance of such dreams might be founded on realities, to be sure, realities which he had not himself experienced. These things, then, as actualities, not as dreams, were revelations to him. He had not really understood that females could be such, or that there might be places where they were such. To be sure, he had heard of such things, as, for example, having a woman at one's feet, but, as is well understood, to hear of having one there is one thing, and to have one there, in actuality, is quite another. Brenner wanted to scream, to cry out with exultant joy, but instead he had ordered her to withdraw, with which command, as we noted, she did not comply, but only clung to his leg the more closely.

The proprietor, back at the desk, stood up, sliding his chair, or seating device, a rather heavy, stable object, cut in such a way as to accommodate his tail, backward on the wooden floor. He then came about the side of the desk. Although the girl had not turned to see, she had undoubtedly heard the movement of the chair, or seating device. Brenner felt her cheek press more closely against his thigh. Her small hands held him more closely, too. He noted that the zard, in leaving the desk, had picked up the quirt. But he had done so, as far as Brenner could tell, as much as a matter of habit as anything else. The zard, in its soiled, pocketed apron, was now moving toward them, with its characteristic, stalking gait. It was of average height for a zard, which was some seven Commonworld feet in height, a foot or so taller than either Rodriguez or Brenner. Brenner could mark

its approach, its measured steps, the heel pads of its rear
legs making contact with the floor first, and then its claws.
Brenner felt the girl now press even more closely against him,
and hold even more closely to his leg. She seemed to be very
afraid. Then the steps passed them, as the zard, apparently
not even noticing them, or being concerned with them, went
to the door of the establishment, and, stretching his neck a
little, peered out into the night. Outside the paneling of the
door one could see the rain in the light of the establishment's
sign. Then, in a moment or so, the zard turned about, and
stalked back to his desk. The night was not a good one for
business in Company Station.

The girl drew back a little, but kept her cheek in contact
with his thigh, her head down. Too, she held to his leg, as
before. Brenner could not forget the feel of her body, the
softness of it as it had been pressed so closely against him
in the girl's terror, her apparent fear of the proprietor, that
unspeakable, luscious softness which was doubtless intended
to be betrayed by the bit of yellow silk she wore. How that
softness had alarmed him, and disturbed him!

Brenner took another drink, angrily.

He was furious that he had agreed to come with Rodriguez.
He had originally resolved to remain in the hostel. He
realized now he should have done so. Too, he could have
gotten something to eat there. But he had decided not to
remain there. He had been afraid to stay there, not that there
was any real danger. And he had certainly been pleased
to follow Rodriguez to the hostel. The day had been, as it
remained, chilly, and what with the rain, and enough wind
to drive the chill through one's jacket, he had been miserable.
When Rodriguez and he, soaked and cold, with their bags,
had entered the hostel, he had seen, behind, and above, the
desk, squatting in a large ring, suspended on a chain hung
from the ceiling, a small, large-eyed, furred creature. He
had originally taken this to be a pet of some sort but it had
swung down from the ring to the desk, and, in a bit, had
welcomed and registered them. Shortly thereafter, too, it
had with one small, prehensile, black-toed foot, punched

a bell, in response to which a large, shambling, slothlike
creature hove into view, who seized up their bags and began
to ascend the stairs. Ascending rings hung to one side, for
the use of those who might prefer them to the stairs. The
stairs were broad, and coarsely carpeted, to accommodate
various sorts of grasping or locomotory appendages. The
desk clerk, if Rodriguez was right in his identification, as it
seemed probable he would be, was a Chian lemet, whereas
the porter, if we may call him that, was a hirsute, three-
toed veripus, an unpleasant creature of unusual strength,
thought to have been originally native to Pergamum. Before
one forms any possible contempt for either of these species,
however, it is well to keep in mind that both life forms had
independently, long ago, achieved interstellar capability, a
feat which the species of Rodriguez and Brenner, presumably
because of various historical reasons, had never managed. In
the hallway, leading to their room, Rodriguez and Brenner
passed a female of their species, who was standing near a
cart. On a projection at one end of the cart, and within
two containing rails, one lower and one higher, were some
cleaning implements, brooms of various sorts, dustpans, one
long-handled and one short-handled, and, standing in a pail
of liquid, a mop. The top two shelves of the cart were laden
with various objects, implements and supplies. Amongst
these were brushes of various sorts, and cans and bottles,
filled with various substances serviceable for cleaning and
polishing. There were also such things as toiletries, bars of
soap, and such. There were also, folded neatly, assortments
of clean linen, sheets and such. Two blankets were also
in evidence. The lower portion of the cart back from the
projection, contained a hamper, in which crumpled sheets
could be seen, and another container in which might be
seen such things as discarded paper and the remnants of
packagings of various sorts. At one side of the hall, not on
the cart, was a vacuum cleaner. The woman lowered her
head as they passed. She was wearing that form of garment
which Rodriguez had reminded him was called a "dress."
It was rather stiff, and was presumably starched. It was of

two colors, basically tan, but trimmed with white at the collar and at the borders of the short sleeves. Brenner had seldom seen a woman's arms, as home-world proprieties had required that those small, lovely, rounded limbs should be concealed. Naturally that her arms were bared disturbed him. The dress, too, far worse, came slightly above her knees. This, too, disturbed Brenner, and even more than the baring of her arms, for the home-world proprieties were even sterner with respect to the baring of a woman's legs, perhaps because this was thought to lead even more swiftly to lewd thoughts of mysterious, sacrosanct secrecies. Such things, the baring of arms and, even more, the baring of legs, were thought to demean her personness, which was apparently regarded by many as being incompatible with having a body, or, at least, an interesting, attractive one. The porter, for we shall speak of him as that, as he passed her, paid her no attention. Brenner noticed that the woman was barefoot, as had been the woman with whom he had so inadvertently and unfortunately collided earlier in the day, she who had been so angry. But about the ankle of this woman, the left ankle, was a small, sturdy chain, doubtless a decoration of some sort. She had apparently fastened this on herself with some sort of short, thick, cylindrical lock. Completing the decoration, about an inch in diameter, was a small, flat, circular metal disk, itself fastened into one of the links. This unpretentious little getup at the ankle seemed to Brenner an unusual sort of ornament, particularly in its plainness and sturdiness, but he did admit it was attractive.

It disturbed Brenner, of course, that the woman should be seen in the company of such tools and implements.

The door to the room was ajar and the porter thrust it open with his foot, that Brenner and Rodriguez might enter. In the room were two more women who, looking up, as they entered, and then looking down, quickly completed their work, turning down the second of the two beds in the room. Something in the attitude of the women had suggested to Brenner that they might be frightened of the porter. The porter put their bags inside the room. The two women now hurried out, one of them glancing over her shoulder at Brenner as she left. The porter had not acknowledged their presence. They were dressed the same as the woman he had encountered in the hall, and so he came to understand that their dresses were, in effect, a sort of livery or uniform. Both, too, as had the woman in the hall, had worn the tiny decorations on their left ankle, the sturdy little chain, with its lock, and disk. As one of them had left Brenner had heard a tiny, metallic click, presumably that of her disk, or its fastening, interacting with the chain.

Brenner looked after them.

"Maids," explained Rodriguez.

"Maids?" said Brenner.

"Yes," said Rodriguez.

This, too, upset Brenner, as such work had been outlawed for women on the home world, where it was regarded, in its servility, and meniality, as demeaning. Such work, on the home world, was now done by men.

"I do not understand," said Brenner.

"This is Company Station," said Rodriguez, by way of explanation.

"But they are women," said Brenner.

"It is fit work for them," said Rodriguez.

"Surely you are joking," said Brenner.

"Not at all," said Rodriguez. "Let them get down on their knees and scrub floors, let them dust and clean, and sweep, and cook, and launder, and sew. Such servile tasks are fit for them."

"I cannot believe what I am hearing," said Brenner.

"I am not a politician," said Rodriguez. "I am an anthropologist."

Most positions of importance and authority on the home world, as far as Brenner knew, were now occupied by women. There were many explanations for this, such as the remote successes of various militancies and activisms, numerous discoveries of rights, countless stunning advances in social, political, and economic justice, landmark decisions by judiciaries, reformations in education, institutionalization of much-needed public conditioning programs, media control, censorship, the domination of major political parties, and the eventual control of all significant political processes, at least on the surface. Further, as every schoolchild knew, the natural superiority of women, and their right to rule, and be dominant, had been demonstrated scientifically in a number of ways, for example, by means of carefully conducted experiments, as a consequence of numerous tests of various design, and by open, objectively conducted public-opinion polls. Interestingly enough, in spite of an apparent control of power on the home world it was rumored that many men remained in positions of power in the metaparty, if it existed, and, indeed, interestingly, that certain women in the metaparty served these men in secret, much as might slaves masters. He knew a number of highly placed women. He wondered if some of them, in secret, had their masters. Then he dismissed such a horrid thought. There were some reservations about the scientific aspects of matters, of course, such as the difficulty of replicating certain crucial experiments, of which little more than the purported consequences were published, difficulties connected primarily with the classified nature of the experimental designs and controls. There were similar reservations on the part of some with respect to the reliability and, more importantly, the validity, of the tests. Historians, largely in obscure monographs, often privately published, had noted interesting correlations, spanning several thousand years, between the pronouncements of objective science and the requirements of various political establishments. The ports at which the ship of science called were often determined by the rudder of politics. Similarly the cargos it carried and the goods it pretended to deliver were often determined by those who, in effect, owned the ship.

Some social scientists, perhaps in virtue of the limitations of their less vast perspectives, tended to find difficulties elsewhere, as, for example, in the redefinition of the parameters to be assessed. For example, if one changes the meaning of a locution 'A' to that of locution 'B,' while retaining the original expression 'A,' it is natural one would then discover numerous bits of interesting and important information about A's, never before noticed. For example, if one changed the meaning of, say, 'tigrons' to that of 'tidwit', then it turns out, of course, that the true tigron would have the properties of a tidwit. To be sure, this is not likely to have any effect on what used to be called a tigron, and, as a consequence of reformational definition, was no longer a tigron, unless, of course, it could be convinced that it must either be, or pretend to be, a tidwit. Recalcitrance, or dissent, of course, would be rare in science, for various reasons, for example, the objective nature of the enterprise and the publicness of its validation procedures. The control of access to graduate education, and the control of professional certifications, appointments, reappointments, tenure, fundings, grants, staff, facilities, equipment, outlets for publication, and such, would also be helpful. Lastly it might be mentioned that various attempts to reform language itself had been attempted, the object being to make it impossible for divergent axiological viewpoints to be expressed, and, ideally, and more importantly, if all went well, even to be thought. This program, for better or for worse, had been largely unsuccessful, because language, in its cognitive richness, as always, and even in its engineered versions, proved itself better adapted to be the accomplice of thought than its jailer. Too, for example, the removal of a word, say, 'tigron', if one wished to do so, from a language, did not, after all, remove tigrons. It would just make it a bit more of a bother to talk about them. Too, the hole left in the lexicon tended to draw attention to itself. And so the old words, or variants of them, would return, to talk about the old things, which had not gone away. To be sure, the linguistic reformers still had at their disposal numerous time-honored devices, such as slander, denunciation, and censorship. But it is aside from our narrative to enter into detail on these interesting matters.

Rodriguez obtained the fiscal number of the porter, and punched him a credit. He had had his Commonworld credits, as had Brenner, converted to company credits. This had been done in their in-processing at the agent's office, at the depot.

The porter then turned about and left the room.

Brenner closed the door, carefully, after him, and locked it, fastening it, too, with a chain.

"You do not tip the maids for their services," said Rodriguez.

"Their services?"

"No," said Rodriguez, throwing his bag on one of the beds, and opening it.

"Changing sheets, and such," said Brenner.

"And such," said Rodriguez, absently, tossing some linen on the bed.

"Their dresses," said Brenner, the word sounding strange in his mouth, "are rather revealing."

"They are intended to be such," said Rodriguez, attending to his business. "If you think that sort of thing is revealing you should see slave garb, when they are permitted garb."

Brenner thought to himself that Rodriguez had probably seen slaves, real slaves. Brenner was uneasy even with the thought of such. He had heard that such women were even branded.

"Did you notice the maids?" asked Brenner.

"Of course," said Rodriguez.

"They are a comely lot," said Brenner.

"They are picked to be comely," said Rodriguez. "There is a bell there," he said, pointing. "You can ring it, if you want maid service."

"'Maid service'?" asked Brenner.

"Yes," said Rodriguez.

"I do not understand," said Brenner.

"Surely you noted that they were barefoot, and noted their left ankles."

"Yes," said Brenner. "They wore some sort of ornament there."

Rodriguez came about his bed and went to the wall where he pushed in the button for maid service.

In a moment or two there was a small knock at the door, and Rodriguez, loosening the chain, drawing back the bolt, had it open.

One of the maids was there.

"Come in," said Rodriguez.

She entered.

He closed the door, behind her.

"Get on the bed," said Rodriguez. "On your stomach."

Brenner almost cried out with protest, but no sound escaped him.

The maid, with no hesitation, but apparently with some apprehension, with some timidity, obeyed.

Rodriguez had put her on Brenner's bed. Brenner noted this with dismay, and, to be sure, another feeling which he would been hard put to describe. To be sure, there was some point in this. There was already a suitcase on Rodriguez' bed.

Rodriguez then, with his left hand, brushed the maid's uniform up a few inches, revealing more of the backs of her legs. Brenner gasped. This thing, small in itself, had a very great impact for Brenner. He had never seen so much of a female before, except perhaps in the performance circles of his imagination, and on the sales blocks of his dreams. She lay very quietly on the freshly made bed, which she had helped turn down but moments ago. Her small hands, at either side of her head, clutched the sheets. "Look," commanded Rodriguez, seizing her left ankle in one hand, and pulling it up, bending the leg forward. "See?"

Brenner looked at the ankle, encircled closely by the small, stout chain. Certainly it could not be slipped, not as it was on her. Too, with misgivings, he regarded the cylindrical lock. That lock, if he were not mistaken, actually fastened the chain on her ankle.

But Rodriguez' interest, it seemed, was in displaying the small metallic disk, about an inch in diameter, which was fastened to the chain. "See?" he asked.

On the disk was a tiny number, but this number, more importantly, was below another sign, larger, impressed in the metal. "Do you know this sign?" asked Rodriguez.

"Of course," said Brenner. It was one of the best-known signs in this portion of the galaxy. It was the company *logo*.

"This, in effect," said Rodriguez, shaking the ankle in his

grasp for emphasis, as though this might the better impress the matter on Brenner, which forcible motion brought a small cry from the woman and was accompanied by a tiny jingling from the disk on the chain, "is company property."

"The chain, the lock, the disk?" said Brenner.

"What they mark!" said Rodriguez, impatiently. "The woman!"

"She is a free person," said Brenner.

"She is a contract slut," said Rodriguez. "You can tell that from the chain. "For all practical purposes she is company property."

He then, angrily, flung the woman's ankle back to the bed. It struck the covers with a sound, and the disk made a tiny noise against the chain. Brenner observed that she had a small foot, and then, closely about her ankle, was the chain, and then came her calf.

"It's part of your job to make our stay here pleasant, isn't it?" asked Rodriguez.

"Yes, sir," she whispered.

"Do you understand "maid service" now?" asked Rodriguez.

Brenner thought it wise not to respond. It was at this point, incidentally, that he decided he would not remain at the hostel that evening but would accompany Rodriguez outside, even in the weather, to find a bar.

Rodriguez dropped his hand to the back of her thigh, and touched it, gently.

Her eyes opened very wide, and she made a tiny sound.

Again Rodriguez touched her.

She closed her eyes, and uttered a tiny moan.

"Get your ass down," said Rodriguez.

She moaned, and pressed herself further down, into the covers.

"You can ring for her later, if you want her," said Rodriguez.

"No, no!" said Brenner, alarmed.

"Get out," said Rodriguez to the maid.

Quickly she left the bed, and pausing only a moment to smooth down her skirt, she hurried from the room.

Brenner, sweating, locked the door after her, and put the chain in place.

He turned about, to face Rodriguez. "How could you have done that?" he asked him.

"What?" asked Rodriguez.

"What you did to her!" said Brenner.

Rodriguez looked at him, puzzled. "I didn't do anything to her," he said.

Brenner regarded him, aghast. But Rodriguez, carrying a robe, was making his way to the bath. A little later Brenner heard the shower running.

For a time Brenner did not even sit on the bed. He stood there, rather, looking at it, and at the place where the maid had lain. There were some small disarrangements in the covers there, sloping up to the sides. Too, there were some tiny wrinkles where she had clutched the sheets, her small hands on either side of her head. He tried to look away, but he found it difficult to do so. He recalled the hem of the dress, as it had been pushed a little above the back of her knees, and the disturbing exquisiteness of what had consequently met his view. The wholeness of what had been revealed had been particularly striking to him, the way the curves, from the foot to the ankle, to the calf, to the back of the knee, and above, blended into one another. He had suddenly understood how, on some barbaric, monstrous worlds, men could kill for the possession of women. To be sure, he did not think that the women of the home world, so miserable, frustrated, smug, inhibited, petulant, and cold, would be in great danger. It was hard to imagine them stripped and roped in the grass, prizes awaiting the outcomes of savage contests. Still, he did not know. They were, after all, women. Perhaps, somehow, under proper conditions, their psychological disarrangements, or improvements and perfections, so carefully wrought by subtle, pervasive conditioning programs, might be torn down and the female might then be freed to find herself as she might be in and of herself, as a female. Then Brenner dismissed such horrid thoughts. But found it hard to forget the chain and disk, with the lock, on the maid's ankle. Too, he remembered how she had made tiny noises when Rodriguez had touched her. He scarcely dared conjecture what might have occasioned them. One of the great breakthroughs of the past several millenniums had been the scientific proof that human beings did not have sexual needs, but that such needs had been invented by insidious men as devices wherewith to dominate, oppress, and enslave women. Accordingly, even if, as Brenner seemed to, one had such needs, one must realize that they did not exist. Certainly almost no one on the home world would admit that they had such needs, and the public admission of such in a public figure was tantamount to disgrace and ruin. Many biologists and even social scientists, who, because of the sensitivity of the issues with which they dealt, could usually be relied upon to produce findings congenial to, and supportive of, current political orthodoxies, whatever they might be, had lost posts for pretending to have come up with politically dubious results. For a time some recusants had embraced a "Two-Truth Theory," namely, that there was scientific truth and political truth, which many scientists accepted because it let the chips fall where they might, rather than in prescribed configurations, but the dishonesty of this distinction was quickly detected by various political establishments. This was succeeded by the "Two-Opinion-One-Truth" Theory, which was to the effect that there was only one truth, the political truth, whatever it might be on the world in question, but that there might be two opinions, according to one of which truth might *seem* to be "A" and according to the other of which truth might *seem* to be other than "A." This approach, too, was quickly suppressed in the best interests of the community, party, people or whatever, and replaced with the "One-Opinion-One-Truth" Theory, which, in an intellectual *tour de force* of unity, simplicity, and elegance, successfully restored *one* qualified opinion, identical with the one correct truth, the political truth, whatever it might be at the time. The theory, incidentally, that human beings lacked sexual needs superseded a somewhat less politically effective theory, which had earlier also been indisputably proven scientifically, the theory that there was only one sex, the human sex. This theory had been quite useful in its role of reducing gender differences which, because there was now only one sex, the human sex, were then regarded as either minimal or nonexistent. The flaw with this theory was that one then had to recognize two varieties of human sexuality, or two sorts of individuals, for example, the egg-carriers, or "eggers," as it was said, and the sperm-producers, or "spermers," as it was said. Astute, politically progressive critics saw in this a concealed version of the old, troublesome two-sex theory which had been so politically divisive, in which men, in particular, thinking of themselves as different from women, might find it more difficult to recognize that that their true best interests lay in the inhibition, suppression, and denial of their own sexuality, in the surrender of manhood, or, perhaps better, in merely discovering that hundreds of thousands of generations of masculine forebears had been mistaken as to its nature. The new theory that sex did not exist, and thus that sexual needs did not exist, was clearly superior. Men and women were now seen as "sames" or "identicals." To be sure, there might be certain anatomical differences amongst human beings but these were negligible. For example, some people were taller than others, some had different-size feet, and such. It is interesting that populationalism remained a political issue in a world in which sex did not exist. But, as some historians had pointed out, generally in underground monographs, such apparent discrepancies in world views have not been unprecedented. Brenner, it might be mentioned, recognized that he himself had sexual needs, or, at least, seemed to have them. Often however, particularly on the home world, he had felt very isolated in this particular. And naturally it would have unthinkable to have uttered an admission to this effect. And so Brenner, and perhaps others, pretended not to have sexual needs. And, though Brenner did have the decency to be sensitive about these needs, he was not one of the more moral sorts who struggled not to have them. As usual, the most moral, or, at least, the most socially controlled, tended on the whole to be the most afflicted, miserable, and guilt-ridden, fighting to be whatever the current stereotypes told them they should be, lying awake at night tormented, troubled, and weeping, denouncing themselves for countless slips, errors, shortcomings, failings, and inadequacies, punishing themselves in orgies of self-castigation, self-contempt, self-scorn and such, which activities provided some gratification, but not much, and, of course, frequently resolving to do better but, for one reason or another, and probably for a very good reason, usually not managing it.

"You haven't changed," said Rodriguez, coming out of the bath.

Brenner could hear the vacuum in the hall outside. One of the maids must be cleaning the corridor.

He was still standing near the bed, in his wet clothes, his bag on the floor near him. The carpet was wet.

"No," he said.

Brenner was disturbed by the sound of the vacuum cleaner, even though it must be some doors down the hall.

"Rodriguez," said Brenner.

"Yes," said Rodriguez, getting dressed.

"When you touched the maid," said Brenner, hesitantly, "she moved a little, she made tiny noises."

"Yes?" said Rodriguez, sitting on his bed, pulling on a boot.

"Why was that?" asked Brenner, uncertainly.

"Surely it is obvious," said Rodriguez, looking over at him.

"No!" said Brenner.

"She was responding to my touch," said Rodriguez, "and probably to the entire situation in which she found herself, and to what her condition is, and so on."

"'Responding'?"

"She couldn't help herself, she's hot," said Rodriguez, working on the second boot.

"I don't understand," said Brenner.

"Frigidity is not acceptable in a contract slut," said Rodriguez.

"I wish you wouldn't use that expression," said Brenner.

Rodriguez stood up, and stomped twice.

"Are you intimating that her behavior was—*sexual*?" asked Brenner.

"Certainly it was sexual," said Rodriguez, irritably.

"Do you mean to suggest that she might have sexual needs?" asked Brenner, carefully.

"Of course she has sexual needs," said Rodriguez.

"But sexual needs," said Brenner, "do not exist."

"Do not be naive," said Rodriguez.

"Surely you are aware of the official position on this matter," said Brenner.

"Of course," said Rodriguez.

"Do you have sexual needs?" asked Brenner.

"Certainly," said Rodriguez. "And so do you, unless you are crippled, or insane or sick, or something."

Brenner was silent.

"What about it?" asked Rodriguez.

"What about what?" asked Brenner, uneasily.

"Do you have sexual needs?"

Brenner was silent.

"This is Company Station," said Rodriguez. "This is not the home world."

"Yes," said Brenner. "I have sexual needs."

"Good," said Rodriguez. "Now say that again, and to another person."

"I have sexual needs," said Brenner.

"Excellent," said Rodriguez.

Brenner felt happier, and freer, then than he had in years. It was as though a great weight had been thrown from him. He wanted to laugh, and cry, with relief.

"But we must be rare, and terrible," said Brenner, though, at the time, given his elation, he did not feel, really, either rare or terrible.

"Then everyone must be rare and terrible," said Rodriguez, "that is, everyone who is not crippled, or insane, or sick, or whatever."

"But what of the indisputable scientific proofs that sexual needs do not exist?" asked Brenner.

"One supposes, except politically, that the existence of such needs takes precedence over the proofs that they do not exist. For example, the existence of one tree takes precedence over the proofs that trees are impossible."

"Then the proofs are not really proofs," said Brenner.

"A proof is a proof, by definition," said Rodriguez, "but, similarly, by definition, what is not a proof is not a proof. A pseudoproof, for example, is not a proof."

"But what of the decisive experiments?" asked Brenner.

"Much there depends on definition, the politician's ally," said Rodriguez. "For example, if a need is operationally defined as, say, something which must be satisfied within two hours or the organization perishes, then one has a certain number of needs, for example, for oxygen, for blood flowing to the brain, and so on; if one operationally defines a need as something which must be satisfied within three days or the organism perishes, then one has additional needs, and so on. For example, on the first definition, one does not have a need for water or food. On the second, one does not have a need for food, and so on."

"But the frustration of sexual needs does not lead to death!" said Brenner, triumphantly.

"Or at least not to immediate death," said Rodriguez. "There are, of course, numerous statistics, muchly suppressed now, in the best interests of the public, of course, that the failure to satisfy sexual needs may tend to shorten life considerably, by several years, in fact. To be sure, the matter is obscure, as the failure to satisfy these needs may be merely a part of, or a consequence of, a pathological syndrome, or a defective system, tending to be linked to decreased longevity."

"You could have your degree revoked, or be imprisoned for expressing such thoughts on the home world," said Brenner.

"Or be remanded for "smoothing" as a physiological deviant," said Rodriguez, smiling.

"Yes," said Brenner.

"I have declined that offer more than once," said Rodriguez.

"The state would have borne the expenses of the operation," Brenner pointed out.

"Even so," said Rodriguez.

"It is interesting how people resist their own improvement," said Brenner.

"Doubtless that is a symptom of their deficiency, and a proof of their need of a cure," said Rodriguez.

"And this then occasionally necessitates the action of the state, to intervene in the best interests not only of the people but of the particular individual involved."

"Some see it so," said Rodriguez. "But returning briefly to the questions of needs, or drives, or whatever, I think it is important that you understand how definitions enter into these supposedly scientific matters, and, indeed, that the scientific results will depend, in effect, on how the definitions are constructed. For example, there is no point whatsoever, except from a political point of view, to define a need in terms of something that must be satisfied at the expense of life itself, and promptly, or soon, as though one could have only needs for such things as oxygen, food, and drinking water. What if the failure to satisfy a need, or whatever we choose to call it, resulted not in death, or at least not in immediately ensuant death, or whatever, but in misery, in frustration, in discomfort, in pain, in unhappiness, in lack of fulfillment, in psychic disarrangements, and such? I would be willing to call that sort of thing a need. Would a plant, for example, not have a need for a certain mineral, simply because it could drag out a pathetic, stunted existence without it? No, needs, at least as I would choose to understand them, are not simply connected with, say, the basic essentials for some level of metabolism and oxidation, and such, but with what is required for the plant to be fully healthy, and, indeed, to flourish."

"But health, too, and such things, may be variously defined," said Brenner.

"Of course," said Rodriguez, "and doubtless will be defined in various ways, to accomplish various purposes.

Some words are good words, so to speak. They are prizes to be fought over. An excellent example is the word 'health'. That is a good word. That word is a prize. It will be fought over. It has favorable connotations, you see. People have been verbally conditioned to believe that health is good, that they should be healthy, and so on. Thus, the political trick is to take the old word, evacuate it of its customary meanings, replace those meanings with the new political meanings, and then count on the favorable connotations of the word to win over the public to your cause. Naturally this is never made clear to the public. Rather it is presented as a new cognitive discovery, as to what, say, "health" really is."

"That is meretricious and deceitful," said Brenner.

"It is done with many words. Excellent examples are 'good', 'right', 'justice', 'normal', 'mature', 'democracy', 'religion', and such. Sometimes, of course, when it is feared that the absurdity of this may be too obvious, one speaks of such things as "true justice," "real democracy," and such."

"But surely there are realities involved, as well," said Brenner. "It cannot be all verbal manipulation, all fraud, all politics."

"Yes," said Rodriguez. "There are realities involved, and that is why the political fraud, the media manipulations, and such, are so important, to distract attention from them, to conceal them, and such."

Brenner nodded. He even sat down on the bed, forgetting that the maid had been there. He wondered if he should have listened to Rodriguez. The man must be mad.

"The stunted plant deprived of the mineral, you see," said Rodriguez, "is an unhealthy plant, in a quite clear sense, to be sure, perhaps in an old sense, or a superseded sense, even if it is now defined, for political purposes, as being "healthy." Similarly, a plant that is clipped and trimmed into an absurd shape, to conform with an external or alien concept of excellence, may now count as a better plant, or a superior plant, from the external or alien viewpoint, but it is certainly not the natural plant, the plant as it would grow if it were under conditions ideal to its own nature, as it would grow in its own natural health and glory, so to speak."

"I see," said Brenner."

"There is also a distinction between the descriptive and prescriptive use of discourse which is often blurred in these matters," said Rodriguez. "For example, 'normal' might be used to signify what sort of thing actually occurs most frequently, or it might be used to characterize an ideal, rational or otherwise, which is seldom attained in actuality. For example, in the first sense, having sexual needs is quite normal, but, in the second sense, on the home world, the *normal* person, so to speak, or the *truly normal* person, as it might be said, does not have such needs. Those who have them, secretly, of course, are thus expected to regard themselves as, say, abnormal, deviant, in need of a cure, or such. This guilt is useful politically, of course."

"I am prepared to admit that I have sexual needs," said Brenner. "But surely I am unusual."

"Not at all," Rodriguez assured him.

"But what of women," asked Brenner. "Surely they do not have sexual needs."

"You saw the maid, and heard her," said Rodriguez.

Brenner suddenly realized he was sitting on the bed, or, rather, that the maid had been there earlier. He stood up, quickly.

"But she must be a deviant, or a nymphomaniac," said Brenner.

"It is highly unlikely that she is a deviant," said Rodriguez. "It is much more likely that she is simply a normal woman, one with sexual needs. To be sure, her sexual needs have probably been liberated by now from the bondage of her training and education."

"Liberated from bondage?" said Brenner. "She has a chain on her ankle." Brenner decided that he would accept what seemed to be the reality of the maid's situation, rather than pretend to disguise it in his own mind. It had seemed to him unlikely, even from the beginning, that the maid held the key to that chain on her ankle.

"I refer, of course," said Rodriguez, "to the liberation of her sexual needs."

"She is probably a nymphomaniac," said Brenner.

"Is that a derogatory expression?" asked Rodriguez.

"I'm not sure," said Brenner, though he supposed it was supposed to be. He was not exactly certain why. To be sure, he could see how it might be of advantage to a certain form of political establishment to claim it to be such, for example, that it might be used as a device to discourage women from seeking sexual fulfillment, from fulfilling their needs, from becoming themselves.

"I am not sure what you mean by the expression," said Rodriguez, "but as I use it, every woman, properly handled, is a nymphomaniac. She will beg for more, and such."

"Then you think that women have sexual needs," said Brenner.

"Women have profound sexual needs," said Rodriguez. "Sexual needs, biosexual needs, psychosexual needs, it all goes together."

"Even the directress?" asked Brenner.

"That self-important, smug, pretentious, frustrated, miserable, frigid slut?" asked Rodriguez.

"She," admitted Brenner. Rodriguez' assessment met with his approval. Still, he did not personally find the directress, who was a young woman, unattractive. He recalled her as he had imagined her kneeling on the plating of the lounge, on the ship, her hands, the wrists linked together in the bracelets, lifted to him.

"I would suppose so," said Rodriguez, "somewhere, somehow. These needs, you must understand, can be suppressed, fought, resisted, and such. Certainly her frustration suggests that something is being frustrated. Her misery indicates that something is wrong. Her frigidity, as it seems rather of the defensive, hostile, frightened kind, rather than that of simplistic anesthesia, suggests that something, awakened, of which she is at least dimly aware, is being blocked and denied. Too, of course, energies can be thwarted and diverted, and twisted, and turned to other outlets, for example, to the seeking of power, to the grasping for position, to the scratching for authority, such things, or others, in an ill-fated, belligerent attempt on her part, which she knows is doomed to failure, to conform to a culturally prescribed stereotype, in effect, to prove that she is the same as a man, a denouement which, incidentally, in my opinion, she does not really want. Thus, her pretenses, her postures, her behaviors and such, represent in their way not only the uncritical adherence to a perverse conditioning program but more importantly a reaction against something, an attempt to deny something she senses in herself, and fears in herself, that they constitute an attempt, in its way, and a rather hysterical attempt in its way, to repudiate her belly knowledge, so to speak, what she knows about herself ultimately, that she, a female, belongs at a man's feet."

"I am wet, and cold," said Brenner. "I think I will change, and shower."

"Well," said Rodriguez, "you have made progress. You have admitted that you are a human being, that you have sexual needs."

Rodriguez glanced at the bell, which would ring for maid service.

Brenner pretended not to notice. He found a robe in his bag, and some dry clothes. He could no longer hear the vacuum in the hall. But he did not doubt but what there would be a maid on call.

"Your next step," said Rodriguez, "now that you have acknowledged that you have sexual needs, is to satisfy them." He pointed to the bell.

"No, no!" said Brenner, hastily, frightened. The bell seemed very large on the wall, very prominent, very visible. Though, to be sure, it was actually rather small, and discreet.

Rodriguez looked at him, puzzled.

Brenner shook his head. It was, after all, one thing to have sexual needs, and quite another to satisfy them.

"As you wish," said Rodriguez.

"Where are you going?" asked Brenner.

"Out," said Rodriguez.

"Wait for me," said Brenner. "I'm coming with you."

He did not wish to be left alone with the bell. Too, what if there should be the small knock on the door? What if a maid should check with him, to see if he wanted anything? Certainly he would not want anything. No! He would want nothing, nothing!

At the door to the bath Brenner turned. He looked at the disarranged covers on his bed, where the maid had lain.

"I'll only be a moment," he said.

"All right," said Rodriguez.

"Is it true," asked Brenner, "that women have sexual needs?"

"Yes," said Rodriguez, "but in some women they are latent, and must be aroused."

"I see," said Brenner.

"But they are there," said Rodriguez, "like combustible material."

Brenner nodded.

"And once they are aroused," said Rodriguez, "it is done to her."

"'Done to her'?" asked Brenner.

"Yes," said Rodriguez. "They are then with her. She cannot unarouse them, so to speak."

"I see," said Brenner.

"The clearest case is the slave," said Rodriguez. "But then they are given no choice in the matter. Their passions are aroused deliberately and uncompromisingly, even cruelly, with no concern for them, and aroused in such a manner that their emergence is profound and frequent, indeed, in such a manner that they become, in effect, the pathetic, helpless prisoners of their needs, dependent on masters for their satisfaction."

"It is hard to understand," said Brenner.

"I have seen them at a man's feet, begging," said Rodriguez.

Brenner gasped.

"Will they be satisfied?" asked Rodriguez. "It is up to the master."

"I see," said Brenner.

"Those are a slave girl's strongest chains," said Rodriguez.

"I understand," said Brenner.

"But you must understand, too," said Rodriguez, "that eventually the slave girl rejoices in these chains, in whose clasp she continues to remain helpless.

"I do not understand," said Brenner.

"They keep her on the mark, where she wishes to be," said Rodriguez, "even more than more prosaic bonds, such as chains, brands, identifications and such."

"I do not understand," said Brenner.

"She is a female," said Rodriguez. "And it is only in bondage, and such relationships, that her femaleness, both by herself and others, is fully appreciated, understood, relished, and celebrated. There is a wholeness in this. Nothing is isolated. Her entire personal, individual, exciting, beautiful psychosexuality is involved, the full range of her feminine needs, nothing starved or denied, the wholeness of her being, the wholeness of her deepest self, involving such, things as giving, devotion, love, service, attentiveness, a desire to be truly pleasing, profoundly so, and as a *female*, and so on."

"You mean they want these things?" asked Brenner.

"Certainly," said Rodriguez.

"And they accept these things, and relish them, of their own free will?" asked Brenner.

"Yes," said Rodriguez, "but one must there be careful, for it is important to the slave to be a *slave*, and this means that she must then, in a sense, be choiceless."

"Interesting," said Brenner.

"Had she the choice, she would choose to be given no choice, said Rodriguez.

"This seems a paradox," said Brenner.

"Perhaps," said Rodriguez.

"But then," said Brenner, "if she is a slave, then she would have no choice, no choice in actuality, literally no choice, whether she wished it or not."

"Correct," said Rodriguez. "She is a slave. She has no choice. She is choiceless, absolutely. She is a domestic animal, a slave."

"Doesn't she know she is supposed to be free, and such things?" asked Brenner.

"Like a man?" asked Rodriguez.

"Yes," said Brenner.

"I thought," said Rodriguez, "we were discussing psychobiology, not the prescriptions of politics."

"Very well," said Brenner. "Continue."

"The slave may even, in the beginning," said Rodriguez, "use the bondage of her liberated needs as an excuse to submit, for if she does not submit, and in ways suitable to the master's will, she will not be satisfied."

"I understand," said Brenner.

"Not to mention her obvious subjectability to other forms of punishment, as well," said Rodriguez.

"Of course," said Brenner.

"For example, the whip," said Rodriguez.

"I understand," said Brenner, shuddering.

"But soon," said Rodriguez, "as the slave becomes familiar with her duties, her chains and silk, and understands in her belly that she is now a slave, and that is that, and that is all, she senses a great relief and happiness. She is then at her master's feet. She is content, joyful, and fulfilled."

"But surely she must occasionally regret her choicelessness," said Brenner.

"Doubtless," said Rodriguez. "She is, after all, a slave. Doubtless the condition contains its terrors as well as its gratifications."

"But what you have described is a sort of an ideal, is it not?" asked Brenner.

"Of course," said Rodriguez. "Doubtless many are the girls who shiver with cold, naked and miserable, chained in the holds of freighters. Doubtless some are dragged weeping to blocks to be sold. Doubtless some labor long hours in remote, muddy fields, far from public view, or, similarly, concealed from sight, behind the scenes, in public kitchens and laundries. Some doubtless labor in barren, spacious, friendless mills, chained to looms. Perhaps they envy certain of their more fortunate sisters, those with painted lips, chained to their beds in brothels."

"Horrifying," said Brenner.

"More terrifying," said Rodriguez, "is the slave who knows that her master does not care for her, for example, she who is merely taken for granted, who must serve neglected or unnoticed, perhaps even scorned. Too, some slaves find that their masters do not like them, literally, and that these masters are intent upon keeping them at a primitive level of slavery, one more associated with terror and punishment than discipline and love. It is one thing, for example, to subdue and tame a rebellious slave, one not yet in touch with her deeper realities, decisively and effectively, and quite another to relate to a woman whom one makes certain will continue to hate you, say, for the pleasure of the psychological torment one sees imposed upon her, for example, as she must beg you for sexual relief, and such. There are many variations here."

"You seem to believe that there are two sexes," said Brenner.

"Yes," said Rodriguez. "And they are not the same."

"That is not the official position of the home world," said Brenner.

"The official position of the home world is mistaken," said Rodriguez.

"Perhaps," said Brenner.

"Did you believe it?" asked Rodriguez.

"No," admitted Brenner.

I didn't think so," said Rodriguez. "Only idiots take it seriously. The important thing is the lie, and to pretend to take it seriously, for purposes of politics."

"The home world is not as inflexible and uniform in its views as you think," said Brenner.

"Oh?" said Rodriguez. To be sure, he had not spent a great deal of time on the home world over the past several years. As you might suspect, there had been good reasons for this.

"Some on the home world," said Brenner, "speculate that sexual needs may exist."

"How bold!" exclaimed Rodriguez.

"Well, it is something," said Brenner, irritably.

"It is a sop thrown to intellectuals," said Rodriguez. "It is usually brought up at professional conventions, where there are no students about to rush off and report to the morality officers. Also, it tends to reassure sycophantic toads of the reality of academic freedom."

"It is always pointed out, of course," said Brenner, "that these needs, if they exist, are unimportant and negligible."

"That position neglects at least one fact," said Rodriguez.

"What is that?" asked Brenner.

"Sexuality's radical centrality," he said. "It is the engine which powers the machine, the force which gives meaning to the world."

Brenner gathered from these remarks that Rodriguez did not share even the more liberal view of sexual needs expressed in the bold conjecture that such might, if only in some minimalistic form, exist. Indeed, he seemed to regard sexuality as of great importance. Apparently, even if it were politically unacceptable, and thus to be denied, or ignored, it was real, very real. Brenner wondered what a world might be like which openly acknowledged sexual realities, rather than denying or hiding them. Perhaps some of the openly stratified, or "strong," worlds, as Rodriguez might have referred to them, he speculated.

"I will tell you something I wager you do not know," said Rodriguez.

"What is that?" asked Brenner.

"Have you heard of the levies?" asked Rodriguez.

"What levies?" asked Brenner.

"Some ten thousand, or so, women from the home world, each year, are taken in them, for slaves."

Brenner regarded him, startled.

"To be sure," said Rodriguez, "that is only part of the tribute."

"I don't understand," said Brenner.

"You do not think a world as weak as ours, as silly as ours, a world which has made one stupid choice after another, a world which is not capable, even, of defending itself against interstellar attack, a world which has nothing really with which to even make a serious contribution to a defensive alliance of worlds, is likely to be somehow immune from the notice of more efficient worlds."

"Speak clearly," said Brenner.

"The home world is now, as it has been several times in the past, a tributary planet. That goes back even to the time of the Telnarian Empire, which you also probably did not know. After its collapse the home world, which had been a tributary planet within the aegis of the empire, fell amongst the prizes to be sought by ensuant barbarisms. In these times of troubles, so to speak, the home world fell within the sphere of influence of one world or another. In those days, our governments, rather as they like to do today, but then with better justification, preferred, in their high echelons, to think of these disbursements, so to speak, as payments for protection, and, in a sense, formerly, protection was involved. The home world became tributary to world "A" which would then protect it, as one of its tributaries, from world "B." But then, later, in the fallings out of war, and after the failures of various alliances, certain agreements were reached amongstst some of these barbarisms, ones active in this portion of the galaxy, agreements which, in effect, divided this portion of the galaxy into protectorates, as our governments might put it, or into tributary sectors, as the barbarisms put it."

"To what world is the home world tributary?" asked Brenner.

"I do not know," said Rodriguez. "But I gather that it is far away."

"What would they want with women from the home world?" asked Brenner.

"Probably nothing having to do with the women *per se*," said Rodriguez, "who might not even be of interest to them, except, of course, for their value as trade goods."

Brenner could not speak.

"The trade may have a dozen corners, so to speak," said Rodriguez. "The women might be inserted at any given point in a trade network. I really do not know. Similarly they might be traded from one world to several others for a variety of items, or they might be traded about, from point to point, for one good or another, until they came to a world or worlds that wanted them for themselves, as what they would be, slaves, of course."

"I have not heard of this," said Brenner.

"You can scarcely blame the government for being somewhat reluctant to publicize the matter," said Rodriguez. "Besides, ten thousand, or so, women, taken here and there out of the population of the home world annually, is a negligible amount, one scarcely to be missed."

"And there are other tributes, too?" asked Brenner.

"Items of various sorts," said Rodriguez. "Raw materials mostly."

"What is the nature of the women?" asked Brenner.

"On the whole they would seem to be what you might expect," said Rodriguez, "young, beautiful, and sexually responsive."

"How do they know they are sexually responsive?" asked Brenner.

"There are tests," said Rodriguez.

Brenner blushed.

"And interestingly," said Rodriguez, "many of these women do not even realize they are, or would be, under certain conditions, helplessly sexually responsive, and as slaves. It has never occurred to them that the time might come when they would beg a man, piteously, and as a slave, for his least touch."

What secrets, Brenner wondered, lie concealed within women, secrets of which they might themselves be unaware.

"A certain percentage of these women are mothers," said Rodriguez. "It is speculated that these may be of interest as proven breeders."

"I see," said Brenner.

"Do these things come as a surprise to you?" asked Rodriguez.

"Yes," said Brenner.

"They should not come as such a surprise," said Rodriguez. "Surely you know that some slaving has taken place for centuries on the home world, both for export and for internal use."

"I have heard such," admitted Brenner.

"And that certain women of the home world, unwary enough to visit certain worlds, or foolish enough to visit certain districts or quarters of certain worlds, have vanished, presumably having been taken as slaves."

"Yes," admitted Brenner.

"Do you think they were careless?" asked Rodriguez.

"Surely," said Brenner.

"Perhaps," said Rodriguez, "But perhaps, too, rather, they wanted a chain on their neck, and a master."

"Surely not!" said Brenner.

"The levies are much the same thing," said Rodriguez, "only periodic and regularized."

"I understand," said Brenner. He glanced back at the bed, where the maid had lain.

"No," said Rodriguez. "That one was not levied. She is not a slave. She is a contract slut."

"But she is, in effect, a slave," said Brenner.

"No," said Rodriguez. "She is merely under contract. That is quite different."

"How can she be freed?" asked Brenner.

"By paying off her contract with her earnings, which she will not be able to do," said Rodriguez. "Or by her contract holder."

"As a slave might be freed?" asked Brenner.

"A slave—freed?" asked Rodriguez.

"Yes," said Brenner.

Rodriguez laughed, and wiped his face with his arm.

"Is that thought so absurd?" asked Brenner, angrily.

"Yes," said Rodriguez.

"But the contract person's contract might be purchased by someone, who would then pay it off for her?"

"Yes," said Rodriguez.

Brenner continued to stare at the bed.

"Perhaps you are thinking of buying her contract, and then freeing her?" said Rodriguez.

"No," said Brenner.

"Good," said Rodriguez. "That is much better."

"What?" asked Brenner.

"Buying her contract, and not freeing her."

"No!" said Brenner.

"But you would want to try her out first," said Rodriguez.

"No, no!" said Brenner, shuddering.

"She looks like she would make a pleasant armful," said Rodriguez.

"No!" said Brenner.

"I would have thought so," said Rodriguez.

"No, no," said Brenner.

"It is just as well," said Rodriguez. "You could probably not afford to buy it, any more than she could afford to pay it off, given the expenses charged to her for board and room, and such things."

Brenner regarded him.

"Not on an adjunct's salary," said Rodriguez. "These contracts are usually held by businesses, institutions, and such. They tend to be expensive."

"Undoubtedly," said Brenner.

"Because the contract slut is not a slave, but a free woman, and can be held openly on worlds on which slavery might remain a sensitive issue, as it is not on many other worlds, more progressive worlds."

"'Progressive'?" asked Brenner.

"To be sure, an illusive word," smiled Rodriguez. "You may define progress as constant change, even racing from one stultifying madness to another, but it need not be defined that way. For example, it may be thought of rather as the attempt to approximate an ideal. If that is so, then refinement, restoration, and such, if they result in a situation which more closely approximates the ideal, would constitute progress. It is not clear, for example, that continuing to go down a wrong road constitutes progress. Also, you must be aware that on many worlds certain institutions, such as explicit social stratifications, aristocracies, slaveries, and such, have been introduced, to counter the decline, disintegration, bankruptcy, and chaos of failed systems, to succeed them with more honest, more realistic forms. Not every world has to be founded on lies."

"Let us not speak further of these things!" said Brenner.

"It is interesting," said Rodriguez, looking at the bed to whose surface he had ordered the maid.

"What is interesting?" said Brenner.

"On your salary," said Rodriguez, "you presumably could not afford to buy her contract, that of the maid, the free woman, but with the same salary, on many worlds, such as Sybaris and Megara, it would be quite easy for you to own one or more slaves."

"Please," protested Brenner.

"You could do with them what you wish," said Rodriguez.

"Please," said Brenner.

"They are beautiful, and cheap, and hot," said Rodriguez.

Brenner looked at him.

"It is largely a matter of legality, and politics, and supply and demand, such things," said Rodriguez.

"Wait for me," said Brenner. He looked at the bell on the wall. He trembled a little. "Do not go out without me. Do not leave me here alone. Wait for me."

"All right," said Rodriguez, agreeably enough.

Brenner then, carrying his robe, and a change of clothing, entered the bath.

Rodriguez pulled a notebook out of his bag and sat down in a chair. It was nice, in a way, to sit in a chair and stay there, without the webbing.

In a short while Brenner had emerged, dressed, from the bath.

He then accompanied Rodriguez from the room. In the hall they encountered a maid, she whom Rodriguez had ordered to the bed. It seemed their encounter was inadvertent. She had some towels over one arm. Rodriguez did not speak to her as he passed her.

Neither did Brenner. She did not raise her eyes as they passed.

The zard, the proprietor of the bar now patronized by Rodriguez and Brenner, as I have mentioned, had now returned to his desk, from his short journey to the front door, to reconnoiter the weather, which he had done to his apparent dissatisfaction. It was a poor night for business in Company Station. Too, it was not, in general, the sort of weather of which his kind approved. To be sure, it was not exactly the sort of weather which was universally greeted with enthusiasm by the species of Rodriguez and Brenner either. The girl was still at Brenner's thigh, with her head down. She, as I have indicated, clung to his leg, as before. This disturbed Brenner considerably, but he could not deny that there was something in him that was not dissatisfied to have her there. Certainly he was still cognizant of the feel of her body, the softness of it, as it has been pressed so closely against him in her terror, her apparent fear of the proprietor, that unspeakable, luscious softness, which, he had not doubted was intended to be well betrayed by the silk she wore. That softness, as we recall, had alarmed and disturbed him. He had then taken a drink, angrily.

"Get away," said Brenner, angrily, to the girl.

She looked up at him, frightened. "Please do not send me away," she begged.

"Your lips are painted," said Brenner.

They had not been painted when he had seen her before, several streets away, earlier in the day, for, as you have doubtless suspected, this is the same young woman into whom he had inadvertently struck earlier, in their small accident, the one who had cried out so angrily, of whom he had caught but a brief, striking glimpse, the one who had then hurried away, in anger, making her way barefoot through the cold mud, clutching the cloak about her. Naturally she seemed much different now, kneeling at his feet, made-up, in a bit of silk.

"It is called 'lipstick,'" she said.

"What is on your upper eyelids," he asked.

"Eye shadow," she said.

He continued to look at her. "There are various cosmetics," she said, "eye shadow, eye liner, mascara, such things."

"You are *painted*," he said.

"Some men like it," she said.

"I am not a man," said Brenner. "I am a *person*."

"Yes, sir," she said.

"To be sure, Brenner thought of himself as a man, at least secretly, and would surely have referred to himself as such in his conversations with Rodriguez, and with others whom he might well know, and trust, but the title 'man' in this context made him distinctly uneasy, for it suggested something quite different from the creature at his feet, who was clearly not a man, but something remarkably, wonderfully, excitingly, and marvelously different. Brenner was not willing to fulfill any expectations, or accept any obligations or responsibilities, which might seem to be involved with being a *man*, at least in a situation such as this. He did not wish to risk relating to her as might have a member of the opposite sex. He did not wish to insult her. Too, he felt safer clinging to the myth of sameness. To be sure, though it disturbed him, he was not really displeased to be addressed as 'sir' by this delectable creature. If there were some subtle inconsistency here, he did not find it objectionable. Besides, by the waiters in restaurants, by the male attendants in conveyances, in hotels, and such, he would often have been addressed as 'sir'. And the locution, he reminded himself, was probably required of her by her contract holder. He thought of having her address him by the proper neuteristic term of 'pers', but then, for some reason, decided against it. He would permit her, devolved though it might be, to continue to address him not only by an appellation indicative of respect, but by one, in her case, appropriate to a member of an opposite sex.

"Do you like them?" he asked.

"Yes," she said.

"Why?" he asked.

"I think they make me pretty," she said. As she had looked down and whispered this, her thighs had moved slightly under the silk. This suggested to him that there might be more involved here than a simple matter of aesthetics. Rather he suspected that the cosmetics, perhaps because of some meaning or other, also made her feel in a certain way, a way which, it seemed, she might not be likely to mention explicitly to Brenner.

"They demean you," said Brenner.

"Then I like being demeaned in this way," she said.

"They make you attractive, as a decorated animal," he said, irritably.

"It is my hope that they make me attractive," she said.

"And," said Brenner, irritably, deciding to risk a shot in the dark, "they also make you feel attractive."

She looked up, startled.

"And you personally find them arousing, and exciting," he said.

She put her head down, quickly. "Yes, sir," she whispered.

Brenner was pleased with this outcome. His shots, it seemed, had exactly and decisively struck home. To be sure, if Rodriguez, and other renegades, was right, and females really had sexual needs, and such, perhaps the shots, so to speak, had not been fired so much in the dark as he had thought. She kept her head down. He then became vaguely conscious for the first time, in a real sense, of the power he held over this creature. He did not, of course, bother to mention the effects of the cosmetics upon himself. He had heard, incidentally, that on some worlds slaves were by custom refused cosmetics. He thought such worlds must be rather puritanical. To be sure, it seemed strange to think of a world as puritanical on which beautiful slaves might have to labor for months, striving to improve their services, and to become more and more pleasing, before they would be thrown a garment.

"I think you should leave now," said Brenner.

She lifted her head. She looked up at him, frightened. "Please do not send me away," she begged.

Brenner looked down at her. He then became even more conscious of his power over her. This pleased him. She was, in some way he was not clear about, at his mercy.

"Why not?" he asked. After all, he was of the home world. Surely he should not keep this person beside him, in this degraded position, one of respect, at his feet.

"I am sorry I was cross with you earlier today," she said.

"It is nothing," said Brenner. "The accident was trivial. It was of no importance, and it was as much, or more, my fault than yours."

"But I did not behave well!" she said.

This interested Brenner, that she should even consider the matter as to whether or not she had behaved well. Certainly the women of the home world, or the typical women of the home world, never concerned themselves with such things. To be sure, this woman was not on the home world, but on this world, and was under contract, apparently to the proprietor of the bar. Brenner gathered that there might be sanctions on the behavior of such women, those on this world, or at least those under contract on this world. She was not, of course, a slave. He did not doubt, of course, that the sanctions placed on a slave for behaving well might be quite severe, and even extreme.

"You did not expect to see me tonight," said Brenner, "or to find yourself where you are now."

She put down her head, not responding to this. Her hair was dark brown, and glossy. Doubtless it had been washed, and brushed and combed, before she had come to the floor tonight. He considered that dark, glossy hair, and the compact, sweet curves of her in the silk. Her entire body had been washed, he did not doubt. Her feet, which had been in the mire earlier, were clean, except for some dust on the soles. On her left ankle, which seemed the place for such things, there was a chain and disk. It was similar to, but of a different construction from that which the maids in the hostel had worn. Brenner liked her chain and disk better. The chain was black-enameled, as was the lock, and the disk was larger. Indeed, he liked her better than the maid at the hostel. He was glad he had not remained at the hostel. Then he put such a horrid thought from his mind.

She looked up at him.

Brenner found the bar very hot. It was not merely that he was emotionally disturbed by the proximity of the young woman, but the temperature was objectively hot. Zards tended to like warm temperatures, even very warm temperatures, and accordingly tended to keep their dwelling areas, places of business, and such, quite warm. Even the girl, who wore almost nothing, would presumably have felt the temperature to be quite warm, perhaps even too warm.

Brenner sniffed the air. He could not place the aura, but he liked it. He had barely sensed it before. It was quite subtle.

He was not certain of its source, but he suspected it. Had he thrust his mouth and lips to the girl's throat its source would have been clear to him.

"It is perfume," she said. "I have a better upstairs."

"It is a substance you put upon your body?" he asked.

"Yes," she said.

"You are apparently intended to be found delightful by many senses," he said.

"Yes, sir," she said.

"I think you may go now," said Brenner.

"Please be kind to me," she said.

Rodriguez laughed, and she looked at him with fear.

"I have no intention of being unkind," said Brenner.

"I am sorry!" she said. "I am sorry I behaved badly!"

"No apology is necessary," said Brenner. "As I told you it was as much, or more, my fault than yours."

"Please forgive me!" she said.

"No forgiveness is necessary," said Brenner.

"I do not want to be tied naked to a post in the back yard!" she said.

"How is that done?" asked Brenner.

"My hands are tied behind my back," she said, "and I am roped to it by the neck!"

"Excellent," said Rodriguez.

She cast him a glance of fear, as at one who knew the handling of women.

"Barbarous," said Brenner, disbelievingly.

"Do you want me to remove my silk?" she asked, looking up at Brenner.

The thought of seeing her so, then with only the appurtenance on her ankle, the chain, the lock, and disk, almost made Brenner scream with joy.

"No!" he said. "No!"

She looked back, fearfully, at the zard, but the creature did not look up.

"Remove the chain," said Brenner.

"I cannot do that," she said.

This pleased Brenner exceedingly, that she could not remove that device.

At this point the other woman, the blonde, the waitress, or whatever we might wish to call her, she who had seemed to share some secrecy with Rodriguez, emerged from the back, bearing a large tray, steaming with food.

Brenner was famished.

The blonde set the tray on one table, a serving table, and then, carefully, in a certain order, set another table. She glanced back once at the zard, but he paid her no attention. Then she gave Rodriguez a look of secretive confidence which he received impassively and declined to return. In a few moments the other table was prepared, complete with napkins, utensils, drinks, a nail wash and such. These arrangements were traditional with zards. Also, it might be mentioned that zards tended to use females of various species, including their own, for such services. It might also be mentioned that such females must in serving serve the males first and the females second. They are forbidden to do otherwise, and disagreements as to this sort of thing will elicit an invitation from the management for disgruntled patrons to depart. Zard restaurants were not common on the home world.

"Sirs," said the blonde, turning to face them.

The table was prepared.

Rodriguez brought his glass of Heimat to the table, and Brenner followed suit, with his cooler. The girl who had been at Brenner's feet, he noted, followed him, as though he might represent some sort of security for her, to the table. There were two rings set in the floor, one on either side of the table. These made Brenner nervous. Their purpose was not clear to him. One was a bit in front of him to his right, and the other was similarly situated with respect to Rodriguez, to his right, who took his place across from him.

"Is everything satisfactory, sirs?" asked the blonde. To Brenner, it seemed, again, as though she might somehow regard herself as playing a role. He wondered if she might not be speaking more for the benefit of the creature in the back than for theirs. Certainly her posing of the question, its tone, and such, to those to whom the language was familiar at least, had failed to ring of authenticity. Again there seemed to be some secret between her and Rodriguez. She was certainly attractive, however, thought Brenner, with those long legs, with that long, blond hair, and the yellow silk, in spite of whatever real or imagined meretriciousness, or falseness, might be in her manner. Yes, thought Brenner, she was ravishing. The brunette who had been at his feet at the bar now knelt docilely to his right. The blonde, it seemed, scarcely took note of her. The brunette was shorter than the blonde. Both, within the parameters set by their diverse heights, were superbly curved, the blonde in a tall, spare, linear loveliness and the brunette, shorter, with a more compact lusciousness. Brenner supposed that the blonde, from her manner and such, regarded herself as the superior of the two. Also, he recalled she had been summoned first to the floor and, of the two of them, Rodriguez and himself, had addressed herself to Rodriguez, who would have been easily recognized as first between them. The zard had then, perhaps as an afterthought, summoned forth the brunette for Brenner. From Brenner's point of view, however, he was not dissatisfied with the arrangement. As a personal matter he found the brunette far more exciting. If the blonde was ravishing, then the brunette was even more ravishing. The blonde, incidentally, was of a type which many men of the home world, those who dared to speak of such things, professed to admire. Perhaps this had to do with her height and linearity, which tended to be more masculinistic than feminine, or, at least, than typically feminine. In this fashion, Brenner supposed that it might seem to many men of his world to constitute a less dangerous object of consideration, triggering fewer induced guilts, aversions, and such, than would the frank and delicious consideration of the luscious forms of more statistically normal females. Herein, one might speculate, could be found certain consequences of the negativistic conditionings to which the males of the home world were subjected. To be sure it was possible that there might exist another appeal of such a form, as well, a more obscure appeal, to be sure, but one perhaps also connected, ultimately, at least for the most part, with the negativistic conditionings. At any rate, Brenner preferred the brunette. Also, as some sop to his preferences, and as a reassurance to his vanity, he recalled reading somewhere, in a footnote somewhere, into which the most meaningful materials were often inserted, that on the openly stratified worlds, on all of which it seemed there existed the institution of female slavery, that the shorter, more luscious females, such as the brunette, tended to bring the highest prices. Indeed, more linear women, such as the blonde, tended to be held in a certain contempt, and were often consigned to the most menial duties. To be sure, it was admitted that they could be taught to jump and thrash, and serve, as well as their more normal sisters.

"Kneel there," said Rodriguez to the blonde, indicating a place to his right, at the ring.

She looked at him, startled, but did as he had said.

She looked well there. Her back, of course, was to Brenner.

"This stuff," said Rodriguez to Brenner, shoving a bowl

in his direction, "is home-world mush. You would probably like it. Here it is probably fed to the women."

Brenner glanced to the brunette. She put down her head. He gathered that such gruel might indeed be a staple in her fare, and doubtless in that of the blonde. The zard would presumably feed them alike. Too, they would not be likely to thrive on the fare preferred by zards. They were, after all, of a different species.

"Are you going to eat that?" asked Rodriguez.

"What?" asked Brenner.

"That," said Rodriguez, indicating a dish near Brenner. "It is of the flesh of animals."

"No!" said Brenner.

Rodriguez pulled the dish over to himself.

Brenner was horrified.

Brenner picked up a spoon and put it to the gruel before him. Such material tended to be unpalatable and tasteless, unless seasoned with various condiments. Some individuals on the home world, moral individuals, insisted upon eating it without condiments, in atonement for past species crimes.

"Is everything satisfactory, sir?" asked the blonde, again, but now from her knees.

Rodriguez felt under the table, where there was, apparently, under the upper surface, a sort of shelving. Brenner heard the slide, and rattle, of metal. To his horror he saw Rodriguez draw forth what appeared to be, at first, a handful of chain within a metal circle. He freed a tiny object from its housing in this apparatus, and slipped this tiny object into his vest pocket. He then tossed the remainder of the assemblage to the floor, before the blonde.

"Put it on," he said.

She looked down at it, disbelievingly.

Brenner now saw, that it was disarranged on the floor, that two objects were actually involved. There was a short chain, the first object, about a yard in length, with an opened clip lock at each end. At one end, this opened clip lock had been inserted through, and turned, but not closed about, a small, stout, rounded staple emerging at right angles from the flat, metallic circle, the second object. This metallic circle, about a quarter of an inch in thickness, and an inch and a quarter in height, had a hinge in the back, which permitted it to open. It also had a hasp in the front, hinged, which was apparently congruent with the staple.

"Surely you cannot be serious," said the blonde.

Rodriguez looked at her.

"Ah!" she whispered. "Of course!"

Brenner looked back to the zard. He had lifted his head, on that rather long neck, when the metal had struck the floor.

"Of course!" she said, rather loudly, doubtless for the benefit of the zard.

Then, and Brenner gathered it was not the first time she had done this, she snapped the lower lock clip shut about the ring in the floor. She then placed the metal circle about her neck, adjusting it with both hands, the chain, held to the metal circle by the open lock clip, it inserted through the staple, dangling from it. She then removed the upper lock clip of the chain from the staple, closed the hasp over the staple, reinserted the lock clip through the staple, it now with the hasp behind it, in place, and clicked it shut. Brenner seized the edges of the table. There was a beautiful woman before Rodriguez, collared and chained.

"You are clever," she whispered to Rodriguez. Again it seemed there was some secret between them.

Brenner wondered if she were mad. Did she not understand that she was chained, truly!

"Chain me," whispered the brunette to Brenner.

"Never!" said Brenner.

"You must!" she whispered. "Please! He is watching!"

Brenner looked up, as discreetly as possible. It did seem that the zard was regarding them.

"Please!" begged the brunette.

Brenner felt under the table. There was, indeed, a shelf there, and his hand, groping about, encountered chain. Too, there was a curved, flat metallic surface there. He drew forth these objects. They were loosely connected, as they had been for Rodriguez, by a lock clip put through, and turned, but not closed about, a staple.

Brenner looked at the objects. There was a key in one of the lock clips, that put through the staple, and Brenner removed it from the lock clip and put it on the table, beside a plate.

The brunette reached for the chain and circle.

"Put your hands down," said Brenner, sharply.

Instantly she did so. She looked at Brenner, startled.

"On your thighs," said Brenner. "Keep them there."

She put her hands on her thighs.

"What do you say?" asked Brenner.

"Yes, sir," she whispered.

He then removed the upper lock clip from the staple and crouched down, rather in front of her. He attached the lower lock clip to the ring in the floor. He jerked it against the ring. It was well fastened. He opened the collar. She then lifted her chin and looked outward, being careful not to meet his eyes. He put the collar on her and swung the hasp forward, over the staple. There was a small, but clear, rather decisive noise, as he did this. He then fitted the bolt of the lock clip through the staple and, decisively, snapped it shut. He jerked it against the staple. It was on her, well. Quite securely. She was chained.

He then resumed his seat and put the key to the apparatus in his upper, left-hand shirt pocket.

"I am sorry I was cross with you today," she whispered.

"You were more than "cross"," said Brenner. "You were angry, and I did not care for it."

"Quirt her," said Rodriguez.

Brenner looked at him.

"They look well, quirted," said Rodriguez.

"There is a whip upstairs," whispered the girl.

"You may remove your hands from your thighs," said Brenner.

She did so, putting them on the chain, three or four inches below the collar.

"Perhaps you may free me," said the blonde to Rodriguez, "so that I may serve you better."

"You will stay where you are," Rodriguez informed her.

"But perhaps others will come in," she said.

"You will remain where you are," said Rodriguez.

"Yes, sir," she said, uneasily. And it seemed to Brenner that it might have been the first genuine response she had uttered all evening.

"Let us eat," said Rodriguez.

He seized up a pair of zardian tongs. These could lift up a number of objects and could grasp quite firmly. Their width and gripping surfaces facilitated the capture of live food, scurrying about in dishes, for which zards had a taste. To be sure, as Rodriguez and Brenner were not zards, such materials had not been served to them. Zards, incidentally, particularly upper-class zards, tended to regard the use of the tongue to secure food as rude, at least in public. Certain exceptions were made for certain forms of food, of course, for which the use of the tongue was traditional.

Brenner noted the blonde, her hands on the chain, near her collar, cast a glance, and, it seemed, a somewhat uneasy one, at the brunette. He wondered how the women, generally, felt about one another. The blonde, he had surmised, held herself superior to the brunette. Now, however, it seemed that the women were rather in a commonality, and that their current predicament might take precedence over any typical competitions consequent upon their vanity. Both were now chained and collared, and kneeling. He wondered if the brunette knew that she was incredibly beautiful.

Brenner and Rodriguez then applied themselves to their repast, such as it was. In the course of the meal neither paid the women any attention. They did not, for example, offer to feed them. To be sure, at one point, Rodriguez did warn the blonde to silence.

"Not bad," said Rodriguez, eventually, thrusting back a plate.

He then drew forth a letter, folded small, written in a feminine hand.

"No, please!" whispered the blonde, suddenly, terrified, lifting her hand to Rodriguez.

He read the letter, slowly, casually.

"Please," whispered the blonde.

Rodriguez tossed the letter over to Brenner. "It was passed to me at the bar by this slut," said Rodriguez.

Brenner now understood the secrecy, and the confidence, which had seemed imminent in the blonde's manner toward Rodriguez.

"Please!" wept the blonde.

"Shut up," said Rodriguez.

She pulled at the chain, but remained on her knees. She could not move from where she was, nor could she, of course, stand upright.

"It is a note which she wishes me to take with us when we leave Abydos, seeing that it is posted to a certain executive in the middle-management echelons of the company on Naxos," said Rodriguez.

"Surely you will do so," she whispered. "You are strangers here. You will be leaving Abydos. It will be easy for you to do! I have no other way to contact him, what with the censorship here, and the control of my movements! Women such as I are not even permitted within the precincts of the agent's office!" The blonde squirmed, her hands on her chain, as Brenner read the note. It was not difficult, from the note, to gather what the situation was. The woman, now apologetic and willing, contrite, begging for another chance, wishing to be reconsidered, had refused the advances of a given executive. She had then been selected for reassignment. On Thasos, enroute to Aegina, her credits had been canceled, presumably as a matter of clerical error, from Naxos. Fortunately the company maintained offices on Thasos, to which she immediately appealed, only to discover that her identificatory credentials were no longer to be found in the company files. The agent on Thasos, it seemed, could do nothing. To be sure, he had expressed sympathy for her, in her dilemma, for it is surely not pleasant to be found stranded on a distant world, and in particular on one such as Thasos, on which visible evidence of support, sponsorship, or kinship is required. It could have been far worse, of course, for

Thasos is relatively civilized. On some worlds she might have found herself in a slave pit by nightfall. The agent had suggested to her, as a temporary expedient, that she consider placing herself under contract to the company, embarrassing and regrettable as such an act might be, by means of which act she would come again under its aegis, and might once more profit from its power, protection, and solicitude, which contracts he was authorized to prepare and execute. The misunderstanding might then, at a later date, be corrected, all errors rectified, the contract canceled, and such. Indeed, he assured her that she would doubtless receive a profound apology from the company, small compensation though this might be for her humiliation. More tangibly, of course, he suggested that she might expect a full restoration of her canceled credits and, doubtless, a substantial compensatory bonus posted to her account. Gladly then did she put her name and personal number, having to do with her world of birth, species, and such, to the contract, for which act a certain number of credits were immediately posted to her account. "I am now a contract person," she had laughed. "Yes, you are," he had smiled. He had then conducted her to a small side room, which was bare, with no furniture, rugs or such. She was locked in this room. Later, toward the end of the working day, he opened the room, and handed her a small, neatly folded, white camisklike garment. This garment was narrow and fitted over the head. Its sides were open, except that by means of strings, on both sides, on both edges, under the arms, at the waist, and at the thighs, it could be tied modestly shut. It was a plain garment, except that at the left shoulder, tiny, and discrete, was placed the company *logo*. He then retired discretely while she changed. She was somewhat dismayed to discover the brevity of this garment. Also, when he first returned, he discovered she had retained undergarments, leg coverings and shoes. He then retired again, that she might remove these objects, which she did, putting them neatly to one side. She was to wear, it seemed, only the light, brief, white garment, literally that, and nothing else. When he returned, matters were in order, as was proper. He then carried her garments from the room, leaving her disconcerted within, in only the brief white garment. When he returned again he had her put her hands behind her back and put them in bracelets. "Routine," he had assured her. He had then had her sit on the floor at the back of the room and put a small chain and disk on her left ankle, locking it there. "This marks you as company property," he informed her. " I am a free woman!" she exclaimed. "Of course," he had reassured her. He had then gagged her and left her in the room, locked within. That night, still gagged, she was conducted from the room. He permitted her to see her clothing disintegrated. Then, hooded, she was transported from the office to the spaceport in an air car. In due course she found herself in a cell on a freighter, with five other females, none of whom spoke her language, and two of whom were not of her species. When she shrieked or complained, she was not fed. In time she found herself on Damascus where she, or, more exactly, her contract was put up for sale at auction. For the purposes of this sale, of course, not even the brief white garment in which she had been placed was permitted to her. In such sales, as you can easily understand, it is important for the bidder to be in a position to form a reliable conjecture as to the worth of the contract. On Damascus, as on a number of such worlds, although the young lady did not understand it at the time, incidentally, sales of contracts tend to be somewhat informal. Whereas the company would receive its credits for the sale, it would not receive any information, nor would any be kept on Damascus, of the disposition of the contract. In this there is, incidentally, a borrowing from slave handling. Suitable endorsements, however, as one would expect, are kept in the contract itself. Similarly, such endorsements are commonly kept on slave papers, where such papers are kept on a slave. Her contract was purchased by a native of the planet, a zard, who had recently negotiated the opening of a concession, a bar, on Abydos, at Company Station. In his bidding he was assisted by the advice of a fellow of the woman's own species, that his selections, bids, and such, might be judicious. Most of the workers at Company Station, of course, as we have noted, were of the woman's own species. It was thus, apparently, that the woman came to Company Station. We might also mention, incidentally, that on the same night some five other contracts, for similar purposes, were purchased by the zard. Amongst these was the contract for the brunette. The other women, unknown to Rodriguez and Brenner, were in the back. Thus, if one should fear that new customers at the bar might not be adequately served, one may discard such apprehensions. In the author's opinion, the best of the lot were the blonde and the brunette. This might seem to be the opinion of others, as well, as the blonde and the brunette were the first to be sent to the floor. On the other hand, the others, I might mention, were also quite nice. The same night on which their contracts were sold the blonde and the brunette had lost their virginities. This seemed a negligible payment on the part of the zard, indeed, nothing from his point of view, for the services of the fellow who had been so helpful. And thus had the blonde and the brunette, and certain others, in cells, come with the zard and his coworkers, who were lodged in cabins, to Abydos. The blonde had worn the small white garment on the freighter to Damascus, incidentally, for several days before she realized what must have been regarded as one of its major assets, and was certainly a consequence of its design. This had become clear to her when a new girl had been put on at Thera or Rhodes, it was not easy to tell in the cells, weeks before they reached Damascus. This new girl, who was in an adjoining cell, was presumably also a company contractee. At any rate she was clad in the same small white garment, marked with the same *logo*, as the woman we are particularly concerned with here, and her cellmates. Interestingly this newcomer, despite the fact that she had presumably freely entered into contract, and was still a free woman, seemed determined to be rebellious. Accordingly, to the dismay of those in the adjoining cell, who must witness these things, she had been subjected to certain mild correctives, such as bonds and strippings. It was in the course of these events that the blonde had come to realize that the sort of garment she wore, the strings loosened, and such, could be removed from, and placed on, a bound woman, these things without injuring the garment or removing the bonds. She found that feature of interest, if a bit unsettling. In a few days the female's rebellion, even given the gentleness of the admonitions applied to her, was over. She was on her knees to the zard crew members, her head down, cleaning the claws of their feet with her tongue, and such. All the females had learned something of discipline, thusly, either in the first person, or, so to speak, in the second person. To be sure, as they were free women, and not slaves, they could presumably not even begin to conjecture what it might be to be subject to a very different sort of discipline, one which we might, for want of a better word, call "slave discipline," a sort of discipline to which, nonetheless, many females in the galaxy found themselves subject. One should not, incidentally, feel any particular horror or regret at the nature of the contract sales. On Damascus, for example, there are also slave sales, and they are quite different, being on the whole, as you might expect, far more brutal and exotic, which is however undoubtedly appropriate, considering the nature of the merchandise. For those of you who might be interested in the fate of the credits advanced to the blonde upon her signing of the contract, it might be mentioned that they were returned to the company, being used to pay her passage to Damascus. In this fashion she arrived on Damascus, as the agent had doubtless intended, under contract, and with not one credit of her own. Indeed, she arrived slightly in debt, as certain charges had been made against her enroute, for food, and certain minor sundries. These small charges, of course, were paid off by the zard, as a surcharge on his successful bid for the contract. The surcharges, of course, were made clear to the clientele of the auction, as well as, naturally, the house's commission. The contractee's earnings, as Rodriguez had suggested to Brenner, are usually arranged in such a way as to either fall short of the contractee's debits, or to equal them. In this case, as the zard, though severe, was an honest sort, he had arranged matters in such a way that the blonde's earnings, and those of her fellow contractees, as well, were exactly balanced by her debits, for example, those charged against her for her keep and food. In this fashion the blonde, and the others, would remain under contract, could make no progress in paying it off, and would have, naturally, not even one credit of their own. In this the zard was not cruel, as were some contract holders, for example, in letting a contractee seem to make progress toward buying back the contract, and then, again and again, on one pretext or another, at the last moment, levying new and large charges against them, bringing them back to their original position. By now, it might be mentioned, it was clear to the blonde, as it eventually becomes clear to most contractees, that she was absolutely helpless in herself, and that she must depend on others. That was doubtless the motivation for her letter. Out of her earnings, incidentally, the zard had recovered both the surcharge on his purchase of the contract and the broker's commission. He had then raised the cost of her food and lodging to equal her earnings. One need not bother with this sort of accounting in the case of slaves, of course, as they are domestic animals.

Brenner handed the letter back to Rodriguez.

He lifted it up, and looked at it again, and then put it back on the table.

The blonde was in consternation, but she dared not reach over to snatch it up, nor, I think, given the temper of Rodriguez, would this have been a wise action on her part.

"Hide it," she whispered, frantically. "Do not let him see it!"

But Rodriguez left it lying before him, on the table.

Brenner glanced at the brunette. She, too, seemed frightened, though apparently not for herself. Brenner noticed that she had her hands on her thighs, as he had once, earlier, ordered her to place them. The dark collar looked well on her neck, the chain dangling from it, running to the ring on the floor. He recalled he had put it on her. He did not feel for it, but he remembered the key was in his upper, left-hand shirt pocket, away from her.

"You planned to use this fellow, the one to whom the letter is addressed," said Rodriguez to the blonde.

"He wanted to paw me," she said.

Brenner thought the locution was an odd one, considering that the fellow in question was doubtless of her own species, and, accordingly, would be highly unlikely to possess paws. On the other hand, he was willing to grant that the usage was intended to be metaphorical, and derogatory. As such, however, it seemed demeaning to various sorts of life forms, which possessed paws. Did she not realize the equivalence of all life forms, and their equal merits, regardless of such trivial differences as size, weight, quantity of population, frequency of gene replication, nature of consciousness, emotional development, and intellectual capacity? Too, he supposed that the females of some species, at least, might find the touch of paws, and even those which contained claws, as most did, interesting, and even tactually stimulating. Certainly several rational species pawed one another in play and love, and so on. Indeed, he knew, beyond this, that the lovemaking of certain species tended to be quite rough, and even violent. Her use of the locution, however, Brenner decided, was largely internal and subjective, not so much indicative of an external reality, suitably appraised, as expressive of her aversion to sexuality.

"Surely," she said to Rodriguez, "as a gentleman, you can understand!"

Brenner considered the matter. Things were doubtless more complex than the blonde's locution suggested. He decided to dismiss, at least for the time, the expression 'pawing', which in this context seemed to function more emotively than cognitively. Suppose one took another expression, one somewhat more literally intended, but nonetheless certainly explicit, such as 'handling'. He then regarded the blonde and the brunette. Certainly it seemed their bodies invited handling, holding, grasping, seizing, touching, caressing and such. Indeed, it seemed likely, given the selections of nature over countless generations, that they had been designed to be handled, and well. It was natural then that they might be of interest to men, regardless of the danger, or inconvenience, of this to the maintenance of certain political arrangements. If moons were political, thought Brenner, they would perhaps disclaim their effects on the tides. If flowers were political they would perhaps scold bees for having been lured to their nectar. Did the blonde not know she was a female, and an attractive one? Brenner looked at her. Yes, thought Brenner, she has been designed to be handled. Her present brief garmenture, of course, left little doubt as to the matter.

"You wished to use his interest in you," said Rodriguez to the blonde.

"No!" she said.

"You put him off," he said.

"Of course!" she said.

"You wished to whet his appetite," said Rodriguez. "What was it you were out to buy?"

"Nothing!" she said.

"What?" he asked.

"Promotion!" she said, angrily.

Rodriguez leaned back, regarding her.

"The company is not like the home world!" she said.

Rodriguez nodded.

In the company, as in most such companies, men remained important. There were a number of reasons for this.

"A woman must do her best for herself," she said.

"You do not think it is an accident that you were stranded on Thasos, do you?" he asked.

"No," she said. "Not now."

"Nor that the agent there was so cooperative, and such?"

"No," she said, bitterly, putting her head down.

"It seems, from your letter," said Rodriguez, "that you have rethought your original position in this matter."

"Yes," she said.

"And now," said Rodriguez, "if I am not mistaken, you

are willing to crawl back to this fellow on your hands and knees, begging his forgiveness."

"On my belly," she said, bitterly.

Rodriguez fingered the letter, idly.

"You must have it delivered!" she said.

"Why?" asked Rodriguez.

"I must be rescued!" she said.

"And you think this fellow will do so?"

"Of course," she said.

"But I gather from your letter," he said, "that your contract was sold on Damascus."

"I don't understand," she said.

"Why not on Chios or Thera?" he asked.

"I don't understand," she said.

"Both are closer to Thasos than Damascus," he said.

"Yes?" she said.

"Doesn't it seem strange to you then that your contract was sold on Damascus? Indeed, why was it not sold even on Thasos?"

"I do not understand," she said.

"You could not be traced from a sale on Damascus," he said.

She regarded him, frightened.

"Your fellow on Naxos surely knew that," said Rodriguez. And so, too, incidentally, would have the agent on Thasos."

"What are you saying?" she asked.

"Is it not obvious?" asked Rodriguez.

"No!" she said.

"You have been thrown away," said Rodriguez. "Your fellow on Naxos, obviously, has no interest in getting you back."

"No!" she said. "That cannot be!"

"He has doubtless dismissed you from his mind," said Rodriguez. "He has doubtless forgotten about you."

"But I am different now!" she said. "I am contrite! I am willing to do what he wants!"

"You will now do what any man wants," said Rodriguez.

She shrank back, in the collar and chain.

"Quite," he added.

"He can't have forgotten me!" she said. "He wanted me!"

"Your contract was sold on Damascus," Rodriguez reminded her. "He has rid himself of you."

"No," she said.

"Doubtless he has others," said Rodriguez.

"No!" she said.

"Do not be naive," said Rodriguez.

"It is only necessary that I let him know my whereabouts," she said. "He has doubtless, by now, regretted his decision, and will hasten to arrange my rescue!"

Rodriguez smiled.

"Yes!" she said.

"And what do you think you would then be to him?" he asked.

"I do not care what I would then be to him!" she said.

"Do you think he will restore your freedom, your position, your salary, such things?"

"No," she said.

"At most what could you be to him, a maid under contract, at a walled country house, on a world occasionally visited? Perhaps you would be assigned as a hostess in a company resort on some world, where he might, on some vacation or another, see to it that a certain portion of your time was reserved for him."

She looked down, her small fists clenched.

"He might even have you embonded," said Rodriguez. "He might find that amusing."

"No!" she said.

"You might become a brothel slave," he said, "chained to a bed on Sybaris."

"Please see that the letter is posted," she whispered. "I must be rescued!"

"Doubtless," said Rodriguez, "you stole the paper and the ink used in this letter, and the use of its writing implement. I expect such things are not commonly at the disposal of contractees."

"Please," she whispered. "He can hear! He can understand!"

"And since he has this concession," said Rodriguez, "and

must deal with humans here, he is undoubtedly literate, as well."

"Hide the letter," she begged.

But Rodriguez left the letter where it was.

"I must be rescued!" she whispered.

"There are many women under contract on Abydos," said Rodriguez, "for example, the maids at the hostel. What of them?"

"Let them fend for themselves!" she said.

"But what if they are unable to do so?" asked Rodriguez.

"Then that is their misfortune," she said.

"To all fours," said Rodriguez, "and come closer."

She did so, the chain then going back a little, and under her.

"Now lift your chin," said Rodriguez.

Frightened, the blonde did so. Rodriguez then, with the back of his hand, in a swift, sweeping motion, struck her on the right cheek.

"Rodriguez!" protested Brenner.

"To all fours, again," said Rodriguez, angrily.

Quickly the blonde, the side of her face red, doubtless stinging, tears in her eyes, hastened to comply.

"You have a room upstairs," said Rodriguez.

"One I am permitted to use," she said.

"You are normally slept below," said Rodriguez, "in cages or kennels?"

"We are not slaves," she said. "We are put in small rooms, separately, with a straw mat, and blankets, and locked in!"

"You look well on all fours," said Rodriguez.

A tear fell to the floor.

"What do you say?" asked Rodriguez.

"Yes, sir," she said. "Thank you, sir."

"You are ready, it seems, to crawl on your belly to your friend on Naxos," mused Rodriguez.

"Yes," she whispered.

"Is there a whip in the room?" asked Rodriguez.

"Yes," she whispered.

"Will it be necessary to use it?" he asked.

"No, sir!" she said.

"Do you know what I am going to teach you?" he asked.

"No," she said.

"I will teach you to crawl on your belly to any man," he said.

She looked up at him.

"Speak," he said.

"Yes, sir," she whispered.

The zard had his head lifted, in an attitude of interest. But then he returned to his work.

"I will release you now," said Rodriguez, removing the key from his vest pocket and opening the lock clip which had been secured through the staple on the blonde's collar. He then removed the clip from the staple, swung back the hasp, clearing the staple, fastened the bolt of the clip about the staple, inserted the key in the lock clip, these things then as they had been originally, and opened the collar. He let the apparatus lie on the floor. The blonde, frightened, took the key from the upper lock clip and freed the lower lock clip, and put the key back in the upper lock clip. Then, with a look of fear at Rodriguez, and on her knees, she curled the chain inside the collar, and put both items back on the shelf. Neatness, Brenner gathered, might be important to the zard. His own species, as he recalled, was regarded as one of the most slovenly in the galaxy. Brenner, seeing what Rodriguez was up to, similarly freed the brunette, but unlocked the lower lock clip first that she would continue to wear the neck chain longer. He was not certain why he did this. He then let the brunette, on her knees, as had the blonde, put the custodial apparatus back on its shelf under the table. The brunette then went to all fours, following the example of the blonde. "You may clear," Rodriguez informed the women. "Then you may precede us upstairs, each of you bearing a desert, a coffee and a liqueur."

"Yes, sir," said the blonde, from all fours.

"I am returning to the hostel," said Brenner.

"No, no!" whispered the brunette to him. "Please, do not! Go upstairs! You do not need to do anything! Please try to understand! If you do not send me upstairs before you, it will be thought that I have not been found pleasing! I do not want to be beaten, or tied outside in the cold! I know that I did not treat you well earlier today, but I am truly sorry, truly! Do not hold it against me! Forgive me! Please be merciful to me now. Indeed, punish me, if you wish, in the room. There is a whip there. But do not send me away now. Order me upstairs, before you. I beg it! Please be kind! Please!"

"All right," said Brenner. And to be sure, on some level, he was pleased, and exceedingly so, to have this woman, so exposed and scantily clad, who had been angry with him earlier in the day, now, somehow, apparently so much at his mercy.

The women, working together, quickly cleared the table and then hurried to the back. When they reappeared, each bearing a small tray, Rodriguez and Brenner rose up from the table and went to the foot of the stairs leading upward, not far from the desk of the zard. The women were there, at the foot of the stairs, to the right of the zard's desk, as one would face it. Rodriguez brought the letter, opened, with him, and looked at the blonde. She shook her head, wildly. She turned white. The articles on her small tray trembled. He must hide the letter!

"I am not an errand boy," Rodriguez said to her.

The blonde cried out with misery and, putting down the tray on the floor, flung herself on her knees, sobbing, her head to the floor, before the zard.

He picked up the letter, opened, which Rodriguez had dropped on his desk. He perused it.

His expression did not change, and it is difficult for those of Rodriguez' and Brenner's species to read most expressions of zards. We might mention, however, that the tiny ridge of plates on the back of its head and neck did not erect, nor did the mouth open, emitting a loud, hissing noise. His forward right appendage, however, reached out, grasping the heavy quirt.

"No, no, please!" wept the blonde, her head down.

Rodriguez put his hand on the clawed hand of the zard, and shook his head.

The blonde looked up, frightened, at the zard, and then at Rodriguez.

"I expect you will be watched rather carefully now, for some time," speculated Rodriguez. "Perhaps you will not be allowed to wear silk on the floor for some time, and your body may be examined, before you are permitted on the floor, to make certain you are not concealing any such messages. I would not wish, if I were you, incidentally, to be caught attempting such a childish, stupid trick again."

"No, sir," wept the blonde.

"I do not know what might be done to you."

"No, sir," she wept.

"Rejoice that you are not a slave," said Rodriguez.

"Yes, sir!" she said.

"But that can come later," said Rodriguez.

"No, no!" wept the blonde.

"Such is certain to become your eventual fate," said Rodriguez.

"No! No!" she wept.

"I will let you know in the morning," said Rodriguez, "if she is satisfactory."

The zard inclined his head.

"I will try to be as pleasing as I can be to you," said the blonde.

"I am confident of it," said Rodriguez.

"Do not complain of me in the morning, I beg of you," said the blonde.

"We shall see how you perform," said Rodriguez.

"What do you want of me? What must I do?" she wept.

"Pick up the tray," said Rodriguez.

Sobbing the blond picked up the tray. She then stood before Rodriguez. The articles on the tray trembled slightly. She did not meet Rodriguez' eyes. Although she was tall, Rodriguez was considerably taller.

"Do you fear you will be "pawed,"" asked Rodriguez.

She kept her head down, and did not respond.

"Before I am through with you," said Rodriguez, "you will beg to be merely "pawed," and brutally."

"Yes, sir," she said.

"Get your ass upstairs," he said.

"Yes, sir," she said.

She then preceded Rodriguez up the stairs. She looked nice ascending the stairs.

Brenner then looked at the brunette. She was standing, holding the small tray, on which were a coffee, a desert, a small custard, and a tiny glass of some liqueur. Their eyes met. Then she looked down. Brenner recalled how she had been angry with him earlier in the day. He had not been pleased by that. "Get your ass upstairs," he said.

"Yes, sir," she said.

He then followed her upstairs. The blonde had turned left. The brunette turned to the right, and led the way to a room near the end of the hall.

CHAPTER 5

B renner sipped his coffee.

He looked down at the brunette. She was kneeling beside the small table on which she had placed the tray, behind which Brenner sat.

"Remain as you are," said Brenner.

She looked well there, in the silk.

He put the cup down on the tray and leaned forward, reaching to his right. He put his hand fully in the glossy dark hair of the brunette, grasping it, and drew her head a little forward, toward him. Then he released her hair and she knelt back again. She had knelt on the right without having been told to do so. She had been trained to do so, of course, just she had been trained to set a table in the zardian fashion, and such. Most zards, you see, like most in Brenner's species as well, and as he was, were right-handed. In this fashion she would be more convenient to hand. It might be mentioned, however, that, as she was a highly intelligent female, the appropriateness and naturalness of this position, its convenience, significance, and such, were quite obvious to her, quite aside from the sanctions of her training.

Brenner looked down upon her. It was hard for him to take his eyes off her.

"Earlier," she said, "I had thought it disturbed you to have me at your feet."

He regarded her, musingly.

They were in the room to which she had conducted
Brenner.

It was a comfortable room, which contained a large, soft
bed. It contained no window. Brenner had locked the door
on the inside.

"One grows used to it," said Brenner.

"You learn quickly," she said.

There was, incidentally, only one chair in the room, that
in which Brenner sat.

Brenner took a another sip of the coffee, a tiny sip, a lingering
sip. He continued to regard the young woman, kneeling there,
in the revealing silk, beside him, attendant upon him.

"I should not have you there," he said.

"It is where I belong," she said.

"We are sames, identicals," he said.

"That is a pretense I have never found either plausible or
congenial," she said.

"I am a person," he said.

"It is my hope that you are a man," she said.

"You are a person," he said.

"No," she said.

"How then should I think of you?" he asked.

"I am a girl," she said.

Brenner looked at her.

"It is common to think of women under contract, and
female slaves, and such, as girls," she said.

"Surely you find that grossly demeaning," he said.

"I like it," she said.

"Oh?" asked Brenner.

"I find it appropriate, and flattering," she said. "And
surely it is fitting, and obviously so, considering our status."

"I see," said Brenner. "It has more to do with status, and
such."

"Yes," she said, "and with interest, and beauty, and how
it is appropriate to relate to us, that sort of thing."

"Then I shall call you a "girl,"" said Brenner, "that being
appropriate for a woman such as you."

"Exactly," she smiled.

"You seem submissive, and docile," he said.

"I am submissive and docile," she said.

"You did not seem so earlier today," he said.

"I am now," she said.

He regarded her.

"You may beat me," she said. "Implements for that purpose are available in the room."

Brenner glanced about. To be sure, on the far wall there hung a whip, and a quirt. There also hung, here and there about the room, some other articles, a coil of rope, a pair of linked bracelets, some shackles, a chain and collar, and some thongs. There was a ring set in the far wall, and one in the floor, near the foot of the bed. There was also a bar in evidence, the latter fixed in the lower portion of the stout headboard of the bed, to which he supposed a woman, perhaps by tied, crossed wrists, perhaps on her back or belly, might be fastened.

"I shall consider it," said Brenner.

She looked at him suddenly, frightened.

He suddenly realized that he could do that, if he wished. He did not think that the zard would object, assuming, of course, that her value was not reduced. Indeed, perhaps a beating might improve her value. Brenner suspected, for example, that the blonde's value might be considerably increased by something of that sort. In any event, it seemed, at least for most practical purposes, that the zard would not be involved. The matter was primarily between him and the girl, or, as he had gathered from her glance, actually, rather, up to him.

He regarded her.

"You can do with me what you want," she said, "that is, within reason, as I am a free woman."

"And if you were a slave?" asked Brenner.

"Then," she said, looking down, "you could do with me as you want."

"I see," said Brenner.

"I was upset!" she said.

He looked at her.

"Earlier you said you forgave me!" she said.

"I may rethink the matter," said Brenner.

"Do you forgive me?" she asked.

"I have not decided," he said.

"I see," she said.

He regarded her. Her curves seemed incredibly delicious to him.

"I was cold, out in the mud, miserable, and barefoot, and I was not looking where I was going," she said.

Brenner finished the coffee, and put down the cup.

"I should not have lost my temper, of course," she said. "I realize that."

"And perhaps you realize it with a special emphasis now," said Brenner.

"Now that I am here, at your feet, and, as you doubtless must understand, much at your mercy?"

"Yes," he said.

"Yes, of course," she said.

"You were wearing a dress," said Brenner.

"Yes," she said. "Women at Company Station must wear skirts, dresses, and such things. They are not permitted masculine garb."

"But such things," said Brenner soberly, critically, "tend to emphasize gender differences."

"Certainly," she said, puzzled.

"Surely you regard that as wrong," he said.

"I regard it as wrong not to emphasize such differences," she said.

"Surely you object to being forced to wear dresses, and such things," he said.

"No," she said. "I want to wear such things. I love such things. And, too, I am pleased that we are *forced* to wear them. I enjoy having no choice in this matter. Such garmenture, and the coercions attached to it, speak to me of my differences from men, and of my own nature, and of the rightfulness and legitimacy of these differences, and of this nature. Too, it then makes it more difficult for a certain form of woman to imitate men, and to attempt to instill guilts in others, who would prefer not to follow their perverse example."

"You know that women on the home world do not wear such things," said Brenner.

"Perhaps they do in secret, with their lovers," she said.

"Surely such things do not occur," said Brenner.

"Perhaps not," she said. "I would not know."

"Are you from the home world?" asked Brenner.

"Once," she said.

"What of your silk?" asked Brenner. "Surely you regard that as deplorably feminine."

"Why deplorably?" she asked.

"I don't know," admitted Brenner. He didn't. He supposed that perhaps it was his conditioning program which, in effect, had spoken. Conditioning programs are useful in the inculcation of values. They are useful in the production of uncritical, reflexive responses. They have many advantages, such as social control, the manufacture of consensus, and the protection of particular establishments, depending on the program in question. Also, of course, from the individual's point of view, they can produce the comfort of unquestioned certitude and the illusion of knowledge. That they save the time and trouble of thought is another considerable advantage. It is not unusual for a puppet to interpret the jerking of its strings as the deliverances of rational intuition. That is part of the jerking of the strings. How very few individuals, incidentally, are even aware of their conditioning. It is rather as though colored glasses were strapped on them at birth and, as a consequence, they lived their lives seeing the world as green, and not even knowing they saw it as green. In a sense, of course, our sensors are such, too. We see the world in a given way, and few of us suspect, or understand, that it might be seen in an infinite number of alternative fashions. Brenner's species did not live in the same world, experientially speaking, as the zards, or the teswits, or, say, the ant, the bat, and cuttlefish. Returning to conditionings, it must be understood that not all stings and shocks, all negative reinforcements, are as simplistic as those administered through electric grids, nor all rewards as obvious and naive as the food pellet rattling about in the feed pan. And if many individuals are not even aware of their conditioning, taking their conditioned responses as the deliverances of reason, or rational inspection, or insights into the nature of reality, or whatever, it is even less surprising that fewer individuals have the audacity or courage, or simple curiosity, to inquire into the nature, justification, or validity of these programs. That, in virtue of the program itself, part of which is to the effect that it itself may not be questioned, except perhaps in a superficial or token fashion, is dangerous, being attended with various risks to the individual, internal, such as self-doubts, miseries, and guilts, and external, such as social sanctions, which may range from ridicule and exclusion to death. It is not surprising that many individuals who pretend to undertake an inquiry into the validity of their conditioning programs will not cease their endeavors nor rest easy until they find themselves securely returned to the point they started from, whatever that point happens to be in the particular case.

But if conditioning programs are so effective, how is it that they are ever changed, or transcended, even over periods of generations? The answer to this is at least fourfold. First, they are not, as yet, at least, that effective. Second, not all conditioning programs are identical. Accordingly, the inconsistency generated by the collision of competitive conditioning programs necessitates adjustments, not all of which can be resolved easily by exterminating the adherents of the alternative program. Thirdly, such programs often encounter difficulties, such as reality. Fourthly, some individuals can think.

"If you think this is feminine," she laughed, "you should see some of the diaphanous silks in the wardrobe." She indicated a wardrobe against one wall. "Would you like me to silk myself in such?" she asked.

"No!" said Brenner. "Of course not."

"You must understand," she said, "that we are given no choice in what we wear upon the floor."

"If you had your choice, what would you wear?" asked Brenner.

"This," she smiled, "or such, or less."

"It is rather brief," he said.

"Do you object?" she asked.

"No," he said.

"Nor do I," she said.

"You are a very strange woman," he said.

"How so?" she asked, puzzled.

"It seems you do not mind being a woman," he said.

"I love being a woman," she said. "I rejoice that I am a woman. I want to be a woman. But I want to be a true woman, a real woman, a loving woman, a feminine woman, not some political travesty that would make my very nature and body an embarrassment or an irrelevance."

"I see," said Brenner.

"My silk disturbs you, does it not?" she asked.

"Yes," said Brenner. Or, perhaps it would have been more accurate to say that she, in such silk, disturbed him.

"I am sorry," she said.

"Are you wearing anything under it?" asked Brenner.

"A bold question," she said, "coming from one from the home world."

"Are you?" he asked.

"No," she said.

Her response confirmed his conjectures.

"It exhibits you—like an animal," he said.

"I am an animal," she said, "biologically." She looked up at him. "It is my hope that you are one also."

He looked at her.

"I am not an animal legally, of course," she said, "as I am a free woman, and not a slave." Slaves are legally animals, domestic animals.

"Save, of course," said he, "that animals are no longer exhibited." He referred, of course, to the home world.

"Say, then," she said, "that it exhibits me—like a *woman*."

"Yes," he said. "It exhibits you—like a *woman*."

"Yes!" she laughed.

"Do you enjoy being exhibited?" he asked.

"I enjoy being beautiful," she said.

"Do you enjoy being displayed—exhibited?" he asked.

"Yes," she said. "I enjoy being displayed. I enjoy being exhibited."

"I see," said Brenner.

"It is my hope," she said, "that you like what you see."

He looked at her.

"Do you?" she asked.

"Yes," he said.

"You may do with me what you want, you know," she said.

"Within reason," said Brenner.

"Yes," she smiled.

"Reason as determined by the zard," said Brenner.

"Where females of our species are concerned," she said, "he is tolerant and has a very broad concept of reasonableness."

Brenner did not doubt it.

"Do you want me to like what I see?" he asked.

"Yes," she said.

"Because you then think that your chances of being punished might be less?" he asked.

She put down her head. "That, too," she said.

"How did you come to be under contract?" asked Brenner.

"Surely you can guess," she said.

"You were in debt?" he asked.

"No," she said.

"You needed money?"

"No," she said.

"But surely you placed yourself under contract?" he asked.

"No," she said.

"I do not understand," he said.

"It was done to me," she said. "I was sentenced to contract."

"Why?" he asked.

"I liked men," she said.

"Of course you liked men," said Brenner. "On the home

world we not only like all life forms, men, women, sponges, insects, grubs, and such, but we love them. It has to do with the brotherhood of life."

"No," she said. "I liked *men*."

"Oh," said Brenner.

"I wanted to be submissive to men, and docile in their presence."

"As you were earlier today?" said Brenner.

"Certainly you find me submissive and docile now," she said.

"Yes," said Brenner.

"I do not speak of fits of anger, or petulance," she said, "lapses to which I am occasionally susceptible, particularly under conditions of stress, as might be anyone, and for which, if you wish, I may be severely disciplined, but of fundamental, genetically determined, attitudes, and dispositions."

"Genetically determined?" asked Brenner.

"One supposes so," she said, "as they were utterly at odds with the prescriptions of my cultural milieu."

"You do not believe in the "blank tablet" or "hollow body" theory?" asked Brenner.

"No," she said. "I believe there are genetically coded dispositions to respond, and genetically coded criteria for what will fulfill the organism, doubtless the result of natural selections over millions of years, as well as genetic codings for hair and eye color, and such things. Too, I find the alternative frightful, for that would suggest, whether it is true or false, that the human being is nothing in itself, but is empty, and meaningless, that it has no nature, and, as a consequence, that it may be turned into anything those with power wish, and there is no measuring rod or standard internal to the organism with which to appraise these subsequently produced human artifacts. For example, those of the home world, the behavioral engineers, and such, seem to suppose that everyone would choose to produce the same engineered products as themselves, but that is certainly not necessarily the case. It would be just as easy, it seems, if what they believe is true, to produce populations with values quite other than those which they approve, indeed, populations with quite diverse, and perhaps even antithetical, sets of values. Moreover, there would seem to be, from their point of view, no more justification for one of these value sets than for another, except perhaps that one might be found distasteful to them, given their values, as theirs might be found distasteful to others, given their values. It is as easy to fill the hollow body with venom as it is syrup. It is as easy to write cruelty and terror upon the blank tablet as platitudes and nursery rhymes."

"Go on," said Brenner.

"I was curious about men," she said. "I wondered what it would be, to be touched by them, to be held in their arms, to serve them, to have to obey them, to be owned by them."

"Such are forbidden feminine impulses," said Brenner, shocked.

"'Feminine' in the old sense," she said.

"Yes," agreed Brenner. 'Feminine' in the new sense meant, in effect, what 'masculine' used to mean in the old sense. On the other hand, as would be expected, 'masculine' on the home world now meant, in effect, what 'feminine' used to mean, in the old sense. These linguistic alterations were portions of the conditioning programs through which children were forced. To be sure, as we have suggested, these linguistic "reforms," despite their political expedience, had not been successful. People tended to find new words for the old things. People, on the whole, continued to fit language to reality rather than reality to language. In such matters, reality continued to have the last word, so to speak.

"And forbidden, of course," she said, "because they are very real."

"Else there would be no point in disparaging such impulses, or attempting to prohibit them," said Brenner.

"Precisely," she said.

"But surely you are an unusual woman," said Brenner, "that you would have such disgusting and terrible attitudes, or needs, or impulses."

"Why are they disgusting or terrible?" she asked.

"I don't know," said Brenner. Once again, he didn't. Once again, it seemed, something had spoken from him, which was not him. "But undoubtedly," he said, "you are almost unique."

"But why then the pervasiveness of the denunciations, all the social care taken to deny, or, if that is unsuccessful, to frustrate, suppress, and thwart such impulses?"

"I do not know," said Brenner.

"I am sure they are widespread," she said. "To be sure, most women live in terror of them, in fear of them. They are taught to pretend that such things, deep and meaningful within them, do not exist, or, if they sense them in themselves, that they must be ashamed of themselves, for being what they are. So the women think they are alone, and each feels isolated and miserable."

"You think there are others like you?"

"Of course!" she said.

"Why then do we not hear more of this?" asked Brenner.

"Surely you do not mean in the media, which is controlled by the parties, by the establishments?"

"No," he said.

"Many women fear to express these things," she said, "and even those in whom they are recurrent and powerful, not just latent and insinuative, lurking in the shadows. Indeed, these things are so fearful to many that they attempt to prohibit them from even reaching consciousness, and they must do so in distorted ways, in mistakes of the tongue and pen, in recurrent images and thoughts, and, of course, in dreams, those doors to half-kept secrets."

"How came you to contract?" asked Brenner.

"I made the mistake, if mistake it was," she said, "of speaking of these things privately to certain friends, or those I thought were friends. I was reported to the local morality board. I should have denied everything, I suppose, but I did not. Rather I sought advice and counsel. I was given a stern scolding, and warning. Later, when I again appeared before the board, as was required, as I had been placed on probation, I was remanded to therapy, and, months later, by a higher board, to institutionalization. I tried to cure myself, but could not. Perhaps I should have pretended to be cured, but I was too honest, too frightened, too worried, to do so. I knew I was not cured. I still had impulses and feelings which I, at that time, interpreted as being symptoms of iniquity or disease. Why could I not be like others, a true person? Eventually I came under the care of a woman who was kind to me, and informed me that it was not wrong to have such impulses, only that in my case they were directed to the wrong objects, that, as I was a female, they should be directed toward other females, such as herself. I did not know what to make of this. I did not even, really, understand it. I was frightened. I had heard of such things, hints and such, but had always thought them strange, or, at least, uncongenial. Too, it did not seem to fit in with the personism I has been taught, which, presumably, she should exemplify, though she assured me, fervently, it not only did, but fulfilled exactly that personism. It seemed to me rather, however, that both of us, as females, belonged at the feet of men. She flew into a great rage at this and I realized I had touched something deep in her. I do not know if she rejected her sex and wished to be a man, having a woman at her feet, or if she, as a woman, frightened, was reacting hysterically, even savagely, against her own feelings and impulses."

"You resisted her advances?" asked Brenner.

"Yes," she said. "I was then, shortly thereafter, barefoot and in a hospital smock, called up before a disposition board. Based on her report, I was characterized as incurable, and as unfit to remain on the home world. I had to be dragged screaming from the room. Later, by a court, I was sentenced to contract. Months later my contract was put up for sale in Damascus, which is where my contract holder purchased it."

Brenner regarded her. She was lovely. To be sure, he supposed it was wrong to be lovely, or, at least, a failing to be overcome. "So you are unfit to remain on the home world?" said Brenner.

"It seems so," she said. "At any rate, it seems they do not want women like myself on the home world."

"Are such things often done?" asked Brenner.

"It is my impression, gathered from cellmates, and such, that the home world rids itself of many women such as myself."

Brenner thought of the tribute levies mentioned to him by Rodriguez. He supposed that they might play some similar role. Certainly the women chosen were supposed to be, at least upon the whole, if he could believe Rodriguez, sexually responsive, a feature, or defect, which would doubtless jeopardize their careers on the home world, at least if noted, or publicized. On the other hand, he supposed that many women on the home world might be sexually responsive. To be sure, it was one thing to be sexually responsive, and quite another to say anything about it, or do anything about it.

"I did see the woman under whose care I had been again," said the brunette. "I saw her on home world, weeks later, at the holding area. We were both inside the wire, in camisks, and shackled. We pretended not to see one another."

"What was she doing there?" asked Brenner.

"I expect it had to do with some political fallings out, or manipulations," she said. "Competitions, eliminations of rivals, and such things. I suspect more than one woman, even highly placed women, has suffered such a fate."

"At the hands of other women?"

"Of course," she said.

"Perhaps the other women found it amusing."

"Perhaps," she said.

"Do you know what became of her?" asked Brenner.

"No," she said. "I trust she is happy."

"You do not hold your own contracting against her?"

"No," she said.

Brenner nodded.

"Besides," she said, "I have no doubt that I would have eventually, given my nature, and the openness of my case, and such, even without her, have been consigned to contract."

Brenner nodded. That did not seem unlikely to him, given what he had heard.

"The other woman," he said.

"She in whose care I had been placed?" she asked.

"Yes," said Brenner. "Was she, or her contract, sold on Damascus?"

"I do not know," she said. "But I do not think so."

"If her fate were as you seem to conjecture," said Brenner, "that she, too, had been contracted, and that hers was a contracting to which she was an involuntary party, then it seems that she, or her contract, would have been disposed of in a market from which she, or it, could not be traced."

"Yes," she said.

"You know that your contract was vended in such a market," said Brenner.

"Yes," she said.

"And that you cannot be traced?"

"Yes," she said.

Brenner looked down at the liqueur, which he had not yet touched.

"There are many such markets," she said, "Naxos, for example, and Sybaris, and Megara."

Brenner did not take his eyes from the soft, ruby fluid in the small glass. He could see a lamp obliquely reflected in its surface. "And doubtless women might be shipped from such worlds to other worlds," he said.

"Of course," she said, "as I was brought to Abydos from Damascus."

"It is interesting to conjecture the fate of such a woman on, say, an openly stratified world."

She looked at him, puzzled.

"A world, for example," he said, "in which pretenses are not maintained with respect to rank and hierarchy."

"A world on which there might be slaves?" she said.

"Yes," said Brenner.

"Doubtless on such a world she would learn quickly to obey and serve well," she said.

"As would you?" asked Brenner.

"Yes, sir," she said.

He gazed upon her. He found her very beautiful. She put her head down.

"Do you regard yourself as iniquitous, or ill?" he asked.

"No," she said. "I regard myself as a woman."

"That was your crime?"

"Yes," she smiled. "That was my crime."

"Sexual needs do not exist," said Brenner, quoting one of the slogans of the home world.

"I have sexual needs," she said. "And they are such that only one such as you can satisfy them." She looked up at Brenner. "This, you see," she said, "puts me much at your mercy."

"You should have knelt before my friend, Rodriguez," said Brenner.

"He is not of the home world, is he?" she asked.

"Once, I think," said Brenner. "But he has been many places."

"That seems clear," she said.

Instantly Brenner was jealous of Rodriguez.

"It is before him that you should have knelt," he said, angrily.

"No," she said.

"No?" asked Brenner.

"I am not discontented," she said, "that I was called forth to kneel before you."

"Oh?" said Brenner.

"No," she said. "I had no choice in the matter, but had I choice, it would have been before you that I would have knelt."

"Better Rodriguez," said Brenner, angrily. "He knows what to do with a woman there."

"I am sure he does," she said.

"You would fit in well with him," said Brenner. Then he laughed.

"What is wrong?" she asked.

"I was thinking of the women of the home world," he said.

"In what way?" she asked.

"It is absurd!" he laughed.

"What is?" she asked.

"Think of the women of the home world," said Brenner.

"Yes?" she said.

"Rodriguez thinks that women wish to be dominated, to be subdued, to be subjugated."

"Perhaps they do," she said.

"He thinks it is what females want! Can you believe that?"

"Yes," she said.

"How can you believe that?" he asked.

"I am a female," she said.

"Surely it is not what you want," he said.

"I am a female," she said.

"It is what you want?" he asked.

"Do not make me say it," she whispered.

"Speak," he said.

"Yes!" she whispered.

"You want it?"

"Yes!" she said.

"Do not expect such from me," he said.

"No, sir," she said.

"I shall respect you," he assured her.

"Yes, sir," she said.

He looked at her.

"You chained me well!" she said.

He shrugged, angrily.

"Quite well," she said. "And when you unchained me you freed the clip on the floor ring first. Do you not know why you did that?"

"Why?" asked Brenner, angrily.

"To have me in the collar, and on the chain leash, longer," she said.

"Nonsense," said Brenner, angrily.

"And you ordered me upstairs, a female, in suitable fashion, decisively, familiarly, even vulgarly."

"It just slipped out," said Brenner.

"It is interesting that it slipped out that way," she said. "Too, I liked it. I oiled when you said it."

"'Oiled'?" said Brenner.

"Never mind," she said. She put down her head. She blushed scarlet.

"I must be leaving," said Brenner.

She looked up at him, suddenly, genuinely frightened. "No!" she said.

"Yes," said Brenner.

She crawled quickly to him and put her hands, pleadingly, at the sides of his knees. "You cannot leave!" she said. "It will be thought that I have failed, that you do not like me, that I was not found pleasing! Please show me mercy! I am sorry if I was cross with you today. Forgive me! I am on my knees before you, contrite and helpless! I beg it on my knees, helplessly! Please do not go away! Do not abandon me now, unless it be your intent to see me severely punished! Is this your vengeance upon me? To so arrange matters that I shall be severely punished? Please, no! I do not want to be punished! Have pity on me! I am a woman of your own species! If you wish to see me punished, tie me, and do so yourself! It is, after all, you whom I have offended! Teach me then that my behavior will not be overlooked. Teach me then that I may not do such things with impunity! I acknowledge that I behaved badly! I acknowledge that I deserve punishment! But I beg you to be kind, and not to turn me over to the mercies of the zard!"

Brenner regarded her, sternly.

Swiftly she knelt back, removing her hands from his knees, putting them, palms down, on her thighs, bowing her head, submissively.

"I beg you to stay here tonight," she said. "I beg it, weeping, on my knees! The room is warm. The bed is soft. You need do nothing! I will not trouble you! You will not even know I am here."

Brenner smiled to himself. He thought it might be difficult to overlook the fact that such a creature was with him.

"Sleep me naked, uncovered, on the floor beside your bed, or on the floor at the foot of your bed, where you would be less likely to see me," she said.

He rather thought he would prefer to see her on the floor at the side of his bed, where he might occasionally, as it pleased him, look upon her.

"Please, sir," she said. It pleased him to be addressed with respect by a woman. It was not an experience which he had had on the home world. Indeed, in several of the states of the home world legislation prohibited the tendering of such terms of respect by females to males. It was claimed by the morality officers, whose opinions and decisions were often fraught with significant consequences for careers, incomes and such, that they were demeaning, degrading, debasing, devolved, and such things, the usual epithets the intention of which was not to describe the world but to influence behavior. Whereas Brenner, some months ago, might have been willing to regard such terms as perilous anachronisms, or dangerous throwbacks to more primitive, violent times, he was no longer sure of it. What if it were acceptable, or even appropriate, for females to show males respect, he wondered. Certainly he knew enough ethology to recognize that deference behaviors, submission behaviors, and such, were pervasive in the animal kingdom, and were particularly prominent amongstst mammals, and amongstst them, amongstst primates. To be sure, it is one thing for something to be a fact and another for it to be morally justified, and such. For example, from the fact that a human being needs oxygen to live, as a fact, it does not follow logically that it has a right to breathe. That is an independent question. Similarly, from the fact that a male requires dominance to actualize his masculinity, rather than deny it, and thereby render himself miserable and shorten his life, it does not follow that he has any right to be himself. On the other hand, by parity of reason, it does not follow, either, that he has a duty to suffocate or shorten his own life. Two different sorts of things are involved, two realms, so to speak, that of fact and that of morality. These realms appear to be logically independent. It is not logically inconsistent, for example, to prefer the destruction of the cosmos to the fulfillment of one's own nature. Indeed, perhaps it is better, or morally superior, or more fitting, that the cosmos be destroyed than that one be true to oneself. To be sure, Brenner was not satisfied with this approach to matters. Certainly more than logic was involved. There was even the question, an interesting one, as to whether or not there was a moral realm, so to speak, a moral order of existence, objective rights and wrongs, moral facts, like planets and stars, but intangible and invisible, etc., as opposed to preferences, rhetorics, and such. It seemed to be one thing to measure mountains and quite another to take the volume of value, one thing to ascertain the location of iron and another the coordinates of right, one thing to weigh sand and another to weigh competitive moralities. Indeed, who shall we trust to design the scales for such comparisons? But Brenner was certainly not willing to relinquish the familiar stanchions of good and right. He was rather concerned with whether or not they had been viewed askew, or misrepresented, or mislocated, or twisted into odd shapes, to become instrumentalities, or tools, for certain parties. The way people were might also be worth considering, thought Brenner, heretical though the thought was, and the way they really were, he had in mind, as opposed to how it was insisted that they be, to answer to one political purpose or another, purposes externally imposed, purposes subserving the ends of one idiosyncratic, aggressive, organized, power-grasping group or another. Perhaps there was no logical connection between, say, nature, and morality, but there were at least two interesting empirical possibilities. For example, what of a real connection, in virtue of law, such as that between a nature and what would satisfy it, just as there might be a real connection, in virtue of law, between the nature of an organism and a sort of nourishment, given which it would thrive? If there were no moral facts, thought Brenner, short of stipulating them, or creating them, there seemed as much reason to stipulate the facts conducive to health and fulfillment as those inducing to sickness and frustration. And if there are moral facts, as Brenner rather hoped, rationally or irrationally, why should this mysterious moral realm not be, one, *empirically* or, two, *rationally* correlated with nature, if not logically? Such things did not seem actually impossible. Consider, first, the interesting possibility of an *empirical* correlation between nature and a generated morality. Analogously, consider the mystery of the emergence of consciousness, whether in birds, frogs, or men, which seemed an order of being quite unlike that of organic circuitry. There are thoughts. Where are they in the brain? Is a thought four centimeters long? Does it weigh seven grams? If the brain could generate thought, why could nature not generate a morality? Is that any more mysterious? To be sure, the fact would not logically entail the value, any more than matter logically entails the thought. The connection would not be one of logic, one of meanings, unless one rigged the meanings, unless one, so to speak, begged the question. Rather the relationship would be one of reality. This possibility, of course, would at best generate a natural morality in the sense of a natural *conception* of morality. In short, strictly, nature would have it such, in virtue of law, that a given organism would *conceive* of right and wrong in a certain way, at least under certain conditions, such as the possession of suitable information, and such. The naturally generated morality, or *conception* of morality, might or might not be in the creature's best interest. For example, if nature generated, say, a conception of morality which required the organism to commit suicide, this would not be in the creature's best interest, at least if the creature were moral, according to its own lights. Given natural selections, of course, it is unlikely such an unusual morality would be perpetuated. There are, of course, millions of extinct species. Some of these may, in effect, throughout the galaxy, have committed moral suicide, sacrificing themselves to others, starving themselves, denying themselves, and such. Perhaps this could be the consequence of a sort of degenerative momentum, rather analogous to the incurring of a predator's canines, which development, past a certain point, becomes not only useless but destructive, leading to extinction. The other possibility, connected with nature, is more interesting and plausible. On this approach, one *devises* a morality in the light of reflective consciousness, a morality which is natural in the sense of being compatible with nature and designed to fulfill it, but which is not an uncritical consequence of nature. On this approach there is a *rational* correlation between nature and morality, rather than a simple empirical one. This approach would possess at least four desiderata: it would preserve the requirement of commitment, the act whereby one accepts a morality; it would produce a morality subject to rational review, treating it neither as merely another myth, as another obsolescent absolutism, nor as a mere reflexive product of organic interactions; it would preserve a distinction between the realms of "is" and "ought," i.e., between the descriptive and the normative; and it would be not only congenial to nature, but designed with its fulfillment in mind, which, to be sure, in itself, represents a value commitment, but one not obviously inferior to others. In such a morality there would be a place for values commonly neglected by other moralities, such as pride, honor, discipline, responsibility, glory, adventure and victory. Moralities need not have as their object the pacification and taming of men; they may also have as their object their heroism and greatness. To be sure, there are many other possibilities, as well, in such matters. One might accept a morality on authority, for example, one of the numerous moralities purportedly handed down by one god or another, who seem concerned, on the whole, to tell their respective priesthoods what they wish to hear. Another obvious possibility is to accept the morality of one's milieu, as absurd as it may be. This possibility is popular with the ignorant, the simple, and the stupid. Another possibility, of course, is to *pretend* to accept the morality of one's milieu, as absurd as it may be. This possibility is popular with the informed, the complex, and the wise.

Brenner regarded her.

She had lifted her head then and Brenner saw that there were tears in her eyes.

"Very well," said Brenner. "I will stay the night."

"You will take pity on me?" she said, hopefully.

"Yes," he said.

"As a male upon a female?"

"If you like," he said.

"Thank you!" she said, delightedly. "Thank you!"

"Do not approach more closely!" he warned her.

"Yes, sir!" she said.

He was not certain he could trust himself.

She leaned back, on her heels, happily. How beautiful, how sexual, she seemed!

He glanced uneasily at the large, soft bed.

"Oh, the bed is yours, of course!" she said. "I am often slept beside it, naked, on the floor. I would request a sheet, if I might, to cover myself, if you deign to grant it to me."

He regarded her.

"I am often slept there," she said, "when my contract holder's client is finished with me, at least for the time. Then, later, perhaps as he awakens refreshed, he may order me again to his side."

"And you are naked?" he asked.

"Yes," she said. "In that way I am more convenient for the guest. He need not strip me."

"Dreadful," said Brenner, shuddering. On the other hand, he had to admit that the thought of her there, lying there on the floor, beside the bed, naked, perhaps under a sheet, summonable to his side in the night or early morning, was not without its appeal.

"Many women," she said, "are not even permitted the dignity of the couch."

"I see," said Brenner.

"May I rise to my feet?" she asked.

"Of course," he said.

There was a tiny sound of the disk against the chain. Brenner was curious to see that device more closely, but he did not call this to her attention.

She went to the door and checked it, to make certain, apparently, that Brenner had locked it from the inside. Then she stood there, with her back to the door, smiling, and her hands behind her, leaning back against the door. Her hands might have been cuffed behind her, Brenner thought.

She looked at him, happily. "Thank you for remaining the night," she said.

Brenner shrugged.

"You have not finished your liqueur," she pointed out.

He lifted the tiny glass and stood up. He approached to where, now wide-eyed, she stood by the door.

Her shoulders were very white, and soft, and well set off by the yellow of the silk. Her hands, behind her, drawing her shoulders back, accentuated her figure, excitingly, subtly. Brenner supposed that women were sometimes tied in that fashion, for such a purpose, in slave markets.

"You may have half of it," he said.

"No!" she said.

"Please," he said.

"I have not had anything like that since I have been on contract," she said.

"Please," he said.

She drew her hands from behind her back and took the tiny glass, looking up at him. She steadied her right hand with her left. "Thank you," she whispered. Then, carefully, she drank a little less than half of the ruby-colored beverage. "Thank you," she said, again, handing him back the glass.

Brenner finished it, and put the glass back on the table. He then turned to look at her again, she standing by the door. The palms of her hands were now back, at her sides, against the door. "It was not too good, was it?" she smiled. "No," said Brenner.

"This is Company Station," she said.

Brenner grinned.

"But I loved it," she said. "You are very kind. Thank you."

Brenner shrugged.

"Little things mean much to us," she said. "Some men give us a candy, or a pastry, in a wrapper."

Brenner nodded.

"Generally we are fed only with mush or gruel," she said. "The zard has read of diets for us."

"I see," said Brenner.

"For which," she said, "we are muchly charged."

Brenner did not respond.

"If we eat less, we are charged more."

"You are nonetheless paying off your contract?" asked Brenner.

"No," she said. "Things are so arranged that we cannot pay it off. I had not realized that at the time of my contracting. We are helpless. We cannot free ourselves from our contracts."

"I see," said Brenner. He had, of course, surmised this, from remarks of Rodriguez.

"Why did you ask for permission to rise to your feet earlier?" he asked.

"Why should I not have asked?" she asked.

Brenner found it difficult to respond to this. To be sure, she was a female, and under contract.

"Some men," she said, "require us to keep one knee on the floor or ground at all times, except when we are lying down. To be sure, we may depart from this injunction in certain transitional movements, as in ascending to the couch, keeping our bellies in contact at all times with its side or surface."

Brenner regarded her, she standing there, her back to the door.

"I am here for your pleasure, you know," she said.

"You are safe," he said.

"Thank you for staying the night," she said. "Thank you for the liqueur."

"It is nothing," he said.

"Do you not find me attractive?" she asked.

"It is immoral for a man to find a female attractive," said Brenner.

"Why?" she asked.

"Surely you know," said Brenner, angrily.

"No," she said.

"It degrades her," said Brenner, "to see her in such terms."

"Why?" she asked.

"It debases her," said Brenner. "It makes of her a mere object."

"Surely you know that is false," she said.

"No!" said Brenner.

"It is not my fault that not all women are attractive," she said. "That not all are attractive does not mean that it is wrong for some to be attractive, if they are."

"Attractiveness in a woman, as you must know," said Brenner, "is a most deplorable feature, a most unfortunate and dangerous property. It can detract attention from personness."

She regarded him, puzzled.

"It is easy to see why you have been removed from the home world," said Brenner.

"Doubtless," she said.

"As you know," he said, "many women on the home world have had recourse to cosmetic surgery, to control and subdue their beauty, indeed, in many cases, to remove it altogether."

"I know," she whispered, shuddering.

"And this sacrifice did they make in the name of personhood."

"And thus did they improve their careers undoubtedly!" she said.

Brenner shrugged. He did not doubt that, on the whole, the women who were "persons," usually the homely, the fat, the belligerent, and such, discriminated unmercifully against their more beautiful sisters. There seemed to be some sort of instinctual enmity between these "persons" and these other creatures, who were doubtless less than persons. Brenner was not quite clear on the source of this obvious hatred. To be sure, it was true that the more beautiful women tended to bring higher prices in slave markets and such. Did the women who were "persons" hate these others because they feared they might become like them, so pathetically needful and beautiful, or because they suspected they could never become like them?

"Attractiveness in a woman is populationally dangerous," said Brenner.

"Surely you are aware that unattractive women can be

bred," she said, "and that conception in any woman may be controlled."

Brenner shrugged, irritably.

"I could not conceive now, if I wished to do so," she said. "It is chemically precluded. The zard has seen to it."

"Doubtless," said Brenner.

"What is personness?" she asked.

"I don't know," admitted Brenner.

"Surely we must not limit it to such accidents as having had a course in algebra or political science?"

"I suppose not," said Brenner.

"Perhaps it is to be equated with subscribing to a certain platform of political values?" she asked. "Perhaps that is the touchstone of personness?"

"Perhaps," said Brenner.

"But what if those values are treacherous, if they are inimical to, or betray, or deny, or make impossible, the fulfillment of the whole person, in her biological and emotional nature?"

"Such factors are unimportant," said Brenner. "They may be ignored."

"I do not regard them as unimportant," she said, "nor do I choose to ignore them."

"Disagreement with the prescribed values, as they exist currently," said Brenner, "is a sign of immaturity, ignorance, stupidity, iniquity, or insanity."

"And tomorrow," she said, "something else will be a sign of such things."

"Doubtless," said Brenner.

"What is the criterion?" she asked. "What is the standard?"

"I do not know," said Brenner.

"Surely it is what we are, really, our own nature, and what will fulfill us," she said.

"The prescribed values are such," said Brenner.

"You do not believe that, do you?" she asked.

"No," said Brenner, angrily. "I don't!"

"Nor do I," she smiled.

Brenner looked away.

"You are angry," she said. "I am sorry."

Brenner did not respond.

"There may, of course," she said, "be different sorts of human beings. That is an interesting possibility. But if that is true, then it would seem irrational to require all, or the whole, to subscribe to the values of some, or a part."

"If it pleases you," said Brenner, angrily, "the values of the home world are not accepted, even by members of our own species, in many places in the galaxy." This would be particularly true, of course, on the sorts of worlds Rodriguez had characterized as "strong worlds."

"I know," she said.

"You seem highly intelligent," said Brenner.

"I am intelligent," she said. "Do you think we become less intelligent if we are put under contract, or if a brand is put in our flesh, or our throat is encircled with a locked collar?"

"Of course not!" he said.

"I am not stupid," she said.

"I know," said Brenner.

"Does that dismay you?" she asked.

"No," he said.

"I sense that I am not as intelligent as you," she said, "but I am not stupid."

"Come now," he said. "It is well known that women are much more intelligent than men."

"That is ridiculous," she said.

"The tests prove it," he said.

"As they once purported to prove that the intelligence of men and women was identical, by balancing masculine and feminine items in the test, and summating statistically. One begins with the proposition to be proved, and then designs the test in such a way as to confirm it. Very scientific! Some types of items are such that women tend to be better at them than men, but there are also types of items, though this is not much publicized, at which men tend to be better than women. All that is done now is to define intelligence in terms of tests constructed largely in terms of feminine items, on which sort of items, as might be expected, women tend statistically to do better than men, particularly masculine men. The facts seem to be that there is a feminine sort of intelligence and a masculine sort of intelligence, and that they are not identical. It is difficult then to crosscorrelate the tests without summations which blur the interesting differences. Too, intelligence seems well understood as being much richer than a set of responses to a particular test. Surely it has something to do with judgmental assessments in actual situations, sensitivity to numerous factors in a real world, organizational capacity, ability to plan, to look ahead, with creativity, with imagination, and such things."

"Perhaps," said Brenner.

"The fact that I am intelligent, and have feelings, and such," she said, "would, I hope, make me more, and not less, attractive to you."

Brenner was silent.

"I have heard that such things tend to raise the price of slaves," she said.

"I have heard that, too," said Brenner.

"All this talk of objects, and such," she said, "is stupid. It assumes a man would be as content with a mindless machine, or an inflated dummy, as a live female."

Brenner nodded. He had never really understood the value of such propaganda, even to those who devised it. On the other hand, he granted that he might be naive. Perhaps it did have an appeal to certain sorts of minds, perhaps to those incapable of reason.

"To be sure," she said, "it is not unusual for a woman, upon occasion, wearying of the platitudes of personness, the complexities of banal, tortuous interrelationships, and such, to wish to be handled and treated as an object, not a mindless object, or an inflated object, perhaps one filled with air, one without feelings, or such, of course, but rather as an intelligent, fully sentient, fully emotional object, who understands that she is now to be put, whether she wishes it or not, to the purposes of another. In this way, she rejoices to be reduced upon occasion to her feminine essentials."

"I shall not listen to this sort of thing," Brenner informed her.

"It disturbs you?" she asked.

"Yes!" he said.

"But you will still stay the night?" she asked, anxiously.

"Yes," he said.

"You would prefer the blonde?" she asked.

"No," he said.

"You do find me attractive?"

"Yes," he said.

"Even though you suspect it may be immoral to do so?"

"Yes," he said, angrily.

"It is not immoral to do so," she said.

Brenner shrugged. He supposed that was true.

"It is even natural to do so," she said, "I would think, assuming that I am attractive, and that you are sensitive to such things."

"One supposes so," said Brenner. It was all he could do to refrain from leaping up, seizing her, crushing her to him, bruising her lips, and flinging her to the bed beneath him, to ravish her.

"A woman prefers to relate to a male who is more intelligent than she," she said. "This does not mean we think that we are stupid, or anything. It is rather merely that we prefer, no matter how intelligent we are, for the male to be even more intelligent. That is a difficulty faced by some highly intelligent women, to find a male to whom it is appropriate, and natural, for them to subject themselves."

"I see," said Brenner.

"To be sure," she said, "the crucial matter is not really intelligence, particularly in a narrow sense, but the wholeness of the relationship, and her needs. In the human species, males, if not crippled, are dominant. There are in our species, as in all others, dominance/submission ratios, and, in ours, as in several others, a significant sexual and psychological dimorphism between the sexes. In our species, as in many others, the female cannot be fulfilled without, in one way or another, in effect, being in the power of the male. To be sure, there can be various pathological substitutes for the male, such as a myth, another woman, a movement, a religion, the state, and so on, but these are always ultimately inadequate. Accordingly the crux is the domination which she requires. And thus, for example, even slaves who doubtless upon some occasions are far more intelligent than their masters, squirm beggingly, pleadingly, helplessly, rapturously, in their arms, owned in a sense far deeper than those to which experts in property law are accustomed. To be sure, the ideal is that she shall be, or know, or sense herself to be, less intelligent, at least in a full, generalized sense of intelligence, than he within whose sphere of domination she finds herself."

"I see," said Brenner.

"And I," she said, "not only in the narrower senses of intelligence, but also, more importantly, in this larger sense of intelligence, accept you as my master."

Brenner did not respond to this. Although he certainly did not regard her as stupid, but, rather, indeed, as of extremely high intelligence, he did not, in virtue of their interactions, and his sensing of them, feel inferior to her. He was intellectually, if not ideologically, comfortable with her. He regarded himself, indeed, in some subtle sense, as her master. Certainly it was clear that she belonged at the feet of someone, and perhaps someone such as himself.

"But it is not my intention to disturb you," she said. "Rather let me reiterate my gratitude that you will remain the night, and for the liqueur, which is much more appreciated than I suspect you can understand." She smiled at him. "I can still taste it," she said.

Brenner wondered if he kissed her, if he, too, might taste the liqueur, its syrupy, ruby sweetness lingering on the softness of her lips.

"Is there anything that I might now do for you," she asked, "any way in which I might serve you?"

"You are prepared to serve me?" asked Brenner.

"Of course," she said. "I am a female."

Brenner regarded her, standing there, by the door.

"May I serve you?" she asked.

"No!" said Brenner. "No!"

"Then, if I may," she said, "and you have no further need of me, I think I shall retire for the night."

"It is early," said Brenner.

"But if you have no further need of me?"

"Of course," said Brenner. "You may retire."

"Thank you," she said, approaching him.

"What are you doing?" he cried. He stepped back, quickly, frightened.

She had come to kneel before him, and had put her head down , to his feet. She looked up at him. "It is customary," she said, "that we exhibit deference to the clients of our contract holder, before retiring."

"What was it your intention to do?" he asked.

"To press my lips to your feet, to kiss them, thus, in one of many ways, exhibiting deference," she said.

"Do not do so!" he said.

"Yes, sir," she said. She stood up, near the bed.

"What are you doing!" he cried.

She looked at him, puzzled. "I am preparing to retire," she said. "I am removing my silk, that it not be soiled."

Brenner sat down in the chair. He looked away. He heard a rustle of silk.

"May I have the use of a sheet?" she asked.

"Certainly," he said.

He heard a sheet drawn from the bed. In a moment then, he understood that she was lying beside his chair, to the right, between the chair and the bed. She would be to the left of the bed, as one would face its foot.

He heard the movement of the sheet, a tiny noise, and the sound of her body, lying to his right, almost within reach.

"Are you naked?" he asked, not looking.

"I have the sheet," she said. "It covers me."

"Aside from that?" he asked.

"Of course," she said.

He still did not dare to look at her. He found the thought of her lying there, naked, within the sheet, on the dark, hard, polished boards of the floor, disturbing.

"You do not care to look at me?" she said.

Brenner did not answer.

"Have I been displeasing?" she asked.

Brenner did not answer.

"There are instruments in the room which may be used in my subjugation," she said.

Brenner was silent.

"What is it you fear?" she asked.

"Nothing!" said Brenner.

"Do you fear you will be tempted to call me to your side in the night?" she asked.

"No," said Brenner. "No!"

"I would have to obey you, you know," she said.

"Do not even speak so," he said.

"Do you fear rather that it would be I, that it would be I who might approach you in the night," she asked, "piteous, begging, perhaps even daring to touch you?"

"You?" said Brenner.

"Yes," she said, "I."

"That would be absurd," he said.

"It is not absurd," she whispered.

Brenner clenched his fists.

"You may prevent that," she said, "by gagging and chaining me, and putting me where I cannot reach you. I will then be unable not only to reach you but even to beg for the assuagement of my needs."

"Sexual needs?" inquired Brenner.

"Of course," she said. "And in the profound and holistic sense in which a woman has such needs."

"Such needs do not exist," said Brenner.

"Is that why the home world must go to such lengths to deny them, to thwart, and suppress them?" she asked.

"You may have the bed, of course," said Brenner.

"It is I who am under contract," she said, "not you."

"I shall sleep on the floor," said Brenner.

"The bed is for the client," she said, "and for me, only upon his sufferance."

"I can order you to its surface," he said.

She was silent. Brenner gathered that he could, indeed, do so.

"Please get into the bed," said Brenner.

"Yes, sir," she said. He heard the sound of the bed, receiving her slight weight.

"Please look upon me," she said.

Brenner turned about. She was small on the large bed, kneeling on its surface, the sheet clutched about her.

"The bed is large," she said. "There is much room. We can both lie upon it. We need not touch. You can bind and gag me, if you wish."

"It is early," said Brenner, uneasily.

"What are you going to do?" she asked.

"I will sit here, and think," said Brenner.

"May I have permission to leave the bed?" she asked.

"Of course," said Brenner.

"May I beg to sleep upon the floor?" she asked.

"I suppose, if you wish it," he said.

She moved gracefully, with a silken movement from the bed, and went to the wardrobe. Brenner refused to watch her at the wardrobe. He heard a tiny noise, as of a glass stopper removed from a bottle. A sudden fragrance, subtle but insinuative, indefinable, exciting, permeated the room. He heard the stopper replaced in the bottle, and the bottle returned to a shelf. She, and this scent, approached, and then she, half sitting, half lying, was again at the side of the bed, to Brenner's right.

"Do you like it?" she asked.

"What have you done?" he asked.

"I have freshened my perfume," she said. "We often do that, when we have a guest."

"It is a different perfume," he said.

"Yes," she said.

"It seems you desire to appeal to many senses," he said.

"Of course," she laughed. "Do you like it?"

"Yes," he said.

"Even though I am a free woman?" she asked.

"I do not understand," he said.

"It is a perfume of slaves," she said. Then she snuggled down on the boards.

Brenner was alarmed. The perfume was heady, and the understanding that it was a slave perfume made him almost scream with need.

"You torture me," he said.

"I am doing nothing," she said. "I am just lying here. You may beat me, if you wish."

"A cuffing might do you good," he said, angrily.

"Quite possibly," she said.

"I think you would make an excellent slave," he said.

"If I were a slave, I would hope so," she said, "as I would wish to live."

Brenner growled, angrily.

"I may one day be a slave," she said. "It is my understanding that that is a common fate for women under contract."

"Perhaps," said Brenner.

"If I were a slave," she asked, "would you like to own me?"

"No!" said Brenner, angrily.

"You are apparently not ready to retire," she said.

"No!" said Brenner. How absurd seemed the thought of trying to rest, let alone getting any sleep, lying there in the darkness, with that perfume in the air, understanding its meaning, knowing the proximity, and the nature and femininity, of the woman who wore it.

"I gather," she said, "that with one such as you I may do much what I please."

"For the moment," said Brenner, carefully.

"I am not accustomed to being treated with such lenience," she said.

"If you are going to be up," he said, "get dressed!"

Quickly, clutching the sheet about her, she rose up and went to the wardrobe again. He did not, of course, watch her, as he was a gentleman, so to speak.

"I am dressed," she announced.

Brenner regarded her, stunned.

"Cover yourself!" he said.

Laughing, she put the sheet again about her. Beneath it now she wore not the yellow silk, but another, a clinging, diaphanous scarlet silk. Her shoulders and belly were bared, and her left thigh. Her breasts were beautiful, sweet and full, in a soft halter of crossed silken bands. The drape of silk, open on the left, was low on her belly. It swirled about her ankles.

She sat on the floor, her knees drawn up, her back against the side of the bed, near him, the sheet wrapped demurely about her. She even tucked it more closely, more modestly, about her. This irritated him. She looked up, smiling. He could see her bared feet, and ankles, beneath the sheet. On her left ankle was the chain, and disk. He would have liked to have looked more closely at that. He did not do so, of course. He turned his eyes away.

"It is warm in here," she said.

That was true. It probably had to do with comfort zones somewhat other than those which those of Brenner's species might regard as optimum.

"With one such as you, it is true, is it not," she asked, "that I may do much what I please?"

"Of course," said Brenner.

"May I not then remove the sheet?" she asked.

"If you wish," said Brenner, angrily.

"Surely it does not matter," she said, "as you do not look upon me."

Brenner kept his eyes away, angrily.

"And as you are of the home world," she said, "it cannot matter anyway. One such as you, a true person, of the home world, merely accidentally male, anatomically, would scarcely notice such a thing. It would be meaningless to him."

"Of course, of course," said Brenner, sweating.

"With one such as you I am safe."

"Of course," Brenner granted her.

He heard the rustle of the sheet. He also sensed that she had changed her position. "There," she said. "That is better."

He looked upon her, and gasped. She had moved a little, and now, where she had earlier knelt, half sat, half knelt, her weight much on her right thigh and the palms of her hands. The sheet had been put on the floor about her, in a circular pattern. In this fashion it contrasted with the dark boards of the floor, and the scarlet of the silk. As she was positioned, her left thigh was bared, a consequence of the draping of the silk doubtless, which silk, it seemed, doubtless inadvertently, like the sheet, was arranged flowingly, and beautifully, one might even have thought, did one not know better, artfully.

"It seems," said Brenner, angrily, "that you choose to torture me."

"You are of the home world," she said. "Surely, in virtue of your conditioning, how I am, or might appear, does not matter. In virtue of your conditioning you cannot see me as what I am, a woman."

"It seems you wish to be seen as an object," he said.

"A woman," she said.

"An object!" he said.

"An object of desire, I trust," she said.

Brenner was silent, angry.

"A woman, the whole woman," she said, "wishes to be seen as an object of desire."

"You are sexual," he said, angrily.

"Is that a reproach?" she asked.

He did not answer.

"Yes," she said. "I am sexual! I do not deny it any longer. I am tired of denying it. I am tired of pretending to be what I am not."

"You must keep such weaknesses to yourself," he said.

"That is no more a weakness than the fact that I can think, that I can feel, that I breathe, that my heart beats."

"Then it is an ugliness," said Brenner.

"No!" she said. "No more than those other things, no more than thought and feeling, no more than breathing and the beating of the heart!"

Brenner regarded her.

"It is not ugly," she said. "It is beautiful!"

Brenner did not respond to her.

"Do you find me ugly?" she asked.

"No," said Brenner.

"I am pleased," she said.

"Doubtless many men have put you well to their purposes," he said, angrily.

"Yes!" she said. "They have! And I have served them well, or to the best of my ability, and sometimes in terror!"

"I see," said Brenner.

"They get what they want from me," she said. "They take it, if they wish."

"Doubtless the zard also uses you," said Brenner.

"Certainly women of our species figure in the perversions of many other species, as you must suspect," she said.

"I see," said Brenner, bitterly. He did not doubt but what certain aliens could simply take the women of his species away from the men of his species, and use them as they wished. The men of his species, it seemed, were on the whole quite weak. They could not even keep their own women for themselves. On the other hand, he did not think that aliens would attempt that on the occasional strong worlds where his own species was dominant. On such worlds, as he understood it, men of his species kept their women for themselves.

"But the zard does not so touch me," she said. "It is not that he is kind, or noble. It is just that he is not interested in such things. In this fashion he is a quite normal zard. He is not a pervert. Surely you are aware of the rareness of interspecific attraction."

"Yes," Brenner admitted. This rareness was to be expected, of course, given genetic selections.

"Do you think you would feel attracted to a female zard?"

"I do not think so," said Brenner. He had once seen one, on Naxos, at a spaceport, or he thought he had seen one.

"It is the same sort of thing," she said.

Brenner nodded.

"Would you like me better if I had scales, bulging eyes, and a tail?"

"No," said Brenner. To be sure, this was not the answer required by his conditioning program, which was that it would not make a difference. This had to do with the equivalence of life forms, and such.

Brenner regarded her. He did not doubt but what beauty might be species relative, for example, that he and the zard might not agree on the nature of feminine charms, but that did not mean that it did not exist, either for him or for the zard. Fruit does not become unreal because there is more than one variety. Certainly Brenner found the young woman before him extremely beautiful. Indeed, she seemed to him, now, to be the most beautiful female he had ever seen. And he did not think that he was isolated in this sort of thing. Even men on Naxos, he was sure, with their rifles and whips, would agree. And even many other life forms, he was sure, though they might not find her of sexual interest, might recognize that she was an unusually lovely specimen of a human being, and would be more marketable than otherwise on that basis.

"Consider the scandalous silk you wear," said Brenner, angrily. "It is the sort of thing in which a slave might be put. In such silk it seems you belong upon an auction block!"

"We might ascend a block in such silk, or more," she smiled, "but it is not likely it would be upon us when we left the block."

Brenner regarded her.

"I have been upon such a block, on Damascus," she said, "when my contract was sold."

She changed her position, to kneel. She arranged her silk. Then she again looked up, at Brenner.

"On the block, though we were free women, instant and perfect obedience was required of us," she said, "even as it is of slaves."

"Did you not demur?"

"No," she laughed, "or at most once, briefly."

"Oh?" asked Brenner, interested.

"They have whips," she said.

"Not sophisticated electronic devices?"

"No," she said. "On Damascus, as on many worlds, they are very traditional."

"I see," said Brenner.

"But the whip is very effective," she said, "perhaps in its primitive simplicity and meaning even more so than more complex electronic devices. We understand the whip."

"'We'," asked Brenner.

"Females," she said. "At least once we have felt it."

"I see," said Brenner.

"Yes!" she laughed.

"Did you demur?" he asked.

"I did not really need to feel the lash," she said, "but I was curious about it and so once I was hesitant. Then, instantly, I felt the lash. I did not know it could be like that. Then, I assure you, I was hesitant no longer. Too, to be sure, I was stung by the laughter from the buyers, the onlookers, and such."

"Who were the auctioneers, the brokers?"

"On Damascus, zards, of course," she said.

"But they would presumably have, as it seems you have earlier suggested, little or no interest in your movements, your posings, and such—such things I presume being expected of you on the block—"

"Yes," she said. "As contract women we were well put through our paces."

Brenner looked at her.

"There were men of our own species in the house, of course," she said, "buyers, and assistants to buyers, and such, who would help to appraise us."

"I see," said Brenner.

"It seems you find the vending of my contract of interest," she said, shyly.

"Were you appraised highly?"

"I think so," she said. "But I am not even sure of the value of the units involved, their relationship to the Commonworld credit, and such."

Brenner nodded.

"I did not bring as high a price as she whom your friend now doubtless has well at his pleasure," she said.

"The blonde woman?" said Brenner.

"Girl," she said.

"Your contracts were vended in the same sale?"

"Yes," she said.

"Was she struck?"

"Three times," she said.

"It seems she was less quick than you, to grasp what was required of her."

"Perhaps," she said.

"Perhaps she is less intelligent than you," said Brenner.

"Perhaps," she said. "I do not know. But in the end she obeyed as quickly and perfectly as the rest of us."

"The rest of you?"

"Yes," she said, "all of us who were being exhibited, whose contracts were being sold."

"I see," said Brenner.

"Perhaps you would have enjoyed seeing her perform— naked," she said.

"Perhaps," said Brenner.

"As she doubtless is for your friend now," she said.

"Perhaps," said Brenner.

"Perhaps you would have found it amusing," she said.

"Perhaps," he said. To be sure, he would have been, he did not doubt, much more interested in seeing the brunette perform. He looked at her. She put down her head, and blushed, beautifully, all of her body that was not covered with the silk.

"I think that on many worlds your contract might have fetched a higher price than hers," said Brenner.

"On the worlds of which I suspect you speak," she laughed, "I gather that it would be we, indeed, ourselves, and not our contracts, which would be vended."

"Perhaps," said Brenner.

She smiled.

"On such worlds, as I understand it," he said, "they buy the female, and that is what they are really interested in, the female, and the female female, so to speak, she who is most female, biologically, hormonally, emotionally, and such. That is what they are out to acquire, what they are bidding for, what they covet and desire, what they truly want, the real female, the female female, so to speak."

She smiled.

"How truly frightful, how truly dreadful—for that sort of woman, the true female, for the female female, so to speak," said Brenner.

She put down her head. "Perhaps not," she said.

"You were exhibited—on a block," he said.

"Yes," she said. "On Damascus."

He regarded her. He found her face very beautiful, so softly rounded, with the dark eyes, looking up at him, questioningly, and the dark hair, so soft and glossy, framing the exquisite features, and the whiteness of her throat and shoulders, and arms, the sweetness of her breasts within the silk, the bared midriff, the rounded latitudes of her belly, the silk low on it, the hips flaring before being captured by the silk, her left thigh bared, the right under the spread silk, and, behind her, her calves, the ankles, the chain and disk on the left, her small, white feet.

"Do you wish to see what they made me do, how they made me stand and pose?" she asked.

"No!" he said. Then he said, "How?"

"Like this!" she said, delightedly, leaping to her feet. "The bed shall be the surface of the block!" she said. "It is soft, and will not give me the best of footing, but it will provide the required elevation. You will get the general idea of matters."

"I am sure of it," said Brenner. How could he have asked 'How?' he asked himself. But how could he not have asked 'How?' he asked himself. "Retain your silk!"

"Do you think such things are permitted to us on the block?"

"Retain it," said Brenner.

"I shall do so," she laughed. She seized up the sheet from the floor, and hurried to the other side of the bed.

"There are many ways in which these things may be done," she said. "In our case, we were chained together by the neck in the waiting area, and our hands were braceleted behind our backs. We came to the block one by one, after being freed, one at a time, from the chain and bracelets. Covered with a sheet we are conducted to the surface of the block." She flung the sheet over her head and body and crept carefully to the surface of the bed, on which she stood, upright. "Various details, then, pertinent to ourselves, and our contracts, are brought to the attention of the crowd. After this the sheet is lowered to reveal our head and face, the nature of our hair and such. At this point bidding begins. Then, little by little, cunningly, as the bids continue, the sheet is rearranged. I assure you we do our best to keep it about us. First our ankles and calves are revealed, and then our shoulders. Then the sheet is raised so that our legs are well revealed. Following this it is lowered to our hips. Then it is removed from us altogether, and cast aside, to be used by the next girl." She then illustrated this matter, taking her time in doing so, for example, folding, and rearranging the sheet, first freeing her head and hair of it, then lifting it to reveal her calves and ankles, and so on. She even held herself motionless at times, as doubtless she had been commanded to do, that bidders might not be rushed in their assessments. Too, she behaved as though she had been turned about, doubtless that the diverse perspectives of her might adequately displayed. To be sure, she was, beneath the sheet, silked, not nude as doubtless would have been the case upon the block. On the other hand, Brenner, as she had anticipated, had little difficulty in grasping the general idea of matters. "It is at this point," she continued, having cast the sheet aside, "that one of the auctioneer's helpers produces a whip. The mere sound of this, when it is snapped, encourages in us a desperate desire to do whatever is required of us. We have been coached, and have been well rehearsed, of course. We know the various movements, the postures, the attitudes, and such, required of us, and the commands appropriate to their elicitation."

"Aii," said Brenner, softly.

"Yes," she said, "such things, such movements!"

"Stop!" cried Brenner. "No! No! Do not stop!"

"Like this," she said, "and this!"

"It is like a sale of slaves!" said Brenner.

"I am sure the sales of slaves are quite different," she said, "but I think it is true that these movements and attitudes, even though we are free women, have been carefully designed, with the object in view that a potential bidder will have an excellent idea as to the value of the contract on which he might bid."

"I do not doubt it," said Brenner.

How marvelous were her calves and ankles. How they flashed, and turned, and moved! How marvelous were the archings and extensions of her body, how beautiful were those numerous excitements, the softnesses of her and the movements of her, the flexing of a knee, the motion of a wrist, the pointing of a foot, rounding a calf, the turning of a hip, the drawing in of her belly, the very breathing of her, its effects so subtly, yet so beautifully, so unmistakably evident in her figure; how marvelous even the upsweeping of her hair, so small a thing, and that display of curves in the bent-back bow of her body, that attendant, lovely lifting of the line of her breasts! "And then," she said, "we were surprised! We were merely told to "be desirable." This had not been rehearsed! The whip snapped!"

"What did you do?" asked Brenner.

"We must improvise," she said. "We had not expected this. We were confused. The whip snapped again!"

"What did you do?"

"We must draw upon our most secret and deepest thoughts," she said, "upon the deepest secrets of our most secret belly!"

"What did you do?" asked Brenner.

"Such things!" she said.

Brenner looked upon her, stunned. Never had he dreamed a woman could be such. Categorically it denied all he had been taught. This was no "same," no banal, meaningless "identical"! This was something different, something utterly different, from a man. Something marvelous and wonderful in its own right, in its own nature, something not the same as a man, but complementary to a man, something special, something unique, something more precious and desirable to a man than anything else, something priceless, a treasure, a living jewel, the sort of thing to acquire which expeditions might be launched and wars fought, the sort of thing for which a man might kill, to possess which he might willingly die.

"Kneel!" cried Brenner, leaping to his feet.

Startled, she knelt where she was, on the surface of the bed, on the edge nearest to him. He seized her by the upper arms, and drew her toward him. He saw that she was frightened. Perhaps she had not understood her own marvelousness, and what she might mean to a man! Then, with a cry of rage, he flung her back, to her side, on the bed. He then turned away, facing the wall. His fists were clenched. He would not now look at her. "Remove your silk," he said. "And begin again."

In a little while he heard her behind him, from across the room, from the other side of the bed. "I am ready," she said.

Brenner turned about.

She stood on the other side of the bed, the sheet clutched about her. To the left, on the foot of the bed, discarded, lying in a small, crumpled pile, partly folded over one another, were the silks she had worn, those silks with which, though they had covered much of her, she had been less clothed than adorned. Such, Brenner gathered, was the function of such silks, certainly insofar as they approximated those of slaves.

She regarded him. She trembled a little. Her eyes were wide.

Brenner clenched his fists. He must surely stop this. He must not permit her to express herself as a woman. How demeaning that would be to her, to fulfill herself, to be herself! How wrong to do what honestly, and in reality, shows oneself! Must one not forever keep the self hidden, and if not deny, at least keep, the secret of one's own being? Must lies forever form the foundation of civilization, he wondered. Can people really be that stupid, he wondered, to believe all they are told? Do the captains, and the kings, and such, believe the people believe them? Can they believe themselves? Is hypocrisy really the price of order? It does not seem so in nature. Is self-deception so necessary, really? Is truth so dreadful, so terrible, he wondered, as to generate its own denial? Would it really, in its light and heat, so obviously pierce and melt, and thus destroy, the carefully wrought crystalline structures of a world, those conventionalized architectures of absurdity, those defenses theoretically constructed to protect us from ourselves? Even if so, perhaps it were not irrational to transcend such accidents of time, to strip away the artificial accretions of ages, to let them subside and drain away into the swamps from whence they derived their pestilential origin. Perhaps it is time for a newer, and more joyful, science, a less eccentric, apter wisdom. Perhaps it is time to recognize that reality is not held in orbit by the conventions, the declarations, the decisions, the pronouncements, or even the needs, of men, but rather that men, and their needs, are held in place, in the very cosmos, even in their most strained and grievous ellipticities, by the nature of reality.

"Sir?" she asked.

She regarded him, questioningly.

He must not permit her to do this!

A wave of resolve, of merciless volcanism, welled up in him momentarily. This thing came from his deepest brain, from the foundations of his existence, antedating conditioning, antedating politics, antedating the capture of fire, the bending of heated wood, the shaping of stone, the insight that a sound might mean, that one could make words.

He pulled the straight-backed chair before him, turning it about, so that its back was between him and the woman, like a fence, like a rail, a wall, and then he sat upon it. He was sweating. He grasped the sides of the back. He closed his eyes. He then opened them. "Begin," he said, quietly.

She ascended to the surface of the bed, standing upon it.

"Do not cover your head with the sheet," he said.

"Yes, sir," she said.

He supposed that sometime he, or others, might wish to hood her and use her, enforcing a decisive anonymity upon her, keeping her a prisoner in the hood, in this fashion perhaps reducing her, in their minds and in her own, to certain basic feminine essentials, but at the moment he did not wish her features to be concealed. He did not wish to lose sight of her lovely face for even a moment. Was it not, in its way, properly understood, an essential of her, as well, as was the whole totality of her? How could she be ever, in a sense, less than her wholeness? To be sure, the part is sometimes easier to relish, to appreciate and understand, when it is conceived in isolation from the whole. Too, occasional localizations, selective isolations, and such, may lead to a more enhanced understanding of, and a more appreciative comprehension of, the whole. A woman, hooded, of course, finding herself in this situation of anonymity and helplessness, is likely to waste little time in becoming sensitized to what is going on in, and with, her body. She becomes, in virtue of this device, and various devices, psychological and physical, such as respect and obedience, garments and bonds, and such, sensitized to her sensations, her feelings, and emotions, and, through these, of course, she comes to a much deeper understanding of her own sexuality, and, *ipso facto*, of her own life and meaning. These things tend, on the whole, to be consequences of certain biological complementarities.

"You must understand," she whispered, "that various details, pertinent to ourselves and our contracts, have now been brought to the attention of the buyers."

"Continue," said Brenner.

She lifted the sheet a little, that her ankles might be glimpsed, and, shortly thereafter, her calves.

At one point Brenner half rose from the chair. "Stop!" he cried. And then he cried, "No! Do not stop!"

In a few moments she knelt upon the bed, half crouched down, the sheet discarded, her hair about her, wildly, her hands now, as though with a sudden, belated recollection of terror or reserve, incongruous with the recent demands of her display, crossed over her breasts.

Brenner rose from the chair, hurling it to the side, only seizing control of himself at the edge of the bed. She looked up at him.

Their eyes met, those of male and female.

He was angered that she knelt so, so crouched down, so covering herself.

He seized the silks from the bed and held them, clutched, in his hand, and then hurled them from the surface of the bed, to the side, to the floor. She looked after them, she naked, they no longer within her reach. He took her by the shoulders and thrust her to her back on the bed. She lay there, looking up at him. Then, perhaps fearing what she saw in his eyes, frightened at what effects she might have had upon him, she whimpered, and turned away, drawing up her knees, keeping her breasts covered with her crossed arms.

He went about the bed and, as she suddenly gasped, startled at the audacity of his action, pulled a collar and chain from the peg on which it hung. He snapped the collar shut about her throat and then fastened its chain to the bar at the head of the bed. The chain was some eighteen Commonworld inches in length. He then turned her from her side to her back. Still she kept her breasts covered, she lying there now on her back, on the bed, fastened to the bar at its head.

"Would you have bid for me?" she asked.

"Yes," he said.

"You have chained me," she said.

"You are in effect a slave," he said. "It is fitting that you be chained as one."

"I am a free woman," she said.

He laughed. Did she not know herself? Could she not understand herself? Had she been unaware of how she had appeared, of how she had had herself seen, of how she had acted, of the obvious revelations, the obvious meanings, of her behavior? In the face of such things how suddenly pointless, how suddenly empty, irrelevant, and absurd became the accident, or mere technicality, of her official legal status.

"Would you have bid high for me?" she asked.

He went again to the wall at the side and took a pair of bracelets from their peg. He pulled her right wrist away from he body and she instantly covered her breasts with her left arm. He snapped the bracelet on her right wrist. He then turned her to her stomach and drew her right wrist behind her. He then drew he left wrist, too, behind her, and, with the second bracelet, fastened her wrists together. Three links joined the bracelets. He then turned her to her back, again, and looked down upon her. She pulled against the bracelets a little, and then lay there quietly, looking up at him.

"Yes," he said.

Then, suddenly, he turned away from her. It was in agony that he forced himself to do so.

Surely he must immediately free her I

What mattered her needs, or wants? What mattered his?

Needs and wants were to be defined by others, not those with them, not those suffering from them, not those exalted by them, and defined in such ways as to obtain political goals frustrative of nature and biology. That much was clear from the politics of a thousand years. Certainly reason, as properly conditioned, the term shifting its meaning with the requirements of various establishments and ideologies, should take precedence over instinct, over blood, over need. What did fulfillment, satisfaction, the summons to heroism, the call to greatness have to compare with conventionalized proprieties, invented, and inculcated by the weak, the sickly, the hating, the envying, the frustrated, the resentful, the petty, and pallid, that they might remake the world in their own image? Surely the lie must be substituted for the truth, the illusion for the reality, thought Brenner, else it will not be a good world for the small, the petty, the weak, the hating, the frustrated, the resentful. Was that not clear? And surely that is the way we should pretend the world is, in order that such entities will be pleased, that they will not be alarmed, and that we shall not be denounced. How shrill are those shrieks, how frenzied and hysterical, like the squeaks of bats, fluttering about, blinking, disturbed in their caves, daring to go out only at night. Yet, thought Brenner, for those who do not fear the sun, and its light, there is much to be said for clear skies and bright mornings.

But then Brenner turned about, agonized. He seized the sheet and thrust it quickly up, muchly covering the woman, tucking it even about her neck. He then, angrily, again, turned away.

How marvelously successful are conditioning programs, thought Brenner, even in his agony pausing to admire the crime, its subtlety, its insidiousness, its sophistication, its effectiveness, that had been committed against him. Who can bind a person better than himself, and in his own name? Who can watch him more closely, and punish him more terribly, than himself? And how few individuals can transcend these programs? How few even understand what has been done to them? How few understand more than the misery, the frustration, and pain? Do not love the bats. Do not attempt to lead them from their cave. Do not tell them of the sun, and of bright mornings. They will only howl and shriek, and, as they can, lacerate you with their tiny, foul teeth.

He heard a sob from the bed.

He turned about, startled. "Do not weep," he said.

She lay on the bed, under the sheet, red-eyed, staring up at the ceiling.

He approached her, and she turned her head away. There was the fresh path, narrow and wet, reflecting light, of a tear's descent on her left cheek.

"I do not understand you," she said.

Brenner was silent. He did not suppose he was so different from other men, at least those of the home world.

"Do you like the way you are?" she asked.

Brenner would not reply to this question.

"I have met men other than you," she said. "You need not be as you are."

"I do not think I am so different from other men," said Brenner, "at least those of the home world."

"Your friend does not seem like you," she said.

"He has been on other worlds," said Brenner.

"It is true," she said, "that you remind me of many of the putative males I met, I do not say "men," on the home world."

"I have striven to be a true person," Brenner admitted.

"I had hoped you might prove to be a man," she said.

"I am not an uncivilized brute," he said.

"That is true," she said.

"Doubtless you would prefer a rough, callous, insensitive beast," he said, "a tyrant who would make demands upon you, and treat you as a thing."

"A thing of beauty," she said, "whom he will have serve him according to his dictates."

"Do not joke," said Brenner.

"What you do not understand," she said, "is that there is no ultimate incompatibility between refinement and the beast, nor between learning and power, that one need not languish that the other may thrive, that it is possible to be both cultivated and strong, sensitive and forceful, intelligent and strict. Civilization need not imply weakness. Civilization need not be rejected. It, rather, can be the setting in which nature finds its grandest fulfillment. There is no ultimate antitheticality between the poem and the whip, between the sonata and the chain."

Brenner was silent.

She sobbed.

"Do not weep," he said, angrily.

"What of my needs?" she asked.

"They are not permitted to exist," said Brenner.

She threw her head back, against the covers.

"They are nothing," said Brenner.

"And what of yours?" she asked.

"They, too," said he, "must be nothing."

"But you have chained me," she said.

"A moment's aberration," he said.

He then, suddenly, turned away, again. He went to the side of the room. He kept his back to her.

"You act as though you are weak," she said. "I wonder if you truly are."

"Weakness is true strength," said Brenner. "The proper employment of masculine power is self-subversion. Manhood's greatest triumph is to overcome itself. The truest man is he who is least like a man."

"That is stupid," she said.

Brenner did not respond to this. The slogans he had uttered had, to be sure, rung hollowly, even in his own ears. He supposed they had been invented as political instruments, to serve one end or another. Too, they provided valuable rationalizations for certain sorts of males, for example, those whose low drive levels would never enable them to comprehend greater forces, those active in creatures of stronger passion. It seemed they did not even, really, share the same form of life. For a moment Brenner envied the creatures of low drives, those who had never experienced more than ripples and stirrings, those who had no concept of tidalities, of hurricanes, of raging seas. Then he did not envy them, no more than the hawk would envy the worm, no more than the lion the lamb.

"You chained me," she said.

Brenner was silent.

"You chained me," she said. "Come, look upon me."

Brenner did not move. He did not even wish to turn about, to see her lying there, covered with the sheet.

"From the first moment you saw me," she said, "surely you must have been curious as to what I would look like, in chains."

Brenner was silent. There was a sense, he supposed, in which this, or something like it, was true. He had found her attractive, even as long ago as their brief encounter in the rain, in the muddy street. And chains, though they are surely, indisputably, effective custodial devices, both from the point of view of he who chains and she who is chained, are, perhaps even more, a symbol amongst symbols for a symbol-using animal. They speak of a relationship, of a propriety deeper than those of convention, of a claim of an animal of its rightful complement, and the expression of this claim in terms as graphic, as explicit and real as the piling of stones to mark a border, as the touch of steel in the conferring of knighthood, as the exchanging of a handful of earth between lord and vassal. He had, of course, wondered what she might look like, stripped, and his, and, in the sense in which chains would make clear by whom she was claimed, to whom she was subject, it was in its way true. In this sense one might, metaphorically, consider the woman as, so to speak, "in chains." Earlier, of course, when he had imagined the directress on the ship, and later, of course, when he had been downstairs in the bar, his thoughts along these lines had been much more explicit. Then he had, not only symbolically, and metaphorically, but literally, thought of explicit signs of claiming, and ownership, and chains, of course, in their beauty, their primitiveness, their simplicity, like vines, like cords or ropes, come quickly, naturally, to mind.

"You chained me," she said, irritably. "Surely you must have been curious to see what I would look like, in chains."

Brenner was silent.

"So, come, look upon me," she said.

He turned about, angrily, and went to the side of the bed. She looked up at him, defiantly.

"Look upon me!" she challenged.

He drew down the sheet a little, from about her throat. He could then see the metal collar on her neck. To the side, half lost under her hair, was the ring by means of which it was attached to the chain. Then the chain went up, behind her, to where it was fastened about the bar at the head of the bed.

"Look upon me!" she challenged.

He put his hand to the sheet, and then, after holding it a moment, tore it down and away. She cried out, startled, a little frightened, for she had not anticipated that this action would be done so suddenly, so decisively. She lay there before him. He noted that she seemed frightened, now. She was not as bold, it seemed, as she had pretended. Then, again, she spoke boldly. "Do you like what you see?" she asked.

He did not respond. Never had he seen anything so tantalizing, so beautiful, and, in its way, so ungracious, so unpleasant, so irritating.

"Unchain me!" she said.

He regarded her.

"Unchain me!" she demanded.

He looked her over. His eye rested on the chain and disk, that fastened on her left ankle. He had been curious about that. He had not dared, really, hitherto, to look at it.

"What are you doing?" she asked.

He took her left ankle in his hand and lifted it, and looked at the device fastened there. He ran his finger about, under the chain. He examined the small, stout, cylindrical lock. Then he turned the metal disk, from one side to the other, it with its own link to the chain, looking at it. It was about an inch and a half in diameter, larger than that worn by the maids at the hostel. On one side Brenner read the inscription giving the name and address of her contract holder. On the other side was another inscription, perhaps with the same content, but one unintelligible to Brenner. It was, of course, in one of the several zardian languages. She tried to pull her ankle away from Brenner, but was unable to do so. In a moment, realizing her inability to free her ankle, that her strength was insignificant as compared to his, she turned her head to the side, desisting in the contest which could have been continued only to her further embarrassment. He then considered the smallness of her foot, the slenderness of the ankle, encircled by the chain and disk, the lovely curve of the calf, above the chain. He then again regarded the chain and disk. "You are under contract," he said. He then opened his hand, letting her pull her ankle away. She put down her leg, flexed, so that the sole of her foot was on the bed.

She looked up at him, angrily.

"Unchain me," she said.

"You are under contract," he said.

She struggled up on her left elbow, half lying on the bed, the chain now looping back to the bar.

"You wished to see me in chains," she said. "Now you have done so. Now release me."

"You are under contract," he said.

"I do not understand," she said.

He undid the top button at his collar. "Do not protest, or make noise," he said.

"And if I do?"

"Then you will be gagged," he said, dropping his shirt to the side.

"What is your intention?" she asked.

"Surely you are woman enough to guess," he said. He touched her lightly, at the side of the leg, and she pulled her leg back, higher. And then she struggled back, half sitting up, thrusting her back against the back of the bed, pulling her legs up.

"You will beg my touch," he said.

"Is that a command?" she asked.

"No," said Brenner, stepping from the clothing at his feet, "it is a prediction."

"Never!" she said.

"Am I to gather," asked Brenner, "that it is your intention to be found less than fully pleasing?"

She turned white. "No!" she said. "No! Please do not report me to the zard in the morning as not having been fully pleasing!"

"I have no intention of doing so," said Brenner.

"Thank you!" she breathed.

"Do you know why?" he asked.

"No," she said.

"Because you are not going to be less than fully pleasing," he said.

She looked at him, startled, stunned.

He then went to the wall and took down a short, stout whip which hung there.

"Do not strike me!" she begged.

Brenner gathered that she must, at one time or another, have felt the touch of such a device, surely at least once, for example, on the block, on Damascus. "I trust that it will not be necessary," he said.

"You, you, could not strike me!" she said.

"Do you wish to put that to the test?" he asked.

"But you are a true man," she said, suddenly, "tender, soft, kindly, weak, gentle, mild, indecisive, vacillating, compliant, anxious to please women, obedient to their wishes!"

"I am tired," said Brenner, "of being denied, of being hungry, of being humiliated and tormented, of being cheated of my rights."

"You have no rights!" she cried.

"If not," said Brenner, "I now create them."

"It will not be necessary to whip me!" she said. "Let me rather kiss the whip, to show my deference, my respect, my submission!"

"'Submission'," said Brenner. "I like that word on your lips. It well becomes them."

He held the whip to her lips, and she kissed it, and then, softly, licked it, and then looked up at him.

He then replaced the whip on the wall.

"See where it is?" he asked.

"Yes," she said.

"It may do you good," he said, "from time to time, to look over here, and see it."

"Yes, sir," she said.

He entered upon the bed.

He drew her down a little, from the head of the bed.

She looked up at him.

"If you are going to be a man," she said, "then I will have no choice but to be a woman."

He touched her, softly, delicately.

"Ohhh," she said, softly.

"A woman under contract," said Brenner, "should be beautiful, humble, and useful."

"It is my hope that I am beautiful," she said.

"And?" asked Brenner.

She, now on her back, turned her head to her right, and looked at the whip, on its peg on the wall.

"I am humble," she assured him.

He again touched her, and she squirmed, helplessly. "Oh," she said, softly, "oh!" Her small wrists, encircled in the bracelets, moved behind her back. "Oh!" she breathed.

He kissed her.

"It is my hope," she whispered, "that I will prove useful."

"I will see to it," said Brenner.

"Yes, sir," she whispered.

Some time later he had freed her wrists of the bracelets, but he had not seen fit, for whatever whim, to release her neck from the clasp of the collar, this, by means of the chain, fastening her to the bar at the head of the bed. To be sure, lest it be feared that he was showing her too little respect, and even treating her as though she might not be free, but bond, a vendible article, a property, a domestic animal, it might be mentioned that slaves are often chained not on the bed itself, but at the *foot* of the bed, on the floor, and used there, upon covers or furs. It is not a foregone conclusion, you see, that a slave is permitted upon the surface of a bed, or couch. It is something of an honor for a slave, or a privilege, for her to be permitted there. It is something to obtain which she may have to strive for months, for which she, though a mere slave, must try to prove herself worthy. The passage to the surface of the couch is one calling for heat, devotion, and dutifulness. It is not something, strictly, which she can earn, for its gift is in the treasury of the master, and no bargains are struck with slaves, but it is something for which she may eventually hope, assuming that her zeal and her increasing slave excellences render such a hope not unrealistic.

"If you bought my contract, would you free me?" she asked.

"I cannot afford your contract," he said. This was clear, as she was a free woman. Such contracts were not cheap. Even a moderate one would cost some thousands of Commonworld credits. It was not like the openly stratified worlds, where slaves were numerous, and cheap, where even a poor man such as Brenner might, if he wished, have had three or four, particularly if they were merely hot and comely.

"Do you wish you could afford my contract?" she asked.

"Yes," he said, "for I should then be well-to-do."

"But if you could buy it," she said, "would you do so?"

"Perhaps I could be convinced," he said.

"I would do my best to convince you," she whispered.

"Yes," he said. "If I could afford your contract, I would buy it."

"Let us suppose you could afford it," she said.

"Very well," said Brenner.

"If you bought it, would you free me?" she asked.

Brenner considered the matter. "No," he said.

"Good," she said, snuggling against him.

Later, Brenner, as the whim had seized him, had again back-braceleted her. This, too, if nothing else, helped to control her active, hot little hands. She was so eager, so exciting, so alive.

Then, a Commonworld hour later, after an intimacy that had taught him something of what it might be, to be a woman's master, he had, after extinguishing the light, dozed off. Then it seemed but a moment later, though doubtless it was more, he had been awakened, by her whimpering. He became aware of her near him. He heard her pull a little, helplessly, against the bracelets which held her small wrists pinioned behind her. She was on her side, on an elbow, leaning over him. "Please," she whispered. "Please!"

He lay there, quietly.

"Are you awake?" she whispered.

"Yes," he said.

"Please," she said. "Please!"

"What is it?" he asked.

"I beg your touch," she whispered. "I beg your touch!"

Brenner smiled to himself in the darkness. He wondered if she recalled his remark to her earlier in the evening. He thought that perhaps she did not now, but might recollect it later. In any event, she had often enough earlier, in one modality or another, begged his touch.

"You beg my touch?" smiled Brenner. He saw fit to remind her, thusly, of his earlier remark. His vanity might as well be indulged, he thought.

There was a pause. He sensed her recollection, and her surprise, and perhaps her chagrin, or embarrassment.

"Yes," she said, suddenly, softly, defiantly in the darkness. "I beg your touch!" Then her voice broke. "I beg it, desperately," she said. Brenner wondered if it had been anything in their last intimacy which had evoked this response, which had discovered something to her, something that now made her as she was. Need and vulnerability had been manifest in her pathetic accents. How much power he now sensed he had over her.

"I think I might know now what it is, or something of what it might be, to be a slave," she whispered.

Brenner was silent.

"I did not know it could be like this," she said.

Brenner was silent.

"I beg your touch," she said, "I think as might a slave whose needs are upon her!"

Brenner did not break the silence.

"Please be merciful," she said. "Do not have me suffer. Do not leave me dangling like this!"

Brenner had heard of such things as slave need, of course. He supposed it possible that something of the sort could occur in a free woman, particularly one under contract, one at the mercy of others. Such needs in the slave, of course, are generally a function of what she is, and her entire condition. Also, cruelly, the slave is sometimes given no choice in the matter of these needs, but must submit to, and acquiesce in, their release and efflorescence, until she finds herself, as was her owner's intent, the helpless prisoner of their implacable, frequently recurrent, profound demands. It is said that such needs, and love, are the strongest bonds to which slaves are subject, that they are stronger than bars of iron and bands of steel.

"Get on your back," said Brenner, with which command she immediately complied. He then rose up, on one elbow. He touched her, lightly.

"Oh, yes!" she said. "Yes, please!"

He then realized how helpless she was, not merely physically, but, more importantly, psychologically.

"Please, don't stop," she begged.

In a few moments Brenner placed his hand over her mouth, that her cries might not carry throughout the establishment, perhaps disturbing the rest of others. How she squirmed, and bucked, and writhed! How helpless she was, so much in the grip of her reflexes, so much in the careless, merciless bondage of her femaleness! Who would have thought there could be so much vitality, so much force, so much strength and power, in so small and beautiful, so soft, so deliciously curved, a body? Beneath the palm of his sweating hand, hastily placed, pressing firmly downward, Brenner felt her lips and, beneath them, her teeth. She could not, beneath his hand, open her mouth, nor could she scarcely move. What would have been screams of ecstasy became no more than tiny sounds, no more, by his action, permitted to her. Then, later, after the subsidence of her tumult, its crisis passed, she lay back, not much moving, and whimpered, pleadingly. He removed his hand from her mouth. His palm was wet, from her mouth, and from his sweat. The side of his hand, too, was wet, as tears had streaked down her cheeks, stopped by its barrier.

She did not speak.

"You yielded," he said.

"Yes," she said.

"Helplessly," he said.

"Yes," she whispered, in the darkness.

He kissed her.

"I love being this helpless," she said, "so much yours."

"You speak as might a slave," he said.

"Yes," she said.

He rose from the bed and went to the side of the room, to the lamp. He turned it on, and up, just a little, setting the shade in such a way as to diffuse the light. He looked back upon her, on the bed, now on one elbow, turned to him, her hands held behind her, in the shadows.

"What are you doing?" she asked.

"I was curious about something," he said.

"Oh?" she said.

"Lie back," he said.

She lay on her back, and turned her head to her left, to look at him.

"Yes," he said. "It is true."

"What?" she asked.

"You are beautiful enough to be a slave," he said.

She half reared up, turning toward him, but then, as though she feared she might be guilty of some subtle infraction of discipline, lay back on the bed. She kept her head straight, her eyes facing upward, toward the ceiling.

"Yes," he said, confirming his former assessment.

"Ohhh," she said, softly, suddenly, moving, but continuing to look upward, "I gush—my Master."

He went to the side of the bed, and, standing to one side, looked down upon her.

She kept her head as it had been, straight, looking up at the ceiling, not meeting his eyes.

"We will be your foes, you know," she said, "if you do not make us your slaves."

Brenner was silent.

"I would be your slave," she said. "I am your slave." Brenner then understood how much a woman can give, and that she will find nothing sufficient short of giving all, that she wills to give all, to give herself, all of herself, unstintingly, unreservedly, unquestioningly, that she can in her heart be content with nothing less than the fullness of love's surrender. Brenner then joined her upon the bed, and very gently kissed her.

"I fear the coming of the morning," she said.

"Be silent," said Brenner.

"Yes," she whispered, "—Master."

CHAPTER 6

"Those are Pons, over there, in their camp," said Rodriguez, pulling on one of the ropes, one of two attached to the mud sled, purchased through the hostel this morning, before light, their luggage now on it.

"They are small," said Brenner.

"They are amongst the slightest, most trivial, most backward organisms in the galaxy," said Rodriguez.

Brenner nodded. Their simplicity, and primitiveness, might make them a trove for the researches of the anthropologist. To be sure, several of the most advanced cultures, too, in their depth and complexity, promised exotic fields of study, but grants for the study of the safer ones, usually reserved, for example, for those well-fixed in credits, who could afford the appropriate disbursements, bribes, and such, or those highly placed in a field's or party's bureaucracy, were not available to the likes of Rodriguez and Brenner, and grants pertaining to the study of the more perilous ones often languished for want of applicants. More than one female anthropologist, for example, had vanished without trace on such a world. It was rumored that one had been found, light years away, months later, in a slave market. It was said that another anthropologist had bought her, and kept her. Anthropologists, of course, need not be concerned with simple cultures, no more than the biologist must content himself with the study of protozoa. On the other hand, Rodriguez, and others, including Brenner, found cultural protozoa, so to speak, of great interest, and, who knew, perhaps one might, if one could understand them, truly understand them, even things so simple, perhaps one might then be better equipped, in time, to essay more profitable inquiries into the nature of more complex cultural structures, into the life of, so to speak, more complex organisms. Brenner thought that the mud sled was not a bad idea, particularly now that he saw how small the Pons were. Surely they would prove unlikely porters. And he, of course, was less than enthusiastic about carrying suitcases, or even encumbering packs, through dangerous forests. It had been enough of a bother to get their goods from the depot to the hostel. To be sure, the load might have been distributed over various porters, if the Pons were willing to serve as such, but Rodriguez was not sanguine about too open a transportation of a miscellany which included valuables such as several bottles of Heimat and two radios, not to mention a forbidden weapon, the disguised Naxian rifle.

It was raining, again. It was a little after dawn.

They drew the sled across the mud, and up, onto the plank road that led to the fence, the gate, and the tower, where the operator was stationed.

The Pons had apparently seen them, for they had emerged from their tiny, tentlike shelters and were hurrying about, seemingly conversing amongstst themselves.

The fence was actually a double fence, with the field between the two sets of wires, so that rational organisms would not be likely to enter the area of the field while it was active. There were postings frequently about, as well, on both sides of the double fence, in various languages, and in one of the common signs supposedly interpretable by all, or most, visually oriented rational creatures, a circle with a jagged line within it, presumably symbolizing lightning, or the flow of some strong current. Occasionally certain organisms, scions of diverse phyla, some of them distinctly unpleasant, for example, often poisonous or carnivorous, had been found dead within the fence. That now was seldom the case. Even the Norwegian rat, as it was called, now endemic on several worlds, the origin of the name a matter of debate amongstst zoologists, manifested the rudiments of a primitive tradition, older animals, for example, warning younger animals away from substances which in the past had been found harmful.

Rodriguez and Brenner hauled the sled along the planks to the foot of the tower, only back a little from the first metal-link gate, it set at the interior perimeter of the double fence, it, too, metal-linked. The top of the gate, like that of the opposite gate, and the fence, on both sides, was strung with coiled blades of metal. Rodriguez waved upward to the operator, and lifted his papers. The matter of their passage, of course, had been arranged. Still, as a matter of course, the papers would be checked. I must not make this sound as though those of Company Station were unusually security minded. They were not. It was rather that it was thought to be important to keep track of what went through the fence, and, in particular, what went through in the nature of equipment. It could be company property. It was not difficult, for most in Company Station, to go back and forth when they wished. Company Station, for most at any rate, was not a prison. Too, it might be mentioned, Pons occasionally frequented Company Station. Horemheb, who was, of course, a Pon, as well as others, had even, upon occasion, spent some time there. Also, as I have suggested, a certain amount of trading and, presumably, a sort of primarily asymmetrical cultural exchange obtained between them and the station. Indeed, had it not been so, the arrangements for the expedition of Rodriguez and Brenner, such as it was, might have been difficult to arrange. Certain of the Pons, at least, too, it should be mentioned, it was conjectured in virtue of these cultural contacts, were conversant in the most frequently employed language at Company Station, which was, incidentally, fortunately, the tongue native both to Rodriguez and Brenner. Our friends, then, anticipated little difficulty in initially communicating with the Pons.

In this fashion a great deal of time might be saved, which otherwise would be consumed in learning the language, even as a child might learn it, beginning with rudimentary ostensions, having to do with material objects, and such. It was not that they did not anticipate learning the language of the Pons. It was rather that they thought this familiarity on the part of at least some Pons with their own tongue would facilitate and expedite their efforts. Brenner looked back toward the low, gray, squat buildings of Company Station. He wanted to see something there, and he did not want to see it. The buildings seemed bleak in the rain, in the dim light. The nearest was some hundred yards back, away from the fence. He felt in his pocket, for the small package he had wrapped and placed there.

Brenner turned about, again, to look outward, through the fence.

The operator, not guard, had descended from the tower, some fifteen Commonworld feet tall, which gave him a view along the fence for some hundreds of yards on both sides, and then out, for another hundred yards or so, to the margin of the forest. He took the papers from Rodriguez and, holding them against the side of the tower, initialed them. He and Rodriguez then exchanged some remarks, many of them good-humored and rough, and some of which Brenner found crude and embarrassing. Such, Brenner supposed, with a twinge of envy, passes for camaraderie amongst boors. Amongstst these diverse observations were several on Pons, not all of which, as the reader may have suspected, were complimentary. The operator, it seemed, doubtless a provincial, or outworlder, had not received an appropriate conditioning, one which would have encouraged him to give certain principles priority over the apparent evidence of his senses, for example, with respect to the intellectual, moral, and social equivalence, once suitably defined, and properly understood, of all life forms, from the flatworm to the meditative, polyplike megabregma, forty percent of whose weight was cerebral tissue. Whereas perhaps there was an excuse for the operator, a company employee, and doubtless a simple, ill-educated outworlder, to manifest inappropriate discourse and express discouraged views, what excuse could there be, Brenner wondered, for Rodriguez? Clearly Rodriguez was not stupid. It is always unsettling when one who is obviously not stupid disagrees with one. One may then, of course, revise one's opinion. Perhaps he is stupid, after all. Or, too, one might more charitably suppose a lack of information, insanity, or perhaps iniquity. Iniquities and insanities, of course, go in and out of fashion. If one wishes to reassure oneself that one is right, of course, it is easy to do so. One need only ask those who agree with one. No, Rodriguez did not respect the Pons. It was only too obvious that he did not take them seriously, that he held them in contempt. On the other hand, he did regard them as of anthropological interest, and perhaps even, for some reason, particularly so. As I have made clear earlier, Rodriguez was not a champion of value-free science. He had too many values. What was important to him was to understand the data, and to theorize about it intelligently, and such. Nothing in this approach requires that he arrive at politically acceptable results, or even that he approve of what he learns.

The Pons, there were several of them, perhaps thirty or forty, it was hard to tell, as they milled about, had clustered a few yards outside the outer gate.

Brenner glanced back toward Company Station. It was a little lighter now. The planks of the road leading to the gate were slick with rain. He again saw only the buildings, the mud, the sky, the rain.

Rodriguez joined him, thrusting the wet papers back inside his jacket. He then waved to the Pons outside the gate, affably. It seemed they did not dare to return his greeting.

"What are they wearing?" asked Brenner. It surely did not seem typical raingear, though, to be sure, it might have been closely woven.

"Robes, smocks," said Rodriguez.

"On their heads, over their heads," said Brenner.

"It appears to be some sort of hood," said Rodriguez.

"It is some sort of ritual veiling?" asked Brenner. He had not, in his research on Pons, not that a great deal was known of them, come on anything of this sort. It was a detail which certainly would not be likely to be omitted, even from a superficial account.

"I do not think so," said Rodriguez.

"Perhaps they are timid, frightened, pathologically shy," suggested Brenner.

"Perhaps," said Rodriguez.

"Are there females amongstst them?" asked Brenner. The clothing of Pons, he had gathered from his reading, and from certain drawings, as there had appeared, oddly enough, to be no film records, or even photographs, of Pons, as that of many parts of the home world, was designed to minimize, or conceal, sexual differences, this having to do with the political desiderata of personistic neuterism.

"Probably not in this bunch," said Rodriguez. To be sure, it was difficult to tell.

The operator had now switched a red light on at the top of the tower, making it clear to all that the current was still on, and that the field was active. The switching from red to green, in color codes the origin of which was lost in antiquity, would indicate deactivation. Green would remain lit while the field remained deactivated. Its flashing would indicate the proximity of activation. The switch from a flashing green to a red, which would be sustained for a short time, indicated reactivation. Then the red light, too, would be extinguished, its illumination being unnecessary given the presumption of activation, the presumed normal condition of the field, and the posting of the area. If one were in doubt as to the activation of the field, of course, there were simple ways in which its condition might be ascertained. For example, one might toss a stick between the fences. If nothing happened, the field was not active. If, on the other hand, the stick seemed to be caught, as if it were lodged in a wall of water, and began to twist, and then, in an instant, burst apart, crackling, and flaming, this would indicate that the field was active.

"They must be terribly shy," said Brenner.

"I think it is rather that they are secretive," said Rodriguez.

"I wonder what they look like," said Brenner.

"We are going to find out," said Rodriguez. He waved again to the Pons.

"I do not understand," said Brenner.

"I do not like dealing with people who wear masks," said Rodriguez.

"Why?" asked Brenner.

"Masks may conceal fangs," he said.

He again waved affably at the Pons, who regarded them, clearly alert, clearly aware of them, but refraining from any explicit reciprocation of Rodriguez's overture.

Brenner was uneasy. "You will not do anything foolish?" he asked.

"We must establish our footing with them," said Rodriguez.

"If they are concerned with secrecy, and such," said Brenner, "how is it that we are here? It seems unlikely they would simply open their lives, or culture, to us, if they commonly conceal it with such care."

"Doubtless they want something from us," said Rodriguez.

"What?" asked Brenner.

"Probably gifts, and such," said Rodriguez. He had brought, of course, the customary trinkets, beads, ribbons, mirrors, and such, with which those of his species were wont to deal with, and impress, certain other life forms, which, in spite of their indubitable equivalence, might prefer colored glass to the abstractions of credits.

"The light is green," said Brenner.

The two gates then slid back.

Rodriguez picked up a pebble and tossed it between the gates of the double fence. He was not the sort of fellow to trust to signals which might be deceptive, perhaps for so trivial a reason as a fault in wiring.

Brenner turned about, to look back toward the buildings of Company Station.

"Why are you looking back?" asked Rodriguez.

"No reason," said Brenner.

"Look forward," said Rodriguez. "Not back."

Brenner did not respond to him.

"Did you sleep well?" inquired Rodriguez.

Brenner did not respond.

"How was the brunette?" he asked.

Brenner did not respond.

"She looked well on a chain," said Rodriguez.

"So, too, did the blonde," said Brenner, irritably.

"They all do," granted Rodriguez. He then turned about and waved to the Pons, to enter through the gate.

"What are you doing?" asked Brenner.

"We have drawn the sled far enough," said Rodriguez. "They can pull it from here." Then he turned again to the Pons. "Here!" he called. "Sled! Sled! Pull! Pull! Hurry! Hurry!"

Brenner looked back again. He caught his breath. He thought, between the buildings, he caught sight of a small figure hurrying toward them, wrapped in a cloak.

"Here!" called Rodriguez to the Pons. They then, first two or three at a time, and then the others, together, like domesticated animals, came through the gates. Some of them looked upward, at the operator, who doubtless to them was a figure of considerable authority. He waved them through.

Brenner could now see clearly, through the lightly falling rain, that a small figure, indeed, was approaching them, hurrying through the mud, bundled in a cloak. Her feet and calves were bare.

Rodriguez was pointing to the ropes and communicating with the tiny figures now about them, trying to convey his desires to them.

One or two of them were poking at the cases and bundles on the sled.

"No!" said Rodriguez, pointing rather to the ropes.

Brenner felt in his jacket pocket for the small package he had placed there.

The small figure had now changed its direction a little, as had Rodriguez and Brenner earlier, the mud being deep

in its path, apparently to reach the more secure footing
of the plank road. Then it was on the surface of the road.
The mud had come up several inches on her calves. She
had had to hold the cloak a bit high, to a point just below
her knees, that its hem not drag in the mud. Brenner had
not objected to this glimpse of her well-turned calves. She
now stood on the plank road, some yards from him. She
continued to hold the cloak high. She could not lower
it, of course, even on this surface, lest it be soiled from
the mud on her legs. Again, of course, Brenner had no
objection to this.

She stood there.

Brenner did not, of course, rush to her. He stood there,
regarding her. He had grasped last night that it was, for
most practical purposes, she who must come to him, that
it is the female who must approach, and present herself to,
the male. To be sure, she was still a free woman, at least in
point of law. The woman under contract, for example, is
not free to utter formulas of self-embondment. Being under
contract, she is not at liberty to unilaterally alter her status.
Such would be in clear violation of the rights of the contract
holder. As a technical point, which might be of interest, if
the contract is not paid off within a certain period, varying
from contract to contract, the woman ceases to be under
contract and becomes property, to be disposed of then as
the contract holder may desire.

Brenner took a step or two toward the figure. She was,
after all, a free woman.

She stood there, regarding him.

But he did not move more closely to her. Even though she
might be free, she was, after all, a female.

It seemed she would move more closely toward him, but
then she hesitated.

Brenner noted that there was a cloth wrapped about her
left ankle, apparently to shield the lock, chain, and disk, to
protect them from the mud. Yesterday, he recalled, in the
street, when they had collided with one another, she had not
been wearing the chain and disk.

Behind him Brenner could hear Rodriguez ordering Pons about.

Brenner wondered why the woman had come to the vicinity of the gate. He wondered if she might come with them for a bit, outside the gate.

There were streaks on her face. Brenner did not know if these were tears, or from the rain.

Brenner became aware of some Pons gathered about him, though he now stood back on the road, away from Rodriguez, away from the sled. He pushed them a bit away. Two or three of them looked up at him, their eyes peering inquisitively, too, it seemed, anxiously, through the holes in the hoods. The Pons were short, their heads on the whole coming only a bit above his belt. One of them pulled on his jacket, looking up at him. It seemed they were eager for him to come along, that he accompany them. Brenner pushed the Pon away.

"Good," Rodriguez was saying, behind him. Brenner gathered that he was making progress with the Pons, that he was succeeding in communicating with them. He was enlisting them, or, perhaps better, impressing them, in the matter of drawing the sled. He was determined they prove useful. To be sure, what he wanted would not require great intelligence to fathom. On the other hand, Brenner did not know what the intelligence of the Pons might be. He doubted that it was particularly high, except, of course, that, whatever it was, it would count, in its type, as being the equivalent of any intelligence existing in any galaxy, or yet to be detected in any galaxy, this having to do with the equivalence of all life forms. Brenner hoped that they would have at least the intelligence of bright children.

Another Pon tugged on his jacket.

"Go away!" said Brenner. Then he said, "I'm sorry." It was bad enough that Rodriguez might contaminate the data. He did not want to risk the same thing.

Yes, the woman's face was wet. Surely it must be from the rain.

Why had she come, Brenner wondered. She has come for

her pastry, he thought. That is why she has come. She had come for her pastry. He felt the package in his pocket.

"We are ready," called Rodriguez.

He thought the woman sobbed, and put out her hand.

Brenner felt he should apologize to her for last night. How shamefully he had treated her! He had not treated her, at least not always, as he should have, as a same. Indeed, unaccountably, astoundingly, shamefully, he had betrayed his own conditioning program, that which had been imposed upon him from childhood. Needless to say Brenner, predictably, had experienced a good deal of misery and guilt this morning, at least after leaving the establishment of the zard. After all, you could not really expect his conditioning program to sit idly by and languish in its own neglect, and, indeed, it had not long delayed in exacting its revenge. On the other hand, Brenner had not suffered as much as certain individuals might have hoped, which such individuals might have regarded as an additional defect on his part.

"Tell her to get her ass back to her room," called Rodriguez.

She trembled there, standing in the rain, a few feet away, barefoot on the planks of the road. She was then looking past Brenner, presumably toward Rodriguez. She feared him, of course. He was the sort of man, and she must have known others, particularly in a place such as Company Station, who would not hesitate to enforce his will on a woman, even with blows. Then she looked to Brenner. He did not order her away. In this, small, and vulnerable, trembling, her face stained with tears or rain, clutching the cloak about her, she seemed to take courage.

They looked at one another.

Brenner supposed she wished her pastry.

Some Pons were about. Brenner heard a squeak of the wooden runners of the sled on the planks. It had apparently moved a few inches. "That's it," said Rodriguez.

Suddenly, clutching the cloak about her, she hurried to Brenner.

"Why have you come?" he asked.

"You unchained me this morning," she smiled, half laughing

through what seemed, unaccountably, tears. "Nor did you return me to my room."

"Oh," said Brenner.

"The rooms have no handles on the inside," she said. "They cannot be opened from within."

"And that is why you have come?" he said.

"Of course," she laughed.

Brenner gathered that the rooms, doubtless stoutly walled and doored, must be, in effect, cells. He supposed that the maids at the hostel might have similar rooms. Perhaps this was appropriate enough for women under contract. There would doubtless be a device which, if engaged, doubtless a lock device, would prevent the closing of the door, for the convenience of coming and going during the day. Thus, there would be times at which the door could not be closed, or at least fully, and, when it was closed, could not be opened from the inside. In this fashion the woman would be, in effect, denied privacy, in the sense that she could not close her door, or granted it at the option of the contract holder, at the price of her own incarceration, an incarceration which, of course, with its attendant privacy, was again at the option of the contract holder, or his agents. Brenner did not think that in the case of the zard's establishment there would be surveillance devices in the room. To be sure, there might be an observation portal in the door, or such. Whereas this might seem to show the free female too little respect, it is well to understand the extraordinary dignity that this affords to her, in contrast, say, with the slave, who, for example, might be kept in a barred kennel.

"Where is the blonde?" asked Brenner.

"Your friend left her chained to the bed, spread-eagled," she said, "too, chained by the neck, as you had me."

Her eyes clouded.

"What is wrong?" asked Brenner.

"Apparently with the permission of our contract holder, he administered a releaser to her."

Brenner looked puzzled.

"It is quite possible she is pregnant," she said.

"I see," said Brenner. "Does she want money? Does she want credits?"

"Things have been arranged between your friend and the zard," she said.

"The appropriate credits have been punched?" asked Brenner.

"Apparently," she said.

"She will bear the child?" asked Brenner.

"That or die," she said. "The zard reveres life."

"As she is free," said Brenner, "the child, if any, would be free."

"If she proves pregnant and comes to term, her embondment, if any, is not to take place until after the delivery."

"And provisions have been made for the child?"

"It seems so," said the woman.

This account interested Brenner. To be sure, he did not doubt but what Rodriguez, here and there, might have sired one offspring or another, on one world or another, perhaps even in similar circumstances.

"Why have you come here?" asked Brenner. "Is it because you want credits?"

"No!" she said.

"I have told you I cannot afford your contract," he said.

"I do not want you to buy my contract!" she said, angrily.

"Why have you come?" he asked.

She put down her head. "What you did to me last night," she said. "What you made me feel!"

"Naturally," said Benner, irritably. "I apologize to you for how I treated you. Surely it was inappropriate, as we are sames."

"We are not sames!" she said. "You are a man! I am a woman!"

"I apologize," he said.

"Do not apologize!" she exclaimed.

"I am sorry if I demeaned you," he said.

"It is now that you are demeaning me!" she said.

Several of the Pons now crowded about them. Brenner, not politely, brushed some of them back. Their eyes seemed inquisitive through the holes in the hoods. She did not seem surprised at the proximity of the Pons. She had, apparently, seen their likes in Company Station before. For most practical purposes, she ignored them. It was easy to overlook them, given their tiny size, their nondescript garb. They, on the other hand, seemed to find her an item provoking intense curiosity. They would look from Brenner to the woman, and then back again. Brenner scarcely registered this, but, as he did, he supposed that they were not that familiar with human females. At Company Station most of their contacts would be with males, of one species or another.

Brenner was curious to know what she might be wearing under the cloak. Too, he was somewhat irritated by her demeanor. For one of these reasons, or both, or perhaps, too, because he was not really the same this morning as he had been the preceding morning, he took in hand the edges of her cloak, where they were about her throat, and, moving his hands apart, drew them to the side. She put down her head and turned it to the left. She was not now in the dramatic, sensuous, so revealing, so provocative pleasure silks of the preceding evening, but in a brown work dress, simple, plain, coarsely woven, which came to a bit above her knees. In it, she would doubtless address herself to numerous domestic labors, cooking, cleaning, laundering, and such, shared with her fellow contractees in the zard's establishment. Brenner had no doubt that women under contract, on the whole, particularly in an establishment such as the zard's, would be well worked. Then in the late afternoon and early evening they could transform themselves into compliant, perfumed objects of desire. Even in the brown garb Brenner found her attractive, the contrast of it against her flesh at the neckline, and the way in which the turns of her delicious body were hinted at, and not at all obscurely, within that coarse cloth's confines.

"Please, not before them," she said.

Brenner smiled to himself. What interest could the Pons have in such a thing? To them would she not be merely a piece of meat, and merely meat, meaningless meat, and not meat in the sense in which slavers, or brutal, lusting men, might laughingly, in rude humor, use such an expression of, say, women chained naked in markets or lying helpless, stripped and collared, at their feet. To be sure, they might appreciate that Brenner might see her with desire, that he, as she was a female of his species, might find her of interest. The Pons, to be sure, were looking upon her. On the other hand, they seemed to look upon many things with curiosity, with inquisitiveness and wonder. They seemed a simple folk. It amused Brenner that she would feel shy before them. On the other hand, he supposed she, and other women, might feel that way, just as they might feel that way before children. They might be embarrassed to be revealed before them. It might not seem fitting to them. After all, it is not to children, nor to Pons, that such as they belong.

Brenner did not close her cloak.

"I thought last night that you were bold," she smiled. "I see now that I was not mistaken."

Brenner drew shut her cloak, and she held it together, about her throat.

They looked into one another's eyes.

The Pons, Rodriguez, the opened gates, the operator, the light, green on the summit of the tower, might not have existed.

"I'm sorry," said Brenner.

"Do not be sorry," she said.

"About last night," he said.

"Never be sorry!" she said.

"I'm sorry," he said.

"Because you did what you wanted?" she asked.

Brenner was silent.

"Why should you not do what you want?" she asked. "Why should you always do what others want?"

"I'm sorry," he said.

"Because you did not do what some anonymous, impersonal other wanted? Because, perhaps for the first time, you behaved in accordance with your real self, not some false self, one imposed upon you from the outside, one taught to you as your own?"

Brenner was silent.

"Can you not see that one generation perpetuates its tortures upon the next, and that that is part of the torture, that the next, too, must be tortured?"

"It is hard to know how to live," said Brenner.

"I do not think it is so hard," she said. "Cannot you listen to your heart, to your blood?"

"There is reason," said Brenner.

"Reason is empty in itself," she said. "It is an instrument, a tool. It can be put to many uses."

Brenner was angry.

"It can be used as readily to thwart life as fulfill it, as readily in the defense of pathology as in the pursuit of health. Do not confuse its employment in the service of negativity with its own nature. Reason is a compass. At your disposal it places paths to an infinity of possible destinations. It itself does not tell you on which path to embark. It in itself cannot decide your direction. That you must decide yourself."

"Some things are more reasonable than others," said Brenner.

"Surely," she said, "with respect to given ends. If you wish to frustrate, starve, and deny yourself, then it is reasonable to behave in one fashion. If you wish to fulfill yourself it is reasonable to behave in another fashion."

Brenner did not respond to her.

Surely he had thought such thoughts often enough to himself. Indeed, he was weary of advocating and defending positions which had come to seem absurd to him. Why should he listen to such things from her, he asked himself. Why should he not simply put her to his feet?

"But it is surely easy enough to tell that what you have been taught is wrong!" she said.

Brenner was silent.

"If torture cannot make that clear," she said, "what could?"

"I must be going," said Brenner, angrily.

"I do not even know your name," she cried.

"It is not important," said Brenner. "We shall never see one another again."

"Do you want to know my name?" she asked.

"Doubtless there is something the zard calls you," he said.

"Yes," she said, "but it is in his own language, and I do not know its meaning, nor can I even pronounce it."

"You respond quickly enough to it, I would suppose," said Brenner.

"Yes!" she said. "I do!"

So, too, thought Brenner, slaves learn quickly enough to respond, and immediately, to the names which, for their master's convenience, or pleasure, are put upon them.

"Do you not want to know my name?" she asked.

As she was free, she would have a legal name, a name in her own right, of course, not a name dependent on the decisions of a master.

"No," said Brenner.

Tears sprang anew to her eyes.

"It is better that way," said Brenner. In this fashion he might forget her the more easily. Too, not knowing her name would make it more difficult, or even impossible, to find her, or trace her, should he weaken. He must never see her again. He must never want to see her again. He told himself he must be like iron. He must regard her as only the meaningless occasion of an evening's trivial pleasure. That was best. After all, was she not nothing, or next to nothing? Was she not only a female under contract? And had he not, even, had her on a chain?

"I do not know your name!" she said.

"I did not tell it to you," he said.

"Who are you?" she asked. "What is your name?"

"It is unimportant," he said.

"I see," she sobbed.

"Come along," said Rodriguez.

"You did such things to me," she said. "You made me feel such things!"

Brenner was silent.

"And now you will not so much as tell me your name?"
"No," he said.

"We are ready," said Rodriguez.

"What are you wearing under the brown dress?" asked
Brenner.

"Nothing," she said, bitterly.

"I did not think so," he said.

"The zard does not permit us such frills," she said.

Brenner smiled.

"I see that pleases you."

"Of course," he said.

"Return for me!" she cried.

"No," said Brenner.

"Tell me who you are!"

"No," he said.

"Oh!" she said, suddenly, pulling back from a Pon, who
had been down on all fours, with one or two others, looking
at her ankle, that with the cloth wrapped about the chain
and disk. It had put its small hands on the cloth, as though
to peep under it. "Get away!" she wept. She kicked, freeing
her ankle from the small, inquisitive grasp. It scrambled
back, quickly, like a small animal, and looked up at her. It
was blinking, this clearly discernible through the apertures
in the hood. Brenner hoped it was not disturbed. The others
about, too, had drawn back, timidly. "Go away!" she said.

"Don't frighten them!" said Brenner, angrily. "Stand still!"

She looked up at him, angrily, but obeyed.

"It is all right," he said to the Pons, soothingly. He
supposed at least one or two of them might understand
him. Hopefully the tone of his voice might reassure them, if
nothing else.

"I do not want them to touch me!" she said. "They are
tiny, nasty creatures."

"They are kindly, benign, social, gregarious, inquisitive
creatures," said Brenner. "We can learn much from them.
Do not frighten them."

How angry she was!

He did not want the Pons to associate those of his

species with violence toward them, or with contempt for them. They must understand that he, at least, regarded them as wonderful life forms, and equivalent to, and wonderful like, all other life forms, regardless of what they might be, whether ponderous megabregmas, wonderful in their way, as what they were, megabregmas, or the two-foot-long, suction-disked blood slugs of Chios, which were wonderful in their way, as what they were, two-foot-long, suction-disked Chian blood slugs. Such insights had figured first in the teachings of mystics, managing to overcome the difficulties inherent in communicating the contents of ineffable experiences, but had later been discovered to be self-evident, at least to minds capable of detecting the self-evidence in question. It was well, too, that these things were self-evident, as they did not seem to be evident in other ways.

"Stand still," said Brenner.

"Yes, sir," she said.

Brenner looked at her, sharply. He wondered if she were being ironic. But it did not seem so. She probably wants her pastry, he thought. That is why she has come. She does not wish to risk losing it.

"It is all right," said Brenner to the Pons, soothingly. "It is all right."

She looked away from Brenner. The Pons crept closer, again, to her ankle.

"They are merely curious," he said.

"Surely they have seen such things before," she said.

"Perhaps," said Brenner. "I do not know."

"I do not like them to touch me," she said.

"They do not even understand such things," he said.

"I do not know," she said. "I do not know."

He saw her suddenly shudder a little. The Pon, doubtless, had again touched the cloth at her ankle.

"Steady," said Brenner.

Brenner looked down. The Pon had unwound the cloth from about her ankle and was gazing closely, inquisitively, at the chain and disk. He turned the disk from one side to the other, and then, carefully, others watching, as well, replaced the cloth."

"You see," said Brenner. "They were merely curious. Too, you note they have put things back exactly the way they were. No harm is done."

"Let us be on our way," said Rodriguez.

Brenner turned half about.

"Wait!" she said.

He turned back to face her. Of course he had forgotten her pastry!

"Do not leave me!" she said. "Not like this!"

"You can come with us through the fence, for a way," he said. Perhaps he would make her wait a little for her pastry, or follow them for a time, not certain as to whether or not it would be given to her. To be sure, he did not wish her to accompany them into the forest, or far into it, for that might prove dangerous. Men from Company Station, he had learned, seldom entered it, unless armed. He supposed it probable that even the operator kept some sort of weapon in the gate house. After all, something unwelcome might appear at the gate if it were open, particularly at night.

"I am under contract," she said. "I cannot go through the gate. It is not permitted to me!"

Yes, that makes sense, thought Brenner. Contracted women would not be coming and going as they pleased. That would not do at all. To some, it seemed, then, such as the brunette, under contract to the zard, this place, Company Station, did constitute a sort of prison. The maids at the hostel, too, he supposed, would not be permitted to exit through the gate without authorization, no more than, say, company property which, for most practical purposes, if he could believe Rodriguez, they were. To be sure, these provisions might be as much in their own best interests as in those of their contract holders. The forests were dangerous. Too, where would they go in them? The only port of exit on this lonely, outflung world was at Company Station. And, too, many of them at least, could be identified on either side of the fence by their chains and disks. To be sure,

their plights were not as hopeless as those of slaves, whose
very bodies were commonly marked. Brenner looked at the
woman, and then down at her ankle. The first time he had
seen her, yesterday, out in the mud and rain, he recalled she
had not worn the chain and disk.

"Do not leave me!" she wept. "Remain here! Stay! Earn
money! Buy my contract! It is for sale!"

"Do not be absurd," said Brenner.

"It is not impossible!" she said. "Here there are lucrative
posts for free men! You earn out-world pay! I am sure you
could buy my contract! I am sure the zard will sell it!"

"You are being ridiculous," said Brenner, angrily.

"Do you not like me?" she asked.

"You have pleasing curves," he said.

"I love you!" she said.

"That is absurd," said Brenner.

"I had rather be a constant joy to one man than a
convenience, or a transient pleasure, to many!"

"You do not care for me," said Brenner. "You merely wish
to escape your contract."

"No," she said. "I love you!"

"That is absurd," he said.

"And what is to become of me, other than eventual
bondage on some far world?" she asked.

"You would look well, serving in a G-string and collar,"
said Brenner.

"In yours!" she said. "In yours! Do you not understand,
as I do, that I am your rightful slave, that you are you are
my rightful master?"

"You are a free woman," said Brenner.

"In my heart I am your slave," she wept.

"I know why you have come," said Brenner. "I am only
surprised that it means so much to you."

"I do not understand," she said.

"The zard, I gather," said Brenner, "does not know you
are here."

"No," she said, puzzled, backing away a step. "He does not."

"Yesterday, when we first met," Brenner explained, "you

did not wear the chain and disk outside, in the rain and mud. The zard, it seems, did not wish it dirtied. If you were on an errand for him now, or had his permission to leave the tavern, in such weather, I would suppose he would have again removed it."

"Doubtless," she said.

"Perhaps the cloth will protect it," said Brenner.

"It is my hope that it will do so," she said.

"I suggest that you hurry back to the tavern before your absence is detected."

"Please do not leave me!" she wept.

"What you really want is clear to me," said Brenner. "You need not cover it with so elaborate a pretense."

"I do not understand," she said.

"What will be done with you, if you are apprehended by the zard, outside the establishment without permission?"

"I do not know," she said. "I suppose I will be stripped, and chained to a post in the back yard, and kept there for a day or two, in the cold, in the rain and mud. Doubtless I will be whipped, such things."

"You are bold to come here," said Brenner.

"I love you," she said.

"I am only surprised that so small a thing means so much to you."

"Even if my love be no more than that of a slave, do not scorn it," she said.

"Do not embarrass me," said Brenner, "so prating of love."

"What you did to me!" she said. "What you made me feel!"

"It was nothing," said Brenner, angrily, "only an evening's dalliance."

"I love you!" she said. "I love you!"

"Do you want money?" he asked. "Do you want credits punched?"

She regarded him, aghast.

"The appropriate credits for your services were punched," said Brenner. "Your use has been paid for. The zard and I are clear. The matter is done."

"No," she said. "Please!"

"Your use has been paid for," said Brenner.

"I am not a whore," she said, "who demeans you for her profit."

"No," he said. "You are under contract, and so your earnings go to your contract holder, who applies portions of them on your behalf, to pay off your contract."

"Our contracts are never paid off!" she said. "We soon learn that!"

Brenner shrugged.

"To you," she said, "I am not a whore, not even a woman under contract! To you I am a slave, only an animal to you, an animal who begs to love and serve, to give all of herself, wholly, devotedly, unquestioningly!"

"I know what you really want," said Brenner.

"And what is that?" she asked.

"Apparently it means much to you," he said.

"I do not understand," she said.

"Surely you hinted about such things last night."

"I do not understand," she said.

"And I understand that you do not have coins, or credits, in your own control, that you might spend as you wish." In this respect, of course, women under contract would be rather analogous to slaves, who are totally, like other animals, without economic resources. They are totally dependent upon the master.

"What are you saying?" she asked.

"Accordingly," he said, "I can understand that even such small things may be important to you."

"I do not understand," she said.

He thrust his hand into his pocket. He drew forth the pastry in its wrapper. He partially unwrapped it. It was somewhat crushed now, from its sojourn in his jacket, and it was not at all likely that it was fresh, for he had obtained it at the hostel. But he did not doubt that it would still, though perhaps a bit dried, be tasty enough, and enough appreciated, given the circumstances. It reputedly housed a custard, and was roofed with a layer of chocolate.

"This is for you," he said.

Some of the chocolate clung to the turned-back, opened wrapper.

"It is supposed to have custard in it," he said.

He felt one of the Pons tugging at his sleeve. He looked back and he saw that Rodriguez had lined up several of the small creatures on each of the two ropes of the mud sled. Some of the other Pons had already gone through the gate and had busied themselves at their small, primitive camp outside the fence, striking tents, sacking belongings.

"Do you think this is why I have come?" she asked Brenner.

He held it out to her. "Take it," he said.

"I love you," she said.

He put the pastry in her hands.

"Don't leave me," she said.

He turned away from her and walked the few feet over the wet plank road to the vicinity of the sled, with its broad runners. Pons clustered about him.

"I do not know how long it will take to reach the Pon village," said Rodriguez. "I can't seem to get that out of the little bastards. I think we had better get started."

The Pons outside the fence, at their camp, their work done, now seemed ready to depart, as well. Several of them stood there, tiny, clustered together, with their burdens. They seemed a dismal, forlorn crew, in the half light, in the rain, in their damp hoods, their wet, gray garb, like apparitions come from the forests, insubstantial like the fog which swirled about them, things only partly real. The Pons about them, though, seemed real enough, like small animals, pressing, urgent, tugging. Perhaps there was some place of safety they hoped to reach by nightfall, some cliff, or cave, where they might perch, or hide, until the morning, until they resumed their journey. Brenner did not think that their village, or villages, were close to Company Station. Everything he had heard suggested that that was not the case. It was supposed to take them days to reach the station. To be sure, they had short legs, and one of Brenner's or Rodriguez' species might cover the same ground in less time.

How primitive were the Pons thought Brenner. Rodriguez had had to explain the sled to them. They did not even make use of the wheel. To be sure, wheeled vehicles would presumably not be particularly practical in the forests. There would be no roads there, at best, narrow trails.

"Let us be on our way," said Rodriguez.

Brenner reached to one of the ropes. They were lifted now, one on either side of the sled, by Pons.

"No," said Rodriguez. "They will do that."

Brenner looked back to the woman.

"Don't leave me!" she called. "I love you!"

He turned away from her. He must be strong. He must forget her.

"I hate you!" she cried. "I hate you!"

Rodriguez, with a wave of his arm, indicated that the Pons should proceed. The sled, with a squeak on the wet wood, began to move. It would not be a heavy weight for the Pons to draw, as there were several of them on the ropes. Rodriguez shook hands with the operator, who then climbed back to his tower. Brenner saw the sled slip down from the plank road onto the mud and gravel outside the gate. This made a different sound as the runners passed over mud and rock. In a moment then Rodriguez, too, had passed through the double gate. He followed the sled. After all, he did not know the way to the village, or villages. Only the Pons knew, *now*, thought Brenner. That would be different later.

He noted the line of march, azimuthlike, with relation to the detectable, but veiled position of Abydos' star at the time of morning. To be sure, this would give him little more than a direction, which might be reversed. And a direction might be easily confused, if only by a degree or two, which, over a lengthy distance, could produce an error which might not be inconsiderable. Too, if the Pons were as secretive and shy as it seemed they might be, their village might not even lie in the direction they set out. Indeed, they might utilize various shifts in direction, to make it difficult for strangers to retrace the journey. On the other hand, Brenner was not really worried about this sort of thing. He could depend on Rodriguez. He and Rodriguez had discussed the matter, even on the ship. Rodriguez, of course, had a compass, and would make a map of the journey, jotting down landmarks and, as he could, distances from point to point. In this way the simple stratagems of the Pons, if they saw fit to employ such, might easily, and without their knowledge, as they would not understand such things, be circumvented. How innocent and simple were the small creatures.

"I hate you!" he heard from behind him, and her sobbing.

He looked up at the light on the tower. It was now flashing green. The operator would not activate the field, of course, while anyone was visibly within its circuits, but, Brenner gathered, this was his way of suggesting to him that it was time for him to be on his way. And so he followed Rodriguez.

"I hate you!" he heard from behind him, once more.

Resolutely he continued on his way, and crossed the gate area, and stepped down into the mud and gravel on the other side. He heard the gates slide shut behind him.

He did not want to look back.

He stopped a few yards outside the gate. He looked to his left. The Pons who had broken their small camp were there. They stood there silently, together, with their burdens. They, apparently neat creatures, had cleared the area of their camp. They had even shouldered their tiny tent poles. In a day or so, with the rains, there would probably be very little evidence left behind that they had been there, perhaps some streaks of ashes, some partly burned wood, some marks on the ground.

Brenner then, not looking back, continued on his way.

Two Pons were close to him.

As Brenner went past, the Pons from the area of the camp fell into line behind him, and thereby behind Rodriguez, and the sled, as well.

The forests, some distance ahead, fog within the trees, seemed thick, and dismal.

Brenner was pleased that Rodriguez had the rifle. Brenner, of course, had, as far as he knew, seldom been in danger. On the other hand, he knew that dangers did exist, at least in certain places. They existed in space, for example, and not merely from such things as equipment failures, the leakage of suits, the jamming of locks, and such, or radiation and orbiting debris, but even from some forms of rational life, for example, from the masters of rogue ships, the pilots of predatory corsairs, and such. Too, there had been dangers, it had been hinted, even on the home world, at least in certain backward areas, in which it was rumored that certain elements of the population had not yet been fully domesticated. Brenner had avoided such areas, of course. But in the forests, he conjectured, there might be dangers, genuine dangers, dangers not always easy to avoid, from which not even a party card, if he had had one, would have served as an adequate guarantee of safety. Doubtless in the forests there were wonderful life forms and such, but wonderful as they might be, they might not be literate, and they might be hungry. But then, he told himself, there is probably, actually, little danger. Such things tended to be exaggerated. Consider for example that the Pons had camped in safety, apparently for days, outside the fence. And they actually lived in the forests themselves, with their primitive culture, their simplicities, and no tools more formidable than, say, pointed sticks and their tiny "scarps," little more than sharpened spoons. No, there would be no real dangers, even in the forests. Surely life, existence in its many aspects, had outgrown danger. But, still, he was not displeased that Rodriguez had brought the rifle. A charge from it could cut through a tree.

Brenner could not, of course, at least now, forget the woman. He wondered if she were still there, back, behind the fence, closed in, on the other side of it. Probably not, he thought. She has her pastry. He wondered why she had cried out that she hated him. He doubted that that was true. Too, why should she hate him? After all, she had received her pastry. He had not even made her beg for it, and perform for it, as might, for a master's amusement, have been required of a slave.

He stopped, but he did not look back. The Pons near him stopped with him, and even, too, those following, with the tent poles, and such.

He must not think of the woman, he told himself.

But what would become of her, he wondered. She had surmised, and doubtless with considerable justification, that her eventual fate would be the anklet, or collar, on some far world. Surely that seemed not impossible. It was a common fate, Brenner had gathered, for women on contract. He had conjectured that she would look well, serving, in a G-string and collar. Surely that was true. He considered her, being handed from master to master, from world to world. He thought she would probably bring an excellent price. He wondered what her brand might look like. Such things are, he had gathered, at least in the case of women, discreet and lovely, enhancing their beauty. They would also be, of course, clear, and easily locatable. He recalled that she had declared herself his slave. It was well, he thought, that Company Station was not a place where such utterances constituted legal enactments. There were, of course, many such worlds. To be sure, in her case, such an utterance, even on a different world, one where such utterances could be taken as legally efficacious, would not be binding. She was under contract. She had declared herself his slave. That was nice, he thought. He considered her, stripped and collared, kneeling beside his bed, begging to be permitted to crawl into it. It was a pleasant picture.

One of the Pons pulled at his sleeve, and he, angrily, shook his sleeve, disengaging its grasp. "I'm sorry," he apologized to the small creature.

He was tempted to look back, but he did not do so.

He continued on his way.

How well she had looked on the bed, removing the sheet, bit by bit, moving before him!

He smiled.

How desperately she had wanted to please him, almost as though he had been, in truth, not the simple patron of an establishment, but her owner, her master!

Forget her, he ordered himself. It is best to be done with her. She is a vile, low woman. She is not a person. She is insufficiently neuteristic. She does not behave as she should, as a "same." She was found "incurable." There could be no place for such as she on the home world. She had thus, appropriately, been put under contract and deported. She was disgusting! She had sexual needs! Brenner was pleased he had treated her as he had, coldly, and abandoned her. It was well that such vile needs be denied and frustrated! Or let her be reduced to bondage, in which degraded condition such needs are not only acceptable, but welcomed. And, indeed, in bondage, they are not only welcomed, but required! But he hoped, in spite of his contempt for her, and her weaknesses, that she would return to the zard's establishment before her absence might be noted. It was still early. Perhaps she could slip in, unnoticed. He did not want her hurt. He recalled the heavy, supple quirt which had lain on the zard's desk. He hoped that would not be used on her. He hoped that the zard would, as would presumably one of his own species, take into consideration her slightness, her softness, and beauty. Surely a chaining, and a switching, would be enough. She was not stupid. That should suffice to reform her behavior. Then he shuddered. He remembered the scaly countenance of the zard, its stature, and the seldom-blinking eyes. How much she must have wanted that pastry, thought Brenner. Brenner did not doubt, of course, that discipline was necessary to keep order in a house, for example, amongstst contracted women, and surely amongstst slaves, but he hoped, too, that the zard would possess at least a modicum of common sense about such matters. It was some consolation to him to suppose that the zard was a rational creature, and a businessman, so to speak. He had, if nothing else, an investment to protect. He would then, doubtless, adopt a policy which would both, insofar as these objectives were mutually achievable, preserve the beauty and usefulness of his contractees, women of Brenner's species, and, at the same time, guarantee the absolute perfection of their service. Then again he shuddered.

He had again thought of the creature's seldom-blinking eyes. Hopefully the zard knew something of his species, and of the nature of pain. Brenner supposed that discipline is best imposed within a given species, that its nature and effects may be more adequately understood. Rodriguez had once told him, with a laugh, that slaves almost universally desire to belong to members of their own species. Brenner now thought he understood that remark more fully than he had earlier. To be sure, there were many reasons for keeping a bondage relation an intraspecific one, for example, the master's knowledge of the nature of the slave's nutrition and physiology, her exercise and rest needs, the limits of her small strength, her parameters of performance, her requirements with respect to atmospheres, her tolerances with respect to climatic conditions, and so on, not to mention such obvious things as the ease of communication and the mutual intelligibility of behaviors. Too, of course, in many cases, as was the case in Brenner's species, the female can be a source, in many ways, of enormous pleasure to the male. That is another advantage of intraspecific bondage.

Brenner's foot slipped to the side in the mud, but he quickly regained his balance.

Yes, thought Brenner, that is doubtless one of the major reasons one buys them off the block, for the pleasure one will derive from them.

He would not look back.

If she was serious about loving him why had she not cast aside the pastry? Why had she kept it? That proved it was the pastry she wanted, that the rest had been a pretense.

He would not look back.

Surely she would be gone by now.

He would not look back.

He trusted that she would have turned about by now and run as quickly as her small, sweet, shapely legs would carry her, back to the establishment of the zard. Hopefully she would manage to return unnoticed. That would be clever of her, to both obtain the pastry and escape a beating.

He would not look back.

She must be gone by now.

He would not look back. But then, as he ascended a small hillock, some yards before the beginning of the trees, he did stop, and he did turn about, and he did, over the heads of the Pons, look back.

Her small figure was still there, on the plank road, behind the double fence, not far from the tower.

For a moment he had not seen it as the area had been obscured by fog. Then the wind had stirred the fog, whipping it softly away from the gates. Now he saw it clearly, small, through the soft rain, clutching the cloak about itself.

How stupid she is, he thought, angrily. Let her hurry back before she is caught out of the house without permission! But he was glad he saw her. He was glad she was still there. She must have seen him, too, on the hillock, turned, for she lifted her arm to him. He did not return the gesture. She still, in one hand, held the pastry. She had not cast it away, she had not relinquished it. That is what she wanted, thought Brenner. That is why she came to the gates this morning, why she risked so much. It interested him that so tiny, so frivolous a thing, a trivial sweet, could have been so important to her. He looked at her again. Again she lifted her arm, but, again, he did not respond. Then he turned about, quickly, and descended the hillock. Rodriguez and most of the Pons, with the sled, were waiting at the edge of the trees.

"Are you all right?" asked Rodriguez.

"Yes," said Brenner.

She had said that she loved him, and that she hated him. Surely that was some sort of contradiction. Brenner wondered what love might be, and if it truly existed. One school of thought, of course, held that love was a myth devised by men to oppress women. This position had originated, it seemed, with frustrated women who hated men and wished to destroy them as men, blaming them for all their own difficulties and shortcomings, and, who, in many cases, as it had turned out, interestingly, wanted other women to themselves. Strangely enough they were rival "lovers." One did not hear much of "love" these days. He was a little puzzled, even, that she had heard of it, at least in an intersexual sense. Could it have emerged somehow naturally, spontaneously, within her? But how would she have known what to call it? She must have heard of it somewhere before. That was not impossible. There were, of course, worlds on which love, intersexual love, was accepted and known, but they were, on the whole, worlds in which the position of women was low, "suitably low," as Rodriguez might have said. Love did seem to have something to do with putting women to the feet of men. But he doubted that men had invented this. Rather it seemed to have to do with the nature of love. There had been, at first, it seemed, an attempt to change the meaning of the word, by talk of what constituted "true love," and such, to conformance with the political objectives of certain establishments, but this had not been successful. Unsuccessful, too, interestingly, had been efforts to construe "love" in terms of the civil tepidities, respect, and dignity, and such, prescribed to obtain amongst "sames." Now, generally, however, one did not hear the word, at least publicly and in intersexual contexts. It had become, in such contexts, a word which occurred only infrequently in polite, informed discourse, a word which had become, in effect, to recall an ancient allusion, merely another "four-letter" word. To be sure, love was regarded as appropriate in certain contexts, as for the parties, for the state, and such things, and also for all life forms, of course, regardless of their placement on various phylogenetic scales. It was acceptable for a man to declare his love publicly for coelenterates, for example, and some did, but not for women. Brenner wondered what love might be, and if, indeed, there were such a thing. It must be some sort of emotion, he thought, or something like that, only perhaps much more complex. He did not doubt that there was hate. He had seen a great deal of that, even in his sheltered life. If there were hate, it seemed likely then, though not necessary, of course, that there might be such a thing as love. But surely the whole notion is unintelligible, thought Brenner. Yet she had said she loved him. He had heard, of course, that slaves often loved their masters, even when their masters had forbidden it. That was of interest to Brenner. Surely she had seemed, in many ways, slavelike, so passionate, so beautiful, so helpless, so desirous to please. Perhaps then, as she was such a woman, such a weak, low, helpless, worthless thing, she did love him. Perhaps she was indeed a slave, and that it was precisely in virtue of this that she was capable of love. But too, he reminded himself, she had said she hated him.

"Are you all right?" asked Rodriguez, again.

"Yes," said Brenner, angrily.

Some of the Pons looked up at him, through the holes in the hoods, blinking. Their eyes seemed large, and soft.

"This is as far as we are going," said Rodriguez, "without seeing whom we are with."

"What do you mean?" asked Brenner.

One of the Pons suddenly squeaked, seized by the arm by Rodriguez.

"Stop!" said Brenner, horrified.

But Rodriguez had his free hand on the hood covering the creature's head. It squirmed. It tried to hold the hood over its features. "Grab that one!" said Rodriguez, gesturing with his head to another Pon.

"No!" said Brenner. "Stop!"

"He's a strong little bastard," said Rodriguez.

"Stop!" said Brenner.

Then Rodriguez had jerked away the hood.

"It may bite!" said Brenner.

But the Pon did not bite. Rodriguez held it now, firmly, by the back of the neck and, with his free hand, forced open its mouth.

"Must you do that?" asked Brenner.

"See?" asked Rodriguez, grinning.

"Yes," said Brenner.

"No fangs," smiled Rodriguez.

"It may be poisonous," said Brenner.

"I doubt it," said Rodriguez.

The dendition of the Pon was regular, small, and fine.

The other Pons had scurried back, away from Rodriguez and the sled. They stood about, a few feet back.

"Do not be afraid," said Brenner, soothingly.

Rodriguez released the Pon. Interestingly, it did not run away. It stood near him, looking up at him.

"Do you think you're going to buy it, or sell it, or something?" asked Brenner.

Rodriguez laughed.

Slavers sometimes force open the mouths of captured free women, as a portion of their assessment. The nature of a female's dentition can be informative, providing as it does an index to such things as her general health and condition, her accustomed diet, her age, and, even, in some cases, her former socioeconomic class. Sometimes the mouths of women in markets are also forced open but this is usually merely to remind them that they are slaves, as they, subject to the submission consequent upon their condition, may not only not attempt to prevent, but must, upon any appropriate indication, comply with, and abet, all such inquiries, inspections, and examinations.

"You should not have done that," said Brenner. "You might frighten them. You might make it difficult to win their confidence. You might contaminate the data. You might even be violating some kind of taboo."

"No," said Rodriguez. "I know what I am doing. These little bastards have shown up often enough at Company Station without hoods. I checked that with the operator at the gates."

"The hoods, then, are for our benefit," said Brenner.

"Apparently," said Rodriguez.

"Why would they conceal their faces from us?" asked Brenner.

"I'm not sure," said Rodriguez.

"If they had anything to hide, they surely would not have invited us in," said Brenner.

"I would think not," said Rodriguez.

"They may be afraid of us," said Brenner.

"Possibly," said Rodriguez.

"Perhaps they are pathologically shy," said Brenner.

"Perhaps," said Rodriguez.

"Perhaps it is a custom to welcome guests while hooded?" said Brenner.

"Perhaps," said Rodriguez.

"Perhaps it is really intended to have its full effect later, in rendering familiar, or unsuspect, a concealment for their females," said Brenner.

"That is possible," said Rodriguez. "By hooding all, they might hope to indirectly achieve such a desiderated objective, in an apparently innocent manner."

On many worlds, of course, and in particular on those on which men were untamed, and proud, it was customary for free women to veil themselves, putatively that their beauty not constitute an irresistible provocation to sexual predation. To be sure, there seemed to be cultural ambiguities in such matters. For example, there was little doubt that veiling was in its way, rather like vulnerability and shyness in a woman, often sexually stimulatory to the male. It tended to suggest that she was a concealed treasure, and to enhance her aspects of remoteness, mystery, and inaccessibility. Besides, were veils not meant to be removed? Accordingly, veiling, the intent of which might seem to be to reduce the temptations which might otherwise overwhelm strong, excitable males, did not always have this effect. Too, it might be noted that the free women on these worlds often lavished great care and ingenuity on these veils, treating them less as defensive opacities, behind which they might hide, than as stimulatory accessories to their desirability. As a note it might be added that slaves on such worlds, and on such worlds, where there are strong men, there are always slaves, were commonly denied veiling. That dignity was not to be theirs. Rather, as was appropriate, given the lowliness and degradation of their condition, let them be shamed, refused the security and honor of the veil. Let their faces be bared, exposed to the gaze of any.

"But we do not really know," said Brenner.

"No," said Rodriguez, "but in any event I will not go into the forests with things whose faces I cannot see."

Brenner looked at the Pon. It was tiny, of course, hardly coming to Rodriguez's waist. It was fine boned. It seemed childlike. Its head and face were covered with hair, the face's hair a lighter down. It's eyes were large. Its hands and feet, as its body, were small. It had five digits on each hand, as Brenner would have expected, from the reports. Its nose was not prominent, but broad and flat. Its forehead sloped slightly backward. Its jaw was slightly prognathous. Its appearance, on the whole, was rather simian. Brenner, like Rodriguez, doubted that it was poisonous. It was regarding Rodriguez quizzically, sometimes blinking with the large eyes. It seemed surprising to Brenner that something like that, which resembled the tiny apes of Thera, was rational, that it could think, to some extent, and speak. To be sure, they lacked metallurgy and native pottery. They did have a culture, of a sorts, however simplistic. They were primitive. They were reputedly totemistic. The totem animal, Brenner recalled, was the Abydian mouse, or Abydian ground git, a tiny, stub-tailed rodent. That seemed fitting for the Pons.

"No hoods! No masks!" said Rodriguez to the Pon. "No hoods! No masks!"

He then lifted the small creature into the air, and shook it, good-naturedly, as one might a child.

"We are friends," said Rodriguez. "Friends. There are no secrets between us, no masks, no hoods. We will tell one another everything. In the village you will behave as you always do. Do not be different because of us. In time you will pay no attention to us. It will be like we were not there. We want to find out about you. We want to know all about you. You are interesting. We like you. We will be friends. We will give you gifts, beads, pretty glass, nice things. Do you understand?"

The Pon, lifted up, Rodriguez' hands under its arms, looked down at Rodriguez.

Then Rodriguez set it down, gently.

It then hurried to the others.

"Do you think it understood?" asked Brenner.

"I think so," said Rodriguez. "These things trade at Company Station."

"Do you think it is their leader?" asked Brenner.

"They do not have leaders, at least in the sense you are thinking of," said Rodriguez. "They have little if any social organization. He was the first one I could get my hands on."

"Look," said Brenner.

The Pons, one by one, some of them looking away, or down, pulled away their hoods.

"Good! Good!" called Rodriguez to them. "We are friends, friends!"

Brenner thought they were all males, but he was not sure. The features of many were sufficiently fi ne as to ma ke a mistake in such matters possible. The shapeless, nondescript nature of their garb, too, presented its problems. On the other hand, as they were bipedalian, and mammalian, or mammalianlike, it seemed that some indications of feminine sexuality, if females were amongst them, ought to manifest themselves in even so inauspicious an environment. Yet he did not note such indications. There might, of course, be very few differences between the sexes of the Pons. Rodriguez had conjectured that they approached the unisexual ideal which was so prized, and yet still so imperfectly attained, on the home world. We can learn much from Pons, thought Brenner. His conjecture, incidentally, that they were all males was, in this case, we might note, correct.

"It seems they are cooperative," said Brenner. "I am surprised they did not all rush away and leave us here. You may have jeopardized the entire expedition."

"Not at all," said Rodriguez. "We have something they want."

"What is that?" asked Brenner.

"Beads, hard candy, mirrors, buttons, colored glass," said Rodriguez, "that sort of thing."

"Why did you insist on the removal of the hoods?" asked Brenner.

"Surely you were curious to see what they looked like?"

"Of course," said Brenner. "But you could have waited

until we knew them better, until we had won their confidence, until we had reached the village."

"You have never been in a place like the forest, have you?" asked Rodriguez.

"No," said Brenner.

"I am not going to follow something into the forests whose behavior I cannot interpret," said Rodriguez.

"The forests are dangerous?"

"I think so."

"And so you wished to see if they were unusually alert at times, if they were being evasive, if they were frightened."

"Yes, such things," said Rodriguez.

"You don't trust them, do you?" asked Brenner.

"No," said Rodriguez.

Brenner was silent.

"Too, of course," said Rodriguez, "it is important to rob them of their anonymity, to individualize them, to reduce them to openness, to make them more helpless, more vulnerable to us."

Brenner nodded. It was for such reasons, he supposed, as for many others, as well, that on various worlds slaves were denied veiling, that the least nuances of their expressions, in all their helplessness, in all their subtlety and delicacy, would be available to free persons. This contributes, of course, to their control.

Brenner looked at the Pons. All now, were unhooded. They were approximately the same height. They huddled together, watching himself and Rodriguez. Brenner hoped they had not been frightened.

Rodriguez consulted his compass.

"They seem sexless," said Brenner.

"Back home even the Humblers would stand in awe of them," said Rodriguez. "They would be on all the circuits, they would be celebrated as heroes of the times, they would be held up as shining examples to youth."

"Because they are nothing, and have done nothing?" asked Brenner.

"Pretty much," said Rodriguez.

Brenner suddenly, unaccountably, pitied the youth of the home world. How innocent they were. And how they would be warped and twisted, into what grotesque shapes would they be hammered, what eccentric, pathological, gruesome molds would they be expected to fill, and all to serve the ends of others, mocking them and exploiting them.

Brenner considered the Pons, standing there.

"I do not think I like Pons," said Brenner.

"I would have thought you would esteem them," said Rodriguez.

"How is that?" asked Brenner.

"Are they not, for most practical purposes, "sames"?"

"Yes," said Brenner, guiltily. "I suppose they are."

"So there," said Rodriguez.

One of the Pons had come closer now, to look on.

Rodriguez showed him the compass. "See?" he asked. "Pretty?" Then he put the compass back in his pocket. The Pon, simple creature of the forest that it was, of course, would not understand the compass. At best it would seem to it like some sort of toy. Rodriguez then drew forth a sheet of paper from his jacket, on which he jotted something down. He had begun his map. He showed the paper to the Pon. "Paper," he said. "Paper."

The Pon looked up at him.

"They are illiterate, of course," said Rodriguez. He put the paper back in his jacket. He then clapped his hands together, sharply. Brenner was startled. This seemed rude to him. "Ropes! Ropes! Pick up!" called Rodriguez. He clapped his hands together, twice more. The Pons hurried to the ropes.

"Why are you acting like this?" asked Brenner.

"We will teach them who is master," said Rodriguez.

"You will alienate them," said Brenner.

"No," said Rodriguez. "They are only one step above gits, if that."

"Are you ready?" asked Rodriguez.

"Of course," said Brenner.

"You are all right?" he asked.

"Of course," said Brenner. "Why do you ask?"

"I thought, before," said Rodriguez, "that something might be wrong."

"No," said Brenner.

"Weren't you crying?" asked Rodriguez.

"No," said Brenner.

The woman had not cared for him, of course. She had only wanted her pastry. Women are practical in such ways. She had said she loved him. Such things are easily said. Brenner, of course, did not believe in love, for such, like sexual needs, did not exist. To be sure, one might love a party, or the state, or everything, rather as a rosy, remote, safe, antiseptic, abstract conglomerate. Too, he supposed it was all right to love everyone, and, ideally, everything, including primitive particles. It was only that it was suspect or immoral to love a particular individual, particularly if that entity were of an opposite sex. That was dangerous. For sexuality, as was well known, does not unite men; it divides them.

At a gesture from Rodriguez, the Pons put their small, but cumulatively not inconsiderable, weight to the ropes. The sled moved, over wet leaves and twigs. The trees here, at the edge of the forest were not closely grown. There would be little difficulty in making headway during this part of the journey and, later, hopefully, there would be trails. The mud sled was not wide, only a Commonworld yard in width.

"Those are lantern fruit," said Rodriguez, pointing to some heavy, gourdlike pods, some half split.

"Are they edible?" asked Brenner.

"No," said Rodriguez.

"They are not indigenous to this world, are they?" asked Brenner.

"It is thought not," said Rodriguez.

Most of the Pons were following behind.

Brenner could not, at this point, of course, look back to the tower, to the fence. There was the rise, and there were the trees.

Brenner looked to the Pons drawing the sled. And ahead of them there were some others, strung out, leading the way.

He remembered how rudely Rodriguez had seized up one of the Pons, and removed its hood. Whereas the small creature had squirmed, and struggled, it had not attempted to fight, or defend itself. Too, when Rodriguez had forced open its mouth, it had not resisted. Pons do not bite, thought Brenner. On the other hand, thought Brenner, they do not have very strong teeth either. Perhaps organisms with small, fine teeth are well advised not to bite. At most, they might deliver a small, nasty, unclean wound, one which larger, stronger organisms might find annoying, and punish. Perhaps that was why Pons were good, thought Brenner, because they could not be dangerous. Perhaps morality comes most easily to the weak.

Brenner wondered what was the nature of his own species, and if it had a nature. One theory had it that those of his species were originally filled with a nothingness, and another that they were filled with sunshine. Those who held the "nothingness" theory looked upon this nothingness as an opportunity. If the mind, for example, were a blank tablet, or a blank recording plate, or such, one might then inscribe upon it messages of benignity and beauty. But if the mind were indeed a blank tablet, with no nature of its own, no secrets, no resistances, no internal geodesies, no realities, why might not one, with equal propriety, inscribe upon it messages of terror, of fear and woe, of sickness and hatred? Surely the canvas has no rights with respect to the pictures one chooses to paint upon it. Who decides the plans from which man is to be manufactured? If men had no nature of their own, then they are only putty in the hands of others, whether in the white fingers of angels or the paws of beasts. And where must one stand, outside the domain of man, to see value? Where will he find his patterns and possibilities if not within himself? Where will those who so complacently, so innocently, arrogate to themselves the right to write these messages find their models? Are there plates of graven brass hung between the stars? The stars are silent, burning in space. They are alone, like men. And if such plates were there, who will decipher them, who will read them, and who will ask from whence they came, and if they are true? No, thought Brenner, the theory of emptiness is not a happy one. If true, it is not that man is lost, or that he has not yet been found. Rather it is that he does not exist, has never existed, and can never exist. Rather he would be nothing in himself, not even a material, but rather only a temporary, arbitrary form, only an artifact, meaningless, and perishable. But what of the theory that man is filled with sunshine, thought Brenner. That is a theory, so to speak, of original virtue. Perhaps it is naive, and less plausible than an older, more pessimistic myth, but it might be a benign myth. Believe that man is basically good. Now that might be a useful myth. It could be developed in a number of ways, not all obviously compatible. If one stresses the corrupting influences of institutions and societal arrangements, construed somehow to have arisen surprisingly amongstst these benign creatures, perhaps by magic, then one can absolve individuals, generally on a selective basis, of responsibility for their actions. The victim, for example, is to blame for the crime. On the other hand, in a sterner society, one may blame the criminal, so to speak, for having chosen, somehow, to repudiate his own nature, his natural goodness. On this approach one may hold him responsible for his actions and simultaneously hasten to his correction, the effort to recall him, by various techniques, perhaps punishment, imprisonment, torture, conditionings, pharmacological therapy, lobal surgery, and such, to his forsaken innate goodness. There is an additional difficulty here, of course, which is that of independently identifying the "goodness" which is innate. Who makes this identification, how do we know it is correct, and who decides disagreements which might arise in these matters? Presumably we might not wish to characterize all nativistic dispositions, if there are any, in man as essentially good. If we did that, saying man was essentially good would presumably mean no more than saying that man was essentially man, which might be true, but would not be likely to be of much political utility. Presumably then, if the notion of man being essentially good is to make sense, we have to have an independent criterion for goodness. It does not seem likely that we will be successful in this search, except that we might impose one which pleases us, by force. In this sense, in its ultimate vacuity and bankruptcy, the "sunshine" theory closely approximates the "nothingness theory." It is possible, Brenner thought, that man, innately, is both good and evil, assuming that some external sense could be given to such claims. But it is more likely, he thought, that man is neither good nor evil. Rather, he is something more profound than either. He is real. He is as he is, not in some trivial sense, but in the sense that he has his own nature, which is in its way apart from good and evil, or beyond them, if you like. This is not to deny, of course, that he might not have his own "good," in senses such as those of satisfaction and pleasure, or his own "evil" or "bad," in the senses of frustration or pain. Those things are real enough, and we grant them even to camels and horses, but they do not answer the social needs of a moral "good" and a moral "evil." There may be no common interest; there may be no general will. But without the rules there is only chaos. Perhaps the myths are important.

Brenner was angry, seemingly unaccountably.

Brenner put down his head, and brushed a branch out of the way.

How complacent were those of the home world. How much they claimed to know! How assured they were!

But there must be something beyond the myths, thought Brenner. Beyond the evanescent myths, coming into fashion, going out of fashion. And not just more myths, nor even an ultimate myth, that to which all other myths might point, that to which they might over time, more and more closely, approximate, the myth ultimately fated to be agreed upon by all those in need of a myth, if only investigation could be carried on diligently enough, long enough, the ultimate myth, the fated myth, the ideal myth, lying like a spider at the end of time. No, thought Brenner. Rather a truth. But must we make it ourselves? And how then will that differ from another myth, or even from the ultimate myth? It will be ours, thought Brenner. But the myths, too, are they not ours? There must be criteria, thought Brenner, for truths, even for myths. And who shall decide the criteria? By what criteria shall we judge our criteria, and those criteria, in turn? How long is "until then," how far is the end of time, how shall we come to the last foot of infinity?

Brenner suddenly stopped.

"Are you all right?" asked Rodriguez.

"Yes!" said Brenner.

They began again. That is it, thought Brenner. One must stop somewhere. One must begin somewhere.

What he had been taught, he was sure, was wrong, at least in some basic, fundamental, profound, even if only personal sense. It was productive of frustration; it generated misery; it caused pain.

He thought of the woman, whom he fiercely dismissed as a mere contract slut, in whom he had taken his pleasure, whom he had had well serve him, even to the collar and bracelets. Even she, low, vulnerable, passionate thing that she was, little better than a slave, had reminded him of such things, as though he had needed reminding! If torture could not convince him of the wrongness of what he had been taught, she had asked, what could? Suddenly he was angry with her. What an insult she was to the women of his species! Why could she not have been, like them, a "same"! She cast doubt, even, on her sisters of the home world. Perhaps, too, they were not really "sames." Perhaps, too, like her, they were different from men, something quite different. How horrifying that would be! What if his species was not sexually unimorphic? What if the sexes, really, were quite different? The females of his species, he knew, both by those of his own species, and by those of other species, were kept as slaves, on many worlds. They were easily trained. They adapted quickly to bondage. It was said that within the institution they blossomed, that within it they found fulfillment. What could such things mean?

Brenner looked at the Pons about, so tiny, so weak, so pathetic, so meaningless. And yet they represented, in their way, as Rodriguez had pointed out, the achievement of what was at least a verbal ideal of the home world. That is what the home world wants, thought Brenner, at least of men. It wants to break and destroy men, to make them small and weak. It wants to turn men into such innocent, simple, stupid, harmless things, such tiny, blinking, pleasant, manageable, cooperative, timid, meaningless nonentities. In the Pon, it seemed, was to be found the new idea of the male, gentle, tender, and such, but his very weakness and manageability, and gullibility celebrated as true masculinity and strength. Surely that is an easy route to manhood, thought Brenner, doing what you are told, fulfilling a stereotype, externally imposed, indexed to the utility of those who despised one. Yes, thought Brenner, that is surely an easy route to manhood, doing what you are told, an easy route to strength, being weak.

"Through here," called Rodriguez, pointing out the path through which the sled had been drawn.

A Pon, almost at his elbow, looked up at Brenner.

"Stay with the sled," said Rodriguez.

"Of course," said Brenner.

There must be a truth thought Brenner, a truth for my species, some sort of truth, even it be a truth relative to my species, a truth local or private, in its way, to my species. Then he felt grief for the youth of the home world. To them, such as the Pons, those sweet, insignificant, futile, trusting little aliens, would be held up, as Rodriguez had said, as examples. The youth of the home world, Brenner feared, would be destroyed, in its homes, in its schools, almost in its cradles. How could it resist the uniformity, the pervasiveness, of the conditioning programs to which it would be subjected? Indeed, is not youth, in its beautiful simplicity, and its lack of experience, even more likely than its elders to be devoted to, and defend, the very lies which keep them from their own honesties?

But I was such a youth once, thought Brenner.

To be sure, even when quite young, Brenner had never taken pain as a sign of truth, frustration as a clue to right, misery as a guide to an ideal morality. But perhaps that was because he had been a "vat brat"; indeed, he suspected he might well constitute some sort of anachronism in his species, some sort of atavism, or throwback; his genetic materials, for example, had been generated long ago, in a different, more primitive, more backward time.

Perhaps there is hope, thought Brenner.

Perhaps there is a human nature, with its own truths, its own realities, thought Brenner, even its own goodness and badness.

Perhaps there is hope.

"Help here," said Rodriguez.

He and Brenner, assisting the Pons, lifted the sled up, over some rocks. The Pons then again addressed themselves to the ropes. Brenner noted that the Pons, in this journey, did not make much noise. He did not find that surprising. It seemed fitting for them. On the other hand, perhaps small creatures, generally, in the forest did not make a great deal of noise. There might be a reason for that.

Too, as they had continued in their journey, pausing now and then, he had noted that one or more of the Pons, to the side, rather modestly, back in the brush, squatting down, under the cover of their robes, had apparently relieved themselves. They had then covered this spoor with dirt, gouged up with their tiny, shiny scarps. Predators often covered their spoor, to keep their presence in an area concealed. But the Pons did not seem likely predators. As far as Brenner knew they did not even hunt, their reverence for life deterring them from the chase. This reluctance, of course, need not be symmetrical. In not hunting one does not thereby remove oneself from the category of the hunted. Such unilateral sacrifices are seldom reciprocated in nature. The Pons, in the forest, might not stand at the top of the food chain. There could thus be an advantage not only to the predator in concealing his presence, but one accruing similarly to the prey. But the forest seemed calm. The wind rustled gently through the leaves of the trees. The covering of the spoor, or feces, Brenner supposed, in the case of the Pons, probably had to do with their modesty, or their

embarrassment concerning their own bodies, which they
kept muchly covered, as shameful objects, and the processes
of such bodies, or even with taboos, perhaps their ritual
fear or loathing of touching unclean things, and such. Or
they might just be neat, tidy creatures, intent upon keeping
a pleasant environment.

Brenner struggled not to find the Pons disgusting. He
did not wish to commit a fallacy, imposing his own values,
as uncertain and confused as they were, on alien creatures.
He was not, after all, a Rodriguez, who seemed to feel he
was entitled to his own opinions on such matters. He must,
instead, be scientifically neutral, and rigorously objective,
and keep in mind, too, that all life forms, and all cultures,
and such, were wonderful, the same, and equivalent. To be
sure, there were some exceptions to this. For example, the
science councils and many of the professional organizations
of the home world, which were now in effect branches of
various parties, and were politically active, and responsible,
concerned, and militant, in acceptable ways, had denounced
certain cultures, for example, those of several of the openly
stratified worlds. Indeed, in some cases, vigorous resolutions
had been passed, boldly conforming to various party lines.
In short, in effect, science was neutral, and all life forms,
and cultures, were wonderful, the same, and equivalent,
except for those which were not approved, which were
"bad," etc. Needless to say, the scientific findings on these
matters differed from world to world, and, within given
worlds, from place to place, and from time to time.

From time to time Rodriguez stopped, and consulted his
compass, and made an addition to his map. At such times,
the Pons, too, of course, stopped. Then, again, the party
would proceed.

There must be a human nature, thought Brenner, and a
human goodness and badness, or rightness and wrongness,
one for our species, not for all species, or for no species, not
something external and imposed, but something internal
and real, something with its own teleology, its own impetus,
and viabilities.

But he could not deny the strength of conditioning processes. It is possible to condition an animal to behave in unnatural, eccentric fashions, to starve itself, to frustrate itself, to beat its head bloody into walls, to engage persistently, congratulating itself all the while, in self-destructive, life-shortening activities. Experiments, no longer permitted, except apparently on a global scale with rational species, had made that clear.

Perhaps there is hope, thought Brenner.

It is not always easy, say, to twist trees and bushes into unnatural shapes, however appealing these shapes may be to those with unnatural tastes. Once the eccentric stresses are removed, once the wires, the ropes, and bands are cut, the trees, the bushes, tend to grow again according to their own natures, the ancient natures, never forgotten, lurking in each cell in the body, putting down their roots deeply, into the foundational, sustaining, anchoring darkness, seeking there fluids and nutriments, and lifting their branches toward the light, thus standing in darkness, reaching for the sun. How else can one grow, or become real? Surely neither by repudiating the earth nor by denying the stars. One must have both, the darkness and the light, the polarities, each intelligible, each worthy of veneration, each meaningless without the other. And herein lies a paradox, in which some see tragedy, and others the key to the glory of a species.

But what of reason, asked Brenner. Is it empty, or does it have a content? Is it a way merely to achieve ends, or is it, in its way, an end in itself, or germane to particular ends, more to some than others?

Brenner thought of Rodriguez, who was beside him, to his right.

He is a case in point, thought Brenner. He does not subscribe to what he has been taught, he does not accept uncritically the uncontradicted. Indeed, he seemed genetically disposed to think for himself, a disposition which was rare enough perhaps in any time, but was certainly so in these times. Indeed, in virtue of his weakness for thought, he had encountered difficulties in many matters, almost from the very beginning. He had never been convinced that compliance was reason. Perhaps that was because he thought reason might be required in order to determine with what it might be rational to comply. If reason had an appropriate instrumentality, thought Brenner, rather than merely instrumentalities, surely then one might give some sense to the notion of reason, or better perhaps, to the notion of the "rational." If reason herself were value-neutral, perhaps rationality was not; and rationality might be indexed to nature. To be sure, this involved an axiological commitment. Who is to say that it is not rational for a creature to starve and injure itself, particularly if this starvation and these injuries were instrumental to its moral improvement, namely, in producing an improvement on nature, a twisted, clipped, crippled organism? I, for one, thought Brenner. And who sees words as tools, and weapons, and cloaks of concealment behind which horrors might be hidden? But tell the difference between things and words. They are not the same. Listen to the wind, to the trees, to your heart. Recollect the forgotten languages, learned in youth, the memory of which lurks within you.

Needless to say, as you can see, Brenner was a very confused young man. Had he paid more attention to the Pons about him, his confusions and puzzlements might have been easily resolved. They provided, in their simplicity, inoffensiveness and innocence, the answer to his questions. Too, did they not stand at the "beginning," in their way? Were they not the proof that a rational, or protorational, species, could begin in innocence? Perhaps the results of his labors, and those of Rodriguez, would be to provide such an example of basic, fundamental goodness in a rational species as to be not only refreshing to more complex, confused, jaded cultures, but perhaps even reassuring, or therapeutic, in its way, restorative perhaps. Brenner had gathered, from the directress, months ago on the home world, that it was expected that his researches would have some such utilitarian value, that it would be nice if they provided confirmation in their way of what already needed no confirmation, the value structure of the home world. "Anthropology can be good for something," she had reminded him. Brenner supposed that it would be easy enough to slant the data, and, on a world like that of Abydos, an out-flung world, who would ever know, and, indeed, given the apparent nature of the Pons, it might not even be necessary to slant the data. Presumably they would provide the directress, and her party, through the studies and reports of Brenner and Rodriguez, with exactly what they wished. "Learn from them," the directress had urged him. "We will all learn from them."

Yes, thought Brenner. One must stop, and then one must begin again. Reason, he supposed, had indeed no content in itself. But, indexed to the needs of a species, the decision made, it being stipulated that these were to be satisfied, it could have an appropriate instrumentality, an instrumentality appropriate to that end, as indeed, in a sense, it could have instrumentalities appropriate to diverse ends. It is rather like a knife, he thought. It can be used for various things. For example, it could be used in self-defense, and even to attack. There are better things to do with it, thought Brenner, than to open one's veins.

Brenner looked down at one of the Pons, quite close to him. It, with its small, soft, delicate, gentle, hairy, rather simian face, looked up at him, and blinked.

They are interesting little aliens, Brenner conceded.

The rain had now stopped. The sunlight, here and there, glistened on the wet leaves.

Brenner thought of the brunette. She had seemed a thousand times more a woman than the directress. But then, who knew? Perhaps there was a woman in the directress, too. Perhaps if she had found herself under contract, and put in the light, brief, white camisk of a contractee, chained in a cargo yard awaiting deportation, who knew? Or perhaps if she found herself stripped, save perhaps for a collar, ascending a sales block on an openly stratified world, to be considered by buyers, who knew? Perhaps she, too, later, in a man's house, or at his feet, might recollect her womanhood.

"Look!" said Brenner. "There is another white, rounded rock."

"Have you just noticed them?" asked Rodriguez.

"I have seen several," said Brenner, defensively.

"They began at the edge of the forest," said Rodriguez. "I have been watching. The Pons are following them. They are using them as guide stones."

Brenner was silent, and was rather angry. He, too, should have noticed such things, and long ago, assuming they were actually there. He had been noting them, really, only for the past few minutes. He had been too preoccupied with his own thoughts. The whitish stones were spaced about every fifty feet or so. There were other such stones about, here and there, of course, but what Rodriguez had detected before him, and from the first, perhaps in virtue of having been less preoccupied with his own concerns than Brenner, was the alignment of certain of the stones.

"They probably lead between the village and the gates," said Rodriguez.

Brenner nodded. In virtue of such things the Pons might find their way about in the forest.

"They are apparently so stupid," said Rodriguez, "that they need such things to find their way home."

Brenner smiled. Doubtless Rodriguez was right. But, too, Brenner was quite pleased. Now, he, too, whenever he wished, could follow the stones back to Company Station.

"You will not need your map any longer," said Brenner.

"I will continue to keep it," said Rodriguez. He was, it seemed, a suspicious fellow. Brenner, of course, was pleased, actually, that Rodriguez was going to continue to keep the map. After all, stones could be moved. They might be dislodged, for example, by the movements of water, or even by the passage of some animal, if it were sufficiently large. To be sure, the forest seemed quite empty.

Brenner wondered if the field between the fences was really necessary. Perhaps its main function, in the final analysis, was to prevent the disappearance of company property.

That must be it, thought Brenner.

"Rodriguez," he said.

"Yes," said Rodriguez.

"You remember the little brunette, who came to the gates this morning?"

""Curves"?" he asked.

"If you like," said Brenner. To be sure, the blonde had been well formed, as well, though perhaps more sparely built.

"Certainly," said Rodriguez.

"I gather, from what she said," said Brenner, "that you had the blonde drink a releaser."

"The matter was cleared with the contract holder," said Rodriguez.

"And that you left her spread-eagled, and neck-chained, on the bed."

"I seem to recall that," said Rodriguez.

"Surely that was deplorable," said Brenner.

"It was good for her," said Rodriguez.

"She may be pregnant," said Brenner.

"It is hard to say," said Rodriguez.

"Are you in the habit of doing that sort of thing?" asked Brenner.

"No," said Rodriguez.

"Why did you do that?" asked Brenner.

Rodriguez was silent, walking behind the sled. Brenner could hear his tread on the leaves.

"Why?" asked Brenner.

"Because we are going into the forests," said Rodriguez.

Brenner did not understand this.

Once those ahead stopped, and so, too, then, did the rest of the party. One or two of the leading Pons had their heads back, lifted. They stood very quietly. Brenner went about the sled. Their nostrils were dilated. They seemed very intent. Then, after a moment, seemingly satisfied, they continued on, the rest of the party following.

"What was that about?" asked Brenner.

"Nothing," said Rodriguez.

But Brenner noted that Rodriguez, in the interval, had

gone to the luggage, and to his pack, which was now on top of the luggage. He unzipped the pack. Within the pack, now that it had been opened, on top, at hand, Brenner could see what appeared to be the brass barrel of an optical instrument, a telescope.

CHAPTER 7

"May I see?" asked Brenner, speaking clearly.

The tiny creature, some three Commonworld feet or so in height, looked up from its work, where it was gouging in the dirt, digging for tubers.

Brenner smiled, and extended his hand.

He could have lifted the Pon with one hand, but, unlike Rodriguez, he had chosen not to impress his greater strength on them.

Reluctantly the Pon held the scarp out to Brenner. He did not have enough sense, Brenner noted, to reverse it in his hand, but Brenner took it carefully. It was sharp, but not all that sharp. Small, sturdy, broad, slightly curved, it was less a knife than a gouge, less an instrument for stabbing or cutting, than for digging or scraping. To be sure, Brenner supposed it could be dangerous. It could, for example, administer a shovel-like wound, or scrape flesh from bones.

Brenner looked at the object carefully. He turned it about. To this one, at this time, there clung particles of moist earth. It was the first time he had seen one closely. It was the single most common implement of the Pons. The second most common implement seemed to be the pointed stick.

"Thank you," said Brenner, handing back the tool.

When he rose to his feet he saw that two others of the Pons had been watching him.

There had seemed something unusual about the scarp to Brenner, but he was not certain, at that time, what it was.

He then returned to where Rodriguez was resting.

It was in the vicinity of noon, on the fifth day from Company Station.

He looked back at the Pon who had now freed a tuber from the earth.

Pons did not use the scarps for scraping the interiors of hollow trees, for insects, or for scraping aside damp leaves, or turning rocks, in pursuit of grubs, as might have other forms of simiantype life. The customs of the Pons, or their taboos, or principles, he had gathered, did not condone such predations. The complex worlds could learn much from the Pons, with their reverence for life. Happily, too, the Pons did not seem to realize that the grains, the roots, the vegetables, and such, on which they fed sparingly also shared the chemistries of life. He trusted that Rodriguez would not bring this to their attention. It would not do at all, if the Pons, who seemed to be an unusually consistent sort of creature, decided that they had a duty to starve themselves to death. Too, they need not know of the dangers they posed to small creatures in performing actions so simple as taking a drink of water, washing their bodies, or, indeed, in even breathing. To be sure, lunatic moralities had caught on here and there throughout the galaxy, at least officially, through well-organized political action, by means of which it seemed that anything could be accomplished, no matter how insane or destructive, but even so, sanity, forced into the guise of hypocrisy, had usually prevented the wholesale extinction of peoples. As a case in point, the examples of saints who had murdered their own children, and then as many other people as possible, and then themselves, in expiation, and to provide compensatory justice for worms, and such, despite their inspirational value, and the sentimentality, poignancy, and sympathy with which they were portrayed in various media, were more likely to be objects of public praise than private emulation.

"The Pons do not eat insects and grubs," Brenner had observed to Rodriguez a day or two earlier.

"I don't either," had said Rodriguez.

Brenner could still not place what had seemed to him odd about the scarp he had examined.

Rodriguez rose up and clapped his hands. "Let us be on our way," he said.

CHAPTER 8

"Are you awake?" asked Brenner.

He and Rodriguez lay near the remains of a small fire, surrounded by Pons, the sled, too, within the circle.

"Yes," said Rodriguez.

"They speak the dominant language of Company Station," said Brenner.

"You have known that since the station," said Rodriguez. "They trade there."

This was the sixth day out from the station, and today was the first time that either Brenner or Rodriguez had heard the Pons speak. That some of them, at least, were familiar with the language most spoken at the station had been known for days, of course, as they had regularly understood Rodriguez' instructions, Brenner's questions, and such. Too, they would have found the language useful in their trading at the station.

"You do not understand," said Brenner. "They spoke it amongstst themselves, or something like it. I could understand them."

"I heard," said Rodriguez.

"Surely it is not their common language," said Brenner.

"I would not think so," said Rodriguez.

"What would that be?" asked Brenner.

"I have no idea," said Rodriguez. "The matter is not clear in the records."

"That would seem to be the first thing to be made clear," said Brenner.

"One would think so," said Rodriguez.

"Different parties who contacted them must have spoken different languages."

"One would suppose so," said Rodriguez.

"It is tactful for them to speak only in our language before us," said Brenner.

"Yes," said Rodriguez. "That seems thoughtful."

"That would fit in with their diffidence, and commitment to proprieties, politeness, and such," said Brenner.

"They are excellent mimics," said Rodriguez.

"They would pick up languages quickly?" said Brenner.

"Possibly," said Rodriguez.

"It seems odd that most of them, at least, should be familiar with our language," said Brenner.

"Not necessarily," said Rodriguez. "These may be their traders, their contact individuals. You must remember that they have been in contact with Company Station, and its predecessors, for generations."

"They could be like border peoples, to whom more than one language would be familiar?"

"Possibly," said Rodriguez.

"It would not be spoken in their village or villages?" said Brenner.

"One would think not," said Rodriguez, "but who knows? They may have adopted the language gradually, over hundreds of years. The prestige of superior life forms, such as we, may have influenced this sort of thing. Doubtless we, even such as we are, are like gods to them. Diffusions and interchanges take place, losses, abandonings, accretions, transformations, developments, borrowings, and such, occur. Over generations a language can change beyond recognition."

"You think, then, that they might speak our language," said Brenner.

"There is another possibility, of course," said Rodriguez.

"What is that?" asked Brenner.

"That we speak their language," said Rodriguez.

"That is very funny," said Brenner.

"There are many differences, of course," said Rodriguez, "aside from the difference in tonal quality, the high-pitchedness, the shrillness, and such, differences, literally, in pronunciation, and certainly in vocabulary."

"It is a dialect," said Brenner.

"Each individual," said Rodriguez, "speaks an idiolect, in a sense, his personal language, with its pronunciations, its lexicon, and such. In this sense there are as many languages as there are speakers. If enough idiolects have enough in common, in phonemic quality, in intonation contours, and such, we may speak of a dialect. If the dialects have enough in common we may speak of a language. The division between a dialect and a language is often arbitrary. In innumerable areas, as on a river, there may be ten consecutive villages, or speech communities, any two of which, adjacent to one another, understand one another very well, but the speech of, say, the first village will be clearly unintelligible to that of the tenth village. Thus, in that set of villages, using mutual intelligibility as a criterion, there must be at least two languages, but where does one stop and the other start? You must invent your criterion. Then, with your criterion, it becomes, and only then becomes, a scientific question, a question of fact, as to how many languages are spoken on the river. One criterion may give you ten languages, another five, another two, and so on."

"I wonder what is their native language," said Brenner.

"I wonder what is ours," said Rodriguez.

"There is something about them that makes me uneasy," said Brenner.

"What?" asked Rodriguez.

"There is something remotely familiar about them," said Brenner. "It is as if I knew them."

"Have you been to Abydos before?" asked Rodriguez.

"No," said Brenner.

"Then do not be foolish," said Rodriguez.

"On the first day," said Brenner, "when you took the hood from the Pon, and you looked at its teeth."

"Yes?" said Rodriguez.

"I am curious about something," said Brenner.

"What?" asked Rodriguez.

"Did you count the teeth?" asked Brenner.

"Of course," said Rodriguez.

"How many teeth did it have?" asked Brenner.

"Thirty-two," said Rodriguez.

"That is interesting," said Brenner.

"I agree," said Rodriguez.

"They make me uneasy," said Brenner.

"Hundreds of life forms have that number of teeth," said Rodriguez, sleepily.

"There seems to me something oddly familiar about the Pons," said Brenner.

"There should," said Rodriguez. "You are spiritual brothers. You both subscribe to a morality of lunacy."

"Do you not agree that if you do not regard the bacterium as your equal you have an inferiority complex?"

"No," said Rodriguez. "But if I did regard it as my equal, that would be evidence that I had such a complex, and a severe one. More likely, of course, I would simply be insane."

"There are more of them than you," said Brenner.

"That is true," admitted Rodriguez.

"And you cannot reproduce by fission," pointed out Brenner.

"Yes," admitted Rodriguez, sleepily, "they have me there."

Brenner supposed that if there were no values, no standards, in the universe, if it did not draw a distinction between, say, the bacillus and the megabregma, or was not interested in the differences between them, it was not, then, that the bacillus and the megabregma were equal, but, rather, that equalities and inequalities, so to speak, did not exist. If there are no values, nothing has value, and, in that sense, things cannot be of equal value, unless one counts all as of zero value, or such. But there were values in the universe, obviously. If nothing else, they had been put there as needed, or desired, by various organisms. Values were real; it was merely that they were indexed to species, or individuals. To be sure, they might be incommensurable. But incommensurability did not imply illusion, nor inconsistency, nor unreality.

"If the bacterium has equal value with us, then, so, too, must the Pon," said Brenner.

"Why not?" said Rodriguez, affably.

"But you do not regard the innocent, harmless Pon as our equal?"

"What do you mean by 'equal'?" asked Rodriguez.

"That is interesting," said Brenner. "That is usually left unspecified." He had never really thought about that. Such words commonly functioned noncognitively, usually being used as touchstones to test group allegiances, rather like special signals, pullings on the ear, strange motions with the foot, secret handshakes, and such. You could, of course, use words to mean almost anything. The usual trick was to take a good word, one with favorable connotations, and then change its meaning to something one approved of. For example, if one approves of totalitarianism one simply redefines, say, 'democracy', so that it now means what, or much what, 'totalitarianism' used to mean. Then anyone who disagrees with you is put in the position of being opposed to "democracy," and such. The obvious fraudulence of this tactic, interestingly, seldom acts as a deterrent to its effectiveness.

"The literal meaning of 'equal' is sameness or identicality," said Rodriguez.

"Yes," said Brenner.

"In this sense almost nothing is the same as anything else," said Rodriguez. "Nor need it be, nor should it be," he added.

"We are the same as the Pons in the sense that we both have a single nose, and such," said Brenner. "And we are the same as the bacterium in the sense that we both contain various chemical elements."

"True," said Rodriguez.

"Thus we and the Pons, and bacteria, are equal," said Brenner.

"The fallacy should be obvious, even to you," said Rodriguez. "You shift from sameness or equality in one respect, usually a quite general or trivial one, to sameness or equality in some substantial or totalistic sense, denying differences. I do not deny that you and the bacterium have something in common, for example, that you both occupy space, but it does not follow from this that you are a bacterium."

"I see," said Brenner.

"Be what you are, a man," said Rodriguez, "and be one fully. Do not deny what you are, or let others cheat you of it, or make you ashamed of it. Be what you are, in joy, in freedom, and power. Walk, and run, and climb, as nature intended you should. To do otherwise is to betray yourself. It is to commit treason to your own reality. Let the wolf be a wolf, the man a man."

CHAPTER 9

"**D**id you see it, over there!" said Rodriguez, excitedly.
Brenner peered intently in the direction indicated by Rodriguez.

"No," said Brenner.

It was now the ninth day from Company Station.

"It is the second time," said Rodriguez. "I am sure I saw it before, and this time."

"What was it?" asked Brenner, uneasily.

"It is like a shadow," said Rodriguez. "It is large, very large, out there. I saw it twice, I am sure I saw it twice. You did not see it?"

"No," said Brenner.

One of the Pons looked up at Rodriguez, its small, wide nostrils flat in its face. It blinked twice.

"You are probably mistaken," said Brenner.

For the last two days Rodriguez, and Brenner with him, had remained close to the sled. Brenner had kept this post naturally enough in camaraderie with Rodriguez, that they might the more easily converse as they trekked. Too, he found the humility, kindliness, politeness, and gentleness of the Pons, those ideal, simple children of the wild, clad in all the glory of their unassuming primeval innocence, vaguely disquieting. Too, of course, he told himself that his position near the sled had a practical justification, as well, as it enabled him, and Rodriguez, to assist the Pons with the sled, particularly in steep or narrow places. But now, suddenly, Brenner realized that Rodriguez, himself, might have had a different reason for his positioning himself by the sled. Rodriguez had now removed his hand from the brass instrument, that resembling an optical instrument, which lay in the opened pack on the sled.

"Let us move on," said Rodriguez to the nearest Pon, gesturing ahead.

Again the party moved forward.

"You are certain you saw nothing?" asked Rodriguez.

"Yes," said Brenner. "I am certain."

CHAPTER 10

"**I** have it!" said Brenner. "I now know what it was!"

"What?" asked Rodriguez.

"Some days ago I examined a scarp," said Brenner. He looked about himself. No Pons were close at hand. They had drawn off a bit. It was noon, and the party was resting. "There was something unusual about it, something I could not at the time place, but troubled me."

"Why are you speaking so softly?" asked Rodriguez.

"It was not something on the scarp, not something there. That is what I noticed, not something there, but that something was not there!"

"I do not understand," said Rodriguez.

"The Pons are amongstst the most primitive forms of rational, or semirational life, we know of," said Brenner.

"True," said Rodriguez.

"They do not even have a native pottery," said Brenner.

"No," said Rodriguez.

It might be mentioned here that the Pons did, of course, have a nonindigenous pottery, in the sense of a pottery received in trade from Company Station. Too, of course, they had certain other goods from Company Station, scarps, as we have noted, and, too, naturally, certain other items, for example, pots and kettles.

"Even their form of social organization is primitive," said Brenner. "They lack chieftains, or kings."

"It seems so," said Rodriguez.

"They are utterly simple, utterly primitive," said Brenner.

"Not really," said Rodriguez. "They have had contacts with more advanced cultures, for example." To expand briefly on this we might note that it is difficult for a "primitive society" to remain primitive after it is discovered, because, almost immediately, exchanges occur and influences begin. In this sense, the very investigation of the data tends to contaminate the data. The observer's presence, so to speak, obtrudes into the data, not simply in his categories, his concepts, his judgments, in his interests, and such, but, even more insidiously, at least from the point of view of an objective inquiry, in his own cultural influence. The very beads he distributes create new values. What he chooses to wear and eat, and how and where he sleeps, may constitute implicit criticisms, and so on.

"They are amongst the most primitive peoples known to science," said Brenner.

"They are perhaps more advanced than some totemic cultures," said Rodriguez, "as they are supposed to possess at least the rudiments of an agriculture."

"A primitive level of agriculture at best," said Brenner.

"That would seem to be the case," said Rodriguez.

Some of the Pons on the trek, it might be observed, had supplemented a diet of roots and brush fruit with meal, boiled with water, which practice, of course, tended to corroborate the existence of a native form of agriculture, of some level at least.

"Where would you rank them?" asked Brenner.

"Technologically?" asked Rodriguez.

"Yes!" said Brenner.

"Very low," said Rodriguez. "For most practical purposes they are a stone-age culture, except, of course, that they do not hunt animals, and do possess something of an agriculture. Too, they can weave, obviously. Certain other limitations in their culture are doubtless by choice, such as the refusal to herd animals, or to use them for food. It is even likely they deny themselves the use of bone implements, because of similar reservations."

"You see them then as a mix, as being anomalous in some ways?"

"Certainly," said Rodriguez.

"How do you see them biologically?" asked Brenner.

"That is where in particular I think they are extremely important," said Rodriguez. "I see them as biologically primitive, as basically unevolved, as, in effect, simplistic simian organisms. In this sense I think they are, in their psychic development, in their rudimentary capacities, in their intellectualistic dispositions, in their world picturings, in their mental outlook, in how they think, and such, at a very primitive level. That is what makes them such a beautiful object of study. They do not even have the mental capacity to borrow and adapt the subtleties of later cultures, and not even the subtleties of mathematics and science, but the subtleties even, say, of heroes and gods, of myths and religions. In this sense, as much or more than culturally, I think of them as being, as I said on the ship, "at the beginning." Here, in their thought, in their totemism, I hope to find the seeds of civilization, where it came from, how it arose. Here we revisit the earth, as it was, so to speak, before the Garden of Eden."

"You do regard them as primitive, biologically, and culturally?"

"Of course," said Rodriguez.

"They trade for their scarps," said Brenner.

"Of course," said Rodriguez.

"And for pans and such?"

"Of course," said Rodriguez.

"What do you think the likelihood would be of their possessing a native metallurgy?" asked Brenner.

"Zero, at best," grinned Rodriguez.

"You do not think it likely?"

"No," said Rodriguez. "Now if you were talking about the six-inch Abderan weed snake or the marine slug of Chios that would be different."

"You do not think it likely?"

"The thought is absurd," said Rodriguez. "Look at them. Consider them. Their brains are about the size of your fist. They do not even work clay. They do not even have a native pottery."

"They trade for their scarps," said Brenner.

"Of course," said Rodriguez.

"Where do they obtain them?" asked Brenner.

"Company Station," said Rodriguez.

"I examined a scarp recently," said Brenner. "It did not bear the company mark."

"Is that what this is all about?" asked Rodriguez.

"Yes," admitted Brenner.

"The scarp may not have been marked," said Rodriguez. "It might have been missed, the stamper malfunctioning. It might have been defective, and rejected by quality control before being marked, but somehow, by intent or otherwise, been included amongstst trade goods. The company might not even mark them all. It may have been received through the company, or through a company employer, and had its source in an independent supplier. It might even have been made in a shop at Company Station by a mechanic, and not even be a company scarp."

"Of course," admitted Brenner. "There are many possible explanations."

They walked on, in silence, beside the sled for a time.

"Do you know the one that had the scarp?" said Rodriguez.

"Yes," said Brenner. Over the past few days he had become adept at distinguishing amongst the Pons. As was common with the Pons, as with most sorts of creatures, rabbits, gits, sheep, and such, one recognized them at the beginning only by general, obvious characteristics, and then, later, as one grew more familiar with them, one drew finer distinctions. One begins by recognizing sorts, and, later, individuals within the sorts. Many creatures in the galaxy, incidentally, had difficulty in telling the members of Brenner's and Rodriguez' species apart. Whereas to a member of their species, they appeared quite different, indeed, obviously so, even so acute, if ponderous, an intelligence as that of a megabregma might confuse them. To be sure, there was not much interest in the galaxy, amongstst most creatures, in telling the members of Brenner's and Rodriguez' species apart. Indeed, there was generally not much point in doing so. Whereas Brenner was now adept at telling the Pons apart, he being interested in them, at least to some extent, and having made a serious effort, if only as a scientist, to do so, it must be admitted that Rodriguez, in spite of his considerable intelligence, had given the matter little consideration. He did not have a great deal of interest, certainly at least at present, in individualizing Pons. It did not seem to him important to do so. He regarded them all as rather ineffectual and despicable, and, for most practical purposes, interchangeable. And, in this, Brenner thought he might actually have the most appropriate perspective. For certain purposes of study, one git or slug, so to speak, would do as well as another.

"Which one?" asked Rodriguez.

"That one," said Brenner.

Brenner was naturally intrigued at Rodriguez' apparent interest. Whereas Rodriguez had earlier, at least to Brenner's satisfaction, settled the matter quite adequately, sufficiently accounting for it, appropriately dismissing it for its inconsequentiality, he had not, apparently, at least upon reflection, managed to similarly assuage his own curiosity. It would be something of an anomaly, of course, to find a company object, particularly a manufactured article, an object for sale or trade, which did not bear the company mark. Rodriguez' interest, of course, once expressed, immediately revived Brenner's.

"You!" barked Rodriguez.

The Pons looked up, like small animals startled by a sudden, unexpected, possibly dangerous noise, then holding so still and silent as to be almost invisible.

"You!" said Rodriguez. "Yes, you! Come here. Quick! Quick!"

Rodriguez gestured, impatiently.

Reluctantly the Pon approached, its eyes wide like small moons. It was a small, timid creature.

"Do not be afraid," said Brenner, slowly, clearly, softly, coaxingly, soothingly.

To be sure, Rodriguez could have broken its neck with one hand.

When it was close enough Rodriguez reached out and drew it to him by the robes.

The other Pons watched, curiously. They made no move to intercede for, or to protect or defend, their fellow creature. That was not the way of the Pons. They were not powerful animals, of course, and, too, perhaps, what was one Pon more or less? This sort of reluctance was understood by some on the home world to be a form of cowardice but by many others as a moral sublimity. If offense were wrong so, too, must be defense. Were not all knives sharp? What difference did it make which way the weapons were pointed? Self-defense, then, must be a criminal act, one worthy only of criminals, one by means of which one put oneself exactly on their level. Too, was not such affront in its way a denial to the predator or aggressor of his rights? Benevolence, and love of other life forms, and recognition of the brotherhood of species, was also muchly praised. More than one Humbler saint, for example, had reputedly fed himself to wild beasts lest they go hungry.

Rodriguez pulled the scarp from the little fellow's belt and looked at it.

"There," said Rodriguez.

Brenner looked at the scarp. It bore the company mark.

"You made a mistake," said Rodriguez.

"Yes," said Brenner, slowly, uncertainly. "I must have made a mistake."

Rodriguez stuffed the scarp back in the belt of the Pon's robes. "Go," said Rodriguez, indicating that it return to its brethren, over to one side.

It lost no time in doing so.

"That is the right fellow?" asked Rodriguez.

"Yes," said Brenner.

"It seems strange that you should have overlooked so obvious a mark," said Rodriguez.

"Yes," said Brenner.

"You made a mistake," said Rodriguez.

"Yes," said Brenner. "I must have made a mistake."

CHAPTER 11

Brenner watched the brush. He could hear movements within it. The hair rose on the back of his neck. He did not have the weapon. Rodriguez, a few moments ago, had taken it suddenly, seizing it up and hurrying down their backtrail. The Pons, those with the sled, and the others, and Brenner, had stopped.

"You seem apprehensive," Brenner had said to Rodriguez, earlier in the morning.

Rodriguez had not responded.

"The forest is quiet," Brenner had said.

"It is too quiet," had said Rodriguez.

"I do not understand," said Brenner.

"It should teem with life," said Rodriguez, "but except for a handful of tiny things, some gits, some snakes, some fliers, and such, nothing.

"What is your explanation?" asked Brenner.

"It would seem that our reports on the indigenous fauna must be mistaken," said Rodriguez.

"It would seem so," said Brenner.

"There are other possible explanations, of course," said Rodriguez.

Brenner regarded him.

"Our own passage, for example," said Rodriguez.

Brenner nodded. They, and even the Pons, would be strangers here. The police, on various worlds, for example, in pursuing bandits, insurgents, and such, in jungles, often carried recordings of animal life with them, birdcalls, insect sounds, simian barkings, and such, indexed to the area and the time of day or night, which they broadcast in their search. In this fashion, their presence might not be belied to their quarry by any sudden or unexpected silencing of the local wildlife.

"It could very easily be our passage," granted Brenner.

"We are not a large or formidable party," said Rodriguez.

"There are several Pons with us," said Brenner. To his annoyance, it seemed that Rodriguez was ready, characteristically, to overlook the Pons.

"The men of Company Station seldom, if ever, hunt in the forest, so it is not as if the animals would have learned to fear them."

"True," said Brenner.

"Even when we camp at night," said Rodriguez, "it has seemed to be very quiet."

"At such a time the animals would be expected to resume their normal behaviors?"

"After a few minutes, of course," said Rodriguez. Brenner supposed that Rodriguez might know something about these matters. He had, after all, hunted on several worlds, on some of them professionally.

"Then clearly there must be very little animal life in the forest.

"That would seem so," said Rodriguez.

"Yet," said Brenner, "that contradicts the ecological surveys, sketchy as they are."

"Exactly," said Rodriguez.

"On the assumption that the reports, which seem clear and consistent, are correct, we are left with no alternative other than to assume that it is our presence which has frightened the animals."

"Not necessarily," said Rodriguez.

"I do not understand," said Brenner.

"I do suspect that they are afraid," said Rodriguez, "perhaps even very afraid."

"It is strange that our presence could have so intimidating an effect," said Brenner.

"It need not be our presence," had said Rodriguez.

The movements in the brush were now closer.

Brenner wished he had some weapon, even a stick.

"You!" said Brenner, in relief, as Rodriguez broke through the brush, the brass barrel of the rifle in hand, disguised as an optical instrument.

Rodriguez was not in a good humor. He was covered with sweat. Small leaves and twigs clung here and there to his wet shirt. His face and arms were marked with scratches from brush. One cheek was bleeding. He had turned about, suddenly, and then, with a grunt, seized up the weapon and hurried down the backtrail. Now he was red-faced. He was breathing heavily. He stumbled, and regained his balance. He put one hand out, to steady himself. His paunch swayed. He is finished, thought Brenner. He is done. He is old. That brave animal, that irascible, uncompromising unique individual, that thing that dared to be different in a world of mediocrity and conformity, that hunter, that explorer, that soldier, that thing that lived by its own stars, that acute intellect, that heart of hearts is done. That body, insulted by age, withered in time, abused by Heimat and weed, is cargo now. He had been sent to Abydos to die. But he had come because he wanted to. There was something on Abydos about which he was curious, something he did not understand, something which might have to do with what he thought of as "the beginning."

"Did you see anything?" asked Brenner.

"I had thought I did," said Rodriguez.

"But not now?"

"No," said Rodriguez, sitting down on the ground. "No." He put the tube to one side. The Pons looked at it.

"We will rest for a time," said Brenner to the Pons.

"It has been drifting with us," said Rodriguez, "like a shark following a ship."

"There is nothing," said Brenner.

"It is always downwind." said Rodriguez.

"There is nothing there," said Brenner.

"It is the predator's ambush," said Rodriguez, absently.

"The shadows are subtle in the forest," said Brenner. "There could be a mix of light and darkness, a movement of a branch, such things. It is easy to misinterpret such things."

"You think that is what I have done?" asked Rodriguez.

"Yes," said Brenner.

"Perhaps," said Rodriguez.

"Certainly," said Brenner.

"I do not think so," said Rodriguez.

After a time the party rose up and continued its journey.

"Do you feel better now?" asked Brenner.

"Yes," said Rodriguez.

CHAPTER 12

"It is to be a ceremony of some sort," said Brenner.

It was now night.

On the next day they had been given to understand that the village would be reached.

"The git is apparently to play some role in the ceremony," said Brenner.

"Naturally," said Rodriguez.

"You aren't going to use the camera," said Brenner.

"No," said Rodriguez. This made sense to Brenner. After all, the Pons might be familiar with cameras from Company Station, and the effects of their operation. Some primitive peoples objected to the capturing of their images, so to speak. Some feared this might steal their souls. For such reasons, and because they were still strange to the Pons, Rodriguez and Brenner would not attempt to film the ceremony, that in spite of the fact that the camera was dark-adapted. Rodriguez did have a small recorder with him. That, of course, could be easily concealed.

The Pons were in a circle.

Rodriguez and Brenner stood back, that they might not be obtrusive. They were close enough, of course, for the effective functioning of the recorder.

In the center of the circle of the Pons was a small cage of twigs. Within it, crouching down, was a tiny, stub-tailed rodent, the Abydian mouse, or git. Brenner could have held it, squirming, in his hand. This had been caught in a nest of rotted wood, half under a fallen log, earlier in the afternoon, in a sack, and then placed in the small enclosure of twigs, about which the Pons were gathered.

Rodriguez put on the recorder.

"We love you, father," called a Pon, the voice high in the night.

"'Father'?" asked Brenner.

"The totem animal," said Rodriguez. "It is always referred to as "ancestor," as "father," as "primal father," and such. The totem group regards itself as descended from it."

"That is absurd," said Brenner.

"Surely you are familiar with totemistic theory," said Rodriguez. "The totem bond is regarded by these people as one of complete consanguinity, as one of blood, literally one of blood."

"Forgive us, father, for what we have done," called the Pon. "We are contrite! Show us forbearance! Be kind to us! Cherish us. Protect us! We will refrain from touching the soft ones!"

"That is exogamy, denial of the in-group females to the in-group males," said Rodriguez. Brenner nodded. The two central tenets of totemism were reverence for the totem animal, respecting it, sparing it, and such, and exogamy. Mating was forbidden within a given totem.

"We beg your forgiveness, father!" called the voice.

"What did they do?" asked Brenner.

"Probably nothing," said Rodriguez. "Maybe they have thought about breaking a taboo, or something, who knows?"

"Forgive us, father," said the voice. "Love us! Cherish us! Protect us!"

There was then silence amongst the Pons.

"They are waiting for the response of the father," whispered Rodriguez.

This rather surprising communication made Brenner, for no good reason, decidedly uneasy. There was only a little wind, however, amongst the branches. Some lantern fruit, softly glowing, moved on its stems.

Then, after a time, another Pon, from somewhere in the circle, called out the following:

> Oh, I could get me in.
> I could lay them waste.
> But I will not do so,
> for they are my children.
> I am the father.

"That makes no sense," said Rodriguez.

Brenner was forced to agree.

"Apparently the ceremony is over," said Rodriguez. He turned off the recorder and slipped it into his pocket.

"Tomorrow," said Brenner, "we reach the village."

"It would seem so," said Rodriguez. He then looked about, at the trees, and the clearing.

"You are still concerned that something is out there?" asked Brenner.

"Yes," said Rodriguez.

"Surely the Pons know the forest," said Brenner. "And they do not seem frightened."

"They are stupid," said Rodriguez.

"We reach the village tomorrow," said Brenner.

"It will not be too soon for me," said Rodriguez.

"You are concerned, aren't you?"

"Yes," said Rodriguez.

CHAPTER 13

"Let us take stock," said Rodriguez.

It was their first night in the village, and they were alone in a small hut, on the periphery of an open, circular area in the center of the village.

"The palisade does not appear very formidable," said Rodriguez.

"No," said Brenner.

"The Pons seem friendly," said Brenner.

"One of them rushed up and struck at you," said Rodriguez.

"They seem friendly, on the whole," said Brenner.

"Why did that one strike at you?" asked Rodriguez.

"I have no idea," said Brenner. "As far as I know I have done nothing to generate his hostility."

"He did not strike at me," said Rodriguez.

"No," said Brenner.

"The area of the village is perhaps two acres," speculated Rodriguez.

Brenner nodded. That seemed about right. It was certainly not large.

"The Pons here would number in the vicinity of a hundred or so," said Rodriguez.

"Perhaps," said Brenner.

"I counted ninety-seven," said Rodriguez, "but I may have missed some, and counted others twice. They all look the same, even the females, and they move about a lot, trying to keep the distances between them."

"They do differ one from the other," said Brenner, "if you pay attention. Too, the females are for the most part distinguishable from the males. They tend to be smaller, and their features seem to be different, finer, or more delicate, or less coarse, or something."

"They all dress the same," said Rodriguez.

"One clue as to whether females are present," said Brenner, "is to observe the spatial relationships."

"Of course," said Rodriguez.

"Males will crowd together," said Brenner. "Females usually keep about a yard between themselves and other females. The intersexual distances are at least ten feet."

"Yes," said Rodriguez.

It was sometimes interesting, incidentally, to note the rapid shifting in spatial relationships which might occur in groups, given the entry or exit of various individuals, of one sex or another. This sort of thing, of course, objectively, was no more strange than similar sorts of distance observances in various cultures. Distance arrangements occur also, apparently naturally, amongst the individuals of many species. In some species, literally thousands of individuals could cluster in small spaces, or move about one another, even at high speed, and, almost as if by magic, avoid physical contact. Dominance orders, too, of course, of various sorts, were almost universal. In a flight of birds it is not an accident that the first bird is first, or the second second, and so on.

"You seem to be good at telling them apart," said Rodriguez. "What do you think the ratio of males to females is?"

"About half and half," said Brenner.

"You have noted, of course," said Rodriguez, "that the males and females live separately."

"That makes little sense to me," said Brenner, "as there must be females from other clans, from other totems, in the village. It is only within the same totem that the males may not touch the females."

"You saw no evidence of families?"

"No," admitted Brenner.

"I made every effort this afternoon," said Rodriguez, "where I could tell a female, to ascertain her totem."

"All here are of the gits, so to speak," said Brenner.

"As nearly as I can tell," said Rodriguez.

"That makes no sense at all," said Brenner.

"Where are the other clans, the people of other totems?" asked Rodriguez.

"They must be somewhere," said Brenner. "In other villages? In the hills in the distance?"

"Yes, there must be others, somewhere," said Rodriguez.

"There would have to be," said Brenner.

"Did you see any children?" asked Rodriguez.

"No," said Brenner.

"Nor did I," said Rodriguez.

"That is interesting," said Brenner.

"Yes," said Rodriguez.

"There must be children," said Brenner.

"Hidden away?" asked Rodriguez.

"Of course," said Brenner.

"Outside the palisade, in the forest?"

Brenner shrugged. That did not seem likely.

"I looked about, as carefully as I could," said Rodriguez. "I could find no evidence of children, no representations, no small furniture, no carrying boards, no cradles, no toys, no tiny clothing, nothing of that sort."

"Interesting," said Brenner.

"Amongst fifty or so females, in a primitive culture," said Rodriguez, "it is almost a certainty that some would be pregnant."

"But you did not detect any evidence of this?"

"No," said Rodriguez.

"They, too, could have been hidden away," said Brenner.

"Outside, in the forest?"

"You still think there is something out there?" asked Brenner.

"I think there are many things out there," said Rodriguez.

CHAPTER 14

"By the gods of ten worlds," exclaimed Rodriguez, in fury, rummaging through his things.

"What is missing now?" asked Brenner, looking up.

"The walnut-brained, grapefruit-headed, thieving little monkeys!" said Rodriguez.

"Do not blame them," said Brenner. "They are curious, they like things, they pick them up, they steal them away. It is their nature."

"Inoffensiveness and innocence are apparently no guarantee of honesty," said Rodriguez.

"No more than in a child," said Brenner. "What is missing now? "

"My shaving mirror," said Rodriguez.

The Pons could indeed be nuisances, thought Brenner. But the shaving mirror was certainly less of a loss than that of certain other items which had similarly vanished, usually when he and Rodriguez were out of their hut.

They had now been in the village for several weeks.

The map in which Rodriguez had been recording their journey, and the compass he had used, had been amongst the first items missing. To be sure, they had disappeared in the journey itself, possibly lost in the fording of a small stream. More serious, since the white guide rocks were still visible, like a necklace connecting the village with the vicinity of Company Station, was the loss of the two radios. That had occurred on the eleventh day in the village. Without them there was no way to expeditiously contact Company Station. Similarly, its air cars, and air trucks, would not have a signal on which to home, in case of emergency.

In the beginning Brenner had been somewhat alarmed by these losses, for it had seemed to him that there might be something of a methodicality in them, as the Pons might, at least in some dim way, understand the meaning of the compass and map, and the radios. They had not taken the rifle, but then it was apparently a mere optical instrument, of no more intrinsic potency than field glasses. Perhaps they had not taken it because they did not understand what it was? But later Brenner's suspicions, absurd as they were, had been fully allayed, when trinkets like a watch, a ring of keys, thimbles from a sewing kit, and, now, a shaving mirror, had also disappeared. In this way he understood that the losses were no more meaningful than what might be attributed to the furtive predations of the home-world's burglar rat or the tiny bandit bird of Chios.

"You can use mine, my shaving mirror," said Brenner.

CHAPTER 15

"Rodriguez," whispered Brenner, tensely.

The hut was dark. It was late at night.

"Wake up," whispered Brenner.

There was no sound from his companion.

"Wake up!" whispered Brenner.

"What is it?" said Rodriguez, sleepily.

"There is something outside," said Brenner.

Brenner heard the sliding of metal. Rodriguez, in the darkness, had armed the rifle.

"Get the torch," said Rodriguez.

Brenner reached out and put his hands on the device. It was a camper's torch, based on a Naxian military model, its pack manually rechargeable, the recharging requiring only a few turns of the crank. Such devices functioned under a variety of conditions and would normally last for years. They were outlawed on several worlds because of the threat they posed to certain segments of the economy.

Brenner stood up, and was conscious that Rodriguez, too, had gained his feet.

They went to the opening of the hut.

They stood there, very quietly, listening.

"I do not hear anything," said Rodriguez.

Brenner was silent.

"Do you?" asked Rodriguez.

"No," said Brenner.

"Turn the torch on," said Rodriguez.

Instantly the beam shot forth, throwing a circle of light before it, bright in the darkness, illuminating the cleared area, even huts across the way.

The light swept back and forth.

"Apparently I was mistaken," said Brenner.

"Give me the torch," said Rodriguez.

Brenner handed the torch to Rodriguez.

Rodriguez focused it on the ground.

"The soil is hard here," said Rodriguez. "It is muchly packed down."

Brenner watched the pool of light moving about. The circle of its illumination was intensely bright at that range. The ground seemed white under it.

"It would be hard to find sign here," said Rodriguez.

"I was probably dreaming," said Brenner.

"Ah!" said Rodriguez, suddenly.

"What is it?" asked Brenner.

"Look," said Rodriguez.

Brenner came to stand beside Rodriguez.

"Here is your dream," said Rodriguez. "It left a footprint."

"That is a print?" asked Brenner.

"I am sure of it," said Rodriguez. "See this scratch here, and this gouge here."

"It is too large," said Brenner.

"I think it is a print," said Rodriguez.

"The ground is hard," said Brenner.

"I think it is a print," averred Rodriguez.

"You can't be sure," said Brenner.

"It walks very softly," said Rodriguez.

He shone the light about.

"Here is another," said he.

"They are too far apart," said Brenner.

"That would depend on the size of the object that made the prints," said Rodriguez.

"You are not going to follow them?" said Brenner, uneasily.

"Would you prefer to go back to sleep?" asked Rodriguez. "Surely you understand this thing may be within the palisade."

"I'll take the light," said Brenner. That would free Rodriguez to use the weapon.

"They lead in this direction," said Rodriguez.

Their figures were dark, like shadows behind the light.

"Let us proceed," said Rodriguez.

Sometimes the light ranged forth, striking ahead of them; sometimes it illuminated the ground, darting here and there, as Rodriguez directed, almost as though taking scent.

"The idiots!" hissed Rodriguez.

The gate to the palisade was open.

"They lead outward," said Rodriguez, in relief. Then he set the rifle inside the palisade, against a pale. "Help me shut the gate," he said. "Quickly! Quickly!"

In a moment he and Brenner, the light put aside, had closed and barred the gate.

"At night," said Rodriguez, "we had best check the gate."

"Right," agreed Brenner. He was shaking and sweating. He did not think that Rodriguez was in much better condition.

"We will examine the tracks in the morning," said Rodriguez. "The light will be much better."

"They may not be tracks," said Brenner.

Rodriguez was silent.

"That is surely possible," said Brenner.

"It will be easier to make a determination on that in the morning."

Rodriguez and Brenner then returned to their hut.

Interestingly, in the morning, they could find nothing. No longer could they detect even the traces which they had seen, or thought that they had seen, the night before. It was as though such things might have been swept away. The Pons, questioned, proved to be of little, or no, assistance.

"We were overwrought," said Brenner. "In the uncertain light, we misinterpreted a mark here and a mark there, certain marks on the ground, meaningless scratches, organizing them, seeing them, in a certain way, which marks, now, scattered and isolated from one another, we aren't even aware of, or at least in no sense different from countless other such marks."

"That is possible," said Rodriguez.

"A reason for thinking that," said Brenner, "would be the width of the marks, and the lightness of them, for the width. That would suggest an animal of unusual size and stealth."

"True," said Rodriguez.

"Did you recognize the prints?" asked Brenner.

Rodriguez did not respond.

"Rodriguez," said Brenner.

"I thought I did," said Rodriguez.

"You had seen such things before?"

"Once," said Rodriguez.

"What sort of animal did you think it might be?" asked Brenner.

"No," said Rodriguez. "It makes no sense."

"What shall we do today?" asked Brenner.

"They do not want us to explore the temple," said Rodriguez.

They had tried to do this unsuccessfully before. Naturally they did not wish to force their way in. The temple was a long, narrow, wooden building whose entryway was of heavy timbers, ornately worked and fitted, and colored, with double doors. About the sides of the temple, on the outside, and over it, earth had been packed. The impression was much like a wooden structure built within a small hill.

"No," said Brenner.

"Let us examine the fields about," said Rodriguez.

"Bring the rifle," said Brenner.

"I shall," Rodriguez smiled.

"Do you think the Pons understand that that is a weapon?" asked Brenner.

"No," said Rodriguez.

"They think it is a telescope?"

"For all a Pon knows it holds Heimat," said Rodriguez.

"Did you mention to the Pons about the gate being left open last night?" asked Brenner.

"Yes," said Rodriguez.

"And what did they say?"

"They said that the gate was not left open, that it was closed, as usual," said Rodriguez.

CHAPTER 16

One afternoon, as Brenner and Rodriguez were returning to their hut, they noticed, behind the hut, two Pons. These two individuals, seeing Brenner and Rodriguez, suddenly moved away from one another, each hurrying off in a different direction.

"One of those Pons was the fellow who struck at you the first day here, wasn't it?" asked Rodriguez.

"Yes," said Brenner.

"I wonder what he was doing there," said Rodriguez.

"You noticed the distance between the two?" said Brenner.

"Yes," said Rodriguez. They had been about five feet apart. They were thus farther apart than one would expect for two males together or two females together, but not nearly as far apart as one would have expected between individuals of opposite sexes.

"That is what they were doing there," smiled Brenner.

"I don't like it," said Rodriguez.

"The Pons would not hurt a fly," said Brenner.

"The members of their own group are not flies," said Rodriguez.

Brenner looked at him.

"Primitive peoples do not look lightly upon the violation of taboos," said Rodriguez. "And the Pons are subprimitive. They are even subrational. They are simian, at best."

"I understand," said Brenner.

"Say nothing to anyone about what we saw," said Rodriguez.

"I will not, of course," said Brenner.

CHAPTER 17

"Apparently something called the Festival of the Harvesting of Seed is to take place shortly," said Rodriguez.

"It is fall," said Brenner. "That makes sense, to gather in seed for the planting in the spring."

They were standing in the clearing, in the center of the village. In this clearing, on a table, in a small, open-sided shelter, its thatched roof supported by four pillars, was a tiny, wire-barred cage, presumably obtained in trade from Company Station. In this cage was a tiny, gray git, not the one which had been captured in the forest, which had been released after the ceremony, with elaborate apologies, but another.

"Greetings, little fellow," said Brenner to the git.

It was large for a git. It crouched on one side of the cage, on some crumbled leaves. Its fur was oily. Its eyes were like bright spots.

Brenner tapped the cage, a little.

"Do not put your finger too close to it," said Rodriguez. "They are wild."

"It should be fed by now," said Brenner.

"There are many varieties of totemism," said Rodriguez, looking down at the git. "Even the concept of the totem animal is interesting, and varies from group to group. I assume the Pons are typical, but it is difficult to get clear on the matter. Certainly the totem animal is seldom identified with a particular animal, which might die or be killed. But, too, it is seldom understood as a species of animal, at least in the scientific sense. It is too real for that. The concept seems to be primitive, substantial, and mystical. It is alien to civilized understanding. The totem is an individual, and alive, as alive as that git, but it is somehow present in many places. It is one in many, so to speak. It lives in many houses. It is neither, say, the git as a species nor that git alone. It is more than both, and beyond both. It sees through both."

The tiny animal in the cage lifted its head, and those tiny, bright eyes regarded Brenner.

"Let us return to the hut," said Brenner.

"The keeper should be along soon," said Rodriguez.

"Let us return to the hut," said Brenner.

But Rodriguez was looking down, at the git.

"Totemism is an insanity," said Brenner, suddenly, angrily.

"It is too widespread for that, in too many cultures, on too many worlds," said Rodriguez.

"We have been here for weeks," said Brenner. "We know little more about the Pons now than we did when we first came through the gate."

"We have gathered a great deal of data," said Rodriguez.

"But it does not fit together," said Brenner. "There is no unity in it, no sense, no meaning."

"There is a meaning in it," said Rodriguez. "It is only that we have not yet detected it."

"There is something about these little beasts which frightens me," said Brenner.

"The Pons?" asked Rodriguez.

"Yes," said Brenner.

"What?" asked Rodriguez.

"I do not know," said Brenner. "They are too simple, too kindly, too inoffensive, too innocent, too good."

"You should be pleased," said Rodriguez. "They confirm all the theories which are so important to you."

Brenner was silent. The git seemed to be looking at him.

"They are the beginning," said Rodriguez. "They are the

proof you have always desired, that the rational races did not begin in crime, that they did not emerge bloodily from the wars of nature in virtue of an uncompromising and superior ruthlessness, that they did not survive, and surpass, their competition in virtue of a more tenacious will and greater savagery, that their success is not to be attributed to the darkness of a heart which, in pride and mercilessness, will proclaim itself chieftain and king. The club, you see, is for pounding grain. It is not a heavier, crueler paw. The knife is for the gathering of fruit. It is not a more efficient fang."

"Do you believe these things?" asked Brenner.

"It seems I must," said Rodriguez.

"I am not at ease with the Pons," said Brenner.

"You could not ask for a more harmless form of life," said Rodriguez.

"I am not sure what it is," said Brenner. "Something about them seems familiar. It is almost as if I knew them, as if I had been here before."

"But you have not been," said Rodriguez.

"No," said Brenner.

"Presumably what you sense are affinities," said Rodriguez. "They exist amongst many species, of diverse sorts. Such affinities make comparative studies possible, and occasionally illuminating. Indeed, it is precisely because of such hypothetical affinities that we have come to Abydos. Naturally they might be occasionally sensed, particularly by a sensitive individual, as a bit eerie, or familiar. Indeed, is it not hoped that the Pons will constitute a lens of sorts, with which to look back, into the past of our own species?"

"We have been sent here, and informed of as much, in so many words," said Brenner, recalling the directress, "to confirm current political theories."

"And it appears we will do so, honestly," said Rodriguez. "It does not even seem that we must keep two sets of notebooks, one to be reviewed by the directress and her superiors, in which the data is faked for publication, the other in which the truth is concealed, for those trusted to understand it."

"I am afraid here," said Brenner.

"Do not fear the Pons," said Rodriguez. "They are simple, they are stupid. They do not even have names."

"There is much here that I do not understand," said Brenner.

"There is much here which I do not understand either," said Rodriguez.

"Where are the children?" asked Brenner. "Where are the other totems, the other clans?"

"I do not know," said Rodriguez.

"How can these things live in the forests?" asked Brenner. "How is it that they can survive here?"

"The totem protects them," said Rodriguez.

"Of course," said Brenner.

The git was looking up at Brenner, with its small, round, shiny eyes.

"Perhaps the forests are not as dangerous as is alleged," said Brenner.

"Perhaps," said Rodriguez.

"I think the keeper wishes to feed the git," said Brenner, looking to one side. The keeper of the git, in his smocklike robe, was now waiting, a few yards to the right. Under the scrutiny of Brenner and Rodriguez he turned about.

"He is a polite fellow," said Rodriguez.

The Pons would seldom meet one's eyes directly.

In many cultures direct eye contact is regarded as a sign of openness, of honesty. In many others, of course, it is regarded as impolite, or obtrusive, and may even be interpreted as a sign of hostility.

Brenner and Rodriguez then withdrew from the small, open-sided, roofed structure, returning to their hut.

It was near noon.

CHAPTER 18

"Let us review," said Rodriguez, looking up from the pages of a large, black notebook.

"I have a headache," said Brenner.

"It is the bemat brew you were given last night," said Rodriguez. This was a fermented beverage derived from the bemat grain, which was the common staple, fried, baked, or boiled, of the Pon diet.

"I do not feel well," said Brenner.

"It was not a strong brew," said Rodriguez.

"You have no ill effects?"

"No," said Rodriguez.

"I did not sleep well," said Brenner.

"I slept splendidly," said Rodriguez.

"I had an odd dream," said Brenner.

"What was it?" asked Rodriguez.

"It doesn't matter," said Brenner.

"One of those dreams?" asked Rodriguez.

"Perhaps," said Brenner, angrily.

"Was she pretty?" asked Rodriguez.

"It was not what you think," said Brenner.

"You do not find the Pon females of interest?" said Rodriguez.

"Certainly not!" said Brenner, angrily.

"Good," said Rodriguez.

"They are like monkeys," said Brenner, angrily.

"Members of our species, sufficiently frustrated, have made do with worse," said Rodriguez. "I remember once, when I was a lad, on Abdera."

"I do not care to hear it," said Brenner.

"Stay away from the Pon females," said Rodriguez.

"You need not fear," said Brenner.

"You are a young man," said Rodriguez. "I should have realized how difficult this would be for you."

"I am all right," said Brenner, angrily.

"We should have brought a contract slut from Company Station along for you," said Rodriguez.

Brenner thought immediately of the brunette.

He would not have minded having her along, totally at his mercy, in the forests.

"But I thought it would be too much extra bother," said Rodriguez. "It is not as though they are slaves, who are no trouble, who are instantly obedient, who are desperate to please, knowing that the integrity of their pretty little hides, and, indeed, their very lives, depends on the perfection of their service."

"Slaves?" said Brenner.

"They stay where you put them, they leap to obey, they plead to be assigned further tasks, that they may to some extent redeem their worthlessness, in being of service to the master."

"Contract women are not slaves," said Brenner.

"Certainly not," said Rodriguez. "But, sooner or later, one supposes, on one world or another, they will learn slavery."

Brenner was silent. He supposed that that was true.

"Perhaps we could have brought your little brunette along, handcuffed, on a leash."

"Please," said Brenner.

"If she dallied, or resisted, we could have stripped her, and lashed her. They step lively enough then."

"Please, Rodriguez," said Brenner.

"Like the slaves they are," said Rodriguez.

Brenner was silent, angry.

"You could have used her, to satisfy your needs. That is what they are good for."

"Rodriguez!" said Brenner.

"But I thought it was too much bother," said Rodriguez.

"You wished to summarize certain matters?" asked Brenner.

"What was your dream?" asked Rodriguez.

"It does not matter," said Brenner.

"It concerned the Pon females," said Rodriguez.

"Yes!" said Brenner.

"What was it?" asked Rodriguez.

"I found myself on a low table, helpless," said Brenner, angrily. "I could scarcely move. I was naked. I was strapped down. Pon females clustered about me, with bowls and vials. They addressed attentions to me, with their tiny hands, their lips and teeth, their mouths. I could not resist. It seemed I slept and awakened so, to the same attentions, several times during the night."

"Such things are a nuisance to clean up in the morning," said Rodriguez.

"I was not soiled," said Brenner.

"That is interesting," said Rodriguez.

"You were concerned to summarize certain matters?"

"Review them," said Rodriguez. "I am trying to bring together some of the things that we know, generally, about totemism."

Brenner nodded. Whereas he and Rodriguez had certainly gathered a great deal of data on the Pons it mostly concerned their behaviors, and not, so to speak, their motivations and intentions. They were more aware of what the Pons did, and how they did it, than why they did it, or, indeed, what it might all be about. Furthermore, there were many varieties of totemism, as an interpreted system. To be sure, they all involved the totem itself, with the reverence and attention accorded to it, and, oddly enough, exogamy, which, embarrassingly, from the scientific point of view, did not seem to fit into the picture at all. It was conjectured by many culture scientists to be an accidental, ultimately inexplicable accretion on totemism, and yet, of course, its universal appearance in the totemistic cultures, particularly as the totemistic institutions had apparently developed independently on diverse worlds, suggested a more intimate relationship. What Rodriguez was up to here was to review certain commonly found totemistic elements. Some of these might be pertinent to the Pons. Too, of course, the Pons might have elements in their system which were local to, or possibly even unique in, their own form of totemism.

"The totem is the tribal ancestor of the clan," said Rodriguez. "It is a sort of tutelary spirit, it acts as a guardian, a protector."

"That probably fits," said Brenner. To be sure, these were almost universal traits of totemism.

"In some cases it warns the clan of danger. It sends oracles to them. It can be used to predict the future."

"I think you would need a priesthood, or medicine men, or shamans for that," said Brenner.

"The Pons are presumably too primitive for that?" said Rodriguez.

"I would think so," said Brenner. "Too, as far as I can tell, there seems to be little hierarchy, or differentiation, amongst Pons."

"True," said Rodriguez.

"Go on," said Brenner.

"We know the strength of the totem bond," said Rodriguez.

"That is clear," said Brenner. "The Pons all claim descent from the totem."

"The totem may not be killed," said Rodriguez. "Its flesh may not be eaten. No use may be made of it whatsoever."

"It is sacrosanct," said Brenner.

"In many cases it is forbidden to touch it," said Rodriguez. "Indeed, in many cases, it is forbidden even to look upon it."

"That does not seem to fit," said Brenner.

"No," said Rodriguez.

"Too," said Brenner, "in various cultures one does not even publicly identify the totem. One conceals the true totem. One does not even dare to refer to the totem by its real name."

"That does not fit," said Rodriguez.

"No," said Brenner.

"The totem group has totem dances, in which the movements and actions of the totem animal are imitated, and the dancers may even disguise themselves as the totem animal itself."

"We have seen no evidence of such dances, or feasts, or festivals," said Brenner.

"The totem is almost always an animal," said Rodriguez, "but it may occasionally be a natural object, and, sometimes, though this is unusual, an artificial, or manufactured, object."

Brenner nodded. On some worlds a discarded watch, or clock, or radio, had been treated as a totem by primitives. But, presumably they had taken it as alive. Did its hands not move, or did it not speak? Later, when the hands were still or the device silent, they would wait patiently for it to move or speak again, sometimes for generations, that it had ever done so becoming a matter of faith. Too, of course, to a savage almost any manufactured object might appear exotic, mysterious, divine, miraculous. Who could understand a rubber ball, its regularity, its consistency, its liveliness, or a glass jar, in its transparency, like ice that did not melt? But most totems were animals. The git, of course, was an animal.

"The animal is a much more likely totem," said Rodriguez. "The primitive mind often regards animals, rather as children are wont to do, as fellow creatures, and equals."

"That is now common on several worlds," Brenner reminded Rodriguez.

"No, I mean *really*," said Rodriguez. "I am not talking about moralistic cant, pretentious moral poses, prescribed hypocrisies, vacuous sentimentalities which are not taken seriously except by an occasional lunatic, and such, no, I mean *really*."

"Oh," said Brenner.

"That is quite different," said Rodriguez.

"True," said Brenner.

"The animal is alive, it is conscious, it is real, it seems much the same to the primitive as himself. He respects it.

He talks to it. He worries about its feelings. He wonders what it is thinking. He begs its pardon if he must kill it."

"Interesting," said Brenner. To be sure, from his point of view, there did not seem much difference between the Pons and the git. To be sure, the Pons did have a culture. They could speak, and such.

"Thus it is a natural choice for the totem," said Rodriguez.

"Doubtless," said Brenner.

"The natural-object totem and the artificial-object totem, thus, would seem to presuppose the animal totem. Such totemisms would seem best understood as being derived from, or suggested by, a more primitive institution of totemism, namely, that of animal totemism.

"Their rareness, too," said Brenner, "would suggest that they are more recent developments."

"Yes," said Rodriguez.

"I think it is very likely," said Brenner, "that with the Pons we are encountering a very early, an almost original, a very pure form of totemism."

"I would think so," said Rodriguez, "particularly considering their inferior mentality, their rudimentary cerebral development, their lack of a technology, their general primitiveness."

"Correct," said Brenner. He was thinking about the brunette, and how beautiful she had been in her chains, on his bed, helpless, pleading with him, tears in her eyes, to be merciless with her, to complete her subjugation, without which she could not be herself.

"The animal chosen is almost always a lively animal," said Rodriguez.

Brenner nodded. Some typical totem animals, he knew, were birds, snakes, lizards and mice. The git, for example, was mouselike.

"Why?" asked Rodriguez.

"I don't know," said Brenner.

"Because they are thought to be ensouled," said Rodriguez.

"There you touch on many common theories, of course," said Brenner.

"Specify," said Rodriguez.

"You know them better than I," said Brenner.

"Which do you have in mind?"

"One theory thinks that the totem is a repository for the savage's outward soul," said Brenner, "that he hides it there, to keep it safe, that he himself may in effect become invulnerable. Another is that the spirits of the dead enter into the totem animals and live on in this fashion. Thus the animals may be reverenced, and thought of as ancestors, and such."

"Such theories seem to me unlikely," said Rodriguez. "Surely the savage is familiar with his own vulnerability, or, if not his own, that of others. Surely he has seen tribal members die while the totem animal survives. Thus his soul is not in the totem animal, who keeps it safe for him. Similarly, if he thought it was his own soul which was in the totem animal, it seems unlikely that he would refer to the totem animal as "father" and "ancestor." It also seems quite unlikely that the savage believes that the spirits of the dead enter into the totem animal. There is presumably one totem, so to speak, not many, not thousands, or hundreds of thousands, one for each departed soul. Too, individual totem animals can obviously die. If each contained a departed soul this might seem to suggest that that soul died, too, which consequence would presumably be regarded as at least unwelcome, if not actually unacceptable. To be sure, one can always save any hypothesis with enough ad-hoc qualifications. The soul might hurry to another totem animal, or something."

"That seems unlikely," said Brenner. "They do speak, however, of the totem as "primal father," as "ancestor," and such."

"But that, too, upon reflection, is a clear mark against the multiple-souls theory," said Rodriguez. "Not all departed souls would be those of males, let alone of fathers. Too, even of fathers, presumably there would be many fathers, not just one."

"True," mused Brenner.

"No," said Rodriguez. "We may regard the totem animal

as ensouled, so to speak, but it would have its own soul, so to speak, not someone else's soul. It is its own thing."

"That seems to me most likely," said Brenner. "What of the theory that the totem animal is a guardian spirit acquired by an ancestor, say, in a dream, and handed down to descendants?"

"Such things are seldom bequeathed," said Rodriguez. "They must be earned independently, often in fasting, prayer, and visions. The medicine animal of the father is seldom that of the son. Too, such things would presumably be handed down, if at all, through a given line of descent, not within an interrelated complexus of descent lines, such as those, say, of phratries and subphratries. Similarly the medicine animal is not regarded as an ancestor, or father. It is more in the nature of a tutelary ally."

"What is your theory?" asked Brenner.

"That the totemistic peoples mean what they say," said Rodriguez. "That they conceive the totem literally as the progenitor of their people, that they think of it, truly, as the primal ancestor, as the father."

"Surely they understand procreation," said Brenner.

"What is clear to you may not be clear to someone else," said Rodriguez, "and, if you were in their place, it might not be clear to you. Procreation is undoubtedly mysterious to many primitive groups, in particular, in societies practicing group marriage, and in societies where descent is traced matrilineally, and so on."

"It is easier to know the mother than the father," smiled Brenner.

"More importantly," said Rodriguez, "it is easier to know that there is a *mother* than that there is a father."

"Interesting," said Brenner.

"Animals are presumably unclear about the nature of procreation," said Rodriguez.

"Surely," said Brenner.

"And often children," said Rodriguez.

"True," said Brenner.

"Consider the matter," said Rodriguez. "Coition and

birth are not resembling events. Too, they are separated in time, often by months. The discovery that they are related, as cause and effect, if you stop to think about it, is actually an intellectual achievement of the first magnitude. Indeed, it is not even possible, obviously, to trace descent patrilineally until this discovery has been made."

"The Pons trace descent matrilineally, supposedly," said Brenner.

"That is universal with totemistic groups," said Rodriguez.

"You think they do not understand procreation?" asked Brenner.

"No," said Rodriguez. "I think it is rather because of the great importance of the totem and the fact that it is easier, as you pointed out, to know the mother than the father. In such a group it is extremely important for the child to know his totem. You must understand that. Too, considering the exogamy regulations it is important that the group know his totem, as well. Without the totem an individual in a totemistic society is lost, so to speak, placeless, homeless, metaphysically orphaned, a creature who does not know himself, a refugee, a wanderer, a stranger, an outcast, something without identity or meaning, one who is without status, one who is, in effect, nothing. He will be scorned. He will be held in contempt. He may even be driven out. In totemistic cultures, thusly, it is natural for descent to be traced matrilineally, that it be to the totem of the mother, and not that of the father, who may not be known, that the child belongs."

"I see," said Brenner.

"You will note the anomaly," said Rodriguez, "that the primal ancestor is referred to as "father," although descent is traced matrilineally."

"They do understand procreation then," said Brenner.

"Or have come to understand it," said Rodriguez. "We may be dealing with cognitive retrojections."

"I do not understand," said Brenner.

"The original concept may not have been, and quite possibly was not, that of a father in the simple biological sense of a progenitor, that might not even have been understood, but of something else, perhaps that of a large, powerful, feared, dreaded, dominant male, a tyrant, a governor, an overlord, a claimer of, herder of, and possessor of, and perhaps a jealous and ruthless possessor of, the group's females."

"This would be presumably with single-adult-male, isolated groups," said Brenner.

"They speak of "father," not "fathers," said Rodriguez.

"That form of social structure is quite at odds with that of the Pons," said Brenner.

"Indeed," said Rodriguez, "it would seem to be, for most practical purposes, the exact opposite."

"It is a possible grouping," said Brenner.

"Such groupings exist," said Rodriguez.

"They can perpetuate themselves?" asked Brenner.

"Certainly," said Rodriguez.

"I think I would fear such a male," said Brenner.

"Your feelings would most likely be a mixture of dread and awe, of fear and reverence," said Rodriguez. "That beast is not only lord and tyrant, but, too, it is clearly understood, he is guide, protector. and leader, keeper of the peace, instiller of order. With him, under his rod of iron, in virtue of his jaws, his might, the jungle is kept at bay. Predators fear him. He makes possible his group. He is a source of security and needed authority."

"But it is an *animal* that is spoken of as "father,"" said Brenner.

"We are dealing with primitives," said Rodriguez. "The concept may be mystical. Too, in a world where little is understood, it might not seem impossible that an animal might father a different form of race."

"It seems I know little more about the Pons now than before," said Brenner.

"Having an animal, and one animal, as the "father,"" said Rodriguez, "solves another problem which has been little noticed, a sort of logical, or philosophical, problem, likely to be frightening to a primitive mind."

"What is that?" asked Brenner.

"It avoids the infinite regress of fathering, with its terrors," said Rodriguez. "If the father had a father, and that father a father, and so on, it seems that there could not be a first father, but the primitive mind wants a first father, but it seems that no ordinary father could be the first father. Thus the series might be begun with a different father, the totem. This gives us a beginning to the line, that desired first father, and one which, because of its nature, other than that of a normal father, stands outside the normal lines of fathering, thus not being itself exposed to the same difficult question of the father's father, and so on, which a *normal* "first father" would require."

"One might ask where the totem came from," said Brenner, "or about its father, and so on."

"No," said Rodriguez. "You are thinking of the totem there as though it were only an ordinary animal, a mere biological creature. It is more than that. It is mystical. It is the totem."

"I see," said Brenner.

"Everyone stops asking questions at one point or another," said Rodriguez. "The only question is where. Where the totemistic savage stops asking them is not obviously inferior to a number of other places, even more obscure or eccentric, where one might stop asking them."

"Perhaps not," said Brenner.

CHAPTER 19

"I have found something I want you to see," said Rodriguez.

Brenner put three pebbles down in the dirt, pressing them into the dust like buttons. He counted them, slowly. "One, two, three."

"One, two, three," said one of the Pons, crouching before him. Present, too, were two other Pons, observing closely, intently.

It was shortly before noon.

"I found it yesterday," said Rodriguez. "I would like you to take a look at it."

"You didn't mention it," said Brenner.

"We will talk on the way," said Rodriguez.

"All right," said Brenner.

"It is unimportant, of course," said Rodriguez.

"What is it?" asked Brenner.

"Something," said Rodriguez.

"I am eager to see it," said Brenner.

"If you have time, of course," said Rodriguez.

"In a minute," said Brenner.

Brenner then wedged three twigs, upright, into the dust.

"Ai!" said Brenner, stung by a small stone flung from the side.

He looked up.

"Get out of here!" said Rodriguez, waving his arm angrily

at a Pon, some feet off, which it presumably regarded as a safe distance. "Get away!" said Rodriguez to the small creature. It bared its tiny teeth at him. Rodriguez took one step toward the tiny creature and it spun about and rushed off, scampering about the edge of the clearing.

"You frightened him," chided Brenner.

"If I could move that fast, and change direction that quickly," said Rodriguez, "I would break his neck."

"Bad Pon! Bad Pon!" one of the Pons scolded the fellow who had flung the pebble, he now turned about, again, and standing some yards off.

"That was your friend, wasn't it?" asked Rodriguez.

It was now baring its teeth at the other Pons. It picked up a handful of dust, too, and flung it angrily, petulantly, in their direction. It was dissipated in the wind, of course.

"You still can't tell them apart, can you?" asked Brenner.

"It was, wasn't it?"

"Yes," said Brenner. Rodriguez was looking after the Pon. It had now hurried away, between two huts.

That Pon, and he alone, had seemed hostile toward Brenner, even from the beginning. Brenner did not understand it. As far as he knew he had done nothing to offend it. It had never bothered Rodriguez.

"It bad Pon," explained one of the Pons to Brenner.

"No," smiled Brenner. "It not bad Pon. All Pons good."

"Yes," said another Pon, its small lips moving apart, in something like a smile, seemingly odd in such a face. "All Pons good."

"Yes," said Brenner.

"Yes," said the Pons present.

Brenner saw the git keeper standing nearby, watching the small group. The keeper had a small vessel of water and a tiny bucket, containing bemat seed. It would soon be time for the git, that in the small wire cage, on the table under the open-sided, roofed structure, to be fed.

"Greetings," said Brenner.

The keeper put down his head, not meeting Brenner's eyes, and hurried to his duties.

"They are shy creatures," said Rodriguez.

"One, two, three," counted Brenner, slowly, pointing to each upright twig in turn.

"One, two, three," said the first Pon, proudly.

Brenner then put his left hand over the three pebbles.

"Three," he said.

"Three," said the Pons.

He then put his right hand over the twigs. "Three," he said.

"Three," said the Pons.

Brenner then folded his arms, and said, very distinctly, "Three."

"Three stones?" asked the first Pon.

"Three sticks?" asked another.

"No," said Brenner. "Just three—*three*."

The Pons looked at Brenner, and at one another, puzzled.

"They cannot grasp the concept," said Rodriguez.

"Look," said Brenner. He pointed to the three stones, and said, "Three," and then to the three twigs, and said, "Three," and he then counted the Pons, too. "One, two, three," he said.

The Pons looked at one another.

"They have probably never thought of themselves as objects, capable of being counted," said Rodriguez.

"Do you think they would find it alarming, or demeaning?" asked Brenner. He had certainly not wanted to frighten or offend the Pons.

"No," said Rodriguez. "It is merely that they may very well not have achieved that sort of perspective. Indeed, the adoption of such a perspective, an external perspective, a sort of standing outside oneself, doubtless constitutes some sort of scientific achievement. A baby presumably does not think of itself as being one baby, or even a baby, presumably."

"Three Pons!" said the lead Pon, suddenly. "Three Pons!" It leaped up and down. It said, excitedly, "One Pon, two Pons, three Pons!"

"Good! Good!" said Brenner. "Good!" He held the Pon by the arms and shook it delightedly.

"Good!" said the Pon.

"We shall call that one "Archimedes,"" said Rodriguez.

"Do not be cynical," said Brenner, delightedly. "It is wonderful."

"Look," said Rodriguez to Brenner. Then he turned to the Pons. He pointed to the three pebbles first, and then to the three twigs, and then to the three Pons. Then he did not point to any of the three groups, neither that of pebbles, nor twigs, nor Pons. "Three!" he said.

The Pons looked about, eagerly, but then, after a moment, regarded Rodriguez, perplexed.

"Do you see?" Rodriguez asked Brenner.

"Perhaps," said Brenner.

"Experiments have demonstrated that even rodents can grasp the concept of threeness," said Rodriguez, in disgust. "They can be taught to locate food behind a panel marked with three objects, circles, or lines, or such."

"Pons can do that," said Brenner. "It is only that they have not yet grasped the concept of pure number. That is an abstraction of the second order."

"Do not grow too fond of these things," said Rodriguez. "You do not know what they are."

"What do you mean?"

"You do not know what they think, what goes on in their heads," said Rodriguez.

"That is all for now," said Brenner. He pulled up the twigs, like tiny stakes, and dropped them back on the ground. He stood up. He dusted off the knees of his trousers.

The Pons, too, stood up. They had been squatting down in front of him.

"What is it that you wanted to show me?" asked Brenner.

"You are supposed to be investigating these things," said Rodriguez, "not teaching them mathematics."

"They need help," said Brenner.

"Let others help them, after our work is done, perhaps in another generation or two," said Rodriguez. "You are here to study them, in as original, pure, and untouched a form as is possible. You want to find out how they are now, and why they are as they are, not start them being different. You may be contaminating the data. You may be jeopardizing the study."

"We have made little enough progress," said Brenner.

"Do not change them, or interfere with them," said Rodriguez.

"Is that an order?" smiled Brenner.

"Yes," said Rodriguez.

"I think they like me," said Brenner.

"You do not know that," said Rodriguez.

"They have probably received little enough respect, and little enough decent treatment, from members of our species," said Brenner.

"Do not interfere with them, and do not lose your objectivity," said Rodriguez.

"I want to win their confidence," said Brenner.

"You could as easily win the confidence of the git," said Rodriguez. He gestured with his head toward the git in its cage on the table, in the shelter, in the clearing. Its keeper had now finished feeding it.

"What did you want to show me?" asked Brenner.

Rodriguez looked down at the Pons. "Some pretty rocks I found to the southwest," he said.

The Pons looked up, blinking.

"Go away," said Rodriguez. "Go away."

They scurried away.

"You are prepared to leave now?" asked Brenner.

"Yes," said Rodriguez. "And you?"

"Of course," said Brenner.

The two men then started for the gate of the palisade.

They looked back, once.

"Look," said Rodriguez. "Surely that is your little friend."

"Yes," said Brenner, ruefully.

The Pon, he who had thrown the stone, he who had bared his teeth to Rodriguez, and to the other Pons, had apparently sneaked back to the place of the lesson. He was picking up the pebbles, one by one. He then flung them away, scattering them. He picked up the twigs, too, from where Brenner had left them on the ground, and flung them

away, as well. He then looked up, and, seeing the eyes of
Rodriguez and Brenner upon him, bared his teeth, defiantly,
and then hurried away.

"Pleasant fellow," said Rodriguez.

"He will not let me approach him, or make friends," said
Brenner.

"The recorder is missing," said Rodriguez.

"This morning?" asked Brenner.

"Yes," said Rodriguez.

"Last week it was a buckle and shoelaces," said Brenner.

"The week before that the camera," said Rodriguez.

"We transcribed the material from the recorder," said
Brenner. They had done that in case of damage to, or
deterioration of, the recording. "And we never used the
camera," he added, "so we have not lost any material there."

"They are thieving gits," said Rodriguez.

"They are like children," said Brenner.

"It is one thing to steal a handful of glass beads," said
Rodriguez. "It is another to make off with a thousand-credit
camera."

"To them it is only another belt buckle," said Brenner.

"They are thieves," said Rodriguez.

"No, they are Pons," smiled Brenner.

"There is no one even to complain to," said Rodriguez.
"There are no mayors, no governors, no police."

"No state," said Brenner.

"Good for them," growled Rodriguez.

"Unless perhaps something like a "state of nature,""
mused Brenner.

"Perhaps they can get around to the social compact,
someday," said Rodriguez.

"I have questioned several Pons about these things," said
Brenner, "but have obtained no satisfaction. I am not even
sure they understand what I am talking about."

Rodriguez grunted, angrily.

"They may not have a concept of private property," said
Brenner.

"And thus not of theft?"

"Precisely," said Brenner.

"Even mice have such a concept," said Rodriguez. "They are not good at sharing pieces of cheese."

"Perhaps the Pons believe that property itself is theft," said Brenner.

"Tell that to someone who has worked for it," said Rodriguez.

"They may believe it," said Brenner.

"That is usually said by someone who is preparing to steal something from someone else," said Rodriguez.

"Do not be cynical," said Brenner. "The Pons, of all forms of life with which I am familiar, that is, encultured forms, most closely approximates the ideal of total egalitarianism, and not in political myth, reenacting familiar charades, but in reality."

"They are primitive," granted Rodriguez.

"That is not what I meant," said Brenner.

"Nature is aristocratic," said Rodriguez.

"You suggest then, that the Pons are not, in effect, in a state of nature?"

"Does it seem so to you?" asked Rodriguez.

"How would I know?" asked Brenner.

"Consider nature," said Rodriguez.

"I do not understand," said Brenner.

"In it there is always distance, rank and hierarchy," said Rodriguez.

"Then the Pons would not seem to be in a state of nature," said Brenner.

"No," said Rodriguez.

"Yet they are surely primitive," said Brenner.

"Yes," said Rodriguez.

"Do you think that our little friend, the one who seems to have taken such a dislike to me, is the thief?" asked Brenner.

"No," said Rodriguez. "I don't think he would even touch anything of yours."

"He hates me too much?"

"It would seem so," said Rodriguez.

"Who then?" asked Brenner.

"It need not be one," said Rodriguez. "It could be several of them, one at one time, another at another time."

The two men had now passed well beyond the palisade, and were moving southwest from the village.

"Have you noticed that the attitude of the females toward you has been different lately?" asked Rodriguez.

"No," said Brenner. "Have you?"

"I am not sure," said Rodriguez. "It is something subtle, but I think it is there."

"I did not even know you could tell them apart," said Brenner.

"It is not easy," said Rodriguez.

"I am surprised you didn't strip a couple of them," said Brenner.

"I did, the first week in the village," said Rodriguez.

"No!" said Brenner, horrified.

"They are only Pons," Rodriguez reminded him.

"You told me nothing of this," said Brenner, angrily.

"I was not sure you would approve," said Rodriguez.

"I do not!" said Brenner.

"Why not?" asked Rodriguez.

"It is terrible!" said Brenner.

"It is all in the interest of science," said Rodriguez.

"You should not have done it," said Brenner, angrily.

"It is not like removing the clothing of a free female of our own species," said Rodriguez.

"That is not the point," said Brenner.

"And even there," said Rodriguez, "once they understand there are no two ways about it, and feel the lash once or twice, they are quick enough to comply."

"I see," said Brenner.

"No longer then do they waste your time."

"I do not wish to hear this," said Brenner.

"Surely scientists of other species have seldom hesitated to subject members of our species to such examinations."

"That is irrelevant," said Brenner.

"It makes the point about the interests of science," said

Rodriguez. It was true, of course, that the members of Rodriguez and Brenner's species, as being life forms, were of interest, along with other sorts of species, to various forms of scientist. Members of Rodriguez' and Brenner's species, as we have indicated earlier, were usually held in low esteem, and often actually in contempt, throughout the galaxy. There were many reasons for this, which it would be tedious to recount. They were occasionally removed from vessels for purposes of study. On some worlds they were kept as pets. It was not unusual, either, to find them in zoological gardens.

"What did you find?" asked Brenner.

"Minimalistic, but distinctive, sexual differentiation," said Rodriguez.

"Interesting," said Brenner.

"It seems almost of a vestigial nature," said Rodriguez.

"Interesting," said Brenner.

"You have not noted any difference on the part of the females toward you lately?"

"In maintained distances, or something?" said Brenner.

"In anything," said Rodriguez.

"No," said Brenner.

"I am probably mistaken," said Rodriguez.

Rodriguez and Brenner were now at some distance from the palisade.

Brenner noted that Rodriguez had with him the Naxian rifle, disguised as an optical instrument. That made sense, of course, as they were now in the forest.

"Why are you turning about?" asked Brenner. "I thought we were going southwest?"

"We are going to the northeast," said Rodriguez.

"To see some pretty rocks?" asked Brenner. He seemed to recall that that was what Rodriguez had wanted to show him.

"Don't be silly," said Rodriguez.

"What is it then?" asked Brenner.

"You will see," said Rodriguez.

Brenner brushed aside a low-hanging lantern fruit.

"Is it far?" asked Brenner.

"No," said Rodriguez.

"It could have been reached much more easily from the village," said Brenner.

"Of course," said Rodriguez.

"I do not like keeping things from the Pons," said Brenner.

"I have no objection to doing so," said Rodriguez.

"This is not the way to win their trust."

"Do not concern yourself," said Rodriguez. "They are no more capable of trust than a git."

"I do not believe that," said Brenner.

"They are sly, sneaky, secretive little bastards," said Rodriguez.

"No," said Brenner. "They are simple, innocent, loving, and childlike."

"And they are thieves," said Rodriguez.

"But only like children," said Brenner.

"Or gits," said Rodriguez.

"If we are going to go this way, we should let them know," said Brenner.

"Nonsense," said Rodriguez.

"I do not think this is in the best interests of the study."

"That may be better judged later," said Rodriguez.

They continued on their way. Some minutes later, they were northeast of the village.

"What is it you are looking for?" asked Brenner. "There," said Rodriguez, stopping, pointing. "There it is. I must have passed it a dozen times in the past weeks and not noticed it."

"Where? What?" asked Brenner.

"There," said Rodriguez.

"That?" asked Brenner.

"Yes," said Rodriguez.

"What is its meaning?" asked Brenner.

"I don't know," said Rodriguez.

"How far does it go?"

"I don't know," said Rodriguez.

"You intend to follow it?"

"Certainly," said Rodriguez.

"How did you find it?" asked Brenner.

"It became clear to me almost from the first that the Pons did not want me to explore in this direction. Accordingly, I determined to find out why. Again and again I returned to this area, usually, as today, by a circuitous route. I only located this yesterday."

"What do you make of it?" asked Brenner.

"Be careful of it," said Rodriguez.

"What do you make of it?" asked Brenner.

"It marks some sort of trail," said Rodriguez. "I am sure of it."

"I don't want to be out of the village after dark," said Brenner.

"Nor do I," said Rodriguez. "I am not insane."

"What do you want to do?" asked Brenner.

"We will return to the village, approaching it from the southwest. In the morning we will return, again by a circuitous route."

"I have one amendation," said Brenner.

"What is that?" asked Rodriguez.

"We will do this openly. We will not betray the trust of the Pons. I seriously think that an attempt to deceive them in this matter might doom the study. One of them might see. Everything might be ruined."

"I am going to follow it," said Rodriguez. "I will do it with you or without you."

"And with or without the approval of the Pons?"

"Yes," said Rodriguez.

"Regardless of their wishes, their attitudes, or feelings?"

"Certainly," said Rodriguez.

"You think this is important?"

"Yes."

"I will come with you," said Brenner.

Rodriguez nodded.

"But we must do this openly."

"As you wish," said Rodriguez.

"It is almost as though it were not there," said Brenner.

"It is there," said Rodriguez.

"It is hard to see," said Brenner.

"Do not break it," warned Rodriguez.

Brenner fingered the string, stretched between the trees. It was not easy to see, but it was there, the string.

The Pon who had followed them returned first to the village. Rodriguez did not notice the small prints of its feet on their backtrail.

CHAPTER 20

"Perhaps it is here that they celebrate the Festival of the Harvesting of Seed," said Brenner.

"It is far from the fields," said Rodriguez.

"They might celebrate it here," said Brenner.

"It would be more likely, I would think, to do it in the village, or near the village," said Rodriguez. "Perhaps it is done in the temple."

"Why not here?" asked Brenner, putting out his hand, to the surface of the platform.

"This place does not look used," said Rodriguez. "It could be dangerous here, too, this far from the palisade. There have been beasts about. Look there. There are claw marks on the surface of the platform."

Brenner was not pleased with what he saw. Some of the furrows on the platform were better than a half inch deep. Similar furrows defaced a nearby post.

"Surely this place must have some purpose," said Brenner.

"Or once had," said Rodriguez. "Look at the age of these timbers, the weathering of them."

"You do not think anything occurs here now?"

"No," said Rodriguez. "This place is deserted, forgotten. The Pons may not even know it is here."

"It may belong to their history," said Brenner.

"Possibly," said Rodriguez.

"The string led here," said Brenner.

"That is true," said Rodriguez.

"And surely that is not as old as the platform."

"That is true," said Rodriguez. "But it could be kept up as a matter of tradition, that the string be there, that it lead here, perhaps for no reason even remembered now."

"Such things are not unknown amongst primitive peoples," said Brenner.

"Nor even amongst others," said Rodriguez.

Rodriguez and Brenner had followed the string, that gray, frail, worn, dried strand, strung between trees, to a sort of hemispheric amphitheater, floored with flat stones, carefully fitted together, at one end of which was which was a low, broad, sturdy platform. This platform was apparently very old, and it was surely muchly worn and weathered. Here and there traces of paint were detectable on its surface, these suggesting it had once been the object of careful decoration.

"Why is the platform not of stone, like the amphitheater?" said Brenner.

"I don't know," said Rodriguez.

"Those claw marks are frightening," said Brenner.

"Yes," said Rodriguez.

"This place seems eerie," said Brenner, "with the cliffs behind the platform."

"We might be able to see the village from the cliffs," said Rodriguez.

"You were wrong about one thing," said Brenner.

"What is that?" asked Rodriguez.

"We set off quite openly in this direction this morning," said Brenner, "and no one attempted to dissuade us."

"I assure you they were clear in their attempts to deter me in the past," said Rodriguez.

"You were surprised then this morning?"

"Yes," said Rodriguez.

"There was no interference."

"No," said Rodriguez.

"Nor even, if I am not mistaken, any sign of particular interest."

"No," said Rodriguez.

"You were then mistaken about things before."

"I do not think so," said Rodriguez.

"What is the difference then?" asked Brenner.

"I do not know," said Rodriguez.

"Perhaps they wanted us out of the village, so they could celebrate the Festival of the Harvesting of Seed," mused Brenner.

"No," said Rodriguez. "That much I know."

"How so?" asked Brenner.

"It was apparently celebrated some days ago," said Rodriguez.

"I did not know that," said Brenner.

"They are sneaky little bastards," said Rodriguez.

"It would not be surprising if the rituals, having to do with things of importance to their very survival, the harvesting of seed, and such, were secret. They might fear the presence of strangers might profane their mysteries, or impair their efficacy. Such fears are common with simple peoples."

"There does not seem to be much here," said Rodriguez. His voice, as he spoke toward the cliffs, had an extra ring.

"Rodriguez," said Brenner.

"What?" asked Rodriguez.

"I have an idea, said Brenner.

"What?" asked Rodriguez.

"The Pons did not wish you to explore to the northeast?"

"No," said Rodriguez. "But I did so often enough. I merely took a different route, and then circled about. They are stupid."

"They did not object today."

"No," said Rodriguez.

"Why not?" asked Brenner.

"I do not know," said Rodriguez.

"What was the difference?" asked Brenner.

"I do not know," said Rodriguez.

"I am the difference," said Brenner.

"I do not understand," said Rodriguez.

"Don't you see?" said Brenner, delightedly.

"No," said Rodriguez.

"They trust me."

"I don't understand," said Rodriguez, slowly.

"We are successful," said Brenner. "My efforts, my attention, my kindness, the simple decency of my intentions, my interest in them, my concern for their well-being, my solicitude for their happiness, my desire to be of service to them, to help them, to care for them, have been recognized, and appreciated, and accepted."

"What are you saying?" asked Rodriguez.

"I think they like me," said Brenner.

"Do not be sure of it," said Rodriguez. "They may not be capable of liking anything."

"I have, if I am not mistaken," said Brenner, "earned their respect and trust."

"Do not count on it," said Rodriguez.

"I think this is a day for which I have long striven," said Brenner. "I think I am important to them. I think they will listen to me. I think that I have at last won their confidence!"

"That, if true, may be useful in our inquiries," said Rodriguez.

"It goes far beyond that," said Brenner, angrily. "It is a victory of trust, of emotion, of civilization."

"I think I will climb these cliffs," said Rodriguez, looking up to the steepnesses behind the platform.

"Don't you understand?" asked Brenner. "I may be able to help them."

"They can't understand the concept of "three,"" said Rodriguez.

"Why do you hate them?" asked Brenner.

"They are monkeys," said Rodriguez.

"You said they were at the "beginning"!"

"That is what makes them important, not lovable," said Rodriguez.

"There is more to them than you understand," said Brenner.

"You do not even know what they are," said Rodriguez.

"I do not understand," said Brenner.

"You are romanticizing them," said Rodriguez. "You are reading your own mentality, and interests, and such, into them. You are committing the anthropomorphic fallacy."

"They are on the brink of civilization," said Brenner.

"They are subrational."

"We can help them!"

"Do not interfere with them," said Rodriguez. "You are here to study them, not change them."

"You are cruel," said Brenner.

"You do not even know what they are," said Rodriguez.

"I understand them, and you do not," said Brenner.

"You could as easily understand a git," said Rodriguez.

"And you are good for only Heimat and weed!" cried Brenner.

"There is a sort of path, or trail, here," said Rodriguez.

"I am sorry, Rodriguez," said Brenner.

"I wish I did have some Heimat and weed," said Rodriguez.

"They are totemistic," said Brenner.

"And so are thousands of other life forms, far more advanced," said Rodriguez.

Brenner leaped lightly to the surface of the platform. Its surface, here and there, was deeply, widely scarred, apparently from having been torn at with claws. He stood there for a moment, in something like awe. He had not appreciated the full extent or depth of these things before, as they had not been so evident from his former angle of vision.

"Come along," invited Rodriguez.

"Have you seen the markings on the platform?" asked Brenner.

"Yes," said Rodriguez.

"From up here?"

"Yes," said Rodriguez.

"What could make such marks?" asked Brenner.

"I know something that could," said Rodriguez. "But it is impossible."

"Do you hear something?" asked Brenner.

"No," said Rodriguez. "Come along."

Brenner scrambled up a yard or so behind Rodriguez.

"Do not put your hand anywhere you cannot see," said Rodriguez.

Brenner knew enough not to do that. On ledges, sunning themselves, soaking up the sunlight, even now, in the late fall, there might be various snakes, some of them poisonous. There was the possibility of unpleasant arachnids, as well, tarantulas, in particular, occasional scorpions, and such.

"I hear something," said Brenner.

"I am now sure of it," said Rodriguez.

"You hear it?" asked Brenner.

"Consider the height," said Rodriguez.

"What?" asked Brenner.

"That we will be able to see the village from the top," said Rodriguez. "It is almost certain that these are the cliffs which are visible from the village."

The path up the cliff, while it was rather steep, was not precipitous. Indeed, here and there there was the clear sign of a carved step. Something, at one time, at any rate, doubtless in the distant past, had used that path.

"Ah!" said Rodriguez, hoisting himself to the height of the cliff.

"I hear it quite clearly now," said Brenner, stopping on the ascent, looking about.

"Come up," said Rodriguez.

In a moment Brenner had attained the level and was beside Rodriguez.

"There is the village," said Rodriguez, pointing.

"Yes," said Brenner uneasily. He could see the palisade, and the village within, tiny, thatched, with smoke from cooking fires ascending into the sky, located in the center of a large, environing clearing.

"What is wrong?" asked Rodriguez.

"Surely you can hear it now?" said Brenner.

"You have excellent hearing," said Rodriguez.

"Listen," said Brenner.

Yes!" said Rodriguez.

The sound was faint, but it was clear now. It was a bit difficult to interpret, of course. Something in it sounded like a pack, except that there was no baying, no barking. There were, in it, the sounds of more than one organism.

One thing was clear. They were not silent runners, one of the forms of life in the forest, humped, crested quadrupeds which, in groups of five to ten, were wont to pursue a quarry in deadly silence, if necessary, for hours at a time.

"It is Pons," said Brenner.

"Yes," said Rodriguez.

There was no mistaking the sounds of Pons, that particular vocal timber, that special quality of sound produced by their tiny throats, but these noises, though doubtless of Pons, seemed somehow anomalous emanating from such small, gentle creatures. These sounds seemed unusually shrill, angry, hysterical, even vengeful.

"There must be several of them," said Brenner.

"You would come here openly," said Rodriguez, in disgust.

"I don't think this has anything to do with us," said Brenner.

Rodriguez unslung the Naxian rifle.

"They are coming this way," said Brenner.

"Step back, do not let them see you," said Rodriguez.

"No," said Brenner. "We have nothing to hide."

"There must be another way down," said Rodriguez, backing away.

Brenner heard the arming of the Naxian rifle.

"Do not do anything foolish," said Brenner.

Rodriguez was somewhere behind him. He was not, presumably, as Brenner was, standing on the edge of the cliff, outlined against the sky.

"Something is coming from the trees!" said Brenner. "It is alone! No, it is being followed! It is a Pon. It is being pursued by other Pons!"

"Look here!" cried Rodriguez. "There is a path down here, on the other side. And there is a valley between cliffs. There are openings of some sort in the far cliff."

"Come here!" said Brenner.

"The openings are not natural," said Rodriguez. "They are squared, rectangular."

"It is running this way!" said Brenner.

"I think it is a burial place, a graveyard," said Rodriguez.

The tiny Pon, several yards before its pursuers, hurried into the amphitheater.

"It's below!" said Brenner. "This may be a place of sanctuary!"

"Do not let them see you!" said Rodriguez.

"It is on the platform!" said Brenner.

The Pon below, on the heavy platform, was casting about, wildly.

It is highly unlikely this is a place of sanctuary," said Rodriguez. "Come away. Do not let them see you. There is a path down, on this side."

"It sees me!" said Brenner. "So, too, do the others! They are not stopping!"

"This is no place of sanctuary," said Rodriguez, grimly. He now stood beside Brenner, in full view. He had his arm in the sling of the weapon, to steady it, in firing.

The fleeing Pon, having seen Brenner, now began to scramble up the cliff side.

"What are they going to do to it?" asked Brenner.

"Kill it," speculated Rodriguez.

"No!" said Brenner.

In an instant the fleeing Pon had reached Brenner and, whimpering and howling, clutched his leg, pressing itself against it.

The other Pons, below, on the path up, stopped. The path was narrow, and Brenner and Rodriguez, even without the rifle, could have defended it against such tiny foes, however militant.

"She is frightened," said Brenner. He touched the head of the Pon, soothingly.

"It is a she?" said Rodriguez.

"Certainly," said Brenner.

"You are aware that distances have been breached," said Rodriguez.

The Pon looked up at Brenner, her eyes wide. Her nostrils, almost flat with her face, opened and closed. The downlike hair on the tiny face glistened with sweat.

"Do not be afraid," said Brenner.

She pulled at his pants' leg.

"I do not understand," said Brenner.

"If it was a pet ferric, you'd understand," said Rodriguez. "She wants you to go with her."

"It is all right," said Brenner to the other Pons, several of which were on the ascent, and several others of which were below, on the platform, or on the flooring of the amphitheater. Several carried tiny, pointed sticks. "Nothing is wrong. Everything is all right now." He then said to the Pon near him. "Do not be afraid. I won't let them hurt you."

Again she pulled at his pants' leg.

"She wants you to go back to the village," said Rodriguez. "There is some reason."

"I don't understand," said Brenner.

"It is no accident she is here," said Rodriguez. "The village knew we went this way. She doubtless came looking for you. She wants you to go back with her."

"Then we will go back," said Brenner. He then faced the other Pons, very calmly. "We will go back home," he said. "Things are all right now. There is no trouble. We will go back home now."

They looked at him for a moment, and then those on the path turned about, and began to descend.

"I think you have managed it," said Rodriguez, removing the rifle sling from his arm.

Brenner picked up the quivering Pon in his arms, gently. She weighed no more than twenty to thirty Commonworld pounds. He then, carefully, began the descent, toward the platform, and the flooring of the amphitheater. Rodriguez revolved the plating on the rifle, returning it to its normal guise.

CHAPTER 21

"Get away from him!" screamed Brenner.
The two Pons near the conical cage, suspended from a tripod of saplings, startled, scurried back, the points of their sticks red.

The small female which Brenner had rescued on the cliffs began to howl.

"There is nothing you can do for him now," said Rodriguez.

"It is eerie," said Brenner.

"Seeing such things in another life form?" said Rodriguez.

"Yes," whispered Brenner.

"Such things occur in many life forms," said Rodriguez.

"It is like a hideous mockery, a grotesque travesty, of the cruelty of our own species," said Brenner.

"The Pons are higher on the evolutionary scale than I realized," said Rodriguez. "Only rational species cage and torture their own kind."

"We were too late," said Brenner.

"You came as fast as you could," said Rodriguez. "He was probably dead hours ago."

Brenner regarded the tiny, hairy, bloodied, naked form cramped within the bars of the suspended, conical cage. It must have been poked with sharpened sticks a great number of times. Its fur was a mass of bloody spots. Blood stained the bottom of the cage, and the lower bars. Too, below the cage, the dust was reddened, where blood had apparently run.

"Besides," said Rodriguez, "it is perhaps better if we were too late."

Brenner looked at him.

"We do not know what was going on here," said Rodriguez. "This is a matter amongst the Pons. These things are their business. We should not interfere."

"You can't be serious," said Brenner.

"What you might have been tempted to do might not have been in the best interest of the study."

"The study is not important," said Brenner.

"These are not members of our species," said Rodriguez. "If you saw ten gits biting another to death would you thrust your hand amongst them?"

"Probably not," said Brenner.

"If you saw ten monkeys attacking an eleventh would you feel obliged to rush amongst them?"

"These are not monkeys," said Brenner.

"They are obviously a similar life form," said Rodriguez.

"They are rational," said Brenner.

"Subrational, or, at best, incipiently rational, or protorational," said Rodriguez.

"Rational enough," said Brenner. "Do they not cage and torture their own kind?"

"Even if so, you do not know the nature of their rationality," said Rodriguez.

"Rationality is one," said Brenner.

"That is highly unlikely," said Rodriguez.

"I might have been able to prevent a murder," said Brenner.

"You might have interfered with an execution," said Rodriguez.

The tiny female was whimpering now, and rocking back and forth.

Brenner reached out, to touch her, in sympathy, but Rodriguez held back his arm. "Put your pity aside," said Rodriguez. "Remember that it is only an animal. Too, it is agitated. It might bite."

Brenner looked at him, angrily.

"You have already violated the distances," said Rodriguez.

Brenner straightened up. Rodriguez was right, of course. The distances were doubtless to be respected. He did not wish to risk, either through ignorance or inadvertence, placing the small female in jeopardy. He had just learned, this afternoon, to his dismay, that the benignity of the Pons, exhibited even in such small matters as their respect for, and benevolence toward, insects, and such, need not be invariably extended, under all circumstances, to the members of their own species. This was not unprecedented, of course. Those who flew the banners of love were commonly the first to demand the destruction of those who disagreed with them. A thousand histories were stained with the blood of heretics. Too, in all honesty he doubted that his touch would much comfort the tiny, forlorn beast.

"Look," whispered Rodriguez.

"The git keeper, with two other Pons, was approaching. They carried pointed sticks.

"Do not interfere," Rodriguez cautioned him.

"I have already interfered," said Brenner.

"More are coming," said Rodriguez. They were mostly males. That could be told from the distances, if nothing else. Females hung about the edges of what was now becoming a circle. More than one male carefully approached, avoiding them.

"There must be fifty or sixty of them," said Rodriguez.

Brenner took a step closer, a protective step, toward the tiny female a few feet in front of him.

"I will not let them hurt her," said Brenner under his breath.

"Do not interfere," said Rodriguez, softly, tensely.

"I will not let them hurt her," said Brenner.

"You will ruin the study," said Rodriguez.

"I will not let them hurt her," said Brenner.

"It is an animal, a monkey," said Rodriguez. "That is what they all are. Do not interfere."

"They are not going to hurt her," said Brenner, determinedly.

"Look," said Rodriguez.

Some four Pons were now carrying forth three poles, with some rope. Two more, behind them, held a cage of saplings, tiny, and conical. They came through the males gathered about and tied the poles together at one end, and fastened the cage of saplings to it, by more rope. They then set the poles up, as a tripod, the cage dangling from it. It was set up at the proper distance from the other tripod and cage. One of the Pons then opened the door of the tiny cage, and gestured to the small female to come forward and enter it.

She looked around, wildly, at Brenner.

"Do not interfere," said Rodriguez.

Brenner put out his hand. The tiny female hurried to him, and put her hand in his. Several of the Pons about, in particular those who had not been at the amphitheater, gasped. Their eyes widened in fear.

One of the Pons at the cage angrily gestured again toward the small opening.

"No," said Brenner, firmly. "No."

The Pons looked at one another. Rodriguez was pleased that they were so small.

"No," repeated Brenner, in a kindly, but firm, voice.

"No?" said one of the Pons, puzzled.

"No," said Brenner.

The git keeper, with his pointed stick held in two hands, lifted, the point toward the tiny female, took a step forward. Brenner, with an angry scowl, released the hand of the female and stood squarely between her and the git keeper.

The git keeper, his way barred by Brenner, who to him must surely have constituted a considerable, menacing obstacle, stopped.

"Touching!" cried one of the Pons shrilly, pointing to the crumpled form in the cage and then to the small female. "Touching! Touching!"

"They must have violated the distances," said Rodriguez. "They may even have touched."

It may be recalled that the two central tenets of totemism, its most fundamental doctrines, so to speak, have to do with the veneration of the totem animal and exogamy, that the females of the totem group are denied to the males of the same totem.

"It does not matter," said Brenner.

"It is the violation of a taboo," said Rodriguez. "That is serious here."

"It does not matter," said Brenner.

"The violation of a taboo must be punished by the group," said Rodriguez. "If it is permitted for the taboo to be broken, the example will be contagious. Do you not understand? It is like condoning crime. It is like saying that the bonds of the community are unimportant. It is like saying everything is permitted. It is to threaten the foundations of society. It will produce moral anarchy. Chaos will ensue. There is a reason for these things, even if you do not know it, or they. They are afraid that a taboo should be violated. They fear that the violation of the taboo, the betrayal of the totem animal, and their pledge to it, the sundering of the pact with the totem, if not punished, will being disaster upon the group. They are afraid. Understand them."

"There is nothing to fear," said Brenner.

"They fear the vengeance of the totem," said Rodriguez.

"The totem is a git," said Brenner.

"They are afraid," said Rodriguez.

"There is nothing to fear," said Brenner.

"It is their perceptions which are important here," said Rodriguez. "Not yours."

"I will not let them harm her," said Brenner. "No!" he said angrily to the git keeper, who had inched forward. The git keeper looked about, frightened, at the others. Two of the Pons began to wail. Some looked back to the palisade, and to the forest beyond, which seemed quiet and dark. Again Rodriguez was pleased that they were so small.

"There is nothing to be afraid of," said Brenner, softly, to the Pons about.

"You are threatening their way of life," said Rodriguez. "You do not even know the reasons for these things. They doubtless do not know them themselves."

"It is time they outgrew their superstitions," said Brenner.

"I am trying to explain this to you," said Rodriguez, quietly. "Try to understand it. If taboo is violated, and left unpunished, the pact with the totem, the very foundation of their way of life, is breached. This will call forth the wrath of the totem. It may punish them for their infidelity, for their crime. At the least it will no longer accord them its protection."

"The totem is a git," said Brenner.

"I am not sure of that," said Rodriguez.

"Get back!" said Brenner, angrily, fiercely, to the git keeper. It scurried back, to stand beside the one cage, with its bloodied, crumpled occupant.

"Touched! Touched! Touched!" shrieked the git keeper. With his stick he pointed at the figure in the cage, and then at the female, again and again.

"Maybe no touch," said Rodriguez. "Maybe mistake. Maybe no touch!"

"Saw! Saw! Saw!" shrilled the git keeper.

"It does not matter," said Brenner to the git keeper. "It is all right to touch."

There was then a great silence in the clearing.

"Yes," said Brenner, quietly. "It is all right to touch." It was strange in a way, he thought, that he, from the home world, should be saying this. The home world, for centuries, reeling in pernicious momentum, had discouraged touchings of an intersexual manner, as they were regarded as incompatible with the identity of the sexes, such touchings tending to elicit an outlawed masculinity and a forbidden femininity. It was true, of course, that they tended not to produce neuteristic identicals but, in effect, masters and slaves. Interestingly, masculinity and femininity had supposedly been disproven by science. But Brenner's society, like many, had found it necessary to suppress with vigor what it claimed did not exist. Such inconsistencies are common amongst advanced societies, and idiots. There are, of course, numerous ways to produce offspring without touchings, available in laboratories, and such. Thus one needed have no fear as

to imminent extinction on the home world. The official
views tended to be accepted, at least ostensibly, by those
in Brenner's society who would seek to rise in various
hierarchies. They tended also to be accepted by many moral
individuals who, in virtue of their conscientious adherence to
these directives, were effectively weeding themselves out of
the population. It might be added that the average individual
on Brenner's home world now failed intelligence tests of the
sorts which had been given several centuries ago, but, as
an alarmed bureaucracy had hastened to produce new tests,
it was proven, by identity of scores, that the intelligence of
the population had not declined. Such touchings were not
regarded as taboo on Brenner's home world, of course, but
rather as, depending on the authority, devolved, antiquated,
perverse, antisocial, unprogressive, pathological or wicked.

"It is all right to touch," repeated Brenner. He said this
very softly, very gently, very soothingly.

Several of the Pons looked at one another, frightened. It
was odd, thought Rodriguez. Their eyes. The look in their
eyes was not like that which might have been in the eyes
of home-worlders, amused, skeptical, or puzzled, that there
might seem to be a reversal, perhaps local or temporary,
perhaps in the interests of a party, in a policy which most of
them had never genuinely internalized in the first place. No.
It was quite different. This had not to do with the inanities
of politics, and pressure groups, and what was thought to be
in the best interest of this or that special group, and so was
absurdly universalized for an entire species, but had to do
with something fundamental in their lives. Some of the Pons
seemed terribly uneasy, as though they might have suddenly,
quite unexpectedly, found themselves standing defenseless
amongst enemies. Some glanced back at the females. Their
eyes were not met. Some of the females backed away.
Distances widened appreciably. The eyes of others seemed
frightened, as though they looked down into an abyss, or
outward, into a nothingness. Several of the Pons began to
wail and turn about. Some covered their faces.

The git keeper began to drive his pointed stick angrily

into the ground near the one cage, stabbing again and again with it, down, into the ground.

Brenner looked at him, irritably.

The git keeper's eyes were furious. Then, suddenly, angrily, petulantly, defiantly, he thrust his pointed stick through the bars of the small cage, hard, into the body confined there. The tiny body drew back spasmodically from the blow, whimpering.

"It's not dead!" cried Brenner, wildly, delightedly.

He rushed toward the cage.

"You little bastards!" screamed Brenner, with tears in his eyes. "You little bastards!"

The git keeper fled away.

Brenner, with a strength he did not know he possessed, tore apart the cage. He drew forth the bloodied Pon. The small female moved toward him, timidly, putting out her hand. Brenner knelt down, holding the bloodied Pon in his arms. The female came to the thing in his arms, and pulled a little at its fur, a gesture not unlike grooming.

A ripple of horror went through the assembled Pons.

"It is all right," wept Brenner. "It is all right."

"Yes," said Rodriguez, suddenly, decisively. "It is all right!"

Brenner threw him a look of gratitude.

The small female began to croon over the thing in Brenner's arms.

"Take it," said Brenner to Rodriguez, standing up. "We are going to finish this thing once and for all."

Rodriguez took the Pon.

Brenner went to the tripod from which hung the bloodied cage and threw it to the ground. He then, with his boots, smashed the remaining bars. He pulled apart the ropes. He scattered the poles, the rope, the bars. He then went to the other tripod and threw it down, and crushed that cage, too, under his feet, and then, too, cast the pieces about.

"Come along!" he said to the horrified Pons. "Come with me!"

He gestured with his arm, and strode toward the small shelter in the center of the clearing. The Pons, uneasily keeping the distances, some of them wailing, followed him. Rodriguez followed him, too, the tiny Pon in his arms, the small female running beside him.

Brenner now stood beside the table, that within the open-sided, roofed structure. The tiny wire cage, housing the git, was on the table.

Brenner looked at the small Pon in Rodriguez' arms.

Rodriguez lifted it up and put his ear to its chest. "No," he said. "It's still alive."

Brenner pointed to the git in the cage.

"This is a git," he said. "It is not a totem. It is only a small animal. It is only an animal."

The git looked up at him, with his small, round, shiny eyes.

Brenner regarded the Pons.

"You!" said Brenner. "Come here."

He addressed himself to the git keeper, who had rejoined the group. The Pon approached him cautiously, holding its pointed stick.

Brenner put out his hand for the stick.

Reluctantly the Pon surrendered it.

"You will not need this," Brenner said. He then broke the stick, into four pieces, and flung them away.

"Watch," said Brenner.

"Be careful," said Rodriguez. "It's wild."

Brenner had opened the tiny cage.

"This is only a git," he said. "It is only a small animal, nothing more, only that."

"Ahhh," breathed a Pon.

Brenner had put his hand gently into the cage. With one finger he caressed the glistening, oily back of the small, fat creature.

"Be careful," said Rodriguez.

"I won't startle it," said Brenner. "It's tame."

"Interesting," said Rodriguez.

"See?" said Brenner to the Pons. "It is only a git. It is only a little animal."

Brenner removed his hand from the cage.

"Do you want to touch it?" Brenner asked the git keeper.

The Pon shook his head negatively.

"Are you afraid of it?" asked Brenner.

The Pon looked up at him.

"Do not be afraid of it," said Brenner. "Just do not startle it."

The Pon looked about himself, at the others.

"Do not be afraid," said Brenner.

The Pon looked at him again.

"It is the totem, is it not?" asked Brenner. "The totem does not harm its children."

"You are treading on dangerous ground," said Rodriguez.

The Pon then, slowly, carefully, put its arm into the cage.

"Be careful," said Rodriguez.

"Eee!" screamed the Pon, jerking his hand back wildly, tipping the cage, causing it to fall, with the git, to the floor of the shelter. His finger was bright with blood. He thrust it wildly, in pain, in his mouth.

"You see!" cried Brenner. "It is not the totem! The totem does not harm its children! It is an animal, only an animal!"

The git keeper ran howling from the vicinity of the shelter.

"There are no totems!" said Brenner. "You may touch! You may love! You may do as you please! You are free! I have liberated you from superstition!"

The Pons regarded him.

"They do not understand," said Rodriguez.

"They will later," said Brenner.

"Perhaps it would be better if they did not," said Rodriguez.

"I do not understand," said Brenner.

"You cannot just go about taking people's beliefs away," said Rodriguez.

"I have done so," said Brenner. "The beliefs are false. They must go."

"And what will you put in their place?" asked Rodriguez.

"That is not my concern," said Brenner.

"I thought you might have some developed ideology in mind," said Rodriguez, "something that might be useful in the exploitation of colonials, or something."

"No," smiled Brenner.

"It might be better, if you had," said Rodriguez.

"Be serious," said Brenner.

"Do not expect gratitude," said Rodriguez.

"There are no totems," said Brenner to the Pons. "That is all over now. I am going to free the git."

Brenner righted the cage, where it lay on the ground, and carefully put his hand into it. The git was crouched down, quivering, in one corner.

"Do not corner it," said Rodriguez.

"I won't," said Brenner. Then he held his hand, open, near the git. In a moment or two it moved out of the corner. A little later it climbed onto Brenner's hand. "It's a heavy one," said Brenner.

"Be careful," said Rodriguez.

Then, very carefully, not closing his hand, Brenner lifted the git up and out of the cage, and held it, nestled, against his shirt. "I won't hurt you," he said to it. Then he said to the Pons. "See? It is not a totem. It is only a little animal. We are going to free it now, and as I free it, so, too, you are freed, from misery, from backwardness and superstition. In your world this is a great step. You will begin your climb now toward civilization."

Brenner then slowly walked toward the gate of the palisade. When he reached that point he put the git down, at a point between two of the palings of the gate. It stayed there for a moment, and then, suddenly, rushed out the opening, hurrying away.

"It is gone now," said Brenner, straightening up. "It is all over. Go back to your huts now."

The Pons looked at him.

"Do you grasp what has occurred here?" asked Brenner.

"Three?" asked one of the Pons. That was the one which Rodriguez had derisively christened 'Archimedes'.

"No," laughed Brenner, touching its head. "Billions, and billions."

The Pon looked at him, puzzled.

"There are no totems," said Brenner. "You are free now, to love and grow."

"We go back huts," said Archimedes.

"It seems you have an ally," said Rodriguez.

"We good Pons," said Archimedes.

Brenner pointed to the injured Pon in Rodriguez' arms, and to the tiny female who clung close to Rodriguez. "Good Pons, too," he said.

"Good Pons?" asked Archimedes.

"Yes," said Brenner. "All Pons good."

"Yes," said Archimedes. "All Pons good."

"Go to your huts now," said Brenner.

"Yes," said Archimedes. "We go huts now."

"They are still maintaining the distances," said Rodriguez, as he watched the Pons withdraw.

"It will take time," said Brenner, "for them to understand how far-reaching are the effects of today."

"And what are the effects of today?" asked Rodriguez.

"Billions, and billions," said Brenner. "The opening of a whole new world."

"You were clever with the git keeper," said Rodriguez. "He would either handle it or not. If he refused to handle it, it would seem he feared the totem might injure one of its children, thus betraying a lack of faith in his own dogmas. If he handled it, either it would injure him or not. If it did not injure him, he would, at the least, in his handling of it, have suggested, and perhaps even demonstrated, its simple animal nature, that it was no more than any other animal. And if it did injure him, as perhaps fortunately for you, and not so fortunately for him, it did, that, of course, as the totem animal is not supposed to injure its children, would make clear the fallacy of totemism."

"Precisely," said Brenner.

"It was very nicely done," said Rodriguez.

"Thank you," said Brenner.

"You have ruined the study, of course," said Rodriguez.

"Yes," said Brenner.

"We can always fake the report," said Rodriguez. "It would have to be faked anyway, if it were not politically congenial."

"True," said Brenner.

"What are we going to do with these Pons?" asked Rodriguez.

"We will keep them in our hut until we are sure they are safe," said Brenner.

"This one is asleep," said Rodriguez, of the Pon in his arms.

"He has lost a great deal of blood," said Brenner.

"He is your little friend, is he not?" asked Rodriguez.

"Yes," smiled Brenner. "He is."

"I thought so," said Rodriguez.

"The female," said Brenner, "is the one we saw with him, several days ago, behind the huts, closer to one another than the prescribed distances."

"I thought she might be," said Rodriguez.

"Let us return to the hut," said Brenner.

"There is one thing here which I find hard to understand," said Rodriguez.

"What is that?" asked Brenner.

"It seems surprising to me that the Pons bore the loss of their totem with such grace."

"They were ripe to outgrow it," said Brenner.

"There is still a matter to consider," said Rodriguez.

"What?" said Brenner.

"A taboo has been violated," said Rodriguez, "and its violation has not been punished."

"So?" asked Brenner.

"Did you not see the fear in them, when they returned to their huts?" asked Rodriguez.

"They were uneasy, some of them," said Brenner.

"There will be terror for days, perhaps for weeks, in the village," said Rodriguez.

"I have disproven their totemism," said Brenner.

"Things are in a state of subtle balance," said Rodriguez.

CHAPTER 22

"How is he?" asked Brenner.

"Stronger," said Rodriguez.

Rodriguez looked across the hut, to where the Pon lay, the small female near it.

"He has hardly looked at you," said Rodriguez.

"Pons tend to avoid eye contact," said Brenner.

"He has been awake for better than an hour," said Rodriguez.

"He hates me," said Brenner.

Brenner went to the door of the hut. It was bright outside, the middle of the morning.

"He must understand that you saved his life yesterday," said Rodriguez.

"'We'," said Brenner.

"As you wish," said Rodriguez. "What is it like outside?"

"Things are much as normal," said Brenner.

"Or seem so," said Rodriguez.

"What do you mean?" asked Brenner.

"Do not be deceived," said Rodriguez.

"I do not understand," said Brenner.

"Things cannot be the same—underneath," said Rodriguez.

"It is interesting the influence we have had upon them," mused Brenner. "How they listened, and watched! How dutifully they attended our lessons, despite their radical contrariety to their previous convictions. In what shining authority must we have seemed invested."

"Perhaps," said Rodriguez.

"We must seem like gods descended amongst them."

"That is unlikely," said Rodriguez. "They are familiar with representatives of our species at Company Station."

"Then," said Brenner, "that is better yet. It has nothing to do with us, really. Rather, it is the light of reason which has triumphed."

"You think they are changed?" asked Rodriguez.

"Certainly," said Brenner. "Do you not?"

"I do not know," said Rodriguez.

"We must allow, of course, for a season of accommodation, a period of adjustment."

"The males have gone to the fields?" asked Rodriguez.

"Yes," said Brenner.

"Good," said Rodriguez.

"You seem apprehensive," said Brenner.

"Possibly," said Rodriguez.

"Why?"

"A taboo was violated," said Rodriguez, "and its violation has not yet been punished, or expiated."

"Taboo is superstition," said Brenner.

"Of course," said Rodriguez.

"So dismiss it," said Brenner.

"Things may not be so simple," said Rodriguez.

Brenner looked at him, puzzled.

"Are you aware of the ancient belief," asked Rodriguez, "that a journey on which one stumbles at its beginning is ill-fated?"

"Yes," said Brenner.

"Does that seem to you a superstition?"

"Certainly," said Brenner.

"But in such a case," said Rodriguez, "it may be truth which hides itself behind the mask of superstition."

"How so?" said Brenner.

"On some level the traveler understands, or believes, that the journey is not in his best interest, that it is a mistake, that it should not be made, and thus, unwilling to make the journey, not wanting to undertake it, he tries to keep himself from it, without even understanding what he is doing, by stumbling. The stumbling, then, is taken as a sign of ill luck, and that the journey should not be made. He turns back. It is not his fault. His conscience is clear. He could not help it. No one can blame him. He has been given a sign, from the gods, or whatever."

"I understand," said Brenner.

"Truth can wear the mask of superstition," said Rodriguez.

"You surely are not suggesting that anything of that sort is involved here."

"I do not know," said Rodriguez.

"Do you think they are aware of such things?"

"No," said Rodriguez.

"Do you think such things are involved here?"

"I would not think so," said Rodriguez.

"Then do not be afraid," said Brenner.

"Let us suppose that such things have no application here," said Rodriguez. "Let us suppose, as seems quite likely, that we are dealing with simple, pure, baseless superstition. There is still much to be concerned about. We are dealing with something, I am sure, which is profoundly sensitive, and possibly dangerous, even in the case of such small creatures."

"Do not be afraid," said Brenner.

"I think that you, for one reason or another, perhaps because of your education, your rationality, your youth, or your inexperience, may not fully appreciate the nature of primitive mentality."

"How so?" asked Brenner.

"In particular," said Rodriguez, "I think that you may underestimate what I am particularly concerned with here, the power of taboo. The very nature of the savage's universe is thought to depend on the respecting of taboo. These things, too, are internalized in so deep a manner that you can scarcely conceive of their force in the savage mind. Taboo is a very serious matter, a terribly serious matter. Its violation need not even be intentional to be culpable. Twice, on different worlds, I have seen taboos inadvertently broken, broken quite by accident, in one case by the inadvertent touching of a tabooed object, it was the lost comb of a sacred king, not recognized as such when it was picked up, in the other case it was in accidentally having the shadow of a tabooed person, a fratricide, fall upon one's body. In the first case the fellow died within instants of discovering what he had done, in the other case he died within hours."

"Of what did they die?" asked Brenner.

"I would suppose," said Rodriguez, "of fear."

"Then they did not die from violating the taboo, but from the fear that was associated with the violation."

"I mention it to convey to you, to some extent, the power of the internalization of the taboo, and how seriously it is taken by primitive peoples," said Rodriguez.

"These two," said Brenner, indicating the Pons, "broke the taboo. They have not died of fear. The female is healthy, and happy. The male is recovering."

The female, at this point, had cradled the male's head in the crook of her arm, and was holding a saucer of water to his lips.

"They probably prepared themselves for months for the breaking of the taboo," said Rodriguez. "Their violation of the taboo was doubtless intentional, premeditated."

"I see," said Brenner.

"You understand then, too, of course," said Rodriguez, "that that makes the violation seem far more culpable, and heinous, and threatening, to the group than it might otherwise?"

"I suppose so," said Brenner.

"They are courageous little things," said Rodriguez.

"Is that why you joined me in taking their part?" asked Brenner.

"Perhaps," said Rodriguez.

"But they are only monkeys," said Brenner.

"Brave monkeys," said Rodriguez, with a smile.

"You are all unregenerate iconoclasts," said Brenner.

"You are the one, with the neat trick at the git cage, who disproved their totemism," said Rodriguez.

At this point the female had put down the saucer of water. The male turned his head weakly toward Brenner, and put out its hand.

Brenner rose up and went to crouch beside it.

"Watch out," cautioned Rodriguez.

The male looked up at Brenner, and then reached out, and pinched at his arm.

"That is a grooming gesture," said Rodriguez, "probably forbidden for a thousand years."

Brenner then put out his hand and took some of the hair of the Pon's arm between his thumb and forefinger, and pulled gently at it.

The female made a soft, contented noise.

"He is grateful," said Rodriguez.

"I think he is asleep now, again," said Brenner.

"Let him rest," said Rodriguez.

"Listen!" said Brenner.

"What is it?" asked Rodriguez.

"Pons!" said Brenner. "The sound is coming from the fields!"

Rodriguez leaped up and hurried from the hut, running toward the gate of the palisade. Brenner was only a few feet behind him.

Pons, terrified, were streaming through the gate. Some stopped inside the palings and looked out, back, frightened, toward the clearing.

"What is wrong!" demanded Rodriguez.

"Killer!" screeched a Pon. "Killer!"

More Pons fled past, their eyes wild, their tiny feet scattering dust behind them.

"What happened!" screamed Rodriguez, grabbing at a Pon, missing him.

"Back there!" cried another Pon.

"Where?" asked Rodriguez, trying to get his hand on another Pon hurrying past.

"Field! Field! Came! Took!" cried another.

Several of the Pons, together, began to swing shut the
gate. Rodriguez held it forcibly open, to let another four or
five Pons squeeze through.

"Shut! Shut!" screamed Pons.

"There are still others outside!" said Rodriguez.

More Pons, tiny, across the clearing, could be seen hurrying
toward the gate.

"What happened?" asked Brenner.

"I don't know," said Rodriguez.

"Stealthy one!" said a Pon.

"Came! Took! Hungry one! Stealthy one!" screeched
another.

More Pons hurried through the gate.

Female Pons began to howl amongst the huts.

"No understand!" said Rodriguez.

One of the Pons suddenly, fiercely, for so small an animal,
bared its teeth and held up its tiny hands, the fingers hooked,
like claws. It made a sudden, ugly sound, which, even in its
tiny throat, was frightening.

The gate swung shut, creaking.

Rodriguez' face was covered with sweat. There was much
howling now, from both males and females, in the village.

Brenner looked wildly at Rodriguez.

"It could not be worse!" said Rodriguez. He kicked aside
some of the posts braced against the gate, opening it a few
inches to let another Pon through. "Go to the hut. Get it.
You know what! Bring it! Run!"

Brenner turned about and fled back to the hut. He
rummaged through Rodriguez' things and, in a moment,
from its leather case, drew forth the requested object.

"You must show us where!" Rodriguez was saying to a
Pon when Brenner, gasping, returned to the gate.

"No! No! No!" screamed the Pon.

Rodriguez seized it by the back of the neck, and held it
literally in the air.

"Shut! Shut!" screamed another Pon.

Another Pon squeezed through. It was the git keeper.

"Come along!" said Rodriguez to Brenner. He then

wedged through the gate and, carrying the terrified, struggling Pon, went into the clearing. Save for the footprints it seemed quiet.

"You will show us where!" Rodriguez said to the Pon.

"Let go! Let go!" screamed the Pon, squirming.

"Where, you little bastard?" asked Rodriguez.

"Let go!" it screeched.

"You show," snarled Rodriguez. "Then I let go."

"There! There!" said the Pon, pointing.

"Come along," said Rodriguez, furiously, to Brenner, who carried the weapon.

"There!" screamed the Pon, now thrust ahead of Rodriguez, by the collar of its robes.

They were at the edge of the fields, near the forest.

"The trail is clear," said Rodriguez. He released the Pon, who fled back, toward the palisade.

"Give me the weapon," said Rodriguez.

Brenner handed it to him.

"Stay behind me," said Rodriguez. "You will be my extra eyes. In particular keep watch to the rear."

"Is that necessary?" asked Brenner.

"We do not know what this is, or its intelligence," said Rodriguez.

The brush, torn apart, the trampled leaves, were a trail that even Brenner might have followed. Whatever it was might have approached with circumspection, but it had not concerned itself to conceal its withdrawal.

"You can see where it went," said Brenner.

"Yes," said Rodriguez.

"It does not deign to conceal its trail," said Brenner.

"No," said Rodriguez.

"It did not expect to be followed," said Brenner.

"No," said Rodriguez.

"It does not fear pursuit?"

"No," said Rodriguez.

"It is not afraid?"

"Perhaps you can see why," said Rodriguez.

"Why?" asked Brenner.

"Nothing was dragged here," said Rodriguez. "Thus the thing is of considerable size."

"There is blood on the leaves," said Brenner.

"We will teach it fear," said Rodriguez.

He armed the rifle.

"You are going to kill it?"

"We must attempt to do so," said Rodriguez. "A prey range, once extended, is likely to remain extended."

Brenner nodded.

"It may even grow fond of a new taste," said Rodriguez.

"I understand," said Brenner, shuddering.

"Are you ready?" asked Rodriguez.

"How far away is it likely to be?" asked Brenner.

"It is probably extremely close," said Rodriguez, "perhaps within yards."

"I'm ready," said Brenner.

They had not made their way far into the forest when Rodriguez stopped, and held out his hand.

Brenner stopped, too, scarcely daring to breathe.

Rodriguez put his left arm carefully into the weapon sling. Until then he had carried the rifle at the ready. In this fashion it might be brought instantly into play, in any direction, or attitude. Now, however, he had a fair shot. He wanted the extra steadiness of the sling. It would not do to miss.

The beast was crouched down. It had its head low. One could not see its jaws.

A bird, overhead, took flight.

The beast, at the sound of the rush of wings, instantly lifted its head.

Rodriguez and Brenner did not move.

The beast, a white, starlike blaze on its forehead, looked at them.

"It sees us," whispered Brenner.

"No," whispered Rodriguez.

The ears of the beast were erected, facing them.

Rodriguez' finger began to press gently, ever so gently, on the trigger.

Suddenly the beast leaped up and Rodriguez, with a curse, fired. A passage of light, marking the trail of the charge, burned through the air. A tree, in a ball of fire, seemed to explode and its top, the trunk smoking and severed, crashed down.

"It's gone!" said Rodriguez, in fury.

He jammed another charge into the breech.

In moments Rodriguez and Brenner had reached the spot where they had seen the animal.

Rodriguez plunged into the forest after it.

Brenner lingered behind.

"I've lost it," said Rodriguez, coming back.

"He was finished anyway," said Brenner, wearily.

Rodriguez looked down at the leaves.

"We had best take what is left here back to the village," said Rodriguez.

"I will carry him," said Brenner.

"I should not have missed," said Rodriguez.

"You had no chance," said Brenner. "The beast leaped up."

"At one time, long ago," said Rodriguez, "I would not have missed."

Brenner gathered the small form, torn apart, half eaten, into his arms.

"It may come back," said Rodriguez.

"You frightened it," said Brenner. "It may never come back."

"It will come back," said Rodriguez.

Brenner's shirt and chest were drenched with blood.

"That is not the worst, of course," said Rodriguez, gloomily.

"What could be worse?" asked Brenner.

"How do you think the Pons will understand this?"

"What do you mean?" asked Brenner.

Rodriguez looked at him.

"No!" said Brenner.

"How else can they understand it?" asked Rodriguez.

"We must return as soon as possible to the village," said Brenner, alarmed.

Rodriguez looked at what Brenner held in his arms. He then looked at Brenner, questioningly.

"It is "Archimedes,"" said Brenner.

Rodriguez nodded.

"Let us return to the village," said Brenner.

"We may be too late already," said Rodriguez.

"Hurry!" begged Brenner, tears in his eyes. He looked behind him, over his shoulder, at Rodriguez. "Hurry!" he wept.

"Wait!" called Rodriguez.

But Brenner was already far ahead of him.

Brenner threw back his head and howled with rage.

The Pons had seemed very calm when he had returned to the village. It was as though the terrible event of the afternoon had not occurred. It was as though nothing had happened. Things were much as they usually were. All seemed tranquil.

Brenner had put down the remains of Archimedes in the clearing, and rushed to the hut. The two Pons whom he had left there were gone, of course.

Brenner rushed out of the hut, demanding information. It seemed the Pons did not quite understand him. To be sure, he was much beside himself, and may not have been coherent.

"Things all right," one Pon had assured him, hoping perhaps thereby to assuage his obvious agitation.

In moments, however, Brenner found two trails in the dust, where it seemed that two objects, perhaps baskets, which might have been obtained in trade from Company Station, had been dragged, perhaps on ropes. In the furrows in the dust, too, were reddish stains. Along the paths of these furrows, too, there were numerous small footprints, those of Pons. Apparently a great number of them had followed these objects. Although Brenner was not in the mood, or really in a proper condition of mind, to interpret these prints, a calmer observer might have noted that the smaller prints, presumably those of females, tended to be apart from and outside the somewhat larger prints, those of males. Prom this it might have been gathered that in whatever was going on there had been some attention given to maintaining the proper distances. Although it was difficult to tell from the furrows after a time, it seemed that the objects might have been dragged around and around, in circles. Here the markings in the dust, the stains, and the footprints became very confused. These matters became substantially clearer when, rather close to one wall of the palisade, behind some huts, rather back and to the right of the gate, as one might enter it, two small heaps of bones were found, the shards of skeletons, from which, bit by bit, judging from the nicks and cuts on the bones, the flesh had been scraped. This had presumably been done by scarps, which seemed the most likely instrument for such work in the Pons' inventory of tools.

It was at the moment of making this discovery that Brenner had howled with rage, and perhaps, too, with misery, with regret, with frustration, with grief.

Some Pons had followed him about, puzzled. They looked at him, and blinked.

"You bastards!" screamed Brenner and he, despite his larger size, and his much greater strength, and the moral problematicity of such an act, had struck two of them. These had hastily withdrawn from his dangerous ambit and then, with the others, watched him.

He had then fled back to the hut, to hide, to cry, to be alone.

It was there that Rodriguez, who, of course, had only shortly before arrived back at the village, found him.

"You know?" asked Brenner.

"Yes," said Rodriguez. "I saw."

"I should kill them all," said Brenner.

"The taboo was broken," said Rodriguez. "Disaster ensued. Now the taboo has been expiated. Things are the same again. The balances are restored, the proportions are in order."

"I am leaving," said Brenner.

"There is nowhere to go," said Rodriguez.

"I will not stay here," said Brenner.

"Where will you go?" asked Rodriguez.

"Company Station," said Brenner.

"How will you find your way?" asked Rodriguez.

"I will follow the stones, the white stones," said Brenner.

Brenner rose up and began to throw clothing, and various articles, into his knapsack.

"Wait until morning," said Rodriguez.

"No," said Brenner.

"Take the rifle," said Rodriguez.

"No," said Brenner. "It is yours. You may need it." He recalled the large beast they had seen in the forest. It might return.

"It is insane to go into the forest alone, without a weapon," said Rodriguez.

"I am going!" screamed Brenner. "I will not stay here!" He then, with his knapsack half packed, weeping, crying out, fled from the village.

"Come back!" Rodriguez screamed after him. "Come back!"

Then Rodriguez turned back to the village. A Pon looked up at him, and blinked.

Then Rodriguez returned to the hut. He had one bottle of Heimat left. His hand shook when he poured it.

"Ten years ago," he said to himself, "I would not have missed."

Then he threw out the Heimat on the floor of the hut, and, on one of the stones of the fire pit, at the center of the hut, broke the bottle.

CHAPTER 23

Brenner looked wildly about.

He cursed a world with no moon. The forest loomed about him, lit by the dim glow of the dangling lantern fruit.

The snapping of a twig is a tiny sound, but he had heard it. He had heard, too, from time to time, movements amongst dried leaves, which might have been their stirring in the wind, but might, too, have been the soft, quick tread of paws.

Brenner sobbed and peered into the darkness.

He jerked off the knapsack and held it by the straps. It would be a poor weapon, flung on its straps. It would be an ineffectual shield. Yet it was something to strike out with, or something to insert between himself and the forest.

A stick, a club, would be better.

Brenner stood in the tiny clearing and listened, as carefully, as intently, as keenly, as he could. He could hear only his own breathing.

There is nothing there, he told himself. I am alone.

He saw another of the white stones. He ran toward it. It was late at night, how late he did not know. He fell on his knees and picked up the whitish stone, and clutched it to him, weeping, and then put it down.

He must now search out another.

How fortunate that the Pons were so stupid, and had so little sense of direction, or knowledge of woodcraft, that they needed a trail of stones to find their way between Company Station and the village. With such an aid Rodriguez' compass and map, which had been lost in the journey to the village, were not even necessary.

Brenner stood up.

Anything might have caused a twig to snap, if it really had. If it were small enough, and dry enough, and properly positioned, even the foot of a git might break it. Perhaps he had not even heard the sound. It was late at night. It was dark. His imagination might have played tricks on him.

Brenner looked about for another stone. He saw it, several yards away.

He hurried toward it.

Brenner looked behind him, and to the side.

He stumbled toward another whitish stone.

I have gone miles, he said to himself. The knapsack was now again on his back. In one hand was grasped a stout branch. It would help him to keep his feet in the darkness. There is nothing to be afraid of, he told himself.

Then he cried out with alarm and flung up the stick, and was nearly buffeted by a fleet body which bounded past him, crossing diagonally before him, from his right to his left, one of the tiny, small-horned ungulates of the forest.

He remained very still.

Overhead he heard the calls of a night bird.

Then he went to the next stone.

After an hour or so, Brenner stopped to drink at a shallow stream, one of many which flowed through the well-watered forest. Then, at the edge of the stream, he sat down. He was tired and hungry. He removed the knapsack and put the stick beside him. He leaned back against a tree.

He sat up, quickly, when two of the small-horned ungulates, one larger and one smaller, crossed the stream some yards below him, splashing, and trotted into the darkness. Their heads bobbed as they moved. Had Rodriguez been with him Rodriguez might have remarked on the oddity of the movements of such creatures at night, as they were day-feeders and normally quiescent at night.

Brenner partook of some bemat cakes and dried fruit.

Then, rested and fed, and feeling much better than before, he rose up.

He had, of course, before resting, located the next stone.

Brenner was not clear, at first, that that there was anything out there. It is very difficult to interpret the shadows in the uncertain light of stars, in the dim glow of lantern fruit.

It was his unusually fine hearing that at last convinced him that he was not, as he had hitherto assumed, alone in the forest.

At first it was the soft flaking, and crushing, of dried leaves, closer now, and less mistakable than formerly. It was mostly on his right, and behind him.

A little later Brenner stopped, suddenly, and, to be sure, there was the sound again, but then it stopped, as he had stopped.

He removed the knapsack uneasily from his back. He clutched the stick more firmly.

Then he heard the sound, or a similar sound, from his left.

Brenner hurried to the next stone. It was fortunate that there were such stones. Without them he would have been lost, utterly confused, disoriented, in the forest. Even with a map and compass it would have required skill to find Company Station. Without them, trying, say, to find one's way by marks of weathering, by the growth of moss, by stars, and such, there would have been but small prospect of success. Company Station was no more than a dot in the trackless forests of the northern hemisphere of Abydos. In searching for it, one might pass within a mile of it and never know it. But, felicitously, there were the stones! They would

be his guideposts. They comforted him, providing him with
assurances of Company Station, with its fence and gate.

"Go back!" screamed Brenner. "Get away!"

This was his first clear visual contact with what was out
there. It was a dark shape to his left, as he had turned. It
was not like the thing which had seized Archimedes. It was
quite different. It was not nearly as large. It sat back on its
haunches. It seemed almost, facing him, as though it had no
head, until Brenner realized that what he had taken for the
shoulders was actually a gigantic knot of muscle, humplike,
below which, there emergent from the shoulders, was the
head.

"Get away!" screamed Brenner.

When the beast turned its head to the side, Brenner could
detect that it had an odd silhouette. There was something
running the length of its skull. Brenner spun about. There
was another noise there. Brenner was extremely quiet.

He now heard, clearly, from at least two quarters,
quick, breaths, those which might be expected of animals
with heavy coats, which might have become overheated in
movement. Such creatures perspire primarily through their
mouth, and the pads of their feet.

Then, from the darkness, there emerged another such
beast. Its eyes flashed, suddenly, reflecting the light of one of
the dangling fruits.

"Stay away I" said Brenner.

Then it had backed away, and was crouching down,
watching him.

On its skull, running the length of it, beginning above
and between the eyes, visible in the dim light of the lantern
fruit, seemingly yellowish in its light, was a hairless, serrated
bony plate, or ridge.

Brenner then detected two more of the creatures, farther
back.

The muzzles of these creatures were very broad, and
powerful. Brenner could see teeth, they, too, in the light of
the lantern fruit, appearing yellowish.

"Go back!" said Brenner.

Suddenly one of the ungulates, the fourth he had seen, emerged from the darkness and darted, with odd bounds, through the beasts, and disappeared amongst the trees.

That is it, said Brenner to himself. They do not want me. They are pursuing that. That is what they want. That is what they are after.

Another pair of animals appeared.

They appeared, silently, from the direction from which the ungulate had come, fleeing.

"Get back!" said Brenner.

Brenner backed away, and the nearest animal, crouching down, inched forward.

Brenner could now detect several of these beasts about him. There were, though he could not be sure of it, given the darkness, seven of them.

"Get back!" said Brenner.

Another animal came a little closer. They expected Brenner to run.

Brenner, holding to a strap, flung the knapsack out at the closest animal. It struck it across the face, and it drew back. Then it bared its teeth. Another animal, crouching, head up, teeth bared, approached. Brenner struck out again with the knapsack. Then again, at another animal, he struck out. Then the sack was torn from his grip and he saw the knapsack attacked by two other animals. Three fought for it. Brenner saw the great knots of muscle in the necks bulge, the wide, powerful jaws closed like clamps on the object. Then it was being fiercely shaken by one or another animal, the others, too, rolling, snarling, in the dirt, not relinquishing their grip. Then each had a portion of the heavy leather and canvas object, the contents scattered for yards about, on the leaves, amongst the trees. The great mass of muscles in the back of the neck, of course, a feature in this life form, tended to average out successes in such vigorously prosecuted contests. Doubtless it had been selected for. It was useful in the retention of shares of food. These animals, like many social beasts, acquired food in concert, but its division, except for the young, which in the dens tended to be fed on regurgitated prey, was decided on a much more individualistic basis. Needless to say, the broad jaws, the tenacity of their grip, and such, had similar utilities. Although Brenner was not interested at the moment in such zoological matters it might be called to the attention of the reader that the hairless, serrated ridge on the skull was also of some importance. As these beasts were not merely hunters but scavengers it tended to reduce the danger of contamination from decomposing prey, guarding the head and jaws to some extent as they were thrust into the bodily cavities of carrion. The ridge also, of course, to some extent, enlarged the area within the cavity for the feeder, this giving freer play to the jaws. Its function apparently did not have to do with enabling vision within the bodily cavities, at least in the present form of the animal, as they fed with their eyes closed, a useful disposition to protect the eyes from bone and reduce the possibility of infection.

Brenner moved back, further.

The knapsack was now in pieces.

The beasts who had disputed it now sniffed it. Others, too, crept forward, to be warned away by menacing noises. One beast bit at another, and for a moment there was a flurry of snarling and biting. Then they had backed away from one another. One of the beasts looked up from the knapsack, and then it stepped over it, toward Brenner.

Brenner took another step back.

He raised the stick.

He looked into a yawning maw and thrust the stick at it. It tore into the side of the beast's face and it drew back.

Brenner spun about. Another animal was quite near now. He struck down with the stick, slashing the beast across the nose and muzzle. Another approached and he jabbed out with the stick. It put up its paw, as though to fend it away. But Brenner had neither managed to touch the animal, nor had it touched the stick.

Brenner turned about and, crying out, thrust at another beast, which seized the stick in its jaws.

Brenner could not pull the stick from its jaws.

The beast gripped it near the end, that end emerging from the right side of its jaws.

Brenner pulled at the stick. He backed away. Forward was dragged the beast. The weight of the beast, which seemed fastened to the stick, was some seventy to eighty Commonworld pounds. It looked at Brenner with its left eye. Its jaws moved up an inch on the stick, and then, opening and closing, another inch, toward his hand. Brenner released the stick, and the stick, still gripped in the beast's mouth, flew to the side, the animal turning fully about with it.

Brenner then turned and ran.

The animals hung about him, a few yards back, a few yards to the side, running with him, always leaving an open space before him. This action on Brenner's part, not standing in one place, or not yet doing so, and moving, was familiar, and comprehensible, to them. It returned their world to its normal form. Before, when Brenner had seemed at bay, they had not been fully certain as to how to proceed. It was too early for the attack. It was too early for the kill, for the feeding. The movements of the thing were not erratic. It was not stumbling. It was not panting. It was not exhausted. It had not yet fallen, unable to move, its lungs sucking in air, its eyes wild, waiting for the fangs. But now things were as they should be. They padded along with Brenner. Tenacity and stamina were features of their life form. When it slowed down they would snarl and bite at its heels. They would try to keep it moving. They would try, even, after it had run further, to guide it back toward the den, that they might be nearer home when the kill was made.

This thing, they thought, is strange, as it has only two legs. But it does run. Not well. But it runs.

Too, it was strange, they thought, as it was already gasping.

This was not like the small, horned ones, the leaping ones, whose stamina almost matched their own, whose fleet, bounding gait was so difficult to match, which so often eluded them in the forests, the scents mixing with so many others. No, this chase would be short.

Brenner stumbled and he felt his leg slashed with teeth.
Crying out, he rose to his feet, his trousers torn, his leg wet
with blood and saliva. He ran on. His heart was pounding. It
seemed he could not breathe. In his terror he was only vaguely
aware of the pain in his body. It was like someone else was
in agony. He struck into a tree. He saw another white stone.
He ran toward it. I am going to Company Station, thought
Brenner, wildly. I am going toward Company Station! I will
see the gate! I will see the fence! But he knew, too, that he
was days from Company Station.

Yes, it is nearly time, they thought, were they capable
of such thoughts. But it has not lasted very long. This is a
strange runner. It is too slow. It is no wonder there are so
few of these in the forest.

Brenner spun about, his legs buckling. Things began to
go black.

He began to sob and cry, and gasp for breath.

Then he found himself backed against an outcropping of
rock.

Yes, there were seven of them. He could see that now. He
counted them.

There was nowhere to run.

He covered his face with his arms and crouched down.

Yes, they thought, it is now time. And each thought, I
must not delay, there are the others!

Brenner lifted his head from his folded arms, after a time.

He had not felt the charge, the rending, the tearing.

He looked about himself. There was no sign of the beasts.
They had melted away, back into the shadows, through the
trees, disappearing in the darkness.

It was very quiet.

He stepped away from the rock outcropping. He peered
into the darkness. He turned about, and screamed.

On the rocks, above his head, not yards from where he had
been, he saw a gigantic, terrible shape, a huge, monstrous,
sinuous, catlike form. It was not so unlike the stealthy one
which had seized Archimedes, except in its dimensions.
It was sitting back on its haunches. Its broad head, with

its sharp, erected ears, must have been twenty feet above the rocky level on which it sat. Brenner, with his arms outstretched, could not have begun to measure the span of its chest. Its eyes, which were large, were separated by some eighteen Commonworld inches. They were set forward on the face. It doubtless had excellent binocular vision. Its pupils were black, large and round. The creature seemed excellently adapted for night vision. Such eyes would not need the feeble aid of the lantern fruit. They would have served in darker, more terrible places. Yes, it was not unlike the stealthy one Brenner had seen, that on which Rodriguez had fired, missing his shot as the creature, alarmed, had leaped away. It, too, clear in all its lineaments, in the lithe, beautiful, savage form, was a predator. That it would live by killing, and the death of the slower, the weaker, the less clever, the less fierce, was visible in every inch of its frightening beauty. It was terrible in a way that was beyond ruthlessness or cruelty. It was terrible in a simple, natural way, as lightning is terrible, or fire, or storms. It, like the stealthy one, was a product of evolution, and the coming of kings and terrors, a product of what was to be fed upon and what must be done to obtain it, of how cunning one must be, how secret, how swift, how terrible. It, like the stealthy one, was a handiwork of nature, of nature in all its merciless innocence, and yet, it seemed, of a nature more terrible than that which, over thousands of years, had fashioned the sinews of the stealthy one. Brenner shuddered to conceive the nature that might produce such a shape, and being. This, thought Brenner, is that which is first in the forest. Here, in this world, this majestic horror is king. The smaller beasts, the humped, crested ones, the pack, had slunk away. They did not do contest with one such as this. With one such as this they would dispute nothing.

I am dead, thought Brenner. But he was awed, as well. Better, thought he, to be eaten by this, to serve such a king, than to die beneath the jaws of the pack, to be torn to pieces by the small ones, to die of a hundred wounds, to feel the lacerations of tinier, fouler teeth, to expire choking in fetid breath.

Brenner looked up at the beast above him. "I salute you," he cried, lifting his hand to the beast. "I await you!" He tore open his shirt.

The beast looked down upon him.

"Kill me," invited Brenner.

The beast did not move.

Brenner, in the ensuing interim, suddenly became very much aware of the pain in his body, of the soreness in his leg, where it had been bitten, of the blood in his boot, of how he was breathing heavily, of how his heart was pounding.

"Kill me!" called Brenner.

The beast turned its head to one side, and licked at the fur on its left shoulder.

The others disturbed it, thought Brenner suddenly. Its lair is about. It came out to see what was occurring. It may not be hungry. It may not recognize in me anything that it is accustomed to preying upon!

Brenner's resignation to death, and the perhaps somewhat hysterical bravado which he had managed to muster up, perhaps somewhat belatedly, to face it, suddenly evaporated.

He took a step backward, and then another step.

At this point the beast looked up, observing him, and Brenner stopped.

They faced one another for a time, Brenner not knowing what to do. The best thing, he knew, was not to make eye contact. But that had occurred. Many encounters with predators, particularly with ones which were not hunting, were avoided by so simple an expedient as both turning about, each as though they had not seen the other, and going their own ways. Also, he must not approach within a certain critical distance. But he had already discovered the presence of the beast within what must surely count as a critical distance, that distance within which the beast is provoked to action, either to turn and flee or, in the case of one such as this, more likely, to charge. But Brenner had not been approaching it. That was a point. Indeed, he had drawn back a little.

Brenner stood very still.

Suddenly the beast put down its head a little, and hunched its shoulders, and snarled. That sound raised the hair on the back of Brenner's neck.

Wise or not, Brenner then began to back rapidly away.

It just awakened, it is hungry, thought Brenner, in misery. Then, although it was surely not wise, he turned about, and ran. The foolishness of this, however, for flight tends to elicit pursuit, occurred almost immediately to him, and, miserable, he stopped, and turned about.

His heart sank as he saw the beast lightly, with a swiftness, and agility, and grace, that was odd in so large an animal, descend from the rock.

Brenner turned about and fled through the trees.

It was doubtless not wise, but sometimes one's body makes such decisions for one, not taking the time to weigh the pros and cons involved. Reflection is often useful, and is doubtless to be accorded great respect. In certain cases, however, as when it betrays the animal, it can be the road to misery or death. Some ten minutes later Brenner, gasping, caught hold of a tree, to keep from falling, and looked about himself.

He was lost, of course, but, more importantly, from his point of view, was still alive. If one is not alive, it is not of great importance, after all, whether one is lost or not.

It did not follow me, thought Brenner. It is not hunting me. To be sure, it had descended from the rock. It might be about, somewhere.

It was rationally reassuring to Brenner that it had not brought him down already. Surely anything like that could outrun him, indeed, overtake him in a few bounds, and, too, it could presumably follow his scent, fresh as it was, if it were so inclined.

Whereas these reflections might have brought comfort to a fully rational mind, it must be conceded that Brenner, exhausted, frightened, lost in the dark, only recently having escaped from savage beasts, and having just encountered another, did not fully appreciate their weight.

That his trepidation might not be ill-founded was surely suggested, too, by what occurred almost immediately.

He had scarcely made his best judgment as to the direction of Company Station and started in that direction when, some forty yards ahead, amongst the trees, in the dim light of lantern fruit, he saw the form of the gigantic, catlike animal. It was standing. It must have been some fourteen feet high at the shoulder. It then growled. That sound, low and rumbling, seemed to come from deep within it. In its undulations, it was almost as if it were moving, rapidly crawling, toward him through the trees.

Brenner turned about, hurrying in the opposite direction. For a time the beast was behind him. Once Brenner picked up a rock and hurled it at the beast. He did not manage to strike it, which was perhaps just as well. Brenner also picked up another branch and tore away smaller branches and leaves from it. It might serve as a weapon. He wished he had the electric match which had been in his knapsack. He might then have managed to light some dried branch, and use it to thrust at the animal, if it approached too closely. To be sure, it may never have seen fire. Still it might not care to approach a light so bright, one contrasting so intensely with the darkness, one perhaps actually painful to look at, in its vision's current dark-adjustment. Too, it might find the heat unpleasant, and an actual burn, particularly a severe one, would surely teach it quickly enough the menace, the power, of that bright, flickering stranger in its kingdom.

Then it seemed the beast was gone.

Perhaps it did not wish to risk being struck by the stick.

Perhaps it had lost interest in Brenner.

Perhaps it had been by coincidence that their paths had for a time been conjoined.

There were trails, of course, in the forest. Brenner might have been on one.

Brenner continued on his way. But now, no longer did he thrash through the brush, looking wildly back, plunging into shadows, witlessly toward anything that might be in the darkness. Now he moved with care. He frequently sought cover. He held the stick ready. He stopped often to listen, for little things, mostly, such as the resistances of dried leaves to the tread of soft paws, a breathing not his own. He stopped once, to look at his leg. It was no longer bleeding. He wrapped a kerchief about the wound, to protect it, but it would slip, and he ended, after a time, by thrusting it back in his pocket. He began to regret the loss of the knapsack, with its food. He became aware of how cold it was in the forest now, at night. He frequently looked behind himself. He saw no sign of the animal.

He suddenly became haunted by a new fear. That he might be moving in a circle. The two legs of one of those of Brenner's species are seldom of precisely the same length. Accordingly, if a pace is not measured, if it is not trained, so to speak, there will be a tendency to move ever so slightly, over a great distance, to one side or the other. Over miles this tendency can describe circles, which remain circles, of course, whether they be five or fifty miles in diameter.

Brenner peered upward at stars. It must be hours before sunrise.

Perhaps he should wait until morning.

Suddenly, reflecting the light of a lantern fruit, he saw, like ignited, heated copper, like lamps suddenly illuminated, the eyes of the beast, not more than ten yards away, in his path. It was crouched down, like a small house, its belly no more than a foot from the leaves, its head even lower, the jaws almost at the ground. He saw its tail move behind it, a sudden, nervous movement.

Brenner turned about and began moving away from it, looking back over his shoulder. He saw it move forward a few feet, quickly, then stop, then move forward again.

Suddenly Brenner saw a white stone, and another beyond that.

He had apparently passed between the stones, not realizing it. His heart leaped. He had come again to the trail of stones! There was no mistaking the stone, or the one beyond it, whitish in the woods, like a pale, softly glowing hemisphere. But the beast was behind him. How ironic it was, to have found once more, even by accident, the well-marked road to Company Station, to the fence, to the gate, to safety, only to furnish upon it a repast for a brute!

Brenner put down his stick, and picked up the stone. It must weigh some five Commonworld pounds. It was a not inconsiderable missile. Surely it might bruise even a monster such as threatened him. But, after a time, as the beast had half circled him, but did not attack, he put it down. He picked up his stick and advanced to the next stone. The beast remained where it had been. It was not difficult to see the next stone, and Brenner proceeded to it. The beast was now well back. Brenner eagerly proceeded to the next stone, and then the next.

If it is going to attack, thought Brenner, why does it not do so? But then, too, Brenner was in no hurry that it should come to some firm decision on the matter, particularly one which might be affirmative.

After a time the beast was nowhere in sight.

It is gone, thought Brenner. I hope it is gone.

Brenner was not following the same stones he had followed earlier in the afternoon and evening. I mention that in case the reader might suspect that in his understandable disorientation in the forest, he might, in confusion, be following his own backtrail. This was a possibility, of course, of which Brenner, after a time, was well aware. But these stones, he satisfied himself, were not the ones he had originally followed. The terrain was different. He had passed numerous objects earlier, certain rock formations, particular fallen trees, and such, which he would have recognized, had he met them again. He was quite confident that he was on his way to Company Station, until, later, looking upward through a gap in the trees, he noted a constellation which, by all rights, should have been behind him, not before him. He was then less sure of his direction. Still he was quite sure that he was not following the same stones he had followed earlier in the afternoon and evening. That could not be the case. Things were not the same at all. His uneasy ruminations were interrupted when, ahead of him, through the trees, far off, he saw two small, flickering lights, torches. In moments he came through the trees to the edge of a broad clearing. The lights were indeed torches, one mounted on each side of the gate in the palisade, that encircling the Pon village.

Confused, Brenner stumbled into the clearing.

It was not at all the custom of the Pons to set torches by the gate.

He slowly approached the gate, in consternation. He realized then that stones had been moved. The path which had once led to Company Station now described a loop, a large one, leading back to the village.

He turned about, suddenly.

Perhaps it was suspicion, or fear, or a sense of prudence, suddenly recollected, or perhaps a tiny, subliminal cue, not even consciously registered, but he had turned about, suddenly.

He could see it, a looming shadow, dark against dark, amongst the trees.

It was still with him!

It had followed him!

His astonishment, his perplexity, his frustration, his fury at finding himself once more before the village, dissipated, like dust in a gust of wind, before what was behind him.

He began to run toward the gate.

Rodriguez would be within. Rodriguez had the rifle. He had seen it blast a tree, felling it in an explosion of fire.

"Help!" he called. "Help!"

He looked behind himself, wildly.

The beast had emerged from the trees. He could see it now, the blackness in the clearing, blocking the darknesses of trees behind it.

He had little doubt it could bring him down before he could reach the gate. And it seemed not unlikely that it might decide to do so, before he could reach the security of the palisade. Surely, even in that simple, brute brain, in that small, dark, instinctual surrogate of rationality, it might sense that the palisade might constitute a barrier, that behind it what it had followed for so long might obtain immunity, or refuge. Understanding it must act, or risk the loss of what it had followed for so long, would it not now act, bounding forward with graceful, precipitate violence? Brenner ran madly toward the gate.

"Help!" he cried. "Rodriguez! Rodriguez!"

There were torches out, two of them, one set on either side of the gate. That was not usual with the Pons.

"Help!" cried Brenner.

There was something heaped, large, before the gate.

"Help! Help, Rodriguez!" screamed Brenner, running across the clearing.

To Brenner the gate, the palisade, represented safety and security. He did not consider that the frail, wretched palings of the tiny village would not be likely to constitute a very formidable obstacle to what was behind him.

"Allan! Allan!" cried a voice, from within the palisade.

The gate of the palisade opened a crack and Rodriguez emerged. Brenner was illuminated in the blaze of the electric torch in Rodriguez' hand. He had it in his left hand. In his right was the rifle.

"Aagh!" cried Brenner, falling against the thing heaped before the gate, some yards in front of it. It was stiff, and covered with fur. It lay oddly.

Rodriguez was then behind him. "Ai!" cried Rodriguez, looking out. Then, in the clearing, the light of the electric torch shone on the hideous monster. It backed away two or three yards, and then sat back, on its haunches.

"Aii," repeated Rodriguez, himself backing away.

"It is the same thing that did this, I am sure," said Rodriguez.

Brenner, shuddering, pushed back from the carcass lying heaped before the gate, and, unsteadily, stood. He then went around the carcass, and backed a step or two toward the gate.

"Rodriguez, come back!" said Brenner, hoarsely.

But Rodriguez, on the other side of the carcass, was standing there, very quietly, looking up at the thing some yards away. He flashed the torch about it.

It snarled.

"Come back!" begged Brenner.

"It is incredible!" marveled Rodriguez.

"Come back," said Brenner.

"Magnificent!" said Rodriguez.

Something of the beast, though it was several yards from the gate, on the other side of the carcass, could be made out in the torchlight The play of Rodriguez' electric torch made its hide seem pale, almost whitish, in the darting pools of light. Brenner conjectured that the beast's hide, if seen in good light, would be a variegated pattern of tans and browns. Such a coloration, against a mixed background, tends to obscure outlines. It also blends in well with lights and shadows. Too, on the flanks, it was marked with broad, vertical, darkish bars. These, too, Brenner thought, might make it difficult to detect, particularly against a forested background, particularly at dusk. If the animal were absolutely still, Brenner had the uneasy feeling that one might look directly at it, some yards away, and not see it.

The ears of the beast were erected.

It had a broad, feline head.

"It is magnificent!" said Rodriguez.

Brenner wondered at what might be the nature of the consciousness of such a thing.

Brenner could hear the jabbering of Pons behind the palings.

Rodriguez, keeping his eyes mainly on the beast, backed around the carcass and joined Brenner before the gate.

"We set out the torches for you," said Rodriguez.

"You expected me back?" said Brenner.

"The Pons did," said Rodriguez. "They assured me you would be all right. I have been waiting up all night, by the gate."

"The stones leading to Company Station have been changed," said Brenner. "They lead back here."

"Ah!" said Rodriguez.

"We are prisoners," said Brenner.

"It doesn't matter," said Rodriguez, looking out at the beast.

"What do you mean?" asked Brenner.

"Look!" said Rodriguez, flashing the light on the carcass that lay before the gate. It was very large, and tawny. Its head was twisted to one side, the jaws open, revealing fangs, and lay there, beside the body, as though it had been left there, by accident. The vertebrae of the neck had been bitten through. It was not a complete carcass, as portions of it had been eaten.

"Surely you recognize it?" asked Rodriguez.

He flashed the torch on the head of the carcass, where, on the forehead, above the eyes, was a white, starlike blaze.

"It is the beast that killed Archimedes," said Brenner, stupefied.

"Back away," said Rodriguez, quickly, whispering.

The huge thing which had followed Brenner approached the carcass, and put its nose down to it, and moving its head, turned the carcass a little.

"Yes!" said Rodriguez. "And it was brought to the gate this evening, after you had left, carried limp in the mouth of that beast, as easily as a bask cat might carry its kitten. He deposited it there. He left it there. He left it there!"

The hair on the back of Brenner's neck rose.

"You understand what this means?" asked Rodriguez.

"No!" said Brenner.

"This is an incredible discovery," said Rodriguez.

"We are prisoners here," said Brenner.

"It does not matter," said Rodriguez. "That is not important now."

"It is going to eat it now?" asked Brenner.

But the gigantic feline had now lifted its head away from the carcass.

"No, it is not fresh now," said Rodriguez. "He will leave it for others. When they come we had best be within the gate."

Brenner recalled what might be the nature of some of the others. He shuddered.

"Come inside now," said Rodriguez.

Brenner regarded the gigantic, catlike beast. It was sitting behind the carcass, back on its haunches.

Come along," said Rodriguez.

"I encountered it in the forest," said Brenner.

"I do not think that that was an accident," said Rodriguez.

Brenner looked at him, puzzled.

"We are going to the temple," said Rodriguez. "I have had enough of the secrecy of these Pons."

"I do not understand," said Brenner.

"I will show you what I mean," said Rodriguez, elatedly. "I shall show you what must be the case!"

Rodriguez took down the torches from beside the gate. He thrust them into the hands of Pons.

"Let us get the gate closed!" he said.

Brenner looked once more at the gigantic, catlike beast, sitting there. Now that the torches had been moved, and Rodriguez' light was no longer playing upon it, he could see only its outline against the sky, the erected ears, the broad feline head.

"Come inside!" said Rodriguez.

"It seems almost tame," said Brenner.

"It is not tame," said Rodriguez.

In a moment Brenner was inside the gate. He still clung to the stick he had carried in the forest. Now, inside the palisade, he realized how futile a weapon it would have been.

Several Pons swung shut the gate.

"Greetings," said several Pons to Brenner. But they did not touch him. Pons did very little touching.

The bars, the bottom one with handles, the top with poles, which fitted into sockets, were slid in place, these blocking the gate from opening.

Brenner pressed himself against the lower bar and strained his eyes, looking out, through the palings of the gate.

Rodriguez joined him at the gate and shone his torch through. It illuminated the carcass outside the gate, but nothing else, but a part of the clearing.

"It's gone," said Brenner.

Rodriguez slung the rifle, disguised as an optical instrument, over his shoulder.

"It's gone," said Brenner.

"Come along," said Rodriguez, and strode away, toward the center of the village. Brenner struggled to keep up with him. At the center of the village Rodriguez did not turn left to their hut, but made rather a quarter right toward the northeast part of the village. In moments they had come to the entrance of the temple. As it might be recalled, this was a long, narrow building of wood, much of which had earth banked about it. It had a painted, carved, ornate entrance, with wooden side pillars. A Pon was near the entrance.

"Rodriguez," said Brenner. "This portal, the long axis of the temple. It is aligned with the string, with the platform near the cliffs!"

"Of course," said Rodriguez. "Have you just noticed that?"

The Pon quickly placed himself before Rodriguez but Rodriguez, with one hand, brushed it aside. When it returned, to renew its protest, he seized it by the back of the neck and threw it a dozen feet to the side. Brenner, quite other than he would have been earlier, did not object.

"Come along!" said Rodriguez, eagerly.

Together, they entered the temple. There was no light within it. Rodriguez" torch illumined their way.

"There is little here," said Brenner, following Rodriguez through a corridor.

Rodriguez' light flashed here and there, revealing only heavy wooden walls.

"There will be something here," said Rodriguez, grimly.

"The ceiling is high," said Brenner.

"That gods may better walk here," laughed Rodriguez.

This did not much reassure Brenner. Their footing seemed now to descend.

Rodriguez pressed on, the light darting about.

It was not unusual, of course, for the architecture of temples, with vistas, spacious expanses and lofty heights, to contrast vividly with that of lesser places. How often temples rose grandly above the hovels of the faithful.

"There is not much art here," said Brenner.

"What do you expect of monkeys?" asked Rodriguez.

"There is some carving outside," said Brenner.

"The corridor is widening," said Rodriguez. "We are coming to some sort of room, or hall."

They were now well underground, and probably well beyond the palisade.

They stopped before a large, rectangular portal, now closed, access to which would be obtained by means of two doors, each mounted on its wooden hinges; the interior edges of these doors, when closed, as now, would meet in the middle, and, when open, would swing to a side. These doors with their side pillars, and lintel, were carved, and painted, largely purple and yellow.

Beside the two doors were torches, unlit, one on each side.

Rodriguez, flicking on a lighter, an electric match, reached up and lit the torch to the right. He then snapped off the electric torch and hooked it on his belt. He then lit the torch to the left.

"Give me a hand here," said Rodriguez.

Brenner went to one of the two doors of the portal and pushed against it, while Rodriguez pushed against the other. They swung inward.

Within, to one side, they saw a Pon. It seemed frail. Perhaps it was quite old. If so, this was of interest, because most of the Pons seemed neither young nor old. They just seemed Pons. Perhaps the thing in front of them was injured, or diseased. In the village there had seemed to be little, if any, evidence, of injury or disease. Perhaps that was because the afflicted were hidden away, perhaps locked away in this very place. It was robed, and a hood muchly concealed its face. It was not more than a yard in height, and would not have weighed more than thirty Commonworld pounds. It put up its hands, in a gesture which was not a threatening one, nor one of prohibition, nor of warning, nor even one which was really defensive. It was more as though it were surprised, and wanted to reach out with its hands, as though to touch, to feel, to investigate.

"Do not be afraid," said Rodriguez. "Come here."

The tiny creature approached, its hands outstretched before it.

Rodriguez let it touch his face. Then, with two hands, he put back the hood.

Brenner suppressed a cry of horror.

"Who did this to you?" asked Rodriguez, sternly.

The Pon pulled back.

"Note the scarring about the eye sockets," said Rodriguez, angrily.

"Yes," whispered Brenner.

What had been done there had not been accomplished with surgical neatness. Brenner remembered the bones in the clearing, from the preceding afternoon, the cuts on them, the nicks, where the flesh had been scraped from them, perhaps in some unleashed communal madness, some social passion of mindless vengeance, in some holiday of horror. Brenner turned away from the little thing. He did not want to look at it. It was horrifying enough to look upon one of his own species who had been tortured, or mutilated. It seemed somehow additionally pathetic, if only because so pointless, that an animal, a Pon, should have been treated in this fashion.

"They did this to you?" said Rodriguez, bitterly.

The thing shook its head.

"Do not lie to me," said Rodriguez. "It was done with deliberation."

The Pon pulled the hood again over its head.

"No!" whispered Rodriguez.

The Pon backed away, a step.

"It did it to itself," said Rodriguez, shuddering.

"Why?" asked Brenner.

"There could be many reasons," said Rodriguez.

Rodriguez pointed to one of the torches beside the portal.

"You are going on?" said Brenner.

"Take it," said Rodriguez. He seized the other.

"What do you expect to find here?" asked Brenner.

"I will show you," said Rodriguez, the light of the torch moving ahead.

Quickly Brenner followed him.

"There!" said Rodriguez after a moment. "There! See!"

At the end of the large, underground room, they had come to a heavy, broad platform, quite like the one in the open, at the foot of the cliffs. Behind the platform there was a large opening, which might have led into a cavern, or den, or tunnel. What Rodriguez had particularly called Brenner's attention to was one of two stout posts, set at the front left and right corners of the platform. There had been nothing like these posts at the other platform, the one in the open, by the cliffs. Rodriguez stood at the front, right corner of the platform and lifted his torch. On the top of the post, carved there, painted, very large, indeed., life-size, was the head of an unnaturally huge, terrible beast. The head was broad, and feline. Between the eyes, set rather forward on the head, there were at least eighteen to twenty inches. The iris of the eyes, as the head was painted, was yellow. The pupils were black, narrow and vertical. The eyes had been painted rather in the appearance they might have borne in daylight, rather than at night. Not all features were the same, of course. For example, the head was largely purple, save for the eyes and teeth. Yet, despite such discrepancies, or artistic licenses, there was no mistaking the nature of the beast depicted. It was the same which Brenner had encountered in the forest, that which had followed him to the village. A similar head, carved and painted, surmounted the post at the other front corner of the broad platform. Brenner went and examined it, and then returned to the other side, to rejoin Rodriguez.

"Occasionally I had suspected some such thing," said Rodriguez, "but then I would dismiss it."

"What is it?" asked Brenner.

"Look upon the totem of the Pons," said Rodriguez.

CHAPTER 24

"It is impossible!" said Brenner, looking up at the great, carved head on the post.

"Not at all," said Rodriguez. "And that is the least interesting thing about the matter."

"I do not understand," said Brenner.

"Do you mind if I look a bit into this cavern, or tunnel, or whatever it is behind the platform?" asked Rodriguez. "Such things tend to make me a bit nervous."

Brenner shook his head.

Rodriguez thrust his torch into a nearby rack, or holder. There were many such things about, particularly on the walls. At times, Brenner conjectured, the room might be well lit with such devices. This place did not have look of disuse about it which characterized the platform in the open. Rodriguez then removed the weapon from his shoulder and armed it.

"Come along," he said. "I do not anticipate any danger."

Brenner, holding up the torch, followed Rodriguez about the edge of the platform, toward the entrance, or exit, as it might be, in the back wall.

"If this is a cave," said Rodriguez, "it is almost bound to be empty. If it is a tunnel, it is almost certain to be sealed off."

"Where does it lead?" asked Brenner, after a moment or two. It did, indeed, appear to be some sort of tunnel, or, at any rate, a long, narrow cave, of some length.

"I don't know," said Rodriguez.

They had come to a stout gate of timbers. This was reinforced from the back and, on the side which faced out, away from the room, was guarded by numerous, projecting spikes of sharpened wood, each, at its base, as thick as the body of a Pon.

"The gate suggests that this is a tunnel," said Rodriguez. "And, if so, there is probably a similar barrier at the other end."

"It seems they do not trust their totem," said Brenner.

"The gate, or gates, may not be to fend away the totem," said Rodriguez.

"True," said Brenner. He recalled the tawny brute which had carried away Archimedes, and the beasts in the pack, in the forest. There might be many varieties of creature in the forest, which reportedly teemed with life.

"I see no tracks on the other side," said Rodriguez. "Nothing may have come down that passage in a thousand years."

"Let us go back to the main room," said Brenner.

Rodriguez disarmed the rifle, returned it to its harmless guise, and replaced it, by means of its sling, on his shoulder.

"It is an incredible animal," said Brenner, in a few moments, again looking up at the gigantic, carved head, that on the post at the right, forward corner of the platform.

"It is a most beautiful and dangerous creature," said Rodriguez.

"Yes," agreed Brenner.

"Now it becomes clear why the Pons accepted with such good grace your disproof, so to speak, of the git as their totem. It was not their totem."

"But this!" said Brenner, looking up at the monstrous head.

"It is not that unusual to pick a terrifying, dangerous animal as a totem," said Rodriguez. "There are many points in favor of doing so. Better to be allies with such a terror than its enemies, or prey. Too, you must see the advantage of such an arrangement from the point of view of the Pons, from the point of view of the primitive mind. They are "children of the totem.""

"And no animal devours its own young," said Brenner.

"Precisely," said Rodriguez. "Such a belief, too, interestingly, might even give them some security from the totem. In its presence, they would not be likely to sweat the exudates associated with terror, or to betray fear by awkward, or uncertain, or uncoordinated movements, arousing curiosity and aggression, or to flee from it, inciting pursuit, and so on. And, of course, if a dangerous totem animal does attack one once in a while, or eat one, or whatever, that can always be explained as the result of some hidden fault in the victim, some secret violation of taboo, such things."

"Of course," said Brenner. Such closed belief systems, like circles without openings, not susceptible to clear refutation, existed in their thousands in the galaxy. Interestingly, they tended to be taken seriously by their devotees. Their imperviousness to refutation, their immunity to disproof, a natural consequence of their vacuity, tended to be taken by many as evidence of their truth.

"And it is certainly not as if they were consorting with the beast on a familiar basis," said Rodriguez.

"No," agreed Brenner.

"We had best be getting back," said Rodriguez.

"Why did they conceal the true nature of their totem?" asked Brenner.

"That is not that unusual," said Rodriguez. "The totem animal is sacred. Its relationship to the totem group is quite sensitive. It is to be protected, perhaps even against enchantments or spells. They may not wish the identity of the totem to be known, for fear enemies might try to harm it. The name of the totem may be seldom mentioned. If it is mentioned, it may not be called by its own name, and so on."

"I understand," said Brenner.

"In some groups it is forbidden even to look upon the totem," said Rodriguez.

"The Pon we met within the portal?" said Brenner.

"I do not think so," said Rodriguez. "The Pons outside

tonight, those within the palisade, dozens of them, looked upon the beast. I noted it. I watched them. Too, there are two explicit carvings of it, in this very room. Presumably Pons enter here. It seems certain that there is no taboo, or, at least, no general taboo, against Pons looking upon the totem animal."

"Then what of the Pon we saw when we entered?" asked Brenner.

"I do not know," said Rodriguez.

"His injuries were self-inflicted?"

"It seems so," said Rodriguez.

"But why would he do such a thing to himself?" asked Brenner.

"Perhaps he witnessed the beatific vision," said Rodriguez.

"I do not understand," said Brenner.

"And did not care for it," added Rodriguez.

"I do not understand," said Brenner.

"It is not important," said Rodriguez.

"Rodriguez," protested Brenner.

"Many is the saint," said Rodriguez, "who, granted a glimpse of his god, would cry out with horror."

Brenner was silent.

"That is the "father,"" said Rodriguez, looking up at the great, painted head on the post. "And how many, in any culture, can look on the "father," if they understand it, and see it as it truly is, unflinchingly?"

"But the others look upon it," said Brenner.

"Not comprehendingly," said Rodriguez. "The rarest gift is to look upon such things, and understand them, in all their terror, their mercilessness, their beauty, their reality, to look upon the world, the cosmos, the father, so to speak, and understand it, and then, knowingly, with a hearty will, rejoicing, even with a great laugh, to accept it, to affirm it, to rejoice in it, to celebrate it, to meet it, to make of it a game and a festival."

"You are speaking of more than a totem," said Brenner.

"We all have our totems," said Rodriguez.

"This thing, for you, is only a symbol!" said Brenner.

"But one which is quite exact," said Rodriguez.

"Let us leave, quickly!" said Brenner.

"You think that I am mad?"

"It is hard to understand you," said Brenner.

"It was not my intention to frighten you."

"We should go now," said Brenner. "We have solved the mystery of the Pons."

"That is absurd," said Rodriguez. "We have solved but one mystery, and that the least of all, the mere nature of the totem beast."

"What more is there to learn?" asked Brenner.

"Much," said Rodriguez.

"What?" said Brenner.

"This afternoon," said Rodriguez, "the beast brought his kill to the gate of the Pons, and left it there. I saw it coming across the clearing, roused by the cries of Pons. The Pons, when the beast had left, rushed out, rejoicing, striking the carcass with sticks."

"I do not understand why the beast would have killed the other animal, or brought it here."

"It is quite clear from the point of view of the Pons," said Rodriguez.

Brenner looked at him, perplexed.

"Surely you see?"

"No," said Brenner.

"It is in accord with the *pact*, the *pact*, between the totem and the totem group."

"That is madness," said Brenner.

"You saw the carcass. It is that of the animal which slew Archimedes."

"It is some sort of coincidence," said Brenner.

"The beast followed you, did it not, into the forest?"

"I encountered it in the forest," said Brenner.

"You carried Archimedes back to the village," said Rodriguez. "Your shirt is still filthy with his blood. The scent of Pon would have been on you."

"I was threatened by hideous creatures in the forest," said

Brenner, numbly. "They left, detecting the presence of the huge beast. I ran. The beast followed."

"It protected you," said Rodriguez, fiercely.

"No!" said Brenner. "It threatened me. It would confront me. I would run another way. Then I found the trail of stones. I followed it back to the village."

"Followed by the beast," said Rodriguez.

"Apparently," said Brenner.

"It guided you to the stones," said Rodriguez.

"No!" said Brenner.

"It was your guide, and your guardian angel," said Rodriguez.

"Madness," said Brenner.

"On you was the scent of Pon," said Rodriguez.

"It is a coincidence," said Brenner.

"Here," said Rodriguez, thoughtfully, "it is as though the pact was not mere totemistic mythology. It is rather as though it were real."

"Do not speak madness," said Brenner.

"That is one of the true mysteries here," said Rodriguez, "the pact."

"Have you see such a beast before?" asked Brenner, looking up at the head on the post.

"Of course," said Rodriguez.

"It was the tracks of such a beast we found within the village, was it not?" said Brenner.

"That seems certain now," said Rodriguez.

"But you seemed surprised," said Brenner.

"Certainly," said Rodriguez, smiling.

"'Certainly'?"

"Certainly," repeated Rodriguez.

"Presumably, too, it was the claws of the beast which had torn open the boards, and furrowed the posts, at the other platform, that by the cliffs," said Brenner.

"Undoubtedly," said Rodriguez.

"But you seemed to dismiss that possibility at the time," said Brenner.

"For a very good reason," said Rodriguez.

"Why?" asked Brenner.

"One mystery we may have solved here," said Rodriguez, "is how the Pons have survived in the forest."

Brenner regarded him.

"Such creatures as Pons can exist only in gardens of flowers," said Rodriguez, "and then they had best not look into the grass, or between the stems of the plants, lest they see the jungle there. They live in a world of sunlit, benevolent trivialities, without risk, without challenge, without adventure, sunning themselves like turtles until they die. Such creatures are weak, worthless, soft. They cannot live in a real world unless they are guarded by lions. It is the lions which make their little flower worlds possible."

"And the beast is their lion?" said Brenner.

"It makes such things as Pons possible," said Rodriguez.

"But there have been Pons for thousands of years," said Brenner.

"That is one of the mysteries," said Rodriguez.

"There have been "lions," too, for thousands of years," said Brenner.

"Or things like them," mused Rodriguez.

"Lions," said Brenner.

"No," said Rodriguez. "That is not possible."

"It frightens me," said Brenner, "that such a thing might once have walked in the village, when the gate had been left open."

"It may have been left open by intent," said Rodriguez.

"Doubtless as a gesture of hospitality," said Brenner, bitterly.

"Possibly," said Rodriguez. "But surely you do not think the palisade would be sufficient to keep out that beast, if it wanted in?"

Brenner shuddered.

"Consider its size," said Rodriguez. "It could push through the palings. Consider its agility. It could leap over the fence. Consider its jaws, and the likely might of their grip. It could seize and uproot such palings, such wretched sticks."

"Quite possibly," said Brenner, uneasily.

"Consider, too, its paws, their unusual nature," said Rodriguez.

"I did not notice them," said Brenner.

"I did," said Rodriguez, "this afternoon, and, again, tonight, in the light of the torches. Too, I have seen such things before. They are not the common sort of paw you would expect on a predator. You might have noted the digits, their length, their jointing, the positioning of them."

"What are you saying?" asked Brenner.

"That the paws can grip, not just strike, and hold and tear," said Rodriguez.

"They are prehensile?" asked Brenner.

"With such paws, said Rodriguez, "it could, if it thought in such a manner, push apart palings, snapping them, it could pull them from the ground, it could even reach between them to slide back the bars."

"Do you remember, in the forest, when we first left Company Station, months ago, how the Pons were at first uneasy, even frightened, and then, a little later, proceeded with confidence?"

"Of course," said Rodriguez.

"The beast?" said Brenner.

"Undoubtedly," said Rodriguez. "It was then with them, their secret companion, the angel, secret, dark, and terrible, which would accompany them in the forests."

"The forest was then so quiet," said Brenner.

"It knew more than we," said Rodriguez. "It knew, as we did not, what moved amongst its trees. It was frightened, and hid itself."

"You may have seen it," said Brenner.

"Now, in retrospect, interpreting shadows, movements amongst trees, what seemed, briefly, to appear, an evanescent silhouette, and such, I think I did," said Rodriguez. "But, as with the tracks in the village, the marks at the platform, I would not acknowledge that to which the evidence pointed."

"Why?"

"It did not seem to me possible," said Rodriguez.

"You know this sort of animal," said Brenner.

"Yes," said Rodriguez.

"It is interesting that Pons could manage to train such a creature."

"Such things cannot be trained," said Rodriguez.

"Obviously the Pons have trained it."

"Such things do not train," said Rodriguez. "They kill their keepers."

"Perhaps if taken when young?"

"No," said Rodriguez.

"Something like that must be the case," said Brenner.

"No," said Rodriguez.

"Then we have a fascinating example of zoological symbiosis here," said Brenner.

"No," said Rodriguez.

"Like the warning bird, nesting in the coat of the Chian buffalo, whose cries warn it of the approach of intruders, like the scavenger eels swimming in and out of the mouth of the Abderan shark, cleaning its teeth."

"No," said Rodriguez. "Such relationships involve reciprocities. Each partner derives a benefit. It is clear that the protection of the beast is much to the profit of the Pons, but what possible profit in this accrues to the beast? It does not live with them. They do not shelter it. They do not alert it to the presence of enemies. They do not clean it. They do not groom it. They do not even feed it, nor could they, on their resources, do so. And such things, I assure you, do not live on fruits and porridge. Indeed, in protecting the Pons, it seems the beast is actually acting against its own best interests. For example, the provision of such a service must involve time and effort, which might better be bestowed elsewhere. Too, of course, it excludes a convenient, easily obtained item from its larder, a sacrifice which, I expect, numerous other predators of the forest are less prepared to make."

"Perhaps it keeps the Pons about, rather as bait, to attract other things to feed on?"

"How so?" asked Rodriguez, interested.

"Like the Assyrian panther with the snow does it herds?"

"Or the Milesian corath with the small flocks of females of our own species?"

"Precisely," said Brenner.

"No," said Rodriguez. "That would not explain such things as depositing the body of the animal which killed Archimedes before the gate."

"To reassure the Pons of their safety?"

"It would be more likely to terrify them into remaining within their walls," said Rodriguez. "Bait is normally most effective when it goes about its business, quite unaware of its danger. In the case of the Assyrian panther and the Milesian corath, and other such life forms, too, the hunters, with their bait, angling with it, so to speak, are usually rovers, taking the bait into new and different areas, where their stratagems are likely to be unknown."

"You do not think such a thing, then, is involved in the pact?" said Brenner.

"No," said Rodriguez.

"What then is the nature of the pact?" asked Brenner.

"That is one of the mysteries," smiled Rodriguez.

"We had best get back to the hut," said Brenner.

"Very well," said Rodriguez, retrieving his torch from the torch rack.

But Brenner stood where he was, looking up at the massive, carved head on the post.

Rodriguez, torch in hand, turned back.

"You said," said Brenner, "you knew what sort of animal this is."

"I do," said Rodriguez.

"You have seen them before?"

"Yes," said Rodriguez.

"You seemed familiar with its prints," said Brenner.

"I am," said Rodriguez.

"Where had you seen them?" asked Brenner.

"In the sands of the arenas of Megara," said Rodriguez. "When I was a boy, I raked sand there. It was there, too, where I became aware of the marks of its claws. Some of the marks were eighty feet high, on the barriers, as the beast sought to leap up, and clamber over them. Too, I saw their work on various life forms. One blow of the paw of such a thing can break the back of a mastodon of Thule, another can tear out the belly and backbone of a Thracian dragon. I have seen it."

"I see," said Brenner.

"I have also seen," said Rodriguez, "what it can do to those of our own species."

"Our own species?" asked Brenner.

"In the arenas it is common to match a hundred of our species, derelicts, prisoners of war, captures, debtors, criminals, adventurers, and such, armed with spears, against just one of these."

"Horrifying," said Brenner.

"Perhaps," said Rodriguez, "but the spectacle is popular on Megara. The crowds find it amusing."

"I see," said Brenner.

"The betting usually favors the beast," added Rodriguez.

"I am not surprised," said Brenner.

"Women who come to Megara to see the games, seeking thrills and excitement, sometimes find themselves seized, and set forth as stripped prizes."

"Horrifying," said Brenner.

"They serve as incitements to the men," said Rodriguez. "A woman is one of the nicest things a man can own."

"Undoubtedly," said Brenner.

"Yes," said Rodriguez.

"Do the women participate in these contests?" asked Brenner.

"No," said Rodriguez. "It is theirs merely to watch, naked, and in chains, their fate entirely dependent on the efforts of men."

"I see," said Brenner.

"That is as it should be," said Rodriguez.

"Of course," said Brenner. "What is their fate, if the men are successful?"

"They are, of course, distributed amongst them, as slaves."

"And what if the beast is successful?"

"They are fed to it," said Rodriguez.

"I see," said Brenner.

"Sometimes viragoes appear in the arena, so-called "Amazons,"" said Rodriguez. "They are usually matched against dwarfs. Such matches are used as interludes, as comic relief, between serious contests."

"Such a beast, then, will eat the flesh of our species?" asked Brenner.

"Certainly," said Rodriguez. "At times, eagerly."

"It did not attack me in the forest," said Brenner.

"On you was the scent of Pon," said Rodriguez. "That presumably protected you."

"The pact?"

"Presumably," said Rodriguez.

"It must be difficult and dangerous to capture such a beast for the games," said Brenner.

"I would not wish to go after one with spears and ropes, with torches and nets, and such," said Rodriguez, "but, as it is done these days, on a commercial basis, there is very little danger. Heat detectors are used. The animal is felled with gases or tranquilizing charges. The whole thing is done from a safe distance, from the air. The beast is transported back to a holding compound by air truck, and so on."

"I did not know such a beast was native to Abydos," said Brenner, looking up at the massive, carved head, shuddering.

Rodriguez put back his head, and laughed.

"What is so amusing?" asked Brenner, irritated.

"That," said Rodriguez.

"What?" asked Brenner, angrily.

"Forgive me, my friend," said Rodriguez, "but therein is found another of our small mysteries."

"I do not understand," said Brenner.

"That is why I did not permit myself to correctly interpret what I saw in the forest," said Rodriguez. "That is why I did not allow myself to understand the tracks in the village, or the marks on the platform by the cliffs."

"I do not understand," said Brenner.

"You do not know what beast that is, do you, really?" asked Rodriguez.

"No," said Brenner. "I do not."

"Have you heard of the world called 'Persia'?"

"Yes," said Brenner.

"It is a desert world for the most part," said Rodriguez, "but in its subarctic regions, in the northern and southern hemisphere, there are forested latitudes, much as on Abydos. From that world come these animals. Several varieties are found there. Most are tawny, short-haired and desert-adapted, but there are forest varieties, too, and those of the northern hemisphere are generally marked like the beast you saw this afternoon."

"What you are telling me is impossible," said Brenner.

"The animal you saw today is a Persian lion," said Rodriguez.

"What are you telling me?" said Brenner.

"That the totem of the Pons is not native to this world," said Rodriguez.

"That is absurd," said Brenner.

"It must have been brought here, deliberately."

"Impossible," said Brenner.

"Its presence here is one of our little mysteries," said Rodriguez. "And I will tell you another. Perhaps you recall, earlier, that you said that there had been Pons for thousands of years, which is true, and then, later, you said, in effect, 'lions, too', and I said that that was impossible?"

"Vaguely," said Brenner.

"Have you ever heard of a totemistic group changing its totem?" asked Rodriguez.

"Never," said Brenner.

"Nor I," said Rodriguez. "But the world, Persia, as you apparently do not realize, is a comparatively recent addition to our family of known worlds. It was first discovered, explored, and charted only some five thousand years ago."

"Then the Persian lion, that is, that species of animal, could not have always been the totem beast of the Pons."

"No," said Rodriguez.

"Perhaps they were once not totemistic," said Brenner.

"As far as we know," said Rodriguez, "at least for thousands of years, they have been totemistic."

"They have had, possibly, in that time, a succession of totem animals?" asked Brenner.

"That seems a possibility," said Rodriguez.

"It makes no sense," said Brenner.

"We may be dealing here with a very unusual form of totemism," said Rodriguez.

"I am frightened," said Brenner.

"The Pons may be a subtler, more complex life form than we have guessed," said Rodriguez.

"I am ready to return to the hut," said Brenner.

"The greatest mystery, of course," said Rodriguez, "remains, that with which we are most fundamentally concerned, totemism itself, its origin and its meaning. We know that it is, or is close to, the beginning, that on a thousand worlds, perhaps all, it antedates gods and heroes, religions and philosophies, laws and institutions. Out of its lost, dark soil have sprung civilizations. It is, I suspect, literally the key to the origins of culture, that which frees us from the wheel of nature, that which breaks the cycles of eons, that which most significantly divides forms of life. To be sure, perhaps we have then been entered only upon vaster wheels, grander, more terrifying cycles of growth, and of aging and decay, those of civilizations themselves, but even so, in spite of all, I would understand this totemism, this little, problematic, frightening thing which I think may be the key to culture itself, this strange conception, with its associated practices, which seems so pervasively to lie, often forgotten, secret and mysterious, on a thousand worlds, at the root of civilization itself."

Rodriguez and Brenner then turned about, and walked back toward the two large doors, those through which they had entered the room. As they did so, they detected, to their right, the Pon whom they had met earlier, on their way in. It was half concealed in the shadows, the darkness. They did not raise their torches to illuminate it.

Before they exited, Brenner turned about, once more to regard the platform at the end of the room.

It was hard to see now, far off, in the flickering shadows.

Still, however, one could make out the two painted, massive, carved heads on the posts, one at each front corner of the platform.

"It is a beautiful, savage animal," said Brenner.

Rodriguez lifted his torch. The Pon was coming forth, a few steps, timidly, from the shadows. They could see it clearly now. It put up its hands, as though it might be some sort of gesture of warning. To be sure, it was difficult to interpret such a behavior.

"What does it mean?" asked Brenner.

"Do not mind it," said Rodriguez. "It is an outcast, a pariah. Such, scorned, held in contempt, mistreated, are common in totemistic cultures. They are used for such things as feeding individuals who are temporarily taboo, for example, individuals who have attended to the dead, and such."

Rodriguez then extinguished his torch, and put it in the holder, to the right of the door, as one would enter it.

"We will leave boldly," said Rodriguez, "as though nothing were different."

"Of course" said Brenner. But, of course, too, everything was different.

"Tomorrow," said Rodriguez, "I will go back to the platform by the cliffs."

"Perhaps it is too soon to do so," said Brenner.

"There is a valley behind the cliffs. I saw openings there. I wish to explore them."

"It may not be wise," said Brenner.

"I think I know what I will find there, at least in part," said Rodriguez. "I wish to make certain."

"It may be dangerous," said Brenner.

"I have the rifle," said Rodriguez.

Rodriguez removed the electric torch from his belt, and snapped it on. Brenner extinguished his torch and, with the help of Rodriguez' light, replaced it in its holder, to the left of the door, as one would face it. When they left the temple several Pons were standing about. Rodriguez pushed through them, and Brenner followed him.

In a moment or two they had returned to their hut.

"There is something of additional interest about the totem animal," said Rodriguez.

"You mean the particular beast that followed me back to the village?"

"Yes," said Rodriguez.

"What?" asked Brenner.

"It is old," he said.

Brenner looked at him.

"Is it not clear?" asked Rodriguez.

"No," said Brenner.

"They will need a new one soon," said Rodriguez.

CHAPTER 25

"You should not have come without the rifle," said Brenner.

"You did not need to accompany me," said Rodriguez.

He shone the electric torch about the walls of the long, narrow, cavelike aperture, cut into the side of the cliff.

The rifle, as so many items, now and again, in the past, had been missing that morning. To be sure, the Pons would not have understood its power, its capacity for destruction, its terribleness, even that it was a weapon. Presumably they would not even understand the nature of the optical instrument it was designed to resemble, a telescope, or distance magnifier. It was probably not even, to them, a toy. It was only a shiny object, attractive, and pretty, like mirrors, like colored, multifaceted glass beads. To be sure, it was unfortunate that on this morning, this particular morning, it had disappeared. Brenner, as you might suppose, had then strenuously opposed Rodriguez' leaving the village, particularly considering his proposed destination, but, predictably, Rodriguez, in his impatient, obstinate fashion, had insisted on going. "It will not be better tomorrow," he had said. And perhaps that was true. It was irritating to think that the Pons, with their penchant for picking up objects, usually bright, attractive ones, sometimes smooth, well-fitted complex ones, like boxes or cases, and such, showed so little sense or discrimination. One thing would be to them much as another thing. A radio, for example, would be nothing to them but a fascinating metal object, an aesthetic artifact, not a valuable technological apparatus, a means for speaking across great distances. Most of the things they had taken were of little value, of course, and their loss represented little more than a nuisance or inconvenience to Rodriguez and Brenner, but the loss of some other things, as you might suppose, such as the radios, was quite serious, resulting, as it did, in a severe reduction in their resources. And the loss of the rifle, of course, might actually prove dangerous.

"Do not go!" Brenner had begged Rodriguez.

"Do not come with me," Rodriguez had said to Brenner.

"Very well," had said Brenner. "You shall go alone!"

But, of course, when Rodriguez had left the village, Brenner had accompanied him.

"These places grow less well-hewn," said Rodriguez, shining the light about. "I would say this one dates from some middle period."

"There is a side passage there," said Brenner.

"Yes," said Rodriguez. Some of these side passages, as they had discovered, led to other chambers. Some led to a veritable interlinkage of chambers. Some of these side chambers, as it had turned out, could be reached directly, from their own external entrances, and some only indirectly, by means of other passages.

"Shall we follow it?"

"Of course," said Rodriguez.

"Anything could walk here," said Brenner, looking up at the steep walls, the lofty ceiling.

"But it hasn't," said Rodriguez. "Consider the dust."

"Animals might den in such places," said Brenner.

"But apparently they do not do so," said Rodriguez.

"Why not?" inquired Brenner.

"They are forest creatures," said Rodriguez.

"Come now," said Brenner.

"Perhaps they are afraid to do so," said Rodriguez.

"You do not put me at my ease," said Brenner.

"Perhaps these places are guarded," said Rodriguez.

"By what?" asked Brenner.

"That is a joke," said Rodriguez.

"I am uneasy here," said Brenner.

"Look!" said Rodriguez.

The light shone now on a gigantic marble sarcophagus. Above this object, and behind it, in a sort of vast niche in the wall, there was a gigantic head, carved from marble. It was the representation of a crocodilian animal.

"Behold another totem of the Pons," said Rodriguez.

Brenner shuddered.

"The forest must once have been much more moist than now," said Rodriguez. "More marshlike, or swamplike."

In their explorations in the cliff passages, many of them interlinked, they had found many such sarcophagi, with similar carvings, sometimes in marble, sometimes in limestone, sometimes in wood. The subjects of these carvings had been numerous, but all were of apparently formidable creatures, of one sort or another. The most recent such carving, or that which was apparently most recent, was of wood, and had been found in one of the first passages explored. It was that, unmistakably, of a Persian lion. It might be mentioned that many of the chambers associated with these passages were empty, particularly in the vicinity of the most recent carvings.

"Such creatures are more inert and simple than the current totem," said Rodriguez. "The Persian lion, I would think, constitutes an improvement on such creatures."

"From the point of view of the Pon," said Brenner.

"Of course," said Rodriguez.

"I am afraid to be here," said Brenner, suddenly.

"Why?" asked Rodriguez. "We are safe. We have taken care to protect ourselves."

"Oh, yes," said Brenner, miserably.

"Come along," said Rodriguez, eagerly, starting into another passage.

"Excellent," said Rodriguez, shining his light on another stone representation, in its niche, above and behind another sarcophagus.

"It is a frightening carving," said Brenner.

"It is beautiful," said Rodriguez.

The light shone on what appeared to be the triangular, flattish head of a gigantic snake.

"Early middle period," said Rodriguez.

"Certainly," said Brenner, skeptically.

Rodriguez laughed, delightedly. "Surely you recognize that these carvings do group themselves in terms of technique and conception, that there are differences in style."

"That's true," said Brenner.

"And so I am putting them into periods," said Rodriguez.

"You are incorrigible," said Brenner.

"I wonder if these things are due to Pons," mused Rodriguez.

"Why?" asked Brenner.

"It seems unlikely they could work stone, and with this skill, and, more importantly, with this grasp of what they are doing."

"Do you recognize the snake?" asked Brenner.

"I think so," said Rodriguez.

"What do you think it is?"

"I think it is a Nubian viper," said Rodriguez.

"That cannot be," said Brenner.

"Why not?" asked Rodriguez.

"That is not native to this world," said Brenner.

"Neither is the Persian lion," said Rodriguez.

"Things grow more archaic," said Rodriguez.

"Yes," said Brenner.

There were duplications, of course, amongst the many

carvings in the various chambers, reached by diverse passages. The totems, or representations thereof, if that is what they were, upon occasion seemed to constitute a series. For example, over a considerable period it seemed the totem animal, if these were really totem animals, as seemed likely, had been a form of large, ferretoid creature, and after that some varieties of panther, of sorts probably native to the forest, not unlike that which had borne away Archimedes. These forms of mammalian creatures, quadrupeds, seemed to have been on the whole the most recently favored choices of the Pons, assuming these things to have been done by the Pons. Needless to say, the Persian lion, a representative of which species was the current totem of the Pons, represented an archetype, or exemplar, of such a life form, the quadrupedal predator. Many of the animals portrayed, it must be admitted, were not recognized by Rodriguez, which was interesting, because he was not only a hunter, but something of a gifted, and well-informed, amateur naturalist. Of the animals he was sure he recognized, certain ones, such as the Nubian viper and Persian lion, were not, surprisingly, native to Abydos. Whereas one might have supposed many of the totems to have been purely fanciful, or mythical, or, if not, merely represented, perhaps from pictures or accounts of far worlds, and had perhaps never in actuality roamed the environing forests in one or another of their historical states, there was no doubt, at least, about one thing. These forests, now, in their immediate, present state, did constitute the current habitat of at least one of the beasts represented, the Persian lion.

"As we come to earlier and earlier passages," whispered Rodriguez, "have you noticed how many of the totems have become more Ponlike."

"More simian," said Brenner.

"I had begun to suspect," said Rodriguez, "that these passages, the chambers, the sarcophagi, the carvings, and such, because of the work involved, and the nature of it, could not have been done by Pons, but now I am less sure of it."

"You think something different was here, long ago, that

it made these places, and that the Pons, coming later, or culturally influenced, borrowed their totemism from it?"

"Corrupting and reducing it in the process," smiled Rodriguez, "as I would expect, from Pons."

"But now you are not sure?"

"No," said Rodriguez. "In the totems it is rather like the Pons are concerned, later, more and more, to conceal or obscure any possible kinship, or relationship, between their own life form and the totem type."

"The differences begin rather dramatically at the beginning of what you chose to call the middle period."

"Yes," said Rodriguez. "It is almost as though they wanted to distance themselves from some memory, or event, or insight."

"Or obscure it to others?" said Brenner.

"That is possible," said Rodriguez.

"Why should that be?" asked Brenner.

"I don't know," said Rodriguez.

"Some of the middle totems are not even mammalian in nature," said Brenner. "The later totems would seem more Ponlike, if only in being mammalian forms."

"Perhaps biologically more Ponlike, as they are also mammalian forms," said Rodriguez, "but, certainly at least from the point of view of a primitive mind, otherwise quite unlike Pons, for example, in their cast, their restlessness, their aggressiveness, their savagery, their dispositions."

"Such things might better serve the purposes of the pact," said Brenner, "than certain other forms of totem."

"Yes," said Rodriguez. "I have asked myself how such things as a snake, for example, could be partner somehow to the pact. Surely it lacks the intelligence."

"The Persian lion, too," said Brenner, "is only a mere beast."

"Yes," said Rodriguez, "the mystery remains."

"Perhaps," said Brenner, "in the return to mammalian forms there is exhibited a tendency, perhaps not fully understood, to return to, or hint at, to some extent, the original understanding of the totemic pact."

"Whatever that was," said Rodriguez.

"Yes," said Brenner.

"That is an interesting possibility," said Rodriguez. "There might seem a fittingness to them, after ages, perhaps not really understood, to return to mammalian forms for their totem."

"But such beasts, too," said Brenner, "as we have noted, might constitute more effective totems, in the sense of being more effective guardians, and such."

"That, of course, is true," said Rodriguez. "We might even have a subtle balancing of considerations here."

Brenner shrugged.

"Many, perhaps most, totemistic mammalian groups have mammalian totems," said Rodriguez.

"That is true, too," said Brenner.

"But the Pons have apparently changed their totem from time to time," said Rodriguez.

"That seems to make no sense," said Brenner.

"I agree," said Rodriguez.

"Do you have a theory to explain these things?" asked Brenner.

"Not the specifics of the totemism of the Pons," said Rodriguez. "They seem quite mysterious to me, and not even typical."

"But what of totemism itself, in general."

"There are many theories, as you know."

"Of course," said Brenner.

"All of them obviously implausible," said Rodriguez.

"Do you have a theory?"

"I am interested in a theory," said Rodriguez. "But it is a very ancient theory."

"Oh?" said Brenner.

"It was outlawed, with a number of other theories, ages ago."

"You mean "refuted"?"

"No," said Rodriguez. "It is too real, and meaningful, and too much supports it, to be "refuted," at least in any real sense of refutation. To be sure, it has been claimed to be refuted in a thousand ways. Or used to be. Now, more effectively, it is not mentioned. Most scientists do not even know of it. I came on an old text in which it was referred to, in a derogatory fashion, of course, and it sounded so interesting, and the reasons given against it were so stupid, and so obviously politically motivated, I began a search for the original materials. They were proscribed on a dozen worlds but, at last, on one world, in a black market, I found the forbidden texts."

"What was this theory?"

"It was one of several related theories," said Rodriguez, "pertaining to various things. They have all been proscribed, or removed from libraries, files, and such."

"Why?" asked Brenner.

"They were uncongenial to the ambitions of certain groups," said Rodriguez. "Thus, they were false."

"I see," said Brenner.

Brenner was not unaware of the political constraints to which truth, or, at least, the dissemination of it, and the statement of it, were subject. In most fields, of course, there were fields within fields, the public field, so to speak, which proclaimed the public doctrines, whatever they happened to be at the time, and was thus permitted to exist, and even serve the ends of various parties and groups, and the secret, internal fields, where a small elite of investigators, largely on their own time, and at their own risk, pursued the old quarries of reality and truth. These usually met in clandestine fashion and communicated largely on a face-to-face basis, or in contraband publications, sometimes in handscript, copied as they passed from hand to hand, sometimes roughly reproduced on small machines in basements and attics, sometimes even inscribed within microdots or recorded in invisible inks, responsive to rare reagents. Governments, suspecting such organizations, and realizing the subversive nature of their interests, often attempted to infiltrate them, to expose, and disband them. Many scientists had, as a consequence of these vigorously prosecuted inquiries, been removed from academic posts, which it was now recognized they were unfit to hold. Others, of course, were disbarred from various fields, on the grounds of academic treason. Many others, if the matter was serious enough, were assigned to correction camps, rehabilitation centers, reeducation facilities, and such. With others probation was deemed sufficient. Most scientists, of course, cooperated with the authorities involved, the governments, the parties, and such, and managed, hopefully, for their peace of mind, to enthusiastically convince themselves of the propositions which, in any case, they were required to accept. In the light of such considerations it was remarkable that the pursuit of reality and truth, with all its risks, tended to continue to attract investigators. Many other minds, of course, directed their interests, perhaps wisely, into less sensitive fields, such as physics and mathematics. Some even devoted their time to the pursuit of intricate board games.

"The theory could, of course, independently, be false," said Brenner.

"Certainly," said Rodriguez, "as it is a real theory, a genuine theory, and not an irrefutable theory-surrogate or pseudotheory. Similarly, that a theory must be pronounced false for political reasons does not guarantee that it is true. A fool, for example, for absurd reasons, on the basis of irrelevant considerations, such as Chian sand casting, or the flights of birds, the tracks of insects, and such, might be led to ascribe falsity to a given mathematical proposition, which happens, indeed, to be false. Luck is on his side."

"The fool will not believe it is mere luck, of course," said Brenner.

"No," said Rodriguez. "He is a fool."

"What was this theory?" asked Brenner.

"Which may be false?"

"Yes," said Brenner.

"We are in the process of inquiring into its plausibility now," said Rodriguez.

"Here, on Abydos?" asked Brenner.

"Yes," said Rodriguez.

"You are not being very clear about its nature," said Brenner.

"You might not find it agreeable," said Rodriguez.

"Then it must be false," said Brenner.

"Of course," said Rodriguez.

"Of course," said Brenner, bitterly.

"It is not flattering to the rational species," said Rodriguez. "It does not seem to fit in well with their vanity and self-image. Indeed, perhaps it is too horrifying to be true."

"I see," said Brenner.

"It is sometimes referred to as the "forbidden theory,"" said Rodriguez.

"Quite scientific," commented Brenner.

"Truth is under no obligation to be congenial or appealing, of course," said Rodriguez, "any more than it is under an obligation to be uncongenial or unappealing. It is just what it is. Congeniality and appealingness are predicates more appropriate to our responses to truth than to truth itself. Too, there are those whom truth crushes and those whom it exalts. Truth is what it is. Whether it kills us, or makes us kings, is largely up to us."

"I do not think I am familiar with this theory," said Brenner.

"It is perhaps just as well," said Rodriguez.

"I cannot be of much help to you, if I do not know what it is," said Brenner.

"Whereas it is a real theory, and is true or false," said Rodriguez, "there is no sure way to test it, as the events to which it pertains must, in their nature, belong to a remote past, one which, if the theory is correct, as it pertains to the origins of culture, must antedate culture, at least as we know it."

"And antedate language?"

"Presumably," said Rodriguez.

"But evidence must be pertinent to it, if it is a genuine theory," said Brenner.

"Evidence is obviously pertinent to it," said Rodriguez, "but the evidence which would show it true or false may not be available. For example, we might have a theory as to the first well-formed sentence you uttered, and it is obvious the sorts of evidence which would be pertinent to that, but the evidence just might not be available any longer. The visible and auditory aspects of the event no longer exist. No one may remember, no one may have been paying attention, no records may have been kept, and so on. This is often the case. We then have a theory which is more or less plausible, but can never be shown to be absolutely true or false. This is a merely contingent imperviousness to testability, which is quite different from the imperviousness to testability of a theory-surrogate or pseudotheory."

"There are also considerations of plausibility, of comparative adequacies of explanation, relative to a given set of data, and such," said Brenner.

"And they are quite important," said Rodriguez, "particularly in a case of this sort."

"But you would like harder evidence," said Brenner.

"Of course," said Rodriguez.

"I do not think you would have come to Abydos," said Brenner, "if you had despaired of the acquisition of harder evidence."

"Perhaps not," smiled Rodriguez.

"Legend, myth, custom, practices, ritual, tradition?" suggested Brenner.

"Of course," said Rodriguez.

"And perhaps evidence more fixed and real even than such things."

"Yes," said Rodriguez, shining his light about.

"Physical evidence?"

"Yes," said Rodriguez.

"What is it that you are really looking for here?" asked Brenner.

"The earliest grave," said Rodriguez.

"Did you hear something, back there?" asked Brenner.

"No," said Rodriguez.

"There may be something behind us," said Brenner.

"That is unlikely," said Rodriguez. "Consider the depth of the dust, its undisturbed state."

"Behind us," said Brenner.

"But nothing walked there, for a thousand years," said Rodriguez.

"It might now," said Brenner.

"Unlikely," said Rodriguez. "Listen."

"No," said Brenner, "I do not hear anything now."

"I am going ahead," said Rodriguez. "If you wish, you may go back and investigate."

"I do not hear it now," said Brenner.

"Come along," said Rodriguez.

"Wait a moment," said Brenner.

"Take the light then," said Rodriguez.

Brenner took the light and retraced his steps, for perhaps a hundred yards in the passages.

"Do not get lost," called Rodriguez, his voice echoing through the passages.

In time, Brenner, sometimes calling out to Rodriguez, and being answered, and being guided by t is, rejoined his senior colleague.

"Anything?" asked Rodriguez.

"No," said Brenner. The only tracks which Brenner had discerned were those of Rodriguez and himself.

"I could not examine all the passages," said Brenner.

"If anything was following us, it would use the same passages," said Rodriguez.

"Anything simple," said Brenner.

"I do not think there is anything else in here," said Rodriguez.

"It might just be in here, for its own reasons," said Brenner. "I do not think I would care to meet it."

"The wind plays tricks on the hearing, in passages such as these," said Rodriguez.

"I do not hear anything now," said Brenner.

"In any event," said Rodriguez, "we are safe."

"Of course," said Brenner.

"The totem will protect us," smiled Rodriguez.

"Of course," said Brenner.

"Seriously," said Rodriguez.

"Perhaps," said Brenner.

Rodriguez had such confidence in his theories! This morning, though no love was lost between Rodriguez and the Pons, whom he despised, he had seized up the first Pon, a small male, he could get his hands on, pressed him to his chest, and squeezed him in an endearing fashion. He had also then made certain, following this unusual demonstration of affection, to rub the small body considerably against himself. He had then, as the tiny beast squeaked and jabbered, removed its smocklike garment, it fleeing, shrieking, into a nearby hut, and put it around his neck, rather like a scarf. He had, further, insisted that Brenner, to Brenner's dismay, wear the same filthy shirt he had worn yesterday in the forest, that which doubtless bore on it the scent of Pon. Too, it seemed probable that because of the village, their living in it, the proximity of the Pons, and such, that they would, by this time, have acquired something in the nature of a nest odor or pack odor, or, in this case, perhaps a village odor, so to speak. Accordingly, thusly armed, thusly prepared, they had taken their leave of the village. It was in virtue of these considerations that Rodriguez now regarded them both as having included themselves within the pact of the totem. The point of this sort of thing, of course, was that the pact would protect them from the totem, and the totem, in virtue of the pact, would protect them from other things. To be sure, although Rodriguez had great faith in this theory, he did admit, upon being pressed by Brenner, that he would have preferred the rifle. But the rifle, as we have previously noted, was no longer available. It had disappeared.

"Look at that," said Rodriguez.

"It frightens me," said Brenner.

"These are very old representations," said Rodriguez.

The large, carved head, roughly hewn, looked white, and awesome, in the light of Rodriguez' torch.

"These are surely the earliest passages," whispered Rodriguez.

Brenner regarded the massive head, hewn of limestone.

It seemed primitively executed, but, somehow, the hand of the artist, and his terror, had captured something of what the thing must once have been. Even in the ancient stone, even given the roughness of the work, even given the obvious antiquity of the object, the remoteness of it in time from the present of Rodriguez and Brenner, there was communicated an undeniable, fierce vitality, the savagery, the arrogance, the might, the lordliness of a king of its kind.

"That is unmistakably simian," said Brenner.

"Anthropoidal, primate," said Rodriguez, in awe.

"What do you suppose its size actually was?" said Brenner.

"Consider the size of the sarcophagus," said Rodriguez.

"It could uproot trees," said Brenner.

"I wonder what its intelligence might have been," said Rodriguez.

"The forehead slopes back," said Brenner. "The eyes seem small, and closely set."

"You do not think that Pons could have once been such things?" asked Brenner.

"No," said Rodriguez.

"Have you seen such a thing before?"

"Such things do exist here and there in the galaxy," said Rodriguez. "They may once have existed on Abydos. I do not know."

"That is Ponlike," said Brenner.

"In the sense of being simian, in a general sense," said Rodriguez.

"Yes," said Brenner.

"We have seen similar things in the older passages," said Rodriguez, "but none quite this fearsome."

"The oldest passages have contained representations of other forms of beast, too," said Brenner, "not all of them Ponlike."

"True," said Rodriguez. "But more have been simian in nature."

"It is as though the Pons could not decide on the desiderated nature of the totem," said Brenner.

"Or made use of what beasts might be available," said Rodriguez.

"This is not typical in totemism," said Brenner.

"Certainly not," said Rodriguez.

"Do you think that this is the earliest grave?" asked Brenner.

"No," said Rodriguez.

"But it is early?"

"If we may speak of an early period, and a middle period, and a new period, and recent times, so to speak," said Rodriguez, "I would think this would be late early period."

"And the Persian lion would be relatively recent?"

"Very recent," said Rodriguez, "dating back no more than two or three thousand years."

"These are surely the oldest passages," said Brenner.

"The earliest grave may not even be in these passages," said Rodriguez. "It may be outside them, before the Pons could work stone. It may even be unmarked, or concealed."

"What do you expect to find in it?" asked Brenner.

"The father," said Rodriguez.

CHAPTER 26

"Yes!" cried Rodriguez, excitedly, scrambling down the slope, leaving the passages in the stone, to descend to a shallow valley, not more than fifty yards in width, nestled at the exit, or what might be better thought of perhaps as the first, and perhaps oldest, entrance to the passages. There would presumably have seemed nothing particularly significant about this small valley to an untrained eye, but the spacing of certain grass-grown hillocks, or mounds, or barrows, within it, suggested to Rodriguez that he had here at last discovered the object of his quest.

"There!" said Rodriguez. "And there!"

Brenner, by now, gasping, his boots dusty, had slipped down the descent from the passages and joined Rodriguez.

"The first would be at the center, or in one corner, or at the edge of the place!" said Rodriguez. "Look for that most worn down, the most ancient!"

"What are you seeing here?" asked Brenner. He blinked against the sun, which seemed painfully bright after his emergence from the passages.

"This is a graveyard," said Rodriguez.

"How can you tell?" asked Brenner. There were no visible, or obvious, markers. There was no fence, or gate, or barrier, or such.

"See the nature of the mounds, their height, their uniformity, their spacing!" cried Rodriguez.

"They are covered with grass," said Brenner.

"Look for rocks," said Rodriguez. "Anything that looks like a marker, or an encircling ring of stones, or a blocked entrance. And look for those most weathered!"

"Very well," said Brenner.

"Of course, there may not be such," said Rodriguez.

Brenner's training was in cultural anthropology, and primarily in its academic, as opposed to its field, aspects. He was not an archeologist, and was not sensitive to tiny signs which might, to one who could read them, relate narratives of remote histories, a pin, a buckle, a beam of wood, a handful of beads revealing an unsuspected relationship between kingdoms, a shard of pottery marking the path of a migration, an oddity of terrain suggesting the location of a buried city.

"Here! Here!" cried Rodriguez, excitedly. "It must be this one, or perhaps that one. Come here!"

In a moment Brenner had joined Rodriguez, beside one of the mounds, or barrows, which, to his eye, did not seem much different from the others.

"Are you sure this is a grave," said Brenner, "let alone, the oldest one."

"This is a grave," said Rodriguez, "like the others. Is the barrow, the tumulus, not evident to you?"

"Perhaps," said Brenner, looking at the grass-grown mound. There was a slight wind now, blowing away from them, toward the passages. It bent the grass in that direction.

"I am certain it is the oldest," said Rodriguez. "If not, then it is one of the oldest. If necessary, we can dig them all up!"

"Do you think the Pons know this place?" asked Brenner, uneasily.

"It is doubtful," said Rodriguez. "And, in any event, it would presumably be meaningless to them. Indeed, even the graves, or tombs, in the cliffs, must be meaningless to them. They have been forgotten, or neglected, at least. You saw how no one, in perhaps thousands of years, had walked there."

"True," said Brenner.

"Such places may even be taboo to the Pons," said Rodriguez.

"Yes," said Brenner. This speculation, of course, did little to allay his uneasiness. In the passages he had had occasionally to resist the feeling that he might be something of an intruder there, if not an actual trespasser.

"In any case," said Rodriguez, "what Pons know, or want, is immaterial."

"There are a great many of them," said Brenner.

"Surely no more than a hundred," said Rodriguez.

"No, not so many," said Brenner.

They had never managed to get an exact count of the Pons, as Pons seemed to come and go with some frequency. On the other hand, there was a reasonably reliable village population of some sixty or seventy Pons, and Brenner could recognize most of these, and Rodriguez could recognize some of them. Indeed, to some of the Pons, like Archimedes, they had given names.

"So?" said Rodriguez.

"They might act in concert," said Brenner. After all, even small birds could mob predators twenty times their size. Too, Brenner remembered the tiny bones, and the marks of the baskets, drawn on ropes, near the interior wall of the palisade.

"If only we had a shovel," said Rodriguez.

"If there are bones here," said Brenner, "perhaps we should not disturb them."

"I do not understand," said Rodriguez.

"We may have no business here," said Brenner. "And the Pons might not like it."

"We do have business here," said Rodriguez, "our business, the business of science."

"The Pons might not like it," said Brenner.

"They are monkeys," said Rodriguez. "Do not concern yourself with them."

"I am not a grave robber," said Brenner.

"We are not out to steal rings and cups," said Rodriguez. "This is a scientific investigation."

"What is science to you may be desecration, or sacrilege, to Pons."

"With one hand I could break them in two," said Rodriguez.

"I do not like it," said Brenner.

"Do not be afraid of the Pons," said Rodriguez.

"I do not like it," said Brenner.

"Are you with me?"

"Of course."

"We need a tool," said Rodriguez. He seemed ready, in his eagerness, to attack the small hillock with his bare hands.

"There are scarps in the village," said Brenner.

"There may be something in the passages," said Rodriguez.

"Do you think this place, and the passages, are taboo to Pons?" asked Brenner.

"No, not really," said Rodriguez. "I think it much more likely they do not even know about them. Too, the nearest things, the platform at the cliffs, and the string, were not taboo. You noted, surely, that the little bastards did not avoid them. Indeed, the string must be used as a guide to the platform."

"That is true," said Brenner. This was reassuring to him. He was not eager to trigger any sociological explosions. He remembered the small birds which could mob panthers. Such things could be a nuisance, even to panthers. And there had been the bones, and the marks in the dust.

"Rodriguez!" called Brenner.

But Rodriguez was climbing up the slope toward the entrance to the passages, the entrance from this area, as there were several entrances at various points on the cliffs. He had left the torch, with a pack, at the opening of the passage, as he would not have needed it below, in the small, open valley.

Brenner turned back to look at the mounds.

There was still a slight breeze, blowing back toward the opening in the cliffs.

Brenner looked up, again, toward the entrance to the passages. He could see the pack on the slope. The torch was now gone. So Rodriguez was now within the passages. It did not seem likely to him that Rodriguez would find anything of much use in the passages for digging. To be sure, here and there, there had been one object or another lying about, to a side, usually in rubble. Perhaps he could find a flat, or curved rock, or cornice, or something, broken, or rejected by an artisan.

It was interesting, Brenner thought, how Rodriguez was so confident that this area was indeed a graveyard, that these mounds were barrows or tumuli. To be sure, the area was near the passages, and that alone, actually, would suggest that possibility.

Brenner sat down at the side of one of the mounds. He looked up. The sun was now a few degrees over the trees. It would be best, he thought, to return to the village. They had spent a very long time in the passages. It was getting late in the afternoon. He did not think it was wise to be outside the palisade after dark. He did not have, you see, the same confidence in the pact as did Rodriguez, and, certainly, he was not confident, in any case, even if such a pact existed, that he and Rodriguez would have managed to include themselves within it. It was certain the totem animal was dangerous. And it was possible, of course, that there might be alternative explanations for such things as his return to the village yesterday night, the bringing of the slain beast to the gate, and such.

Brenner stood up, turned, and looked up, to the entrance from which they had descended to the valley

"Rodriguez!" called Brenner.

He thought he could convince Rodriguez of the reasonableness of returning to the village. Too, in the village, they could obtain scarps.

By now it seemed that Rodriguez should have returned.

Brenner, with some difficulty, climbed up to the opening in the cliff.

Now the pack was gone, as well as the torch.

"Rodriguez!" called Brenner, angrily.

How like the fellow, to have returned for the pack, and

to have set off for the village alone, in his impatience. Why had he not called down to Brenner?

To be sure, they were both protected by the pact, supposedly.

Did he intend to return before dark, and work tonight, by the light of the torch?

"Rodriguez!" called Brenner, angrily.

Brenner then entered the passageway, and began to traverse it. It was not dark, certainly not at this point, for the entrance. Moreover, several of the passages, similarly, had an entrance, or, sooner or later, connected with others which had an entrance. Accordingly, whereas a torch would be welcome, certainly in some passages, or for better illumination, it was not as though Brenner were in danger of losing his way, at least for long, in the darkness. Even where the passages were dark one could feel one's way about, and, sooner or later, given the limitations of the passages and the frequency of entrances, one could find one's way outside.

"Rodriguez!" called Brenner, again.

Perhaps Rodriguez had come to the opening and not seen Brenner below. where he had been waiting. Perhaps Rodriguez thought Brenner had entered the passages, looking for him? Perhaps that is when he had retrieved the pack.

"Rodriguez!" called Brenner, no longer angry.

Rodriguez might be in the passages now, looking for Brenner, irritably, thinking Brenner might have tried to follow him in, and perhaps stumbled into one of the side passages and become momentarily lost. Although there were many passages, and chambers, where one would need light, naturally, there were several others, as suggested, where the light, because of the various openings, would range from dim to almost normal. To be sure, at night, given the absence of a moon on Abydos, one would need light.

"Rodriguez!" called Brenner. "Rodriguez!"

Rodriguez must have returned to the village, but that did not really seem likely.

Perhaps Rodriguez had discovered another passage,

one missed earlier, and, in a fashion typical for him, had proceeded on, precipitatously exploring it.

"Rodriguez!" called Brenner. "Rodriguez!" But he heard only the echo of his own voice in the passages. If Rodriguez had heard him, it seemed likely that he would have responded, and that, in the intricate, winding passages, Brenner would have heard the response.

Rodriguez then, thought Brenner, must not be in the passages.

At least it seemed unlikely.

He has looked about, and found nothing useful, thought Brenner, and then he has returned to the village, for scarps, to come back this very night!

He should have told me, thought Brenner. It is not like him to have gone on alone.

But perhaps he did not see me, thought Brenner. Perhaps he thought that I had left.

"Rodriguez!" called Brenner.

Perhaps he did not want to take the time to come back for me, thought Brenner. Perhaps he expects me to wait for him, here.

The pack is gone, thought Brenner. Thus, he must either be looking for me in the passages, or has gone to the village. And it seems unlikely he is in the passages, or he would have responded to my calls. Thus he must have left for the village. Why would he not have called for me? Perhaps he did. Perhaps he thinks I have already left for the village, going back through the passages, thinking that I was following him, or even back about the cliffs, back by the valley, rather than through the passages?

But that did not seem likely.

Brenner then went back to the opening and examined it, carefully. There, by the light, where the wind could blow, there was little dust. It was hard to see footprints there, and, back in the passages, the dust, of course, had been disturbed earlier by their passage. Brenner saw no other footprints, however, as nearly as he could judge.

Brenner then re-entered the passages.

He made his way amongst them for a time.

I will go back to the village, he thought.

Suddenly, for no reason that he clearly understood, in the darkness of one of the passages, one remote from the openings, he began to sweat with terror. He was at that time feeling his way, groping about the walls. Suddenly then, for no good reason, or none that he could understand, he had become panic-stricken.

"Rodriguez!" he cried out, in the darkness. "Rodriguez! Rodriguez!"

Then he cried out, suddenly. "Is anyone there? Is anything there?"

But there was no answer.

He did not know what might be in such passages, if anything, or, really, on the route back, or in the forest.

In the darkness, reaching out, he felt more than one of the giant sarcophagi.

I am lost, thought Brenner, suddenly, frightened.

He had the eerie feeling that perhaps the lids on the sarcophagi might move, sliding to one side, with grating sounds, and that things might emerge, joining him in the darkness.

I will never find my way out, thought Brenner. I will die here!

No, thought Brenner. I must be rational. This is not a labyrinth. These are tombs. It is not as though these were some measureless caverns, which might lead anywhere, even into the bowels of the earth. Too, it is not after dark. That is good. He then counted turnings, and felt the walls at corners, to note any irregularities, to prevent as best he might any unwitting retracing of his path, and then, at last, as he groped his way about, he could see a bit of dimness, or, at least, a space that seemed less dark. In a few minutes, following what seemed to be the lighter passages, he blinked against the light of the outside. He had come to one of the entrances. This was one of those in the side of the cliffs. He could even see the cliffs on the other side, those from the summit of which one could look down and see the platform, and, even, far off, the village.

"Rodriguez!" called Brenner, once again.

Now Brenner was again angry. How rude of Rodriguez, who, to be sure, was noted neither for his tact or civility, to have returned to the village without him, without even informing him of his intention. He resolved to berate his colleague liberally when he encountered him once more in the village. And if Rodriguez was on his way back to the cliffs, following the string, with tools, Brenner would simply refuse to accompany him back to the passages. The morning would be time enough, even if it were not for the dangers of being about at night. Brenner did not care for this joke, or this discourtesy, whichever it might be. But then Brenner was afraid.

He did not really believe, you see, that Rodriguez would return to the village without him. That, at least, did not seem likely.

Rather than return to the village immediately Brenner now walked along the outside of the cliffs, passing the openings on his right. He did not want to go back inside the passages. Too, it was getting darker. The sun was now behind the trees. He did go up to one or two of the openings and call out, but, again, there was no response from within. In a few minutes, about half a Commonworld hour, he had come to the small valley at the end of the cliffs on the right, to where the mounds were. But there was no sign of Rodriguez there, either. Brenner then, the cliffs with the openings now on his left, retraced his steps in the longer valley. Then he climbed up to the cliffs which overlooked the platform below, and the village, in the distance. Here, too, he saw no sign of Rodriguez. He could see the village in the distance. It was now growing dark.

Rodriguez must have left the passages, to return to the village. There was no other possible explanation.

As Brenner stood on the cliffs, above the platform, he saw torches being lit in the Pon village. These torches then, perhaps some twenty of them, left the village. He could see them from time to time, flickering amongst the trees. They were apparently following the string.

They may be coming to search for us, thought Brenner. Or, perhaps, for me. Perhaps Rodriguez has sent them back to find me. Brenner watched the torches. They were definitely following the string, definitely approaching.

In a few minutes Brenner, whose hearing, as we have noted, was excellent, could detect that the Pons were not approaching in silence.

They were uttering strange, keening sounds, sounds as though of misery, or mourning.

Brenner had never heard Pons utter such sounds.

He turned about, facing the valley, and the cliffs, with their openings, across the way. "Rodriguez!" he called. "Rodriguez! Emilio! Emilio!"

He received no answer. There was only the echo, reverberating back from the opposing cliffs.

Then, frightened, Brenner made his way down the cliff, past the platform, and hurried to meet the Pons.

CHAPTER 27

"No!" screamed Brenner, seizing the bloodied shirt from the hands of a Pon, under the torches, near the string.

The Pons with the torches began again their eerie, keening wails.

The pack, too, bloodied, still sticky, was in the hands of another.

Brenner crouched down, his head in his hands. Rodriguez should not have left him. He should not have gone on ahead! He should not have tried to reach the village by himself!

"What happened?" asked Brenner, lifting his eyes, choking.

"Beast, beast," said one of the Pons.

"Darkness, forest, shadows," said another.

"Jump, take, kill, eat!" said another.

The keening was shrill now, almost as though it would cut the leaves from the branches.

"Big beast," said another, gesturing with the torch, lifting and lowering it in what, for him, was a huge half circle.

It must be the totem animal, or an animal of that sort, thought Brenner.

Many of the small, simian faces were streaked with tears. It seemed strange to see these lachrymal traces on such faces. Brenner had not realized that Rodriguez would have meant that much to Pons. Certainly he had never been at pains to treat them well, or to consider their feelings. And Pons did have feelings, of a sort, of that Brenner was much aware. He had seen them throw back their heads upon occasion and utter raucous pleased cries, which may have been laughter, and, surely, upon occasion, he had seen wonder in their eyes, and perplexity, and, once, as yesterday morning in their hut, something like tenderness, or kindliness, or perhaps even love, and, too, he did not doubt they might know frenzy, and hatred. He remembered the small bones, the apparently hideous vengeances enacted upon two members of their own group who had, it seems, violated some rule, or taboo. Yes, they were capable of emotion, Brenner was sure of that, even strong emotion. Very little in the world, Rodriguez had once told him, is accomplished without love and hate.

I am alone, thought Brenner. The only friend I ever had is gone.

"Grief!" said a Pon.

"Sad, sad, terrible, terrible," said another.

To be sure, Brenner understood that their wailing, their keening, their misery, might not be all on the account of Rodriguez, a stranger, one not even of their own group. They might be frightened for themselves, as well. The meretricious nature of the "pact" might have finally become clear to them. Perhaps they now understood, for the first time, the nature of the totem animal. Poor Rodriguez, thought Brenner, how confident he had been in his theories. How little he had been afraid. He could have remained within the palisade, for what protection that might have been worth. No, he had gone on with his work, and then, on the way back to the village, it seemed, he had learned, if he had had time to learn it, that he had been mistaken, that there was no pact, that the beast, after all, was a beast, only that, and that it might be hungry, a force of nature that might be hungry, and that it was no more to be trusted than rushing water or the stroke of lightning.

"When did this happen?" asked Brenner.

The Pons looked at one another, puzzled.

"Where did it happen?" asked Brenner.

Two of the Pons gestured back toward the village. "That way," said one.

"You found the body?" asked Brenner. He had seen, after all, only a bloodied, torn shirt, and the pack, also with blood on it.

"Yes," said one of the Pons.

"Come, come," said another.

"Pieces," said another.

"Not all gone," said another.

The beast, Brenner thought, did not even drag its prey into the forest, to eat it in secret. It was such a lord, such a king, it would feed on it where it laid it low. It had not even, apparently, like certain of the beasts of the forest, dragged it into the branches of a tree, to keep it for later, to keep it out of the reach of others, such as the humped, crested ones. Was it such a hunter, Brenner wondered, that it could feed when it wanted, and eat only fresh meat, and only parts which pleased it at the time. Was the forest such a vulnerable, plenteous larder for it?

"Grief!" wailed a Pon.

Their world may have collapsed, thought Brenner. But perhaps not, he thought. Rodriguez was not of the Pons. Their sorrow may actually be for Rodriguez, or perhaps even for me. It was not as though it had taken a Pon. But what if they thought that Rodriguez had included himself within the pact, and had nonetheless been seized and killed? That would surely undermine their confidence in the pact.

But surely they could find some way to explain it away. Could that not always be done?

But sometimes such explanations do not, truly, satisfy even their propounders.

Are the Pons now as alone, and terrified, as I am, in the forest, Brenner wondered.

"Do not cry," said Brenner, standing up.

"No, cry, cry," said a Pon.

"We will mourn," said another.

"We will love," said another.

"I do not understand," said Brenner.

"Come, come!" said Pons, tugging at his clothes.

"Why?" asked Brenner.

"See pieces," said a Pon.

"They may be gone now," said Brenner.

"No," said a Pon.

"See beast!" said a Pon.

"You know where it is?" asked Brenner.

"Come, come," said a Pon, earnestly. Torches were lifted.

Clearly in evidence was the agitation of the small creatures,
"The beast?" said Brenner.

"Yes, yes!" said more than one of the Pons.

Brenner blinked against the light of the torches. Then the
hair on the back of his neck rose.

"You have cornered it, you have trapped it?" asked Brenner,
suddenly. That might be possible, with the torches. Many
animals fled fire.

"Come, come!" urged the Pons.

"Kill!" cried another suddenly, shrilly.

"Kill the beast?" asked Brenner.

"Yes!" said the Pons.

Yes, thought Brenner, in sudden cold rage, kill it. Kill it.
But how?

"Come, come!" urged the Pons.

Brenner then accompanied the Pons. In a few minutes, to
his surprise, and trepidation, they had led him within the
gate of the palisade itself.

CHAPTER 28

"It is permissible for me to enter here?" asked Brenner.

"Please!" said one of the Pons.

"Please!" said another, gesturing with the torch.

Brenner stood at the door to the temple, that reached from within the palisade of the Pons. In his hands, he gripped a long, pointed stick. It was the nearest thing to a weapon he could find.

"You are sure it is within?" asked Brenner.

"Yes," said one of the Pons.

How terrified they are, how frightened, thought Brenner.

Brenner looked at the makeshift spear, the pointed stick he held. If the thing was indeed within, somehow, what good would the stick be?

So he was a champion to Pons, he thought, towering above them, many of them coming only to his waist.

What would it be doing in this place, wondered Brenner.

Did they hold it within, with torches?

"Kill," said one of the Pons.

Of course, it must be killed, thought Brenner. It has tasted flesh.

He sobbed.

But how could he kill it? He did not have the rifle. And if he had had it, he was not even certain of its operation. Insert the charge in the wrong fashion, and it could blow up in his hands, taking him, and the roof of the temple with him. Too, he was not certain as to how to free the rifle. Certainly its freeing would not be obvious; it would be subtle, at least; it was probably designed with the idea of slipping undetected through customs. Too, he did not know the sequence which prepared the rifle for firing. There must, too, be a safety mechanism. Rodriguez had handled such things. Brenner had not even wanted to know anything, really, about the rifle. It was a sort of thing against which he had been conditioned. This put him, of course, and others like him, at the mercy of those to whom such devices were familiar. But, in any event, he did not have the rifle.

He had, of course, tried to communicate with the Pons pertaining to the shiny tube, the putative optical instrument, even attempting to suggest its latent capacities, but they had, apparently, understood nothing. It was not a pointed stick, not a sharp-edged scarp. How could one explain a rifle to a people unfamiliar with the bow? Would it not be easier to explain fire to a fish? And those with him seemed to know nothing, even about a shiny tube.

And so Brenner, with a pointed stick, with fear, and rage, and desperation, guided by the Pons clustered about him, with their wailing, and torches, had come to the door of the temple.

Several Pons, others from the village, who, it seemed, had been waiting, swung open the doors of the temple.

Brenner could see light within, that of other torches.

He then entered the temple, Pons behind him, those who had come to fetch him in the forest, with torches, those who had opened the doors, and others, too, from the village.

CHAPTER 29

B renner proceeded down the corridor.
The last time he had been in this corridor he had been with Rodriguez.

The torches behind him made his shadow seem long and before him.

He was descending now, and must, by this time, be outside the perimeter of the palisade.

Before him he could see two torches, one on each side of the double doors, within which was the hall of the temple, which he had, only last night, discovered with Rodriguez.

To his surprise there were several Pons at these doors.

The beast, if it is here, must be trapped inside, somehow, thought Brenner. It might have come in here, through the village, frightened by torches within the ring of the palisade, the portal would be large enough. Perhaps it thought the opening was like a den mouth, or a cave, a place to hide. But there seemed no marks in the corridor, the print of moist pads on the floor, strands of hair caught against the wooden walls, to suggest such a journey. Or it might have come in, somehow, from the rear, through the tunnel, that which last night had been blocked by the great gate of logs, with the sharpened spikes, pointing outward. Perhaps that gate had been opened, and then closed behind the beast.

The Pons at the hall doors began to swing them open.

"No!" said Brenner, putting his hand out. "Do not open them widely!"

A beast like that which had taken Archimedes could force its way, fierce head first, then shoulders and haunches, through such an opening with the ease of quicksilver.

But the Pons, nonetheless, swung open the doors.

Within, Brenner surveyed the great hall of the temple. It was bright with the light of more than a hundred torches. Within there were many Pons. Counting those behind him the entire population of the village must be here.

Brenner stood within the double doors, at the height of the aisle leading downward toward the platform.

This was not what he had expected to see.

He had thought there would be nothing here but a frenzied, restless, furious, frightened beast, perhaps in one corner, or at the back, crouching, waiting, eyeing the door, ready to rush forward, or perhaps one prowling back and forth, or circumambulating the walls, tail lashing, confused, snarling, seeking egress, or perhaps one held at bay, snarling, baring its fangs, lifting a threatening paw, one ringed with jabbing, thrusting torches, held in the hands of tiny, terrified Pons.

But it was not like that at all.

The beast, and it was, indeed, the totem beast, as Brenner had feared, sat upon the platform, back on its haunches. Its head, on that long neck, was perhaps twenty feet above the surface of the platform. Its pointed ears were erected. The roof of the hall was not more than a few feet over its head.

The Pons in the hall were in white robes. They turned and looked at him, as he stood there, at the height of the aisle leading down toward the platform. Several of them held lighted candles. Brenner had never seen candles before in the village. He had not realized that the Pons were familiar with such objects, let alone that they might possess them. At the belts of the Pons hung small, polished scarps. They did not appear to be the same sort of scarps as were used for commonplace purposes, such as the digging of tubers. The distance between males and females, he noted, was being maintained, but, presumably because of the number of

Pons in the hall, in a somewhat unusual manner. The males and females were now separated as groups, rather than as individuals; the female group, which was on a higher level in the hall, and farther from the beast, was some ten to twelve feet from the male group, which was lower, and was closer to the beast.

Brenner turned his attention again to the beast.

Yes, thought Brenner, it is old. I am sure it is old. Rodriguez had thought so. He had said so. Brenner now, too, thought so. This was suggested, somehow, more by its general appearance, by its general cast, than by specific indications such as a drab pelt, a grayness about the jaws and muzzle. Yes, thought Brenner, it is old.

The beast did not move.

Perhaps it is dead, thought Brenner, suddenly. It is so quiet.

Its fur moved a little, in some draft, perhaps from the tunnel behind it, moving toward the open doors behind Brenner. But the smoke, too, from the torches, Brenner noted, seemed to be drawn away, mostly upward, somehow. The hall was not close. It was not difficult to breathe here, even with the Pons, the torches, and the candles. The hall is ventilated, somehow, Brenner realized.

He looked again at the beast.

Perhaps it is dead, Brenner thought.

Its pupils, like vertical slits, regarded him.

No, thought Brenner, it is not dead.

Suddenly the Pons behind Brenner, those who had conducted him hither, and those who had opened the various doors, and had then followed him, began to chant:

We will kill.
We will dread.
We will fear.
We will kill.
We will mourn.
We will love.
We will love.

This chant was then taken up by the other Pons. This chant was not done loudly, rather, almost in whispers. It was soft, repetitious, insistent.

Brenner took a step down the aisle toward the platform. He grasped the pointed stick he had brought with him. The stick seemed futile to him. He did not know that he could drive it to the heart of such a beast. He might not be able to reach the heart. He was not even certain of the location of the heart of such an animal.

"We will kill, we will kill," whispered Pons.

"We will mourn, we will love," whispered others.

This is madness, thought Brenner. I cannot kill this thing. It is too large. It is too terrible. In the arenas of Megara, Rodriguez had told him that a hundred men with spears were pitted against one such beast.

But it must be killed. It had tasted flesh.

It was old. Perhaps that was why it had seized Rodriguez. It could not find fleeter game.

It must be killed, Brenner thought.

"We will kill, we will kill," whispered Pons.

"We will mourn, we will love," whispered others.

What is it doing here, Brenner asked himself. Why is it here? Why is it just sitting there?

He approached the beast more closely. He was now some seven yards from it.

"We will kill, we will kill," whispered Pons.

"We will mourn, we will love," whispered others.

How did it get in here, Brenner asked himself. How did it find its way in? Why doesn't it move?

Then, at the foot of the platform, on the floor, where he had not seen it before, his attention so taken with the torches, the Pons, the beast, he saw some objects, gathered together.

Brenner cried out with sorrow.

They were limbs, broken and torn, and a part of a torso, an arm here, a foot there.

The floor was dark with stains beneath them.

Brenner, tears in his eyes, looked up with fury at the beast.

The Pons had doubtless done the best they could. How they had managed to collect, and at what risk, even so many of the remains was remarkable. There was no mistaking parts of the body of his friend, those that were here. He recognized a scar on an arm, the watch on a wrist. The head was gone.

The Pons, in their love, and loyalty, had gathered these things together, and brought them here, and, to the extent that they were capable of such things, had put them here, in state. But above them, on its platform, like a god, was the beast, the totem itself.

"Kill, kill," whispered the Pons.

Of course, thought Brenner. They cannot harm the totem themselves, even if they had the capability of doing so. It is the totem. It is I who must do this. But who better than I, whose friend has been taken from him by this fiend? Who else would I, in suitable vengeance, permit to perform this act? But how can I kill such a thing?

"I hate you!" cried Brenner, in tears, at the beast.

It looked down upon him, but did not move.

It could leave this place, thought Brenner. There is nothing, really, to hold it here. It could kill us all, breaking us with the blows of its paws, tearing us in two with those jaws.

Brenner looked at the makeshift spear, the pointed stick, he held. A hundred men, Rodriguez had told him, were pitted against such beasts in the arenas of Megara.

He would have to climb to the platform, even to reach the beast.

Then, from somewhere behind him, Brenner heard the voice of a Pon:

We love you, father.
Forgive us, father, for what we will do.

This was answered, or followed, by another Pon:

We will be contrite!
Show us forbearance!

> Be kind to us!
> Cherish us!
> Protect us!
> We will refrain from touching the soft ones!
> We beg your forgiveness, father,
> for what we will do.

A third voice then called out:

> Forgive us, father.
> Love us!
> Cherish us!
> Protect us!

After a time another voice, high-pitched, called out:

> Oh, I could get me in.
> I could lay them waste.
> But I will not do so,
> for they are my children.
> I am the father.

Brenner then looked down, to his right. The git keeper was there. Gently, the git keeper removed the makeshift spear from Brenner's hands. Then he turned about and, from a pillow, carried by another Pon, removed the shining brass tube. It had been opened. The rifle was freed. He put it in Brenner's hands. Brenner looked down at it, stunned. The weapon was ready. He was sure of it. He could even see the particular alignment of switches. He was sure, as he now examined it, that they were what he had once seen when Rodriguez had armed the rifle. Somehow, he was sure they would be. The safety, too, doubtless, had been released. Brenner slid back the bolt a little, looking in the breach, then let the bolt move back, automatically. One of the charges, cylinderlike, was in place, its red-capped end forward. The trigger, within its guard, was in evidence, the guard having descended from the barrel. At this distance, standing below the platform, looking up, Brenner could not miss.

The beast was cleaning itself, licking at the fur on its left shoulder.

Brenner grasped the weapon firmly.

The beast looked down at Brenner. It stopped grooming itself.

Brenner lifted the weapon.

The beast's long tail lashed a little, moving back and forth, and then was still.

Thanks to the gods of ten worlds, thought Brenner, echoing a phrase of Rodriguez', that it does not understand this thing, that it does not understand what it can do, that it does not know the danger in which it stands.

With this, I can kill it.

He steadied the weapon, aiming it carefully upward, at the center of the beast's chest.

The beast then, oddly, as it sat there, not really moving much, lifted, and straightened, its body. In that moment it seemed quite vital. It now held its body as might have an animal in its youth or prime. It did not seem old then. It was almost as though it has pride, thought Brenner.

Then he pressed the trigger.

The path from the muzzle of the weapon to its target was quite short, only a few feet.

A sudden, black, startling, seared, cavelike hole appeared, as if by magic, in the beast's chest. This hole seemed ringed in the first instant in a blastlike blaze of fire and light, roaring, incandescent, and torrential. Rocks were gouged out of the ceiling, and showered down behind the platform.

Brenner looked up at the beast. It had not yet fallen. It seemed very still. It was slumped down a bit but, on the whole, retained its sitting position. Perhaps it does not even know, or understand, that it has been hit, thought Brenner. The strike had been made quickly, in a sudden, brief stream of fire, almost a flash of light. It may not understand what has occurred, thought Brenner. It seemed to sit there, the hole smoking, the hair about it burnt away, in its chest. The opening had been made so quickly, so cleanly, that it seemed possible, for a wild instant, to Brenner, that the charge, in its heat, might have cauterized the very wound it made. But then, a moment later, its fur was drenched with blood.

Fall, die, die, thought Brenner. Die, he thought, die!

For a moment he was afraid of it, that it might move toward him. Even in its moments of death such a thing could be terrible.

But it did not move toward him.

It was no longer dangerous.

Brenner, sick, let the rifle slip from his fingers.

The beast lowered its head. It half rose. Its legs seemed uncertain beneath it.

It must fall, thought Brenner. It must die! Are you so hard to kill, mighty beast? Are you so unwilling to die? Do you cling to life with such force, with such tenacity?

Blood then came from about the jaws of the beast. It licked it, running its tongue about its jaws.

Its belly was now almost on the platform.

It looked at Brenner.

"Who are you?" suddenly cried Brenner. "What are you?"

"I am the father," it said.

"He is dead!" squealed a Pon.

"He is dead! He is dead!" cried others.

Suddenly, then, from all about Brenner, there were howls, and leapings about, and shrieks of glee. The Pons, in their white robes, and those in the gray robes, were suddenly intermixed, jostling one another, striking and pulling at one another. Yes, thought Brenner, those raucous, pleased sounds, they must be laughter, or triumph. But how chilling, how maniacal, now seemed what might once have been a mere ventilation of emotion or tension. Brenner saw several Pons tearing off their robes. Some Pons were leaping about now, naked, making menacing sounds, presumably imitative of those of the totem beast. Others were making such sounds, but were moving about, too, in a sort of dance, imitating the movements of the totem beast, its prowlings, it climbings, its charges, even its stretchings and yawns. Many others, dancing about, whirling in their robes, in frenzy, brandished the tiny, polished, wicked scarps in their hands. Brenner would not have cared to walk too close to one.

Brenner felt sick.

The beast was dead. It lay now in its blood on the platform. The blood ran from the platform, and over the floor. In such a thing was much blood. The beast was dead. Brenner had killed it. It was dead, the beast, the ancestor, the primal father, the father, the totem.

Brenner saw one of the male Pons seize a female and pull off her robes. Others, males and females, shrieked with delight. Brenner wondered if this were because the female was not popular, or because she was, to a Pon, attractive, or, perhaps, that it was merely that she was a female, and at hand. The female tried to pull away but the male gave her a sharp bite on the back of the neck and, immediately, with a cry of pain, she crouched down at his feet, whimpering, in a cowering posture. When he turned away from her, she hurried to follow him. He treated another female in the same way, but this one, perhaps more intelligent, or not desiring to be so painfully served as had been her sister, instantly performed the submission behavior. And then the two of them crept after the male, sometimes baring their tiny teeth at one another. Then another male came and seized one of them by the hand and pulled her toward him. She shrieked. The original male and the new male, thrusting the female to one side, then began to circle one another, baring their small teeth. The females, the two of them now, together, cowered to one side. The two males, suddenly, as with one accord, with shrill, angry shrieks, flung themselves at one another, and, with hands and feet, and teeth, fought, grappling, rolling about, twisting, tearing, and biting. Other such altercations, too, began to break out. One fight was apparently over the possession of a given scarp. Brenner heard a cry, and saw a hand drawn back, suddenly bright with blood. He moaned. He sank down on his knees, before the platform. Before him, on the floor, were parts of his friend. Above, on the platform, the beast was dead. Its blood, spilled on the platform, ran to the floor. Brenner's knees were soaked with it. He could see, about himself, tiny, bloody footprints, those of riotous Pons who had walked in it, run in it, or danced in it. All about him rang a bedlam, a madness, of shrieks, exultant and wild. At the periphery of his vision was a whirling flurry of robes, of brandished polished scarps, flashing, reflecting torchlight, and, here and there, of tiny, naked, hairy, spiderlike bodies, with receding foreheads, with small, closely set eyes. Brenner put down his head then, and covered his ears, and closed his eyes. It is festival, he thought. It is carnival, it is holiday. They are glad the father is dead. They wanted him dead. Now they have what they wanted. Brenner shuddered. Had the beast spoken to him? How could that be? He must, somehow, have imagined that. He stood up, shaking, and looked at the beast, dead, on the platform. It could not have spoken. Such things did not speak. Such things could not speak.

Sick, he decided he must leave the place. He turned about, and cried out, with horror.

A few feet from him, on a pedestal, where the floor became level, near the base of the aisle, was a transparent, lidded vat, or large jar, into which various tubes led. In the vat, facing forward, its eyes closed, was the head of Rodriguez.

Brenner spun about, to avoid seeing the object. It must be some form of burial, he thought. Doubtless the Pons are kindly. Their intentions are doubtless benign. They think I must appreciate this! I should not express horror, or disapproval. I would not wish to hurt their feelings. But he sank down again, now to his hands and knees, and threw up, to the side.

The beast could not have spoken.

When Brenner opened his eyes he looked again on the parts of his friend before him.

I must not be impolite to the Pons, he thought. I must not hurt their feelings.

But the Pons seemed to be paying him no attention. Their glee, their cries, their dancing, continued unabated.

As Brenner looked upon the pieces of flesh before him,

he wondered what must be the horror of finding oneself the victim of such an attack, or would it be over so quickly that one would not realize what had happened? But if one did realize, Brenner thought, how horrifying that must be, the sudden blow of the paw, the raking of the claws, like hooks, the biting, the marks of the teeth, the being grasped in such jaws, perhaps the pain of being held down, and toyed with, bitten here and there, licked, clawed, until one could move no longer, squirm no longer, and then the thing might feed. But Brenner, as he forced himself to look at the limbs before him, did not detect the signs of such an attack. There seemed no claw marks, no marks of teeth. The limbs did not seem to have been torn, as in feeding, from the body.

Suddenly Brenner felt very cold.

The beast had not killed Rodriguez. Something else had killed him.

They could not kill the totem themselves, he said to himself. It had to be done by another.

"Emilio!" wept Brenner. "Emilio!"

Another must be brought to kill the beast, he thought, another! And another had done it, another!

The shrieks of Pons continued about him. He heard cries, too, amongst them, of anger, of dissension.

He rose up, tottering, he must flee, he must get away from this place, anything.

He turned about again. He did not want to look at the head, mounted in the jar, on the pedestal. But he did, of course, look, and then, once more, he cried out with horror. The eyes in the head were now open.

Brenner spun about, again, and then, slowly, in horror, sank to his knees once more, before the platform. He did not know if the head had seen him. Does it know it has been cut off, wondered Brenner.

The dancing and exultant shrieks of the Pons continued.

Brenner looked about, on the floor, to where he had dropped the rifle. It was gone. The pointed stick, too, was gone, of course. It had been taken from him, gently, by the git keeper.

It sees, thought Brenner. It sees! It knows it has been cut

off. He turned about, on his knees, to again look at the head. Once more the eyes were closed.

The beast did not speak, thought Brenner.

The eyes could not have opened, thought Brenner.

I have gone mad, he thought.

He looked again to the remains before him. Then he looked again, upward, to the platform.

He was seized with a wild fear, and tensed to leap up, and flee from this place.

It was then that the nets, several, and weighted, fell about him. He could not rise. He could scarcely see through the toils. Ropes were secured, well fastening the nets. Pons clustered about him. He struggled, but his struggles were unavailing. He was now before the platform, on his knees. He could scarcely move his arms or legs. He knelt there, then, caught in the toils, enmeshed, secured. He was totally helpless, trapped as effectively as might have been an animal.

"You killed Emilio!" he screamed to the git keeper.

The small creature, its tiny hands hidden in the sleeves of its robes, did not respond to him.

"You are evil!" cried Brenner.

"I do not understand that expression," said the git keeper.

"Are you all mad, all evil?" wept Brenner.

The git keeper looked at him, puzzled. There had been a pause in the revels.

"Who decides such things?" asked the git keeper. "Is it the lion who is evil, or the fleet one whose selfishness would deny the king its meal?"

"Such things are only as they are!" said Brenner.

"And thus, so, too, are we," said the git keeper.

"Your kindness, your benignity, your lovingness, your innocence, is a mockery," said Brenner.

"No," said the git keeper, "but it has its price."

"Why cannot you be more like Archimedes," said Brenner, "who was truly innocent, and kind, and loving."

"Archimedes could not have lived without us," said the git keeper.

"Be as was Archimedes," said Brenner.

"Archimedes, or he whom you chose to call such," said the git keeper, "was retarded."

Then the git keeper turned to the Pons. He raised a scarp. "We are free, my brothers!" he cried out. "The father is dead!"

This announcement was met with glee from the assembled Pons. Brenner struggled in the net, but could not free himself. He was utterly helpless.

The git keeper then went behind the platform and, on steps there, climbed to its surface, and then came forward, toward its front edge, where he stood beside the slain beast.

"Come, my brothers," called the git keeper. "Let us take onto ourselves the power, the majesty, of the father. He was cruel. He was the tyrant. But now the tyrant is dead. Now we are free, my brothers! We may now do as we wish. We will all become as was the father! We will take his flesh into ourselves, that it become our own flesh. We will drink his blood, that it become our own blood. We will make his substance ours! We will become, through him, him!"

Then the git keeper turned about and, the first of all, dug his tiny, sharp, polished scarp into the great shaggy body that lay on the platform. He crouched on the body, and thrust the tiny bit of meat he had cut free into his mouth. The male Pons then, those clothed and unclothed, swarmed upon the platform and, like flies, or small scavenging rodents, attacked the great carcass with their scarps. Some fed the pieces of meat they cut to others. Brenner was ill. The females, he noted, did not participate in this ritual, or feeding. They hung back. When one of them approached too closely, she was snapped at, and she fled back, to crouch down, to wait with the others. The females looked at one another, apprehensively, while the males fed.

Brenner turned, as he could, to look at the jar. The eyes on the head in the jar were again open. It was regarding the feast. On its face was an expression of horror. Then it, again, closed its eyes.

The eyes did open, said Brenner, wildly, to himself. I saw it.

The mouths of the Pons at the carcass were red with blood. Some of the tiny creatures were half buried in the animal, gouging, feeding. The robes of those who had retained them were spattered with blood. The hair of those who had discarded their robes was similarly spattered. The feet of many, to the ankles, and the hands of many, to the wrists, were soaked with blood.

Trickles of blood ran from the tiny scarps.

Far off, it seemed, from somewhere back, perhaps within, or near, the palisade, Brenner heard the enraged howling of an animal. It reminded him of the sounds he had heard, so long ago, on the ship, from somewhere in its cargo area, before Rodriguez and he had come down to the surface of Abydos. Such beasts, he had understood, like many others, captured on various worlds, brought from various worlds, were transported to diverse destinations throughout the galaxy, such as menageries and zoological gardens, in which they constituted fearsome prizes. Too, as Brenner understood, it was not uncommon to bring them to worlds such as Megara and Sybaris, for use in the games. Brenner heard again the howling. He had never seen the beast in the ship. He had heard it tearing and raking at the steel walls of its confinement; he had heard it roaring, the sound reverberating throughout the ship; he had often heard, when he had lain buckled in his webbing, during his rest periods, its steady, restless, repetitious tread as it moved back and forth in its confinement, sometimes for hours at a time. Brenner did not think the thing he heard now was loose. It did not sound like that. It was probably caged. It could have been brought in, its cage suspended on chains from an air truck, from Company Station, where it might have been landed from a freighter in orbit, brought down in a lighter. Its delivery might have been arranged by Pons at Company Station, even months ago, or perhaps more recently, even by radio. The air truck, if it had brought such a thing in, might have been homing on a signal from the village.

"I have eaten of the father!" screamed a Pon. "I am the father!"

"No," cried another, crouching on the carcass, "it is I who am the father!"

Brenner saw a Pon lash out with his scarp and another Pon draw back, its shoulder bloody. It, too, crouched on the carcass, baring its teeth, lifting its scarp, at the other.

"Peace, brothers!" cried the git keeper. "Peace, my brothers!"

"I am the father!" cried another, back farther on the carcass.

"No," shrilled another. "I am the father!" One could only see its upper body, as its lower body was muchly concealed, it standing within the bodily cavity of the beast. It lifted up something red, and bloody, in one hand. It must be part of the heart, thought Brenner. In the other hand, it brandished a scarp.

"I am!" screamed another.

One of the Pons, its feet bloody, leaped from the platform and ran back toward the females. They shrank back before him, and crouched low. He seized one by the hand, and pulled her away from the others.

"Stop!" cried a Pon from the platform.

But then several of the other Pons, too, some seven or eight of them, as though they feared they might lose their chance, leaped from the platform. These were followed, almost immediately, by several others. The females shrieked, seeing them coming. The males made choices from amongstst them. Sometimes they tore away the white robes, and then made their choices. Some of the females they led away by the hand. Other females were drawn forcibly from the group, their right wrists helplessly in the grip of a male. Some others crept fearfully to indicated places, at so little as an imperious gesture. Some others were literally dragged from the group by an ankle, their robes about their upper bodies, or heads, their tiny fingers trying to catch at the floor of the temple, but gaining no purchase there. Several females, not yet selected, crowded together, crouching down. They were wide-eyed, looking about themselves in terror. They clung to one another. Some tried to hide amongst the others. But other males, circling this group, seized out several of them, too, sometimes reaching into the midst of them, to choose this one or that, one which might strike their fancy, pulling them away from the group. The males isolated their catches, and some had more than one. They then looked about, fearfully, defensively, baring their tiny teeth. There was an occasional dispute as to territory, perhaps as small as a square yard. Teeth were bared. Sometimes scarps were raised. More than one Pon was cut. More than once a female, sometimes more than one, changed hands. The females crouched down at the feet of the males. They stayed very close to the males who had selected them. Most kept their eyes down. Others, warned, did so. In these moments none looked into the eyes of the males. One female, Brenner noted, tried to creep to another male, but she was seen, and bitten at the back of the neck. Quickly she hurried back to her place, where the first had put her. Then the other male, he to whom she had dared to crawl, bared his teeth at the first. They circled one another. They both held scarps.

"Peace, brothers!" called the git keeper from the platform. There were still several males on the carcass, feeding, looking up, then feeding again.

"We are all the father!" screamed one of the Pons on the carcass, its mouth bloody.

"We may all do as we please!" cried another.

"We may all do as we wish!" screamed another.

There was a cry of pain from Brenner's right and, turning, he saw the Pon who had been challenged for the female, he from whom she had attempted to creep away, who had brought her back to her place, clutch at his throat. Blood ran between his fingers. His eyes were wide. He sank down, on the temple floor.

The Pon who had struck him, he who had challenged for the female, himself bloodied, knelt down beside him. He put the scarp to one side.

The female put back her head and uttered a long, keening wail.

There was then silence.

The Pons quietly separated from one another.

"The father is dead!" called one of the Pons from the

platform. This, however, was no cry of triumph, no utterance of exultation, but a lament.

"We will mourn!" called another from the platform.

"We will love," said another.

Brenner saw the females gather to one side.

"The father will be angry!" called a Pon.

"We will fear!" called a Pon.

"We will dread!" called another.

"We will mourn!"

"We will love!"

Those Pons who had discarded their robes drew them on again. The females, too, whose robes might have been removed from them, found them and donned them once more, even torn as they might be. Brenner noted a restoration of the distances.

Basins of water were brought forth and Pons began to wash their hands, drying them on white towels.

Brenner then heard, from somewhere, the voice of another Pon:

We love you, father.
Forgive us, father, for what we have done.

This was then answered, or followed, by another voice:

We are contrite!
Show us forbearance!
Be kind to us!
Cherish us!
Protect us!
We will refrain from touching the soft ones!
We beg your forgiveness, father,
for what we have done!

A third voice then called out:

Forgive us, father.
Love us!

Cherish us!
Protect us!

"The father is dead!" wailed a Pon.

"The father is dead," called out the git keeper.

"Long live the father!" cried a Pon.

"Long live the father!" called out the git keeper.

"Long live the father!" called out the Pons.

Candles, which had been extinguished in the riotous moments following the demise of the totem, were rekindled. Many of the Pons then, in their robes, several of these garments spattered with blood, began, maintaining the distances, to file from the hall.

Some Pons began, one by one, to extinguish the torches in the hall. The git keeper left the platform, by the rear stairs, and came about the platform, to where Brenner knelt, unable to rise, the netting wrapped about him, and secured.

"Long live the father," said the git keeper, looking at Brenner.

"The father is dead!" said Brenner to the git keeper.

"No," said the git keeper.

"He is dead!" screamed Brenner.

"No," said the git keeper.

"I killed him!" said Brenner.

"The father lives," said the git keeper.

"Where is he?" asked Brenner.

"Here," said the git keeper.

"I do not see him," said Brenner. "Where is he?"

"Here," said the git keeper.

"Which one is the father?" asked Brenner, looking about.

"He is here," said the git keeper.

"Who is the father?" said Brenner.

"You are the father," said the git keeper.

"You are insane!" cried Brenner.

He was then put on his side, and his knees were thrust up, before him, almost under his chin, and the net was closed, tightened and tied shut. Ropes were then attached to it.

"Wait!" cried Brenner.

The git keeper gestured that the several Pons in gray robes, those at the ropes, should not yet draw upon them.

"I do not understand what is going on here!" begged Brenner.

"You are the father," said the git keeper.

"That is absurd!" wept Brenner.

"Our males," said the git keeper, "have been unable to procreate for thousands of years. This began as a functional inadequacy correlated, as we now realize, with the repudiation of, the neglect of, and the eventual destruction of, natural relationships. We denied the biotruths of our species. We betrayed our form of life. Once we were a hardy race. Of that you see now only degenerate remnants, clinging to a life, and a bit of technology, in a wilderness."

Brenner shook his head. He looked up, wildly at the git keeper.

"We once lived between angels and fish, where we belonged, but then it was decided by our ancestors, as they grew stupider and weaker, and the quality of their gene pool declined, and the strength of pernicious conditioning programs increased, that this was a mistake, and that we should not be what we were, but that we should be other than we were, that we should be not animals, but angels, that we should deny ourselves and pretend to be what we were not. Weakness soon wore mask of virtue. The least virile were favored for replication, when it was allowed. Worth was assessed in virtue of glandular inferiority. Value was determined by conformance to antibiological desiderata. Our males were forbidden to be males. Our females were forbidden to be females. We could not be ourselves. We must pretend to be other than ourselves. Suffice it to say that what began as a mere functional impotence, prescribed by society, lest our males revert to more primitive forms of life, eventually became, or was replaced by, through selections, a congenital impotence, and, later, over a thousand generations, through similar selections, a complete sterility. Our females, too, suffered. Most are barren, but, some remain capable of conception. Several of these, which ones you need not know, now carry your seed."

"My seed?" said Brenner.

"It was taken during the feast of the harvesting of seed," said the git keeper.

Brenner looked up at him, wildly.

"You are the father, you see," said the git keeper.

"You are an alien life form," said Brenner. "We could not be crossfertile."

"We are," said the git keeper. The trace of a smile seemed to play about that small mouth. "It is not, really, as strange as you think."

"It is impossible," said Brenner.

"This is how we survive," said the git keeper, "and have survived, for thousands of generations. This is how we remain angels, you see, in effect, a travesty, a joke in nature, in effect, bodiless creatures, glandless spirits, simple and loving, benignant and kindly, soft, benevolent, gentle, and such. To be sure, we must be protected by lions. Others must do our killing. Others must supply the seed for our females."

"That is why there are no other clans about, with other totems," said Brenner. "That is why there are no children."

"Every thousand years," said the git keeper, "there are children."

"You are so long lived?" said Brenner.

"Not originally," said the git keeper.

"I do not understand," said Brenner.

"We have retained, in the sacred books," said the git keeper, "some of the advances of our race."

"Do all the Pons know these things?" asked Brenner.

"It is not needful for them all to know," said the git keeper. "It is a heavy burden, and best borne by few."

Brenner moaned.

The git keeper made a small motion, and the Pons about prepared to draw on the ropes.

"Wait, I beg you!" said Brenner.

Another gesture from the git keeper resulted in the ropes slackening.

"I was brought here," said Brenner. "All this has been planned. You had such things in mind, even from before we landed on Abydos!"

"Of course," said the git keeper.

"Why?" asked Brenner.

"That there be a father," said the git keeper.

"But why me, of all?"

"You are fitted for the function," said the git keeper.

"Others might have served as well!"

"Doubtless," said the git keeper. "But your genetic materials are of special interest. They are atavistic, dating from a sterner, hardier time. Also, they represent, although you do not understand this, and might be horrified to learn it, an unusually interesting genotype, one which might not only survive, but might thrive, even flourish, in a natural world, or within a civilization which is an extension and outgrowth of nature, rather than a repudiation of her."

"No!" cried Brenner.

"Would you be so disturbed to own land, to command men, to have women at your feet?" asked the git keeper.

Brenner moaned.

"It is no accident that you are here," said the git keeper.

"More so than you know," said Brenner, bitterly. "The contents of the experimental vats, in one of which I was nurtured, were ordered destroyed, that such genes, putatively dangerous to the security of the regime on the home world, be removed from the gene pool. I was the only one saved, rescued by an attendant technician."

"Does that seem so mysterious to you, or such a coincidence?" asked the git keeper.

"Yes!" said Brenner.

"That it should be you, alone, of all the others, who was saved?"

"Yes," said Brenner, faltering.

"Why?" asked the git keeper.

"I do not know," said Brenner.

"Your genetic materials were selected, thousands of years ago, as being suited for our purposes," said the git keeper. "Their location, condition, treatment, and such, were carefully monitored."

"It was no accident then that I, alone, was spared?"

"No," said the git keeper.

Brenner looked up at him, in consternation, through the heavy netting.

"You have been prepared, so to speak, chosen, if you will, for our purposes," said the git keeper.

"I see," said Brenner.

"The technician was well rewarded," said the git keeper.

"Of course," said Brenner, bitterly. No one, then, it seemed, had cared for him, or loved him. Only Rodriguez, in his rough, unpolished fashion, had seemed to care for him, if only begrudgingly. Tears sprang into Brenner's eyes, as he thought of his friend.

"There must be records kept," said Brenner. "There must be traces of your work, here and there. Some must understand, or suspect, what you are doing!" To be sure, Brenner had wondered, long ago, about the sparsity of records, and reports, and such, pertaining to Pons. On the whole, saving for some obscure monographs, there were little more than fragments, often no more than notes in old texts, and, apparently, some references in company records.

"Did you?" asked the git keeper.

"No," said Brenner.

"The university will have records of our expedition."

"They have been misplaced," said the git keeper.

"The directress?"

"Of course," said the git keeper.

"She was influenced?"

"Yes," said the git keeper.

"It was no accident then that she brought the expedition to my attention, and such."

"No," said the git keeper.

"I might have refused to come," said Brenner.

"Other pressures would then have been brought to bear," said the git keeper. "In one fashion or another you would have arrived here in autumn, before the feast of the harvesting of seed."

"What difference would it have made?" said Brenner.

"None, really," said the git keeper. "But we have our calendar, and are fond of our traditions."

"How could you have purchased the cooperation of the directress?"

"By means of agents, through the company," said the git keeper.

"What did you buy her for?" asked Brenner.

"An interesting way of putting it," said the git keeper.

"I did not mean it that way!" said Brenner.

"That is your disposition for atavistic conceptualization betrayed," said the git keeper.

"No!" said Brenner, angrily.

"She is a female," said the git keeper.

"I was never too sure of that," said Brenner.

"Our agent, who is skilled in assessing such matters, assured us that she was quite female, and profoundly so, but one of those who is frightened of her own femaleness, and attempts, by any means, to suppress it, to conceal it, and hold it in check."

"Absurd," said Brenner. To be sure, he himself had sensed, or imagined, a profound, latent sexuality in the directress.

"She is female enough, it seems," said the git keeper, "to have been fascinated by a handful of Chian diamonds."

Brenner looked up at the git keeper. If pure, and well cut, such diamonds are quite valuable.

"I have heard the cries of a beast outside, from somewhere beyond the temple," said Brenner. "What is it? What is its meaning?"

"That is not important for you to understand now," said the git keeper.

"Is it caged?"

"Of course," said the git keeper. "But do not fear. The

bars are so closely set that it could not even thrust a part of its muzzle through them."

"How could it have been brought here?" asked Brenner.

"By air truck," said the git keeper.

"The drivers will know of this place."

"The truck will fail to return to Company Station," said the git keeper. "It will crash in the forests."

"There will be a search," said Brenner.

"The remains of the crash will be found," said the git keeper.

"I see," said Brenner. He suddenly felt cold, and began to sweat.

"Do not concern yourself," said the git keeper.

"What of the directress?" he asked.

"What of her?" asked the git keeper.

"She is high in a party," said Brenner, "perhaps in the metaparty, the party which controls the others!"

"No," said the git keeper. "She was not in the metaparty."

"She is high in her party!" said Brenner.

"No," said the git keeper. "She was a low-level functionary."

"She is, at least, in a party!" said Brenner.

"No more," said the git keeper. "She does not now even have a name, unless someone has given her one."

"I do not understand," said Brenner.

"Not more than ten days after your departure from your home world she was in the hold of a slave ship, bound for Basra. Later, she was transported to, and sold on, Bokara."

Brenner regarded the git keeper in astonishment.

"The directress' battles with her femininity are at an end," said the git keeper. "She will learn to obey, encouraged by instruments as inexpensive and simple as the lash and chain. She will learn her ecstasy in the arms of a master, and find her fulfillment in selfless service."

"But, as what!" demanded Brenner.

"As a slave, of course," said the git keeper.

"I see," said Brenner.

"It is what she has always been," said the git keeper. "The only difference is that that condition is now no longer deniable, not without absurdity, nor are its appropriate consequences avoidable. It is now overt, satisfying, explicit, and legal."

"And what of the diamonds?" asked Brenner.

"They have been returned to us," said the git keeper, "concealed in trade goods, from that enclave you refer to as "Company Station.""

"Of course," said Brenner.

"If her master chooses to put her in diamonds," said the git keeper, "she will wear them, of course, but I suspect that it will be a long time before she becomes such a slave. In any event, she owns nothing, not even a slave strip, if one is permitted to her. Rather it is she, who is owned."

Brenner wept.

"What is wrong?" asked the git keeper.

"It is madness," he said. "It is all madness!"

"No," said the git keeper.

"What are you going to do with me?"

"You are the father," said the git keeper.

"Kill me with your scarps and sticks," said Brenner. "Or kill me with the rifle!"

"It is wrong to kill the father," said the git keeper. "And the rifle, with its charges, will be destroyed. We disavow such instruments of violence. We disapprove of such things. They are not within our ways."

"You are stinking hypocrites!" screamed Brenner. "You killed Rodriguez!"

"He is not dead," said the git keeper. "We did need his body, to motivate you to dispose of the father."

Brenner felt sick.

"We will give him a less dangerous body," said the git keeper. "We have a use for such as he."

"Release me!" said Brenner.

"Do not fear," said the git keeper. "You will be released."

"I demand to be freed!" said Brenner.

"You will be freed," said another of the Pons, one with his hands on a rope.

"Yes," said another.

"The father must be free," said another.

"Of course," said another.

"How could it be otherwise?" said another.

"I understand nothing of what is going on," wept Brenner.

The git keeper motioned to the other Pons and they, putting their small individual weights collectively to the ropes, began to draw Brenner, on his side, from the temple.

Brenner noted, as he was drawn away, that the pedestal and the vat, or jar, which had been upon it, that in which he had seen the head of Rodriguez, were missing. They had been removed. So, too, had been the body of the slain Pon. Brenner refused to believe, now, that he had seen the eyes in the face open, or that the expression might have changed. Such things were not possible. He wept.

"Why do you weep?" asked the git keeper, indicating that his fellows should pause for a moment in their labors.

"Only one person, my friend, has ever cared for me," said Brenner. "And now he is gone. And this has happened to me, and I have never been loved."

"We love you," said the git keeper.

"We always love the father," said another.

They then drew Brenner from the temple.

When they were in the corridor Brenner heard again, from somewhere outside, the roaring of the beast. The sound was then, naturally, much louder.

They passed, in the corridor, the small figure of a Pon, one which was very small, even for a Pon, and frail. A hood muchly concealed its features. The git keeper and the other Pons, those at the ropes, did not pay it any attention, and it, of course, saw nothing, as it was blind.

At the threshold of the temple, before exiting, the Pons stopped. Brenner tried to pull back his head but, trapped as he was in the net, he could not do so. Then, pressed down over the netting, and held over Brenner's nose and mouth, there was a soft cloth, which had been soaked in chemicals. Brenner was not aware, a moment or two later, that he was taken from the temple.

CHAPTER 30

The lion, for we may call it that, awakened on the cliffs, in the autumn, on a rather wide ledge.

It was not used to this habitat and, after stretching, climbed, with the agility of its kind, to the summit of these cliffs. There, on the height of the cliffs, it surveyed a domain of dark forests. Behind it was a stony valley, and, on the other side of that valley, were more cliffs. In these cliffs were openings, which might serve as lairs. Before it, and about it, and behind it, beyond the other cliffs, seemingly endlessly, stretched the dark forests. Before it, slightly toward the right, in the distance, was a clearing, and, in the center of this clearing, oddly, there was a circle of upright sticks, and, within these sticks, what appeared to be conical heaps of dried vegetation. Such things seemed anomalous to it, but they did not seem to require attention either. It erected its large, pointed ears and drank in the ten thousand tiny sounds of the forest, the rustling of wind in the leaves, the cries of small birds, even the scratchings of a small rodent, of the sort called a git, more than a hundred feet below, off to one side of a large, flat, wooden structure. It lifted its head and attended then to the circumambient symphony of scent, in its ten thousand interwoven traces, as clear, and detectable, and locatable, in their own modality, as would have been individual threads in the pattern of a tapestry. Some of these scents were similar to those with which it

was familiar. Others were unfamiliar. Some of these scents
it did not care for. Others it found intriguing. Others, subtly,
stirringly, spoke to it of warm flesh, and food. Then, when,
in a shifting of wind, a grayish whisper of fog, the dry fog
that chokes the throat and nostrils, and stings the eyes, was
borne to it, from the circle of sticks in the distance, it uttered
a low, disapproving, menacing growl. It shook its head and
fur, disturbed. Somewhere in the labyrinths of its mind it
recalled such ugly fog, not soft with moisture, holding scent
close to the ground, but painfully bright, and glaring, or
loud, and deafening, in its sensory modality, concealing, or
drowning out, a thousand subtler scents. This smell, too,
agitated it, and it lifted its head, for, vaguely, it recollected
then humming, throbbing sounds, flashings, like lightning,
the movement of objects through the air, like birds, the
stinging like hail, and closed caves with shining walls, regular
and cruel, and rounded trees, in alignments, through which
one could not bite or tear. It looked upward, and growled,
threateningly. Fragments of memory, bursting shards of
memory, recollections of an incomprehensible nightmare,
exploded in its brain. And then it crouched down, belly low,
on the cliffs, looking about itself. But all seemed quiet here.
It did not know this place, but it was not unlike the place it
knew. And it could smell food. There was no dearth of food
here, that was clear. This was not a familiar place, but it
seemed suitable. It could make it its own.

CHAPTER 31

IT could tell the feel of oncoming winter, the sharpness in the air. But, too, there were many other signs. Certain small animals, not worth tracking, were storing food. Some others had disappeared, to hide until spring. There were flockings of small birds, anticipatory to departures. And overhead, already, regularly in the late afternoon and evening, and on into the night, calling out to one another, could be marked the flights of others. There were many signs. Even the increasing thickness of its own coat could inform it of the approach of winter.

Things were not, of course, the same here as they had been at home.

Many times it had come to the height of this cliff, as though drawn here.

Often, for hours at a time, perplexed, it would look off toward the circle of sticks in the distance. In one part of its brain, it found such a thing anomalous. But then such things did not matter, really. They did not require attention. They did not impede its movement, they were not edible. They could be accepted as another part of its world, as merely given, and not to be questioned, accepted as facts, like stones, and trees, and the bright spots in the sky, at night. But in another part of its brain, for whatever reason, it found the circle of sticks vaguely familiar, and somehow disturbing. As it gazed upon it, it seemed that something, insistent, but no more than a whisper, struggled to make itself heard.

And then one night, it thought a thought quite unusual for such a beast, which was, "What am I?"

In all its memory there had never been such a question raised, and in such a way. It is not that it had never been perplexed before, for it had often been perplexed, or curious, and had, in its way, investigated one thing or another. But it is one thing to ask, so to speak, "What is that," and another to ask, "What am I?" This sort of thing, as you can see, represents an attitude of inquiry quite other than that expressed in questions, so to speak, such as "Is it good to eat," "Where is it hiding," and "Can I catch it?"

The beast, you see, for the first time, at least as far as it could determine from its memories, had become conscious of its own mystery, its own inexplicable reality, its own unaccountability. That it should be, or that anything should be, had suddenly seemed very interesting to it. It could not recall having concerned itself with such matters before.

One of the very odd things about such questions, and this oddity much disturbed the beast, sometimes making it shudder, was that it seemed to hear these questions in its mind, and understand them. To attempt to make this clear we might point out that it was familiar to the beast that sounds might have meanings, for example, that the breaking of a twig or the dislodgment of a pebble might be pregnant with import, but there was a very different sort of meaning involved here. There seemed no obvious connection or relationship between the sound and what it meant.

From one point of view this seemed preposterous but, from another, it seemed frightfully mysterious, and grand. It was as though a world had suddenly opened up before it, a thrilling world, a world awesome in its possibilities. It grasped, dimly at first, and then with terror, what to you may seem simple, and obvious, namely, that a noise could mean. In a sense, you see, it had come to grasp the concept of a *word*. In considering the greatest inventions of various rational species, on various worlds, it is common to think of such things as a knife or lever. On the other hand, one might also consider the possibility that the most fecund, basic, significant invention of these species is commonly overlooked, perhaps because it is too familiar, or because it is invisible, the *word*. That a noise can mean, in this remote, mysterious, awesome, almost magical sense, is perhaps the most basic and important discovery of a species. Indeed, in that discovery, some might see the quantum leap to a new level of existence. In the beginning, so to speak, may have been the word.

But the beast did not truly believe that it had invented the word. It was rather that it seemed clear to it that there were such things and that, somehow, it understood them. That, in itself, was quite enough for the beast, and surely impressive enough.

It began, over time, to become obsessed with the conviction that the answers to many of the riddles with which it was concerned might be found within that circle of sticks, far off, visible from the cliffs. It was familiar, of course, with the string which ran from the vicinity of the platform toward the circle of sticks. It also read, along the track of the string, now faint, but still detectable, the odors of a beast not unlike itself. Against such a beast it stood ready to defend this territory but the beast did not appear. It had, it seemed, gone away.

The new beast, in claimancy and challenge, with its tread, and the rubbing of its oily fur on trees, and, more explicitly, in the way of its kind, with its feces, and urine, here and there, had marked out its territory. It did not confine itself to this territory, of course. Such markers were not intended to restrict its own peregrinations, which tended to be extensive, but rather to limit the possible intrusions of others. They marked out, primarily, that country it would defend, within which it would regard the passage of certain others as trespass. These borders, to a large extent, followed the lines, and claims, of its unknown predecessor. It was a territory of a nature and range suitable to its kind. The borders of such territories, of course, are somewhat flexible, depending on a number of factors, such as the beast in question, its youth and vigor, the terrain, the game, and the competition from other members of the same species. Within the territory, of course, the beast, following the predilection of its kind, tended to conceal its presence, burying feces, and such. The warnings at the borders, of course, were directed primarily against other predators, and, in particular, against those of its own kind, should they exist, external visitants, possible intruders. A subsidiary advantage of them, however, was that wandering fleet ones within the territory, encountering them, might turn back, thus remaining within the territory. It might be mentioned that the circle of sticks, with its assemblage of dried vegetations, or, as we might say, the village, was close to the heartland of this territory. The absolute heartland, in the sense of being the lair of the beast itself, was a cave in the cliffs, a long, tunnel-like cave which led back, under the cliffs, toward the village.

Often the beast followed the string toward the village, and then followed it back, to its lair. In this fashion, of course, subtle signs of its presence, oil from the pads of paws left on leaves, pelt oil on brush, and tree trunks, a few stray hairs, here and there, the prints of its feet, and such, tended to follow the track of the string. Stealthy ones, wise in their own ways, avoided this area.

The beast's time, of course, was not all spent in subtle, sometimes troublesome, ruminations. Indeed, at times, in the hunt, and in the kill, and in the eager, grisly feeding, and, later, in lying down, sated, sleepy, its consciousness was not other than it had been in the old home. But then, later, the strange thoughts would come. Too, like all beasts it would dream, but it was sometimes puzzled by these dreams, and did not understand them. The beast dreams posed no problems, of course, the running in the forest, the delicious smell of the fleet one, recollections of a successful defense of territory the preceding winter in the old home, against an animal larger even than itself, the feel of wet leaves beneath its paws, the sound of water rushing over stones, where one might drink, such things. In these dreams its legs would twitch, and move, and it would growl. In these dreams there were no words, only things, and doings. But there were other dreams, too, which it did not understand, dreams of places it could not have been, and of other creatures, to whom it, in another form, spoke. It even remembered tastes of a sort which must be impossible, as it could not feed on such things. And it remembered a white softness, supine, trembling, regarding him, frightened, moving, squirming. And then it was again itself and it thrust its snout against that softness, and thrust its head between its legs, forcing them far apart, smelling it, understanding it in its needful, helpless, beast sense. It then drew back and looked at the animal, so white, so soft, so curved. It was before him, supine, in its way, tethered. It was helpless. It would be easy, it thought, to eat it. Perhaps, it thought, that is why it is tethered here, to be eaten. But it licked it, slowly, carefully, with his long, rough tongue. It could not draw away. What strange sounds those tethers made. They seemed excellent tethers. Then it seemed it was again in another form, one recalled from former dreams, one which had appeared even in vagrant memories, and it felt strange sensations, which it did not understand, like promptings in the blood of something not itself, another creature, inexplicable feelings, and there were inexplicable recollections, and it awakened, abruptly, unaccountably furious, and made its way to the summit of the cliff, above the platform, and recollected a distant world, and a broad head, eyes with pupils like knives, a sinuous, agile body, and a maddening, luring odor, and it put back its head, and howled, and howled.

CHAPTER 32

It was now in the depth of winter.

Too, it was late in the afternoon. The beast, the moisture from its breath visible in the chill air, lay indolently on the top of the snowy cliff, the snow melted beneath the warmth of its body, looking toward the village. Perhaps in such weather, and at such a time, one might have expected it to be snug in its lair, asleep, particularly as it had fed earlier, and well, but it could often be found where it was, and, secure in the luxury of its winter pelting, it was not in the least uncomfortable.

Something was coming toward the platform. It was a tiny, frail animal. It was perhaps shedding, strange in the winter, as its outer skin was a different color from its body, and seemed loose about it. Too, it walked in the unusual fashion which the beast, from the darkness of the forest, had remarked upon occasion before, amongst certain animals, on two legs. It interested the beast that the animal could maintain its balance with such ease, given so eccentric a posture. It was much superior in this to one of the other small bipedalian animals of the forest, the tree clinger, which would frequently return to the security of all fours. It did not, on the other hand, seem that it would be adept at climbing, or leaping from branch to branch, or swinging amongst them like a graceful, wingless bird. The footprints of the animal, tiny, and close together, were visible behind it in the snow, even in the half light. It walked as though it were in pain. It is cold, too, thought the beast. See how it clutches its skin about it, how it shivers. The beast doubted that it would be good to eat, at least that specimen. Too, as we have noted, it had recently fed. At such a time even fleet ones could graze within yards of it. The head of the animal, concealed in the strange skin, seemed large for its size.

The beast cocked its head to one side.

It was clear now. The little animal was holding to the string, or, at least, reaching out, from time to time, to touch it, as if to reassure itself that it was still there. Why could it not just look, wondered the beast. Did it expect it to be gone when it reached for it? Was it afraid of that? Where could it go? It was there. Perhaps it had always been there. Perhaps it would always be there. And, if not, what difference would it make? The string was not important to the beast, though it found it interesting. But the string, it seemed, was important to the other animal. It seemed afraid to let it go. Perhaps it needed the string. Perhaps it must hold on to the string, or perish, thought the beast. But ,if so, that is very unfortunate, for the string is very old, very thin, and worn. It might be broken, or taken away.

The beast continued to observe the approach of the small creature.

It must now be able to see me, thought the beast, at least if it looked up. I have made no effort to conceal my presence. But it does not look up.

Yes, the small animal below, making its way, shivering, through the snow, clearly now, was holding to the string, clutching it. Then, when it came to the end of it, it let it go and began, forelimbs outstretched, taking small, shuffling steps, to grope its way forward. This puzzled the beast. It is in the dark, it thought. But it is not in the dark, because it is still light. It is true it is becoming dark. The beast, of course, in its own case, had seldom been in the dark, except when it slept, or closed its eyes. Even with no moon there were the stars, and the beast had little difficulty in seeing by their light. It could see even in most of the passages it had explored in the cliffs, those strange squared passages so unlike a normal cave, and those rooms off the passages, some of which contained large boxes and strangely formed stones. When the stars were obscured by clouds, it was more difficult, but even then there was normally some light, filtering through the clouds, and, too, one could tell much by smell, by hearing the currents of air moving about objects, by noting the effect of drafts on the hair of one's body.

The small creature had now come to the platform, and had put out its forelimbs, touching it.

Its presence there, of course, from the point of view of the beast, was not an intrusion. Only certain presences would have counted as intrusions, providing occasions for activity. Many animals came and went in the beast's territory, and in the thousands of subterritories, maintained by other animals, within his territory, without concerning it. What did it matter, so to speak, that ants might be found in the world of wolves? They did not count. The beast was even fond of a small git, which it occasionally watched, which nested near one of the posts of the platform.

"Are you there?" called a small, shrill voice from below, that of the tiny creature which had groped its way forward to the platform. How strange that high, thin, shrill voice is, thought the beast. If a creature is so small, it thought, better perhaps that it be silent.

"Are you here?" called the small animal.

Suddenly the beast rose to its feet, disturbed. The hair on the back of its neck rose up, like the collar of a cloak behind it. Its fur shook, as if casting off water. It had, for the first time, realized suddenly, comprehending it consciously, that these noises it heard, diminutive, and pathetic, but in their way as real as thunder and rushing water, not like the puzzling, mysterious noises in its mind, those which the ear could only seem to hear, were, like the noises within, intelligible. They could be understood, and it understood them. Such things were words, and they came from without, not from within.

The small creature was now looking up. It must surely

see him. Perhaps it had heard, above it, the scratching on the rock, as it had sprung up, and the snapping of its hide and fur, like leather shaken in the wind.

"Are you there?" called the tiny voice.

The beast resumed its recumbent posture, uneasily. It must put such things from its mind. There were mysteries enough. What had such things to do with food or drink, or shelter, or such things? But it was odd, and unsettling, to hear the noises of the mind, or things like them, coming not from within, but from without, from the outside, in recognizable form, and from so odd and deformed a creature as stood below.

"Are you there?" called the creature.

The beast now rose again to its feet. It was agitated, for this presence was not as harmless as it might seem. Somehow, in one way or another, it seemed to threaten its peace, perhaps even the foundations of its world. I am angry, thought the beast. One bite could finish such a creature, it thought. It made its way, lightly, down the cliff toward the platform. Gently it padded across the platform. Then it crouched down, belly low, on the platform, tail lashing behind it. But I am sated, it thought. Why had it come down? It was angry. But, too, it was curious. And, too, it was a little afraid, because there was some threatening linkage, it knew, between this thing, this pathetic, insignificant, tiny thing, and the strange thoughts, and the strange dreams, with which for the past months it had been troubled.

"Are you there?" whispered the small creature.

The beast looked at it. Its body was very small, but the head, comparatively, was large, or at least large for the body. Would it not be heavy, that head, to be carried by such a body? The head had a tiny face, much too small for it, much like the faces of some of the little, loose-skinned, two-legged creatures it had seen in the forest. But the back of the head was large. In the tiny face, seemingly lost in the larger head, there were two holes. No eyes gleamed out from those holes. They were empty.

"Are you there?" whispered the tiny thing.

The beast growled, menacingly.

The small creature thrust an object onto the platform, and then turned about, and, as it could, feeling its way, fled. The beast saw it reach the string, and grasp it, and then hurry away.

The beast, with its teeth, and holding it down with one paw, tore open the object on the platform, and smelled it. It could not eat such stuff. It lifted it up, and shook it, scattering grains about.

It looked after the small animal, which had now disappeared through the trees. How odd, it thought, that such a thing, and others like it, could live in the forest.

It then stood on the platform.

Some small birds alighted on the platform, and, here and there, and some almost at its feet, pecked at the material which had been flung about.

CHAPTER 33

With a certain form of throat, and oral cavity, a certain type of tongue, and a certain arrangement of teeth, of course, it is not easy to reproduce many sounds which would be the more natural and appropriate issuances of a different form of apparatus. This obvious fact makes clear the importances of translation mechanisms, of one or another level of sophistication, throughout the galaxy. Some of these are responsive to auditory inputs, and others, of course, to visual inputs, and others, yet, to inputs such as the traces of complex chemical exudates. But, invariably, aside from certain constructed devices and certain marvels of biochemical engineering, speech was an overlaid function, utilizing an apparatus obviously developed for other purposes, such as holding, tearing, grinding, tasting, swallowing, breathing, and such. On the other hand, amongst organisms utilizing a vocal apparatus, as opposed to those utilizing the modulation of wing speeds, the rubbing of chitinous limbs, frictions amongst adjacent platings, the articulation of patterns of moisture, condensing in cold air, expelled from blow holes, the secretion of chemicals, and such, it was usually possible for one organism to produce sounds which, once certain adjustments were made, could be accepted as surrogates of others. This is particularly easy to do, if the throat, for example, has been prepared, or altered, in a certain way.

Since that winter day, several weeks ago, the beast had been much disturbed by its insights into its own unusual capacities, which seemed to have been acquired in its new habitat, as, in its deepest memories, and even in its dreams, it could not recall them from the old home.

It was not at all pleased with many of the sounds it made, as they were quite different from the sounds which came to it from time to time in his mind, and in the unusual dreams, when he spoke such sounds, and in another form. Indeed, it often put such things from itself, impatiently, and contemptuously. Why should it not amuse itself by trying to chirp like birds or squeak like gits? But the riddles remained, and the curiosity remained, and so, on the cliffs, and in the forests, it would, from time to time, concern itself with such things.

One day, on the cliffs, it looked out, toward the village. "What am I?" it asked. It heard that sound. It was outside, outside, and yet it was not too unlike the sound from inside, that which the ear could only seem to hear.

The success of this effort, its first in such ranges of endeavor, far from exhilarating the beast, terrified it, and it put such experiments far from itself for several days. It had no business with such nonsense. Such things were not for it. But then, of course, perhaps they were, for it was no longer confident of what it was. It was angry. In the old home it had never encountered such problems. They had not arisen.

It may have been toward the end of winter, when the small creature again approached the platform.

This time the beast, having perceived its approach, came down to the platform, and sat on the platform, awaiting it.

The small creature, so tiny, so ugly, eyeless, the face so tiny in the larger head, put the tiny bag of grain on the platform, almost at the feet of the beast.

He looked up, although he could not see. "Are you there?" he asked.

"Yes," said the beast.

CHAPTER 34

Through the dusk of the winter evening the small figure trudged back toward the village, holding to the string. Behind him, like a gigantic shadow, and as noiseless as one, came the beast.

The small figure, slowly, carefully, departing from the string, his hands outstretched, crossed the clearing. In a few moments, he touched palings, and, feeling his way about, came to the gate.

The beast remained back from the gate. It sat some thirty or forty yards back.

There seemed soon, in spite of the lateness of the day, and the nature of the season, much movement, much agitation, within the palings. Lights moved back and forth within them. Sitting there, it could smell smoke from fires within the village. It did not care for that smell.

The beast asked itself why it had come. What could there be here of interest, or importance, to it? It had, of course, followed the small figure.

It did not understand the village, which seemed a poor lair, or nest. It did not find the inhabitants of that place, which it had observed, from time to time, here and there, from the darkness of the forest, of great interest. They were surely amongst the most miserable and weakest, and worthless, creatures of the forest. Their jaws, and teeth, were small. They lacked claws. They could not fly. They were poor climbers, poor runners. There was little to be remarked about them, other than the ease with which they could maintain their balance on two legs. That was impressive, like the unusual form of locomotion practiced by certain amphibians at the edges of streams and ponds. To be sure, standing on the hind legs did raise their heads higher than they would otherwise be, and this might be of some advantage in looking about oneself, particularly if one had inferior hearing and smell. All in all, the beast held the small creatures in contempt. They were edible, of course. But it was confident it would prefer the fleet ones, or even stealthy ones.

Why have I come here, once more the beast asked itself. But, in its heart, it knew. It had come because of the thoughts, the riddles, the mysteries, the dreams, the troublings. These small creatures hiding in their lair, or nest, were surely, on the whole, of little interest. They were small and weak, and slow and awkward. They could not fly. They could not climb well, or run well. But they did do something that the other creatures of the forest did not do, something that was, in its way, more impressive than climbing well, or running well, and more impressive, too, than the possession of an upright posture. They spoke.

Have I been here before, the beast asked itself? And strange memories occurred to it, of giddy sensations, of swingings about, like a tree clinger, but without grasping a branch, of flying, like a bird, but without wings, of seeing trees, it seemed, from the top, not from the ground, of grating, clanking sounds, of a ground it could not claw through, even less than stone, of hard, narrow, closely set trees, of stuff like the floor, through which it could not press, through which it could not bite, through which it could scarcely see.

The beast growled, in anger.

The gate to the palisade opened a bit and some of the small creatures, Pons, emerged. Some of these held torches. The beast lowered itself to its belly, tail lashing. It remembered, from somewhere, such lights, and others, powerful, from above, seeming to emerge from terrible sounds, like beams darting back and forth through the trees.

The eyeless one was thrust toward the beast and, slowly, foot by foot, while his fellows remained by the gate, approached it, hands outstretched.

The beast growled once, to guide it.

It growled again, in a moment, menacingly, to halt it. It was close enough.

But the figure took another step forward.

The beast backed away a step, belly low, growling warningly.

Again the figure came forward. It did not seem afraid. This puzzled the beast. This was the first time it had been approached in such a fashion. It snarled, warningly. But it would not give ground further. It opened its jaws. It lifted a paw from the ground, in its agitation the claws springing out. But the figure, perhaps as it could not see, came forward still. It came forward with small, slow steps, reaching out. Again the beast snarled, menacingly, warningly. But the figure continued to approach. And then the figure was beside it, standing beside it, at the very side of its jaws, which were close to the ground. The beast did not understand this. It did not understand this, at all. Why had it not killed it? Kill it, thought the beast. But it did not kill it, as easy as that would have been. Somehow, not understanding why, it was permitting this insignificant creature to stand near it. He felt its small hands at its muzzle. The beast's ears flattened back. It growled. But it was permitting this creature to touch it. The small figure then, weeping, embraced, as he could, the head of the beast, and laid his own head against the beast's head. By this the beast was much troubled. It understood little, or nothing. How was it that it had permitted this? How strange this all was, how unlike the old home! Why had it not killed this thing? Why did it not kill it even now, or, if this seemed impossible, back away from it, or run from it? The small creature held to the beast, sobbing. The Pons, seeing this, gasped, thrilled, and looked wildly to one another.

The beast heard, from somewhere in the vicinity of the gate, the voice of one of the small creatures:

We love you, father.
Forgive us, father, for what we have done.

This was answered, or followed, by another such voice. While this second voice was heard, calling out its phrases, enunciating them in measured tones, more, and more, of the small creatures emerged through the gate, taking their places before it. Some of these, too, carried torches.

We are contrite!
Show us forbearance!
Be kind to us!
Cherish us!
Protect us!
We will refrain from touching the soft ones!
We beg your forgiveness, father,
for what we have done.

The beast, of course, understood this, at least in the sense of understanding the words. To be sure, it made little sense of it beyond that. It all seemed quite puzzling. Surely it could have nothing to do with it. Somehow, however, something in these words, like thunder from far away, like the humming, roaring sounds which had, at first, seemed so far away, like the small, moving lights, which had, at first, seemed so far away, disturbed the beast.

A third voice then called out:

Forgive us, father.
Love us!
Cherish us!
Protect us!

The beast now half crouched, its tail lashing. Obviously it was becoming agitated. The small figure which had held it so closely could not hold to it now. The head had pulled away, it was too high for it to reach.

The torches were too much like candles. Things furtive, like phantoms, flew, and shrieked, about the edges of its memory. Its huge heart began to pound. The Pons were now spread out, about the palings, in the vicinity of the gate, some lifting their torches. They did not have strange skins. They wore robes. It recalled, from somewhere, robes of snowy white, wooden walls. Claws sprang into view. Its lips drew back, baring fangs.

Once more the voice called out:

> Forgive us, father.
> Love us!
> Cherish us!
> Protect us!

The beast, crouching down, its hind legs gathered under it, tail lashing, surveyed the gathered Pons, the tiny figures, the torches.

> Love us!
> Cherish us!
> Protect us!

It recalled the parts of a body, somehow meaningful, before a platform. Polished scarps.

> Cherish us!
> Protect us!

It recalled another form, somehow itself, but which could not have been itself, and a strange thing, from which had emerged, bursting forth, a blast of ringing fire, and it drew back, recoiling inadvertently, even in this memory from that sight, and it recalled a gaping, monstrous cavity appearing black, then red, and flooding, in a mighty chest.

It crept forward again.

It recalled a vat, or jar, and, within that container, odd, with no body, a head.

Cherish us!
Protect us!

It did not understand these things, but it was not pleased.
It growled with terrible menace.

It was as though something crept closer now to the corners
of its dark mind. It was as though there were something
quite close to it now, but behind a curtain. It was close, as
if it might be just behind a door, which had not yet been
opened.

"Cherish us!" called a Pon.

"Protect us!" called another.

Again the beast growled. There was no mistaking the
menace in that sound.

"Stop!" cried the small figure to the Pons near the gate.
"Stop!"

But the Pons continued to call out their phrases.

The beast in its agitation, in its mounting fury, looked
upon the Pons.

"Cherish us!" they called.

"Protect us!" they called.

The beast then addressed itself to the small creature who
stood quite near it.

"What am I?" it asked.

"You are the totem!" screamed the small figure near it.

"Who am I?" it demanded, in a voice almost unintelligible
in its form, in a voice heavy with wrath, in a voice which
could be native only to a beast, in the accents of a creature
who lived on flesh, in sounds which might have come from
a storm.

"You are the father!" cried out the small creature.

In that moment then it seemed as though the cliffs
had broken open, splitting apart, and a thousand forms,
violent, and hideous, uncompromising, had burst forth,
howling and screaming. It was as though all the fathers,
all the victims, loved and hated, revered and betrayed,
had come forth, and all thirsting for blood. And now, in

the person of the beast, in the person of this terrible thing, the injuries done onto all these might, in one night of carnage, be avenged. It is that which I am, now thought the beast, the most recent in a line of progenitors, one required for life, who gives life but is to be destroyed by the life it gives, who is doomed to be servitor to ungrateful seed, who will be feared and hated because of the scepter which must be borne, and which he, alone, can bear, he doomed to be protector, defense and shield, tyrant, lover, king, victim.

The Pons, shrieking, fled toward the gate.

The beast, in all its terribleness, had reared up on its hind legs, more then than forty feet in height, clawing at the dark sky, roaring in fury, and pain, understanding what it was, and what had been done to it, and what it could now do, if it wished.

The beast stood there then, a moment later, very quietly, eyeing the gate.

This stillness in it, somehow, seemed even more menacing than its rage of a moment earlier.

It was not a simple beast, of course. It was a beast, but, too, it had a mind capable of firmness of purpose, capable of planning, of attention to detail.

This made it additionally terrifying.

The gate shut. The bars were put in place. Only the small figure of the eyeless one was left outside the palings. He had fallen, twice, trying to flee toward the gate. It had been shut before he could reach it.

The beast walked toward the gate. The small eyeless one, sensing its approach, backed against the palings.

"Where is the rifle?" asked Brenner.

The eyeless one looked up toward the beast. "It was destroyed," he said.

"Good," said Brenner.

"I saw it done before I was given this body."

"That was their mistake," said Brenner.

"It is their way," said the eyeless one.

"A mistake," said Brenner.

"They are at your mercy, like infants," said the eyeless one.

Brenner could see torches within the palings, and the faces of some of the Pons through the gate.

"What are you going to do?" asked the eyeless one.

Brenner did not respond to this but went to the palings at the left of the gate and, with his shoulder, pressing against them, snapped several, and forced others, rupturing the dirt in which they had been planted, from the ground. He then moved to his right, toward the gate and then past it, and, carefully, putting his head to one side, with his teeth, drew up some four or five palings. He dropped them, one by one, like sticks, outside the former perimeter of the fence. Pons drew back from those parts of the fence. Brenner then went to the gate itself and, with the huge prehensile paws of the form of life which he now shared, or had become, with its nature, its instincts, and its memories, seized the gate. Then, with a growl, he reared up, yanking the gate from the fence and, turning, hurled it a hundred feet behind him, across the clearing. He then entered through the hole where the gate had been. Pons shrank back before him, toward the village clearing.

The eyeless one, feeling his way about the palings, groping his way, followed the sounds, the tiny sounds of the retreating Pons, the soft, exultant, anticipatory growls of the beast, in effect, herding them before it.

Brenner sat down, at the edge of the village clearing. He could see the small, open-sided shelter where the git cage had been. He could see the hut he had shared with Rodriguez. He surveyed the Pons.

"Where are you?" called the eyeless one.

"I am here," said Brenner.

The eyeless one came to him, and put his hands out, feeling the beast.

"What are you going to do?" asked the eyeless one.

"I am going to kill them," said Brenner. "I am going to kill them all."

The Pons shrank back, further,

"If I should miss one or two," said Brenner, "others in the forest will finish the work. I will not kill you."

"You will not do this," said the eyeless one.

"Who can stop me?" asked Brenner.

"One who is your equal," said the eyeless one.

"He was old," said Brenner. "He would not have been my equal. And I killed him."

"There is another."

"Bring him forth then," said Brenner. "We shall adjudicate the matter."

"He is here," said the eyeless one.

"Where?" said Brenner. He knew there could be no other. Could their sense of smell not inform them of that.

"You," said the eyeless one.

"You are mad," said Brenner, licking at his fur, on the left shoulder.

"Surely you understand," said the eyeless one.

"No," said Brenner.

"You are the father," said the eyeless one. "No beast devours its own kind."

"These are not my kind," said Brenner.

"They are at your mercy," said the eyeless one.

"Excellent," said Brenner.

"They count on your protection," said the eyeless one.

"They have miscalculated," said Brenner.

"You cannot hurt them," said the eyeless one.

"You are mistaken," said Brenner.

"You will not hurt them!" said the eyeless one.

"Why not?" asked Brenner, puzzled.

"They are your children," said the eyeless one.

"They are not my children," said Brenner.

"Some carry your seed," said the eyeless one.

The beast turned about, in fury. It fled through the hole where the gate had been. Outside the remains of the fence it stopped, and roared in defiance, in anger. Then it put back its head and howled toward the dark sky.

From within the remains of the fence, a voice was heard, high-pitched, calling out:

Oh, I could get me in.
I could lay them waste.
But I will not do so,
for they are my children.
I am the father.

The beast looked back toward the palisade. It then turned about and disappeared into the forest. It was its intention, at that time, never to return. It wandered a long time in the forest, tirelessly. It drank now and then, at one stream or another. But it did not pause to hunt. Oddly enough, as though understanding this, fleet ones, very still in the forest, looked up from their feeding, watching it pass by. It came to a line of white stones and stopped before it. Here something inside it, different from itself, wept, in memory of a mighty creature. It then looked down, again, at the white stones. It did not need the stones, of course, to find its way back to the village. Its sense of direction would have seemed uncanny to most species, and particularly to many which regarded themselves as rational, some of which prided themselves on the substitution of cogitation for the compass of the instincts. And it could, in any case, if it had wished, have followed its own backtrail, which lay as open to its senses, soft on the leaves, almost steaming there, as might have a paved road, a succession of blazed trees, a line of stones, to other forms of life. Shortly before dawn, not following the stones, it had returned to the edge of the clearing, that within which the village lay.

It sat there, amongst the trees, at the edge of the clearing, in the darkness. Torches had been set about the breaches in the fence. It could see figures moving about, mostly within the palisade. The Pons were laboring to restore the gate, the palings.

It thought the following:

Oh, I could get me in.
I could lay them waste.

But I will not do so,
for they are my children.
I am the father.

It then returned to its lair.

CHAPTER 35

"This," said Rodriguez, eagerly, "is the theory!"

"Why did you take their part?" asked Brenner.

"It was your part, as much as theirs," said Rodriguez.

"Are you not horrified at what has been done to you?" asked Brenner. It was revolting to Brenner to look upon the small, eyeless creature, the tiny face lost in the larger head, disproportionate to the body. In such a casing he found it hard to think of Rodriguez, the wreck of whose body, even when Brenner first knew him, had been still large, formidable, strongly built. Brenner recalled that the git keeper had informed him that Rodriguez would be given a less dangerous body. The Pons had feared him, with that large, frightening body. The present body was harmless enough, indeed, small even, and weak even, for a Pon, and without eyes. Pons needed no longer fear the thing that had once been his friend.

"Yes," said Rodriguez.

"What of the Pon whose body that formerly was?" asked Brenner. He remembered that Pon, from the temple.

"They did not need him any longer," said Rodriguez. "He was disposed of, the brain. I saw it removed and destroyed."

"You saw this?" asked Brenner.

"From my jar," said Rodriguez.

Brenner's body shuddered, the fur rippling over it.

"It had been placed on a shelf in the laboratory, overlooking the operating table."

"The placement of the jar there was doubtless not an accident," said Brenner.

"No," said Rodriguez. "I do not think so."

"Did you know what they intended to do?" asked Brenner.

"None had seen fit to inform me," said Rodriguez, "but it was not difficult to divine their intention."

Brenner was silent.

"One sees. One knows," said Rodriguez. "But one can do nothing. One cannot scream. One cannot speak. One is moved about, here and there. One is done with, as others please."

"I understand," said Brenner.

"As you know," said Rodriguez, "decapitory incarceration is used in maximum-security prisons on several worlds."

"Yes," said Brenner.

"It is interesting, in its way," said Rodriguez. "One continues to feel one's body, at least for a time, though it no longer exists, whether it is warm or cold, how the limbs are positioned, and such. It requires an effort to accept this, that the body no longer exists."

"I understand," said Brenner, shuddering. Sensation was located predominantly in the brain, and then extradited, so to speak, to various parts of the body. Indeed, even a disembodied brain, properly stimulated, could have experiences, visual, tactual, and otherwise. Indeed, a common form of paranoia, developed in his species over the past thousands of years, was the suspicion, or conviction, that one might be such a brain, in some ensconcement, being stimulated by aliens, who would then study it, or, perhaps, participate vicariously in its experiences.

Brenner lay on the summit of the cliff. It was a favorite place of his. He had carried Rodriguez upward, Rodriguez clinging to his fur. From where they were, Brenner, even reclining, could see over the forest, to the village. Behind him, at the foot of the cliffs, was the valley, and, on the other side of it, the cliffs with the openings, which he and Rodriguez, one fateful afternoon, had explored.

"Why did they do this to you?" asked Brenner.

"I could thus be of use to them," said Rodriguez. "It was I who knew you, who was your friend. Thus it would be I, the least likely to be torn to pieces, who would approach the new father. You do not think they would wish to risk one of themselves, do you? Some, in the past, I gather, had perished in such a fashion. There was only this body about, almost less than occupied. It would do."

"How is the body?"

"It is painful and feeble. I do not think it will last long."

"They should all be killed," said Brenner.

"They are your future," said Rodriguez.

"Forgive me," said Brenner. "But it disgusts me to look upon you."

"It is a gruesome prison," admitted Rodriguez. "In it I am little to be feared. Too, perhaps it amuses them that I should be kept in this fashion."

"In the village," said the beast, "had you said to me, 'Kill', in that instant, they would have learned you were more to be feared than they had thought."

"They read me well," said Rodriguez.

Brenner did not respond to this. The Pons, he knew, to his fury, had read another well, too.

"Do you have the memories of the beast?" asked Rodriguez.

"Yes," said Brenner.

"Then it is not dead," said Rodriguez.

"It is gone," said Brenner. "Its memories remain. I have appropriated them. In a way it survives, in me. In a way it still lives. In a way we are one. Yet my consciousness is my own."

"But your instincts, your needs?"

"Those of a beast, which I am," said Brenner.

"You are my friend, Allan, as well," said Rodriguez.

"It is very strange," said Brenner.

"Not really," said Rodriguez. "Some sort of enmeshing of brains has taken place, of a quite sophisticated sort. Your brain, it seems clear, or portions of it, doubtless the upper brain in particular, with its consciousness and memories, has been enmeshed with that of the beast, presumably primarily with its lower brain, together with portions of its upper brain, memory tracks, and such."

"The consciousness is that of a beast," said Brenner, "but somehow it is also mine, mine as I remember it, I mean, but mine now in a new manner, as that of a beast."

"Were it not for this mercilessness, this terribleness," said Rodriguez, "you could not be so effective as a guardian."

"The Pons have planned well," said Brenner.

"They have had millenniums to perfect these techniques," said Rodriguez.

"For a long time I could not recall Allan," said the beast. "Sometimes, even now, I forget him."

"You make me afraid," said Rodriguez.

"I could never harm you," said Brenner. "You are the only person who has ever cared for me."

Rodriguez did not respond.

"What is your life?" asked Brenner.

"I am the pariah," said Rodriguez, simply. "Such are not unoften found in totemistic villages. They serve a useful social function. They provide the community with something to look down upon, something to despise and ridicule. Too, they may be utilized to perform tasks which others might find unwelcome, distasteful or repulsive, even taboo. For example, they may make contact with, and care for, and wash, and feed, those who are temporarily taboo, for example, from having attended to the burial of the dead."

"Pons die?" asked Brenner.

"They are quite mortal," said Rodriguez.

"Where do they keep you?"

"I stay in the temple."

"In the darkness?"

"I have my own darkness. They feed me. I have my thoughts."

"Never leave me," said Brenner. "I do not want to be alone."

"I will one day leave you," said Rodriguez.

"Stay," said Brenner.

"Do you think I find this form of life acceptable?" asked Rodriguez. "Do you think I care for the darkness, the weakness, the pain? Do you think I am not aware of this ugliness, this tiny face at the bottom of a head, of the revolting thinness, the shrillness, of my speech, of my disproportions, my ungainliness? Do you think that I am not aware of this pathetic, ludicrous, diminutive monstrosity I have been made? Do you truly think I will continue to indefinitely submit to this humiliation? Do you think I care for these things? Do you think I will grant the final victory to Pons?"

"Do not leave me," said Brenner.

"In any event," said Rodriguez, "the days of this frail house, this humiliating prison in which I have been placed, are numbered."

"Do not speak so," said Brenner, alarmed.

"But there is something I want to learn first," said Rodriguez.

Brenner was silent, troubled.

"Are you now wholly the beast?" asked Rodriguez.

"I do not know," said Brenner.

"Surely you are still curious," said Rodriguez.

"Concerning what?" asked Brenner.

"That which we came here to learn," said Rodriguez.

"Would that we had never come here!" cried Brenner.

"I would have come again," said Rodriguez.

"How is that?" asked Brenner, horrified.

"The answer is here!" said Rodriguez. "It is within our grasp!"

"I do not understand," said Brenner.

"The theory! The theory!" said Rodriguez.

"I do not understand," said Brenner.

"Take me to the graveyard," said Rodriguez.

"I do not understand," said Brenner.

"We will learn the truth!" said Rodriguez.

"You are blind," said Brenner.

"You shall be my eyes," said Rodriguez.

"They have come for you, to take you back," said Brenner. He could see some Pons, three of them, in the vicinity of the platform."

"No!" protested Rodriguez.

"Yes," said Brenner.

"It is late?" said Rodriguez.

"Yes," said Brenner.

"Are you afraid to look into these matters?" asked Rodriguez.

"Perhaps," said Brenner.

"Are you are afraid to learn the truth of the fathers?" asked Rodriguez.

"Perhaps it is a truth best not known," said Brenner.

"You must help me," said Rodriguez.

"It is late," said Brenner.

"Allan," said Rodriguez.

"We will descend now," said Brenner.

"Of course," said Rodriguez.

Rodriguez then seized the fur of the beast, at its shoulder, and, clinging to it, was borne to the platform, and then to the level. The three Pons who had come to the vicinity of the platform, seeing the descent of the beast, withdrew well into the trees.

"Hold to the string," said Brenner. "I fear stealthy ones may be about." It was spring, you see, and that is a time when intrusions are most frequent, when animals tend to range, young ones seeking to mark out territories for themselves, older ones, robust animals, seeking to extend theirs. Another dangerous time is the depth of winter, when food is scarce, when one must sometimes range out of one's own country, to find it. To be sure, it was difficult enough, at any time, to police the territory effectively, as it was quite large, and there were many beasts, like sinister itinerants, which came and went within it. Too, some predators, almost negligible to the beast, constituted serious threats to animals as small as Pons.

Brenner watched the tiny, eyeless one grasp the string. It then went toward the village, followed by the Pons.

"What could the small, eyeless one want in a graveyard?" the beast asked itself. That seemed very strange. It then decided that it was sleepy, and returned to its lair, for a nap. "How had it all begun, what did it all mean?" Brenner later asked himself. But then the beast curled up, and fell asleep.

CHAPTER 36

The beast, after a time, after some weeks, forgot the small, eyeless one, who had not returned to the platform. The spring was a very hard time for it, for no reason that it clearly understood. It often howled in misery, on the cliffs. It became restless. It left its own territory, from time to time, for no other purpose than to meet stealthy ones, and kill them.

The summer came, and then the fall, and winter. And then one day, after a rain, on a cold day in early spring, it found a small, sodden sack of grain on the platform.

It then recalled the small, eyeless one.

Swiftly then did it take scent. Yes, the scent was that of the small, eyeless one! Well did the beast recall it. But the trail did not lead back, parallel to the approach, to the string. There seemed but a single trail, where there should have been two, the approaching trail and then, somewhat fresher, of greater insistency, a returning trail. That was odd. The beast turned about, almost frantically, here and there. It detected no signs of a stealthy one. Then, to its surprise, and apprehension, it discovered the trail, which did not return to the village, but ascended the cliffs. The beast looked upward, alarmed, at the heights. "Rodriguez!" screamed Brenner, silently. The beast put its paws against the cliff. The small, eyeless one had, presumably on its hands and knees, feeling its way, ascended the cliff. In an instant

the beast had scrambled to the height of the cliff and stood
there, looking wildly about. It erected its ears. It distended
its nostrils. It became an alert, living web of apprehension.
The trail led down, over the edge of the cliff. It looked down,
fearing to see a small, crumpled body below. Then, hastily,
it hurried down, and, at the foot of the cliff, picked up the
trail again. It went across the valley, to the cliffs. Then it
went along the cliffs. The small, eyeless one had used them
as a guide. It might have taken the small, eyeless one hours
to grope his way along the cliffs, but the beast, in moments,
had bounded beside them, pausing only an instant, now
and again, to confirm the trail. Footprints soon became
visible in the mud. Panting, its lungs gasping for breath, it
surmounted a rise, and came to the graveyard at the end of
the cliffs. In its center, standing as though lost, amongst the
grassy knolls, a scarp in its hand, bent over, its robes soaked
in the cold rain, shivering, was the small, eyeless one.

"Allan, is that you?" it asked.

"Yes," said Brenner.

"You did not meet me at the platform!"

"You have not come for months," said Brenner.

"They would not let me come," it said.

Brenner was silent.

"I have run away," it said.

"You should not have done so," said Brenner.

"I must know!" it said.

Brenner did not respond to this.

"I have stolen a scarp!"

"To what purpose?" asked Brenner.

"That I might use it to kill any who might try to stop me!"
it cried. "I tell you I must know, and I will know!"

"You are ill," said Brenner.

"I am dying," it said.

"No!" said Brenner.

"Which is the oldest grave?" it asked. The rain now, again,
was pouring down. "Tell me!?" it cried. "Tell me!" Brenner
was silent.

"Do not let the Pons have the final victory!" it cried.

"We thought that one," said Brenner, "or perhaps that one."

"Open it," said Rodriguez. "Open them both. Open them all."

"Out here you will die," said Brenner. He himself shivered. His own fur was soaked with water and the cold wind whistled through it.

"My life is not important," it cried. "Can you not understand that?"

"It is important to me," said Brenner.

"Help me!" it cried.

Brenner shook his great head. The small one, of course, did not see this movement.

"Before I die I would know the truth!"

"To whom will you tell it?" asked Brenner. "To the grass, to the rain, to a beast?"

"Help me!" it cried.

"You cannot stay here," said Brenner. "You are ill. You will die here."

"You are only a beast!" it cried. "Go away! Leave me! I do not need you! I do not want you! Go away! Go away!"

Brenner then watched the small figure, in its sopped robes, the rain streaming over its head, bending down, unsteady, half falling, grope about, with its free hand and scarp, and locate the side of a grassy knoll. It then, on the side of this knoll, fell to its knees and begin to gouge at its side with the scarp. In moments the small figure, tiny, frenzied, coughing, was covered with wet grass and mud.

"Emilio," said Brenner.

"Go away!" shrieked the tiny, high-pitched voice.

Brenner reached down and, turning his head to one side, gently picked up the small figure in its mouth. It struck at him with the scarp, again and again, and Brenner tasted his own blood, running inside the inner, lower lip.

"Let me learn the truth! Let me die!" it begged.

Brenner carried him back to the village and put him down, gently, before the gate. He then withdrew so that the Pons might be more willing, given the security of this distance, to emerge through the gate. He saw them come out, and retrieve the scarp, which the small figure surrendered, and then, gently, take him within. Then Brenner came to the gate. He saw the faces of Pons within. They were frightened, that he should be at this proximity to them. "Care for him," said Brenner.

The beast then returned to the valley.

It went, in the driving rain, to the place of the grassy knolls. There, with its great claws, and might, it tore open what seemed likely to be the oldest grave, and peered within. It then went to the other graves in the place of knolls and, one by one, opened them. With its large eyes, in that broad, monstrous head, it looked into them. Then it turned about and returned to its lair.

Behind it, as it returned to its lair, lay the graveyard. Stones and clods of earth were strewn about. There was a great deal of mud in the area now and much of the grass was flat and slick with rain. The sky was dark. There was a cold wind. Rain continued to fall. It pelted into the graves, and, from the sides, trickled into them. The graves naturally became quite muddy. Soon, puddles formed, their surfaces reacting to the descent of the rain.

Just within its lair the beast shook its fur, spattering water about. It was cold, and miserable. It then lay down, and rather curled about itself, rather as though it would warm itself with its own body. In a moment or two, it was asleep.

The graves had all been empty.

CHAPTER 37

"What is this theory?" asked Brenner.

It was now a warm afternoon, in the late summer. Rodriguez had wished to be carried to the summit of the cliff. He could see nothing from there, of course, but the sun was pleasant there, on the rock, and there was a gentle, refreshing breeze moving over the forest, and, perhaps most important, he recalled, that if he had had eyes, there would have been, from this point, a most impressive and beautiful view. We may conjecture that he saw this view, so to speak, in his memory.

Although the body of the former Pon in which his brain found its current habitat was a frail one, one wretched and vulnerable, and subject to infection, and cold, and misery, it was, at this point, within its limitations, healthy and sound. Rodriguez had been, several weeks ago, recovered from the door of death. He had been nursed back to health by the Pons with care, and with what skills remained to them of such matters, from long ago.

Before coming back to the height of the cliff Brenner had, at Rodriguez' request, accompanied his friend to the graveyard. Rodriguez had himself clambered down into several of the graves, slipping down their now crumbling sides, as though to verify for himself that they were indeed empty.

"The sarcophagi in the chambers are also empty," Brenner

had informed him. "I examined them, opening them, and reclosing them, in the weeks after I returned you to the village."

"All empty?" Rodriguez had asked.

"Yes," had said Brenner.

"The Pons are in crisis," said Rodriguez.

Brenner looked over the forest, toward the village.

"They have been treating you well?"

"They have treated me well, since you brought me back to the village," said Rodriguez.

"They would let you come here, when you wish?"

"Yes, now," said Rodriguez.

"But it is dangerous," said Brenner.

"There is the string," said Rodriguez. "I can hold to that."

"It is only a string," said Brenner.

"No one has more," said Rodriguez.

"In what ways are the Pons in crisis?" asked Brenner.

"Sesostris, who was the keeper of the git," said Rodriguez, "is a reflective fellow. Sometimes we talk."

"I can remember," said Brenner, "when you thought Pons lacked names."

"He is aware that things must change."

"In what way?" asked Brenner.

"Do you know what occurred here a thousand years ago?" asked Rodriguez.

"That which has recurred most recently," said Brenner.

"After that," said Rodriguez.

"No," said Brenner.

"They did not speak to you of it?"

"No," said Brenner.

"A thousand years ago," said Rodriguez, "in the beginning of his generation, some of the offspring were less than Pons. They would fall to all fours."

Brenner turned to regard Rodriguez.

"In the generation before that, one such incident had occurred. But in the last generation, several."

Brenner looked out, over the forest.

"These offspring were destroyed, of course."

"I do not understand," said Brenner.

"They were monkeys, literally," said Rodriguez.

Brenner shuddered.

"Do you recall," asked Rodriguez, "how we thought the Pons were at the beginning?"

"Of course," said Brenner.

"They are not the beginning," said Rodriguez. "They are the end."

"They are totemistic," said Brenner.

"Yes," said Rodriguez.

"Then this makes no sense," said Brenner.

"There is a darker, more terrible sense than you understand here," said Rodriguez.

"Continue," said Brenner.

"There is an ancient theory of totemism," said Rodriguez. "I have spoken to you of it, often. It is not a pretty theory, and it is not politically acceptable. Most do not know of it, because of the effectiveness of its suppression. As you know, nothing is permitted to be truth other than that which serves the purposes of those in power."

"Continue," said Brenner.

"We do know, of course, the pervasiveness, and ancientness, of totemism, recorded on a thousand worlds, of how it seems to lie, betrayed in its vestiges, at the base of civilization after civilization, of how it apparently antedates gods and heroes, religions and philosophies, codes and laws."

"Yes," said Brenner.

"We may then suspect," said Rodriguez, "that it is correlated with, and reflects, something very profound in the psychology of various rational, or protorational, species, in particular, those whose propagation involves at least two sexes and a period of parental care."

"Naturally," said Brenner.

"What could this be?" asked Rodriguez.

"I do not know," said Brenner.

"You never knew your mother and your father."

"Of course not," said Brenner.

"I did," said Rodriguez. "I knew both."

"You killed your father," recalled Brenner.

"He abused my mother," said Rodriguez. "That, in any event, was my excuse. It served at the time."

"Your excuse?"

"It was not, really, that he had not abused her," said Rodriguez, "but rather that I hated him, for she belonged to him, and not to me. I wanted the wholeness of her attention and love, with all the uncompromising, merciless greed of a child. He was the intruder, the enemy. That was why, really, I slew him. Do you think this was so terrible?"

"You were a child," said Brenner. "You did not know any better."

"I had been insufficiently socialized," said Rodriguez. "But, other than that, do you think that I was so much different from others?"

"Perhaps not," said Brenner. "I do not know."

"I do not think so," said Rodriguez. "They would tell you that I am strange, that I am rare, and that anyone who even suspects he might be like me is terrible, and must conceal this at all costs, and pretend to be pure and innocent, but that is not really true. That little drama, that triangle, of father, mother and son is thematic in our species, and, I think, in several others."

"I do not know," said Brenner.

"This, in its time, was known by many names," said Rodriguez, "the Oedipus Complex, the Oedipal Conflict, the Oedipal Syndrome, and such."

"I have not heard these expressions," said Brenner.

"That is a tribute to the effectiveness of the suppression of the theory," said Rodriguez. "When it was found the theory could not be refuted, it was banned."

"I understand," said Brenner. "Where do such names derive from?"

"Ultimately from ancient literature," said Rodriguez, "from the story of a king, Oedipus, who, unbeknownst to himself, slew his father and, later, also unbeknownst to himself, mated with his mother. Rather than face what he had done he gouged out his own eyes."

"What did the mother do?" asked Brenner.

"She hung herself," said Rodriguez.

"But neither were to blame."

"Of course not," said Rodriguez. "That is the point. These things, the resentment of the father, the desire for the mother, are natural, like breathing, like the circulation of the blood. Guilt is unwarranted. Guilt is absurd. But guilt occurs, particularly when these things are concealed, hidden. Particularly when it is pretended they do not exist. It is little wonder that individuals, lied to, made to feel isolated, and alone, made to feel degraded and debased, fear to recognize these things in themselves. These insights, these recognitions, on one level or another, often not clearly recognized, terrifying the individual, frightening him, exert their influence. They erupt, dreadfully, denied in a thousand ways, in a thousand neuroses and compulsions."

"Would it not be simpler to accept such things, if they are true, and simply move on and forget them?"

"Yes," said Rodriguez, "but that, you see, the acceptance, is what is forbidden! That would be to admit that we are as we are, not otherwise! It would be to admit that resentment, jealousy, possessiveness, hatred, lust, such things, are not strangers to us, but fundamental, congenital dispositions. That would be to admit that we are animals, and of a certain sort!"

"Surely such insights are to be avoided at all costs," said Brenner.

"The cost of their avoidance is often sanity," said Rodriguez.

"What have these things to do with totemism?" asked Brenner.

"What are the major tenets of totemism?" asked Rodriguez.

"Such things as the sparing of the totem animal, its being regarded as the primal father, its veneration, and such, and exogamy, of course, the refusal to engage in sexual relations with members of the opposite sex who share the same totem."

"Do you not see the interesting parallelism?" asked Rodriguez.

"I am not sure," said Brenner.

"It gives us, at the least," said Rodriguez, "a surrogate of the Oedipal Conflict, symbolically transformed."

"I do not understand that," said Brenner.

"Consider the ambivalent feelings toward the father, that one loves him and respects him, that he is protector and provider, that one needs him, and is dependent upon him, and admires him, and identifies with him, but that, too, one fears him and hates him, and resents him and is jealous of him, and envies his authority, his strength, and power, and the painful, internal inconsistencies, and the confusions and guilts, which these ambivalent feelings generate. One denies such feelings, one refuses to acknowledge them. One then, in reaction, naturally enough, venerates the father and, of course, renounces all explicit rights to the mother."

"There are some similarities," said Brenner.

"Now," said Rodriguez, excitedly, "let us suppose that there is a primitive family group."

"One such group?" asked Brenner.

"Or ten thousand such groups, on a thousand worlds," said Rodriguez. "This little drama I am going to suggest may have been enacted innumerable times in numerous places."

"But the species are similar?"

"Of course, rational, or, more likely, protorational, at least two sexes, offspring requiring parental care."

"Go on," said Brenner.

"The nature of this primitive group is not clear," said Rodriguez. "It could be an isolated group, with a single dominant male, with his females, and certain subordinate males, brothers, as in some primate species, or it might be, in effect, a group of such groups, as in other species, the dominant males of which, collectively, would constitute a power structure of the larger group, or tribe. Considering the need for unified authority commonly felt in most rational primate species, their tendencies, as they emerge from the cycles of a simpler nature, to found offices such as that of chieftain, king, and emperor, I think we may presume the likelihood of a genetic predisposition for submission to the authority of a single dominant male, one, to be sure, now open, given the developing complexities of life and culture, to consultation, and, indeed, one who may eventually find his role usurped by his most mythical surrogate, the state."

"Very well," said Brenner.

"Consider now the young males," said Rodriguez, "the brothers. In some groups, and perhaps in the primitive group, particularly if it is a single-dominant-male group, they would, possibly, when of age, as in many types of species, be driven from the group. This is not necessary, of course, but it is useful to suppose. It would give them a common cause, and an opportunity to share their resentments and pool their resources, and such, outside the purview of the dominant male. Some of these young males may, of course, in time, be successful in forming their own family groups. They might acquire stray females, or, more likely, surprise them, and lead them away, in effect, capturing them, stealing them. They would do this, of course, at risk."

"What has this to do with totemism?" asked Brenner.

"Let us suppose that the young males, living apart from the group, hate and envy the father, who has driven them away, and desire the females. They might then, and this does not require language, for it might be done with mimicry, with leaping about, seizing branches, and such, or it might even occur as a spontaneous movement of the group, rather like mob action upon occasion, attack and kill the father. Perhaps he is old. Perhaps he is weak. In any event, he succumbs to their collective might. Who now will be the father?"

"The father is dead," said Brenner.

"Precisely," said Rodriguez. "Each wanted to be as the father, to be the father, but now they are all equal, or rather so. None is strong enough to be the father. None are permitted to be the father. The authority is gone. What will become of the group? What will replace the father? They look about. They see only one another. Are they brothers now, or are they not, rather, all rivals, all enemies? Suddenly, in victory, are they not all sundered from one another? How is the victory to be exploited? Authority is abolished. Chaos reigns. There is no one, even, to allot the females. Shall they kill one another for them? Suddenly they feel their loss, their misery, their vulnerability, their danger, their isolation, their separation, their aloneness, their guilt. They must now, in effect, in words or not, form what one might speak of, and not entirely metaphorically, as the social compact. They must understand, with or without words, how they are to live. What can replace the father? No one of them. The father is dead. What must now govern them is something different, not the fist of the father, but the authority, the weapon, of the agreement, of the compact. Here we see the beginning of ethics, of law, perhaps of civilization."

Brenner shuddered.

"Yes," said Rodriguez. "It is thus that history, linearity, novelty, release from the cycles of nature, may have begun, with an act of murder. Culture itself may have its roots in an ancient crime. It is plausible that there is blood on the first step to civilization."

"It need not have been so," said Brenner. "Let us suppose, for the sake of discussion, that we grant three controversial points, all denied by the official theories. Let us suppose, first, that the organism is not hollow, so to speak, but that it has a complex, profound genetic heritage, involving numerous behavioral dispositions, as is the case with other species, that it has, so to speak, a nature. Two, let us suppose, granting this to your heretical theory, as opposed to the official theories, that this nature, in its complexity and profundity, the result of thousands of generations of selections, may not be totally irrelevant to the culture, institutions, and such, developed by the organism in question. Thirdly, let us grant that there might possibly be something to your theory of totemism, namely, that it might have some connection with the Oedipal syndrome. Even granting all this, it would still not be necessary that civilization began, so to speak, with a crime, with murder. The father need not have been killed. Totemism could then be seen as a symbolic rejection of the Oedipal impulses.

Sensing the Oedipal ambivalence toward the father might have been sufficient to generate totemism."

"As in the case of the neurotic, substituting a symbolic action for a suppressed impulse?"

"Possibly," said Brenner.

"Do you think this could have been done with the father's knowledge?"

"That would seem unlikely," said Brenner. "It would seem possible, however, that something like that might have occurred after the death of the father, perhaps as a way of dealing with ambivalent feelings."

"There are at least two reasons for doubting that," said Rodriguez. "First, you may not understand the childlike mind, and the primitive mind, as you are trained in reflection, and rationality. For you there is a clear and immeasurable chasm between impulse and act, between thought and deed. In the childlike mind, in the primitive mind, and, more importantly, in the animal, or animal-like, mind, which is presumably what we are dealing with here, it is unlikely that there is any such chasm. The relationship between seeing and touching, wanting and taking, hating and striking, if one can do it with impunity, is very close and intimate. It seems to me much more likely that the stone, or the club, or the teeth, were actually stained with the blood of the father."

"But you do not know that."

"No," said Rodriguez. "I was not there."

"What is the second reason?" asked Brenner.

"The traditions of the totemistic peoples," said Rodriguez, "and the nature of the totem feasts."

Brenner shuddered.

"In the totem feast," said Rodriguez, "the father, under the form of the animal, is literally killed. There is rejoicing, a relaxing of the bars of custom and taboo, chaos, and license, and then, soon, given the ambivalence of feeling, for the father is loved, as well as feared and hated, and the sense of loss, the frightened comprehension of the collapse of authority, the trepidation before the looming debacle of anarchy, the misery, the guilt, and such, you have the dismay, the terror, the misery, the sorrow, the grief, the mourning, and, of course, soon thereafter, the restoration of the ways of the group, the veneration of the new father, the renunciation of the females, and such."

"The feast, then, you think, is a commemoration, and reenactment, of the original totem feast, that following the crime, the murder of the father?" said Brenner.

"That seems to me likely," said Rodriguez.

"But why the substitution of a totem animal?" asked Brenner.

"There could be many reasons," said Rodriguez. "I shall suggest three, which are rather obvious. First, the father is dead. There is no new father. Thus, something else must be used. And surely, as none of the brothers can take the father's place, and, indeed, most would not wish to share that fate, an animal, or some other object is chosen. It stands in place of the father. Secondly, over time, the use of the animal tends to conceal what was actually done. Most totemistic peoples, and perhaps most of the Pons, may have lost touch with the origins of these things. They accept the totem animal as the father, and such, and kill it, and celebrate the totem feast, and so on, without really understanding it, or its possible connection with things in their remote past. How few rituals are truly understood. Thirdly, the substitution of an animal, and often a large, frightening animal, for the father, is a common symbolic substitution, frequently found in children. The child develops a fear of a certain animal, and can flee it, be comforted in its terrors, and such, with impunity, it not being understood, normally, by either the child or its parents, that the real source of fear is the father. The hostility toward the father, the fear of father, and, indeed, the child's admiration of the power of the father, and its envy of his authority, and such, is neatly, safely, displaced onto the animal. What here takes place often enough in children, we might speculate also took place, long ago, in primitive, or even animal, or animal-like, minds. There are surely affinities here, between the childlike mind, naive in its understanding of the world, and such, and the primitive mind, similarly naive, let alone the animal, or animal-like, mind."

"There seems a frightening plausibility to these things," said Brenner.

"Symbolic transformations, and substitutions, are quite common," said Rodriguez.

"It is strange that a theory so simple, so clear, so precise, so consistent with all we know, which reconciles so much data, so rich in explanatory power, so superior to its competitors, is false," said Brenner.

Rodriguez laughed.

"The evidence of the graves, of course," said Brenner. "They were empty."

"Of course," smiled Rodriguez.

"In the oldest grave, if in no others, you should have found the bones of a Pon, of the first father," said Brenner. "But they were not there."

"True," smiled Rodriguez.

"You do not seem too dismayed at this disproof of your theory," remarked Brenner.

"It is getting late, is it not?" asked Rodriguez.

"Yes," said Brenner.

"I must be going," said Rodriguez.

Rodriguez then stood up, and reached out, and fastened his hands in Brenner's fur and, clinging there, was carried down the trail, to the platform, and thence to the side of the string.

"As you are standing, facing me," said Brenner, "the string is to your left."

Rodriguez touched the string. "Yes," he said. "It is here."

"Are they coming to fetch you?" asked Brenner.

"I think so," said Rodriguez.

"Wait for them," said Brenner.

"I think I will go ahead," said Rodriguez.

"Do you not want me to come with you?"

"No," said Rodriguez.

"Will you not come again, to see me soon?" asked Brenner.

"Perhaps," said Rodriguez.

"You said that the Pons were in crisis, before."

"Yes."

"They seem a strange form of life," said Brenner.

"You do not know who they are, do you?" asked Rodriguez.

"No," said Brenner.

"Were you not curious that they could be crossfertile with you?"

"The chances of that were exceedingly slim," said Brenner.

"Not really," said Rodriguez.

"I do not understand," said Brenner.

"It is unusual, is it not," asked Rodriguez, "that their speech is intelligible to us?"

"Not necessarily," said Brenner, hesitantly. "Most of those at Company Station speak our language, and the Pons could have adopted it from them."

"In this remoteness, this wilderness, so isolated, with no sign of an underlying native tongue?"

"What are you suggesting?" said Brenner.

"Does there not seem something vaguely, remotely familiar, to you about the Pons?"

"I had such feelings once," admitted Brenner.

"Why, do you think?"

"Perhaps from certain physiognomical similarities to our species, or emotional affinities with it, or such," said Brenner. "It is hard to say."

"Do they not remind you of certain illustrations, of certain artist's conceptions, of certain artist's reconstructions," asked Rodriguez, "based on fossilized remnants, bits of a jaw, a few teeth, a bone, the shards of skull, such things?"

"Of course," said Brenner. "Pons seem much like the sorts of creatures from which we ourselves, as a species, once arose. That is one of the things that makes them so interesting."

"You suspect then that they may have great promise, that there is an evolutionary ascendancy before them?"

"Hopefully so," said Brenner.

"Perhaps it is behind them," said Rodriguez.

"I do not understand," said Brenner.

Rodriguez was silent.

"You are suggesting that the Pons are the result of devolution?" asked Brenner, suddenly.

"Yes," said Rodriguez.

"But we are supposed to learn from them. In many ways the Pons, in their innocence, gentleness, and inoffensiveness, are supposed to give us lessons. They are supposed to prove that species such as ours are naturally good, "good" as understood by, and defined by, current political doctrine. Indeed, they are supposed to provide us with a beacon, too, for the future. They are supposed to epitomize the values proclaimed by our society as characterizing the veritable pinnacle of evolution."

"They represent the decline of a race," said Rodriguez. "They are tragic remnants of a once rational species. There is not one morality, but many, and they are incommensurable. One is a morality of nature, an aristocratic morality, a morality of lions, of beasts, and gods, a morality of warriors, of hunters, of pioneers and seekers, a morality of pride, power, honor, loyalty, responsibility, discipline, and courage, and striving, a morality that summons to adventure, and calls for heroes. Another morality is that of insects and mice, and flowers, a morality for a homogenized species, effete and weary, introverted, subjective, examining its conscience incessantly, of false humility, of sham pity, of emotional wallowing, of ostensible self-effacement and secret self-congratulation, of pretension, a morality of species self-betrayal and self-treason. It is the morality of weariness, and preparation for death. In the ascendancy of a species the first morality is dominant, that of the conqueror and lover, the explorer, the hunter, and warrior. Later, in the glorification of the puny, in the wreathing of the mouse in the laurel of the victor, in the substitution of guilt for projects, in the teaching that it is good to be little, and wrong to be grand, in the lie that all are the same, in the denial of, or concealment of, rank, distance, and hierarchy, you have the decline, the descent, of the species. It is without projects, unless they be those of negation and leveling. It begins to live from day to day. The horizons no longer beckon. The songs of the mountains fall on deaf ears. There begins, then, the retreat to the cycles of nature. And it ends by falling again to all fours."

"This is not the home world!" said Brenner.

"You do not know that," said Rodriguez. "This may be the home world."

"No!" said Brenner.

"A species may have a life span, like an individual, like a culture," said Rodriguez.

"No!" said Brenner.

"Millions of species are extinct," said Rodriguez.

"Maladaptation," said Brenner.

"In some cases," said Rodriguez, "apparently a loss of adaptability, the simple lack of ability in the gene pool to cope with change, in others, perhaps, a genetic momentum which could not be corrected, in others, it would seem, afflicted with certain social or political momentums, suicide."

"You are surely not suggesting that the Pons are our own species," said Brenner.

"Chromosomal and molecular analyses suggest it," said Rodriguez.

"Then they are not the "beginning,"" said Brenner.

"No," said Rodriguez. "Rather they would seem to be the end."

"We need not degenerate into such things," said Brenner.

"I would think not," said Rodriguez. "It seems there are choices involved. Perhaps one can learn from the Pons."

"If we could have returned to the home world," said Brenner, "we would have had to extol the Pons and hold them up as exemplars."

"At least we have been spared that hypocrisy," said Rodriguez.

"You said the Pons were in crisis," said Brenner.

"Some of them," said Rodriguez, "the more reflective ones, the ones that can think, like Sesostris, the git keeper. They realize that something must be done, or that, in all likelihood, they will vanish. They will die, or subside, unregretted, unmissed, into the cycles of nature."

"What is to be done?" asked Brenner.

"The selection of your genes," said Rodriguez, "which are regarded as dangerous, has already been done."

"They must be desperate, indeed," said Brenner, ironically.

"Do not be angry," said Rodriguez. "In their way they care for you. You were apparently the first individual in thousands of years to treat them as something other than monkeys to be ridiculed and swindled, or specimens to be examined. You liked them, somehow, and this they sensed. What has been done to you they did, I am sure, with a certain regret."

"I am touched," said Brenner, bitterly.

"I am no longer angry with them," said Rodriguez.

"After what they have done to you?" asked Brenner.

"No," said Rodriguez. "I have found out what I came here to find out."

"I do not understand," said Brenner.

"Incidentally," said Rodriguez, "I have heard them speak of a feast of gathering eggs. Does that make any sense to you?"

"No," said Brenner.

"Nor to me," said Rodriguez.

"Perhaps they are going to raise domestic fowl," said Brenner.

"That would seem rather unlike Pons, would it not?" asked Rodriguez.

"Yes," said Brenner. It did not seem in accord with the ways of the Pons. Meat, for example, and eggs, and such things, were not common constituents in their diet. To be sure, they did not object to being protected by creatures which might require flesh, and such things. But such inconsistencies were not unprecedented. The sweetness, the softness, the gentleness, the innocence, the loveliness of the Pons, and their way of life, was possible only because of the vigilance, the readiness to act, the severity, the ferocity of creatures quite other than themselves. Some gardens cannot grow unless sheltered within rings of iron. Some worlds cannot exist unless nestled within the territory of carnivores. To be sure, the Pons might change their ways.

"I think that in some subtle way," said Rodriguez, "the Pons have become different over the past months."

"How is that?" asked Brenner.

"The other father," said Rodriguez, "saved your life in the forest."

"I killed him," said Brenner.

"He must have understood what you were doing here," said Rodriguez.

"Yes," said Brenner.

"And yet he protected you, and saved your life. That said something to the Pons of love."

"He came to the temple," said Brenner.

"To die," said Rodriguez.

"He died well," said Brenner. He recalled the sudden, startling, arresting regalness of the beast, drawn up, proudly, awaiting the blast from the rifle.

"He was the father," said Rodriguez.

"Yes," said Brenner, "he was the father."

"And, too, the Pons, who have been concerned with little, really, but survival, a mere clinging to the thread of life, pretending it is important in itself, and not because of what may be done with it, were moved when you returned me to the village. In this, you, too, you see, taught them something of love, more than survival, more even than the pursuit of truth."

"I did not want you to die," said Brenner.

"Put down your head," said Rodriguez, putting out his hands.

Brenner put down his great, broad, shaggy head and Rodriguez, with great tenderness, embraced it, and placed his own head against it. Then Rodriguez drew back. "I am going now," he said.

"Will you not wait for the others?"

"No," said Rodriguez.

"I will accompany you," said Brenner.

"No," said Rodriguez.

"Are you sorrowful?" asked Brenner. Rodriguez did not seem as he usually did.

"No," said Rodriguez.

"You do not regret what has occurred?"

"Certainly not," said Rodriguez. "I have found out what I came here to learn."

"The fate of the theory?"

"Yes," said Rodriguez.

"Are you sorry that it was false?" asked Brenner.

"'False'?" asked Rodriguez.

"Of course," said Brenner. "The graves were empty."

"So?" said Rodriguez.

"If the theory was true, the body of the father, the first father, a Pon, would have been found in the oldest grave."

"That the grave was empty," said Rodriguez, "does not refute the theory. It is rather the strongest possible evidence of the truth of the theory. Indeed, it is precisely what the theory in its fullest and most exact form, in its most perfect form, would call for, a form in which I had not even anticipated it might be corroborated."

"I do not understand," said Brenner, in consternation.

"Why would the body not be in the grave?" asked Rodriguez.

"I do not know," said Brenner.

"It was eaten," said Rodriguez.

Brenner shuddered.

"You are dealing here with something extremely childlike, extremely primitive, something with a very powerful appeal on a very deep emotional level. The rationale here is, or is similar to, that of cannibalism or ritualistic omophagia, as in the mystical eating of a god, usually under the form of a beast, or such, the devouring of the divine, so to speak, to take into oneself the courage, the power, the mana, the traits, the spirit of the other, to make its substance yours, to add to yourself by its consumption. Obviously every day one gains strength by eating, by making the substance of others yours. It is only natural then for the primitive or childlike mind, or even for a more sophisticated mind functioning in this respect, perhaps unconsciously, on a childlike or primitive level, to conceive of the eating of the god, or of the enemy, or the father, as a way of identifying with them, of making their substance theirs, of becoming them, or like them."

"But why, then, the graves?" asked Brenner.

"They presumably serve various purposes," said Rodriguez. "For the sophisticated, assuaging guilt, and such, they may serve as atonements to, and as memorials to, the fathers. For the less sophisticated, they may provide loci for the spirits of the fathers, places where they may theoretically be contacted, places which they may occasionally visit, or haunt. Surely one would not wish their vengeful spirits to plague the village. And, of course, for outsiders, they serve to conceal the evidence of the crime. Later, the graves, their preparation and such, may have even become no more than a part of a tradition, the origins of which, and the meanings of which, were lost in antiquity."

"In the totem feast," said Brenner, shuddering, recalling the Pons clambering about on the carcass of the father, crouching upon it, crawling within it, cutting loose pieces of it to eat, "the children fed upon the substance of the father."

"And thus it was, undoubtedly," said Rodriguez, "even in the beginning."

"But this fact," said Brenner, "the emptiness of the graves, does not mean that the theory must be true."

"No," said Rodriguez. "It does not. In the end, of course, we do not know. In the end we are left, as always, with the ambiguities, the opacities, the mysteries."

"But you do not regret having come here?"

"No," said Rodriguez.

"It seems the final victory belongs to the Pons," said Brenner.

"Between myself and the Pons there are no final victories," said Rodriguez.

"You are content?"

"Yes, I am content."

It seemed Rodriguez would lift his hand again, once more to touch the shaggy fur of the beast, but then he lowered it.

"Good-bye," he said.

"Come again, to see me soon," said Brenner. "For I am lonely."

"I love you," said the small figure.

"I love you," said Brenner.

"Goodbye," said Rodriguez.

"Goodbye," said Brenner.

The small figure turned away.

"Hold to the string," said Brenner.

"Of course," said Rodriguez.

CHAPTER 38

Perhaps it was a whisper of scent, carried over the trees. Perhaps it was a sound, so far off that one could not be sure it was heard. Perhaps it was a sudden sense, or fear, or understanding, or something even subtler than these, as one commonly thinks of such matters, but, suddenly, the beast stood up, frightened, on the height of the cliff.

Something within it had seemed to shriek with misery, with a refusal to believe, with a rejection of an insistence. It was an inward shriek, or scream. It was as though of one forlorn, and abandoned. It was like the scream of a terrified child in the darkness, a bereaved child, in an empty house. It was a scream of terrible, profound, chilling loneliness. The beast stood, risen up, the wind cold in its fur, on the height of the cliff, lonely there, against the sky.

Then, in an instant, it had, in one or two movements, leaping, endangering even a body such as its own, as though insane, descended the cliff, left the platform behind, and bounded along the string, toward the village. In a moment or two it encountered three Pons making their way toward the platform. These small things cried out in fear, seeing it coming, and with such swiftness. It bounded past them, even before they had, in their terror, been able to react, even before they could flee into the brush or hide amongst the trees, so quickly had it come upon them. They turned, then, to watch it pass.

Scarcely a hundred yards from where the beast had encountered the Pons, coming to the platform, and cliffs, it stopped. There the trail of the small, eyeless one departed from the string. The string was not broken. He had not been pulled away from it, clinging to it. The string had not failed him. His trail left the string and set out, perpendicular to the string, leaving it behind. He had, it seemed, at this point, left the string of his own will. He had made his way into the darkness of the forest, enclosed in his own darkness. The footsteps, the beast noted, did not seem hesitant or fearful. It had left the string, it seemed, with a good heart. In the forest, as far as it could, within its limitations, it had not crept, but strode, even marched.

In a short while the beast came upon the first stains of blood, a moist darkness on the floor of the forest, and, a little later, uttered a terrible roar, and a stealthy one, scarcely pausing to discern the origin of that hideous sound, and without the least inclination to defend his dinner, or, indeed, to dispute any matter of significance, sprang away from a small form and disappeared in the brush.

The beast who had driven the other away did not make the prey its own. It did not crouch down to feed upon what it had won in one of the ways of the forest. Rather it stood over the small form, torn to pieces, half eaten, and howled with anguish. It then picked it up gently in its mouth, the head dangling to one side, half gone, and carried it to the village, where it deposited it before the gate. It then turned about and, rapidly, returned to the place where it had found the form. It would have been difficult to say how far the beast followed the trail of the stealthy one, or how soon the stealthy one, to its astonishment, as it had surrendered the prey, detected the renewed presence of the beast. We may conjecture that it fled before the beast for a long time. But one suspects, in spite of the speed, the stamina and cunning of the stealthy one, that there was really no escape for it, that it might have been, had it been required, pursued for days, for months, even for years, that it would have been followed beyond forests, beyond deserts, across grassy plains, and through arctic wastes, that it would have been followed, if necessary, to the very ends of the world, such was the tenacity of its pursuer. But in the morning, shortly before dawn, where two torches, perhaps in mourning, had been set at the gate of the village, the beast returned. In its jaws were the shreds of the stealthy one. Little but skin and threads of sinew held together the remains of it. It had been not only killed, but serrated, and disjoined, and ripped into ribbons of flesh. It had, apparently, long been fiercely shaken, as though in some frenzy of rage, or grief. These remains, such as they were, little more now than hair and hide, some loops of trailing intestine, and such, were left in the clearing, back from the gate. The beast did not put these remains in the same place where it had laid the small form earlier, but, rather, somewhat before that place, rather in the fashion of a token, or offering.

For several nights thereafter the Pons, even in their village, could hear the beast howling on the cliffs, seemingly in anguish.

CHAPTER 39

The summer passed, and then the winter, with its cold, and its snow, came. The forest was white. Gits, and some other creatures of the forest, hibernated. On the ground, covered with snow, lay the husks of fallen lantern fruit. At night, however, even Pons could see dimly, in spite of the moonless sky, simply in virtue of the light of stars, reflecting from the snow. Branches, weighted with ice, laced with crystalline structures, occasionally snapped, and, with a very clear sound, carrying in the cold air, fell to the ground. The floor of the forest was carpeted with white. The tread of fleet ones, dainty, and the tread of others, less delicate, could be detected here and there. During this time the Pons stayed much in their village. The beast, during the winter, roamed much abroad. It was warm in its winter coat, and it enjoyed the cold, and the snow. Without the leaves the forest, the trees like dark, giant posts, was very open to it. The beast, however, it must be admitted, also enjoyed the fall, with the changing of the leaves, and the summer, with the fullness of the forest's majesty. It was only the spring that caused it great pain. This may have been, in part, because it was in a spring, long ago, on a far world, that Rodriguez and Brenner had first set out for Abydos. But it seems more likely that there was another, and simpler, reason for the pain, a reason which was a beast's reason.

In the course of time, given the orbit of the planet, the

angle of its axis and such, ice, drop by drop, fell from the branches, moistening, and then creating tiny rivulets in, the forest floor. Streams flowed faster, filled with melted snow from far away. The heads of gits poked out of their nests. Buds began to form on the trees. Grass began to sprout here and there. Certain birds reappeared in the sky, some in flocks, and others in lines, their presence once again indicating the location of ancient routes. Pons, with pointed sticks, and scarps, emerged from their village to essay the first working of the soil. All in all, it was once again, in accord with the physics of worlds, to which many rhythms of nature were attuned, and the expectations of calendars, spring. As I have suggested this was a difficult time for the beast. It was restless. It seemed irritable. It tended to be unusually aggressive. Pons had the good sense not to approach it in these times.

It was one evening in early spring when the beast, troubled by dark dreams, stirrings and shadows, half understood, from the old home, had awakened roaring. After this, uncomfortable, miserable, it had not wished to return to sleep. It did not wish to be tortured again by such dreams, or the shapes it sensed in them, or the maddening scents they carried, as clear to it in its sleep, as penetrant, as though they were borne in the actual air of the forest. Before this the beast had wandered from his own territory, as it occasionally did, and had been gone for several days. It had only returned this afternoon. It had sought stealthy ones to kill, for the pleasure of it, but had found few. They avoided him now, almost all of them. And he, in spite of his fury, his frustration, if they would not stand against him, had not long pursued them. The beast in it, you see, was now ascendant, and it tended to obey the laws of the beast. A more reflective form of life, a more thoughtful form of life, might have been much more implacable, much more relentless, in such matters.

Troubled, restless, angry, the beast left its lair and climbed, scrambling up, to the height of the cliff, where it might look down on the forests that were its world. In the distance, it could see the light of a fire or two in the village.

It sat for some time on the height of the cliff.

Suddenly, almost unaccountably, the hair on its body erected, its nostrils distended, its ears lifted, it snarled. It looked down, beyond the platform, to the dark trees beyond.

Something, it sensed, was there.

Amongst the trees, amongst his trees, somewhere, not far, was something, something which moved with a stealth, a subtlety, not unlike his own.

The beast snarled, warningly.

"Be warned, intruder," bespoke that sound.

No response came from the forest.

The beast strained all his senses, but it could apprehend nothing. Perhaps it had been mistaken. Perhaps there was nothing there. The wind was blowing from the cliffs. If there was something there, it was approaching from upwind.

The beast then emitted a mighty roar, a roar which rang out as might have a trumpet over the forest, an unmistakable sound, of claimancy, of territoriality, of sovereignty, of readiness to do the works of war.

The beast then listened with care. It would have had excellent hearing, even amongst its own kind. It heard nothing. Could it have been mistaken? Far off, Pons were disturbed by the roar. The fastenings on the gate would be checked. Torches would be lit, and placed at the gate, and, here and there, about the palisade, that frail bulwark. Stealthy ones about, if any lurked near, would presumably now withdraw from the area. Certainly they would not be likely to mistake the menace, and meaning, of that sound. Indeed, had not the beast given them warning? Was it not now, in the common customs of beasts, allowing them to withdraw with furtive grace, as though they might never have been there? But the beast could not detect the sound of movement, of either rushing forward, then stopping, then approaching again, of challenge, or of retreat. There seemed to be nothing, not even the stirring of leaves or the rustle of undergrowth, it being thrust aside.

Once again it roared, that there might be no mistake about matters.

Again there was silence.

Then the beast quickly descended from the cliff, leaped to the surface of the platform, listened there for a moment, and then leaped from the platform and moved toward the trees.

Every sense was alert.

It moved into the trees.

It was elated.

On the cliff it had not been displeased by the silence.

Rather it had been pleased.

Too, it had not interpreted that silence as we might have, that there had been nothing there, or that it was now gone. Rather it understood that silence differently, understanding it to mean that whatever had been there was still there, that it had not withdrawn. It was certain, you see, as you or I, and even a more rational particle of its own nature, might not have been, that there had been something there, and that there was still something there.

The explanation for its elation, as it entered the trees, seeking, hunting, was not difficult to determine. It had to do with various primitive excitements, such as the eagerness to rend and the lust for blood.

In a moment or two it detected, before it, dark amongst the trees, hard even for it to discern, a large, dark, sinuous shape. This thing was much larger than a stealthy one, or, at least, those it had hitherto encountered.

The beast, as one might suppose, was much surprised by this.

The beast did not deign to conceal, or to attempt to conceal, its presence.

It approached with caution, but frontally.

It had roared. It had emitted its challenges. It had made its intent clear, and all the dark, terrible menace of that intent.

The intruder, crouching down, its belly close to the ground, backed away, a step or two.

The beast then circled the intruder, which turned about, belly low, so that they might continue to face one another. The beast now, in the stirring of the wind, soft against its face, took in the scent of the intruder, which was surely, as the beast would have anticipated, the scent of a stealthy one, or akin to such a scent.

Suddenly Brenner thought, Rodriguez was mistaken! He thought this form of life was not indigenous to Abydos. But it is! It must be!

The beast growled, and the intruder responded with a snarl, tail lashing.

Is this to be driven away, wondered the beast. I must kill this, thought Brenner.

You see, something in the beast, on a level more primitive than the conjectures of Brenner, which remained rather rational, was profoundly shaken, both by the lineaments of the newcomer and by its scent. It seemed it had seen such things before, and had experienced that scent, or something like it, before, in its dreams, and, perhaps, in its memories, those from long ago, from the old home.

It was only half the size of the beast, but it was, nonetheless, an extremely large animal. Its markings, as Brenner could discern, were similar to his own.

The beast growled, menacingly, at the newcomer, which responded in kind.

Yes, thought the beast, obedient to the imperatives of interspecific aggression, this is to be driven away.

This is extremely dangerous, thought Brenner. I am confident that I can kill it. I must do so.

What had originally motivated Brenner in his rapid descent from the cliff no longer swayed him. The eagerness to rend, the lust for blood, the appetition for destruction, originally felt, for whatever reason, no longer burned in his heart. It seemed that the beast now thought, merely, this perhaps in accord with the customs of its kind, in dealing with its own kind, this thing is to be driven away. If this thing is to be killed, thought Brenner, it will have to be killed with intent, with fixed purpose.

The beast then approached the newcomer, growling. It put its face down, toward the newcomer. The newcomer, the stranger, the intruder, raised its head, snarling. The beast put its snout against the newcomer, growling. The newcomer remained extremely still. The beast continued its investigations. The newcomer turned about, suddenly, angrily, almost like a striking snake, fangs bared, and the beast, with a cry of rage and pain, leaped back, its shoulder bloody.

The newcomer crouched there, snarling.

The beast sat back and licked its own blood, at its shoulder, regarding the newcomer.

The newcomer now crouched very low.

The beast then, without warning, sprang suddenly forward and with a blow of its great paw smote the head of the newcomer forcibly to the side, and, following this, with its fangs, twice lacerated its flanks, taking two bloods for one.

The newcomer whimpered.

The beast, angry, moved to one side, that the newcomer might now flee into the trees.

But the newcomer did not move. It remained where it was, flanks bleeding, belly low.

The beast growled, a threatening, informative, cruel, lordly sound. This was answered by a sound from the throat of the newcomer. Its sound, however, was more in the nature of a whine, or whimper. In it might have been read a note of fear, of penitence.

The beast remained where it was for a time, leaving an avenue of escape open for the newcomer, of which it declined to make use.

I shall have to kill it, thought Brenner.

The beast continued to regard the newcomer.

The newcomer whimpered again.

Then the beast, in the fashion of the sovereign it was, closed off the retreat of the newcomer. It could now withdraw only to the cliffs, where, trapped, it might be dealt with as the beast pleased.

The newcomer presumably was not familiar with this territory, and would not realize the implications of what the beast had now done.

In regarding the newcomer, you see, the beast, had

begun to be swayed by imperatives which, though scarcely
understood, were quite as forcible in their impact as those of
interspecific aggression.

It lunged forward a step, violently, snarling, and the
female leaped up, turning about, and fled.

In a moment, of course, she realized the cliffs were before
her and the beast behind her.

She stopped suddenly, and turned about, frightened,
frenziedly, two or three times, having nowhere to go, and
then crouched down, whimpering.

The beast then took her by the back of the neck and
dragged her bodily to the surface of the platform. There,
lying on her side, at his feet, she looked up at him in terror.
She lifted one paw, pleadingly, the claws retracted. She
whimpered.

No, no, thought Brenner, I must not do this! What could
come of this could mean the doom of the Pons! What could
come of this but the terror of beasts uncomplicated with
thought, innocent in their appetites and might, not fathers
but hunters and killers, carnivores, predators, who in
merciless innocence would claim the forests for themselves!

The female whimpered.

Yes, thought the beast, I remember! And it smelled then,
suddenly, the readiness of the female, and it enflamed it like
storms and wine. Here was the meaning of the dreams and
the memories!

Here was the female!

Here was what something in it had been waiting for,
what it had longed for, yearningly, on the cliffs, during the
long nights.

Now it was here, at his feet. Its petty attempt at resistance,
frightening even her, who must have instinctually recognized
its possible consequences, had been, at the pleasure of the
beast, he having permitted her to consider the matter for a
time, and anticipate his response, utterly crushed. Her flight,
ritualistic or not, had been abruptly terminated, stopped
short, before bleak, towering, seemingly impassable, walls
of stone. Now she lay before him, on her side, dragged

bodily to where he wished her. She lay before him, helpless and submissive. His power over her was complete, effective, uncompromising and ruthless. She squirmed a little. She made a tiny, mewing sound. The beast looked down upon her. She was clearly in estrus. The beast sensed not only the apprehension in her, but the need in her, the readiness in her, her heat. The scents, and the sight of her, were heady. The flanks! The lines of her body! The smells of her! These things were maddening to the beast. Why then had she not assumed the position, wondered the beast. It then, with its prehensile paws, positioned the female. She seemed to cry out, startled, held, helpless. Is she so young, asked the beast. No, it told itself. Clearly not. Can it be that a female this trim, this beautiful, this exciting, does not understand the meaning of this? Can a female this lithe, this attractive, not have been so had many times before? Surely many such as I have used her previously for such purposes, to sate our lusts? How, then, is it that she is reluctant, or perplexed? Are her instincts confused?

As she seemed distraught he exposed his claws somewhat, entering them a bit into her body, not to hurt her but to hold her the more securely, and that she would understand herself the more securely held. His grip, anchored now, was quite tight. She made a pathetic little sound, as though pleading for mercy. She was absolutely helpless.

She felt then the touch of him and, suddenly, terrified, she tried to free herself.

This, of course, her struggles, was unavailing. It only resulted in the tightening of his grip upon her. She whimpered in pain.

The beast found her behavior puzzling.

She was then very still.

She had learned that she could not escape, even if she wished to do so.

She did not wish to deepen the hold of the claws in her.

She felt then again the gentle, exploratory, and prodding touch of him.

This is a strange female, thought the beast.

Then the female uttered a small, soft, surprised noise. Now she is beginning to understand, thought the beast.

She squirmed a tiny bit.

There is no escape for her, thought the beast.

But the female uttered a soft noise, one it seemed at once of curiosity, of surrender, of petition.

She is an unusual and interesting female, thought the beast.

The female then, feeling his touch, began to whine beggingly.

Yes, it is a normal female, thought the beast.

I must not do this, thought Brenner, wildly, agonizingly. Am I naught but a beast? Is this what I have become! How is it that I, of my race and kind, should find beauty in this form? How is it that I can find this attractive, that I can respond to it? What have I become? What am I? How horrifying that I should find this thing so beautiful, so wanted, so perfect! How is it that I should find this lithe, alien form, this glossy pelt, these movements, these sounds, these odors, so exciting? Would it not be better to be forever condemned to loneliness? And what but pain and horror might come of this? Is this not death to Pons? Should I not, in my lonely vigilance, in the discharge of my dark stewardship, drive this thing away, or, failing that, destroy it?

It seems a quite satisfactory female, thought the beast. It will give me much pleasure.

The female, held, intensified her supplicatory whines.

Brenner found himself excited, half maddened, even frenzied, by these sounds, and by the sight and the scent of her. He could not believe the feel of her body. He was delirious with joy at her proximity.

I must drive her away, thought Brenner.

She is quite satisfactory, thought the beast. I will never let her escape.

I must drive her away, thought Brenner.

I shall claim her, thought the beast.

I must not do this, thought Brenner.

Then the beast uttered a mighty roar, of joy, of triumph,

of exultancy, of jubilation, of satisfaction, and the pretty one, so helplessly held, uttered a sound of great surprise, and perplexity, and then, in a moment, again and again, yowled in ecstasy.

Later the female licked at the blood on the beast's shoulder, cleaning it for him, and he, in turn, licked her flanks, where he had, in the forest, punished her for her insolence, or resistance. On her hide, too, at the flanks, there were the bloody marks of his claws. These marks, too, he attended to, with his large, rough tongue.

He later made use of her again on the platform, and then, again, after having driven her up the trail, nipping at her, on the height of the cliffs. He then, toward morning, drove her down to the valley, and thence herded her to his den. There, within those walls, and near the outer gate, that closest to the valley, he again, from time to time, pleased himself with her beauty.

In the morning, before they rested, she lay at his feet and looked up at him, lovingly. She lifted her head and licked at his leg.

You are mine, pretty one, thought the beast.

You are mine, pretty one, thought Brenner.

They then rested, curled about one another.

CHAPTER 40

From that point on, which we might signify as that of the beast's acquisition of a mate, life was much better for Brenner. The misery and the frustration were now muchly dissipated. At an end now were numerous pains of deprivation, the torture of powerful needs left unsatisfied. There was now little point to howling on the cliffs, except, perhaps upon occasion, as Brenner was a rational being, to vent ancient griefs, to deplore the cruelties of fate, to acknowledge the mysteries, to inquire information of the stars, knowing they would give none, and to remember a friend. But perhaps even more important than the mere assuagements of certain physical requirements was his simple joy in the company of the female, his gratitude that she should exist, that there should be something such as she, that she was about, that she was near. Now when he roamed the forests, she was with him. Together they trod upon the leaves, padding softly beneath the branches. They drank at the same streams. They hunted together. They fed together, their heads side by side.

Brenner, in so far as he could, with snarls, and warnings, and by example, for he was clearly afraid of her only too natural instincts, and the ways in which she, untutored, might define her prey range, made clear to her the eccentricities of his office. Pons, the small, strange creatures who walked upright, who lived within their puzzling nest of sticks, were not to be attacked, killed, or eaten. Moreover, they were to be literally protected.

Those who might prey upon them, those who might attack them, or kill them and eat them, were to be driven off, or killed. Moreover, the track of the string, which he showed her, and the region of the platform, and the flat places where the strange grasses grew, where the small creatures often came with their tools, and the clearing, and the village, were to be guarded with particular care. These things, as far as Brenner could tell, the female accepted, or, at least, did not question. To be sure, they must have made little sense to her. In the first weeks he did follow her upon occasion, usually in the morning, when she had arisen earlier and gone out to drink. On one of these occasions she had encountered a Pon near the string, and Brenner had tensed himself to interfere, if he had time. But the Pon had fled and she had merely looked after it. She could have brought it down easily, but had not done so. Brenner then, muchly relieved, had returned to the lair. You do not have to kill her, he had thought to himself. But he wondered if he could have brought himself to do so. But what can be the nature of such reservations, he asked himself. She is only an animal, a beast. If she interferes with the discharge of the fathership, if she threatens the pact, she must die. But he wondered if he could have injured her, regardless of what she might do. But I must be strong, thought Brenner. The children come first, and the fathership. He was terrified at the thought of returning to the loneliness, like an arctic wasteland, he had known before. He was horrified at the thought of injuring what he had come to love so much. But, he said to himself, remember that she is an animal, a beast, only that. If she threatens the pact, she must die. Do not make me choose between you and the fathership, he begged her silently, in his mind. But it did not seem likely that that decision would need be made. She had not pursued the Pon. She respects my will in this matter, he speculated. How problematical, and puzzling, and even unintelligible, my wishes in this matter must seem to her, he thought. He did not expect her, of course, to share the stewardship, the guardianship, which might seem even more absurd, or meaningless, to her. All he really asked of her was that she refrain from killing and eating Pon. And it seemed that she would refrain from such things, at least at this time. He did not know, of course, really, whether this was because of him, the result, say, of deference to his wishes, or of some natural disinclination, or indifference.

There were things that puzzled him about her, such as her occasional restlessness in the night, her movings about, the stirring of her limbs, doubtless in dreaming, roars, snarls, unusual noises, such things.

He learned from her to lift fish from streams, with a scoop of a paw. This was useful. It had not been in his beast memories.

To be sure, he did not care much for water.

It interested him that Rodriguez had been mistaken about such forms of life, regarding them as not indigenous to Abydos. This did not seem the sort of mistake which Rodriguez would have made.

Yet here she was.

He was pleased that she was here.

There was, of course, a lingering loneliness in Brenner, a longing for someone, or something, which might understand him, with whom he could truly communicate. This is not to say that there was not a profound companionship between the lovely female beast and himself. This was an unspoken thing, a primitive thing, deeper and, in its way, doubtless more profound than words. There were feelings here, and interdependencies, as ancient as the beauty of pair bonding itself, a bonding, a loving and needing, and wanting and caring, more permanent than, and exceeding, the casual couplings of heedless beasts. In its way it was the fundamental reality, primeval, and basic, compared to which linguisticisms must seem almost superficial accretions, save in so far as they might point to the deeper realities, and feelings, beyond them. How trivial, and meaningless, in themselves, are the words, 'I love you'. And yet of what

moment they are when they call attention to that which is
beyond words, older than words and deeper than words,
which no words, in any language, can express.

One evening Brenner was lying on the height of the
cliff, as was his wont. In the distance was the village of the
Pons. Near him, also recumbent, was the sleek female. On
this evening, for no reason he clearly understood, he felt
the isolation of his being, how alone, in a way, he was. She
was there, of course, but she was only an animal. Brenner
looked to the village. How he longed to speak to her of
what had occurred there, how he longed to tell someone,
how he wanted to express so many things she could not
comprehend. He wanted to share his grief, his history, the
story of his office. He wanted someone to understand what
he had been, and what he now was. He wanted someone
to understand that he was not a mere beast. He wanted
someone to whom he might tell the secrets he knew. He
looked over to the female. Her jaws opened, revealing the
white fangs, the long, rough tongue, and she yawned, and
blinked, sleepily. Brenner turned away, angrily. I am alone,
thought Brenner. I am alone! And he was angry, for a
moment, selfishly, irrationally, with Rodriguez, for having
left him. He might have continued to bear the burdens of
that wretched body, the pain of it, its blindness, to bear
me company, thought Brenner, angrily. Then he put such
thoughts from him. How unworthy they were! A wave of
hatred swept over him for the female, in her simplicity, that
she was what she was, that she could never understand. She
could never comprehend his pain, his suffering, his sorrow.
She could never understand the knowledge that was his
burden. To one such as she, a simple beast, a mere animal,
with no thought beyond the day, he could never make clear
the intent, the meaning, of thousands of years, the fates of
civilizations, the hopes and fears of a race. To one such as
she he could not even make clear the intent, the meaning,
of the duties which were incumbent upon him. He looked
toward the village. There, as in a cradle, rested a race, a
declining, perishing form of being that was his own. Was

it his role to be only another shepherd of its dying days, to protect it, watching over it, in his turn, as others had in their turn, while it quietly vanished in the darkness of a vast forest, not even noted? He felt great sorrow.

The female rose to a sitting position.

How Brenner then hated her!

You do not understand me, he thought. You cannot understand anything. You are stupid! You understand nothing!

He looked up at her, she sitting there, from where he lay. She had her large, broad head lifted, as though she might be regarding the stars. The wind moved gently in her fur, making tiny ripples in it.

How is it you dare to lift your head in such a way, Brenner thought, as though you were regarding the stars.

I hate "you, he thought.

But you are very beautiful, he thought.

Angrily he stood up. He looked to the village. Then, in anger, in frustration, in loneliness, in desperation, to himself, to the female, to the stars, to the forest, to the moonless sky, he cried out, "I am the father!"

"I am the mother," she said.

CHAPTER 41

"My contract was purchased by Pons," she said. "I was brought from Company Station handcuffed, and on a chain. In the village I was kept muchly gagged, chained in a small box."

"Probably a slave box," said Brenner.

"Perhaps," she said.

"Once I was brought forth to view a large cage, in which was a terrifying animal, that which I now occupy, or am. I was then taken back to my box and placed once more within it."

"You did not know what they intended?"

"Not at that time," she said.

"I sometimes had strange dreams," she said. "I did not understand them."

Brenner nodded.

"Or I thought they were dreams," she said.

"How is that?" asked Brenner. To be sure, he himself had once experienced something like this.

"In one dream," she said, "I dreamed that I was knelt naked before my small captors. I was on several leashes, held to the side and back. I was tightly bound. It was explained to me that I was to be the "mother." I did not understand this."

"What seemed so strange about this dream?" asked Brenner.

"In the morning," she said, "when I awakened, there were rope marks on my body."

"Go on," said Brenner.

"They spoke of a feast of gathering eggs," she said.

"Reproductive cells were removed from your body," said Brenner.

"I gather so," she said, shuddering. "But if Pons are sterile, as I was informed, I thought in my dreams, to what purpose could be their seizure of these cells?"

"It is your understanding, is it not," asked Brenner, "whether from a recollection from your dreams, or whatever, that this feast has been celebrated?"

"Yes," she said.

"Go on," said Brenner.

"I awakened one morning," she said, "in the beast's cage, but it was gone, and I was the beast. I thought that I had gone insane, but I gradually realized what must have occurred."

"Did you have beast memories?" asked Brenner.

"Yes," she said, "of fishing in fast-flowing streams, and such, but they were strangely mingled with my own."

"What was in the cage?" asked Brenner.

"I was in the cage," she said.

"What were you," asked Brenner, "you, or a beast?"

"I was I," she said, "as a beast."

"How long were you kept in the cage?" asked Brenner.

"Three days," she said.

"Long enough for you to understand your helplessness," said Brenner.

"Yes," she said.

"Continue," said Brenner.

"Then, in the darkness, I awakened to a tiny sound. The gate to the cage was open. I fled away, into the forest. There, in a short time, apprised by, startled by, sensations quite new to me, but familiar from my memories, I discovered I was treading in lands that belonged to another. I became frightened, and apprehensive. There was another meaning, too, of course, beyond those of claimancy and territoriality, that of maleness.

Something in my new body, or old memories, found this disturbing. And I, as imprisoned in the beast, was terrified. But I could not help myself. I felt strange heats coming upon me. I knew then I would seek out this beast."

"Did you know it was I?" asked Brenner.

"No," she said. "I assumed it was only a male beast, of the species of which I now was, to be sure, one apparently strong enough and vigorous enough, and terrible enough, to maintain a territory. You can imagine my terror, my misery. I was frightened of this thing. And yet my body, in spite of myself, would have me run panting to it. The rest you know."

"Your feelings must have been frighteningly ambivalent," said Brenner.

"I tried to resist, in my fear, my resentment. Even the beast in me, it seemed, tried to resist for a moment, if only to test the strength and will of the male. But that was a mistake. She was cuffed. She was twice bitten. He did permit her a moment to escape, if she wished, but she did not do so. She remained. He then, this matter clear, drove her to the cliffs, and pulled her to the platform. No longer was there escape for me. I was seized, and I became his mate."

"You realized these things were in accord with the intentions of the Pons?"

"Yes, but I did not understand these intentions. It all seemed madness to me. Perhaps it was some mad joke of Pons, perhaps they found it amusing, to take me, to treat me as they did, to do these things to me, and then, most amusing, to give me over as a mate to a wild beast."

"You understood very little of what was ensuing," said Brenner.

"No," she said. "Indeed, I thought that that was all there was to it, that, for whatever reason, I had merely been given to a beast."

"You were," said Brenner.

"And I bear my fate in joy," she said.

"Would you not have preferred brief silk, and a collar, on a distant world?"

"Had I not met you," she said. "But, you see, I love you."

"Perhaps I might have owned you on such a world."

"I would have striven to be a good slave to you," she said.

"Or to any master," he said.

"Of course," she said.

"We have been put to the purposes of Pons," said Brenner.

"I do not object, as long as I am with you," she said.

"Nor do I," said Brenner, "now that we have one another."

"I do not understand the Pons," she said.

"They are struggling to survive," said Brenner. "Their males are sterile, as you have been informed. Some of their females, apparently, can conceive. They are of our species, or what it could become. We are crossfertile with them. Seed was taken from me, to be implanted in certain females, that the next generation be produced."

"But what of the eggs removed from me?" she asked.

"It seems likely that they will have been fertilized by this time," said Brenner.

"How so?" she asked.

"Doubtless not all my seed was required for the usual purposes of the Pons," he said.

"We could have children," she asked.

"Quite possibly," said Brenner. "Embryos might be raised *in vitro*, as I once was. Pons are aware of such techniques, and, possibly, their technology makes them available to them. More simply, host mothers might be used."

"But why would they do such things?" she asked.

"It might be a kindness toward me, or you, or us," said Brenner. "It might be an experiment. It might be a desperate venture to invigorate their gene pool. It might be all three. It might be something else. Who knows?"

"I am then twice your mate," she said.

"Yes," said Brenner.

"Are you content?" she asked.

"I would not have it otherwise," he said.

"Put your face to my belly," she said.

Puzzled, Brenner did so, placing his snout down to her belly, and then, softly, putting his cheek against that soft, rounded sweetness.

Brenner suddenly sprang back. "It cannot be!" he said.

"Is it so hard to understand?" she asked. "You see, I am indeed twice your mate."

"No!" said Brenner.

"I am the mother," she purred.

"They must be killed," he said. He had felt, against his cheek, stirring, the movement of living creatures, hidden within her.

"Why?" she asked.

"Surely it is clear!" he exclaimed. "They will not be of us. They are of these other bodies. Whatever they are, they are not ours. They are lions. Lions, I tell you. Wild, terrible beasts. Their genes are not ours. They will be alien to us. They are bred for the hunt, the kill."

"They are ours now," she said. "Is the seed within us not ours now, as the memories, the bodies, the limbs, the tongue, and claws?"

"They are not ours!" said Brenner.

"They are from our seed, yours and mine, as we are now," she said. "Thus, they are ours. Or, if you prefer to think of the matter in this manner, we will merely keep them and love them, in memory of those majestic, innocent, lost beasts whose bodies we now occupy. We will care then for our children, or for their children, if you wish, or, perhaps better, simply for the children, who are both ours and theirs."

"They must be killed," said Brenner.

"You will not harm them," she said. "I will defend them with my very life."

"Why?" said Brenner.

"I am the mother," she said.

"It means the end of the Pons, the death of the other children, mine, and ours," said Brenner.

"Not at all," she said.

"It means the end of the pact," said Brenner.

"It means," she said, "a new pact."

Brenner walked away, and turned, and came back.

"You could not kill them," she informed him.

Brenner considered the matter, in confusion, in turmoil. Then he said, "No, I could not kill them."

"We will teach them to speak," she said, confidently.

"They will not have the intelligence for that," he said.

"You have beast memories," she said. "Do they seem those of a stupid animal?"

"No," admitted Brenner.

"They probably just never thought about speaking," she said. "That is really a very unusual sort of thing, not the sort of thing that a beast would be likely to think about. Suppose a baby was raised in the woods. Do you think it would be likely, apart from others doing such things, to think about speaking?"

"I assume not," said Brenner.

"If they cannot form suitable sounds," she said, "we will teach them another way to speak, by use of the head, or paws, or by making marks on the ground, such things."

"We could drive them away, when they come of age," said Brenner.

"Or inform them that they must leave," she said.

"Yes," said Brenner.

"They might come back," she said.

"Woe to the Pons," he said.

"Not necessarily," she said.

"You seem very optimistic," Brenner observed.

"I am a mother," she said.

"I do not understand how this could come about," said Brenner, suddenly.

"Why not?" she asked, puzzled.

"The Pons are not stupid," he said. "They must have understood such a thing could happen."

"I see," she said.

"Of course," said Brenner.

"You were not neutered," she pointed out.

"That would not have made sense, given the intent of the pact," said Brenner. "It would have rendered me more passive, less aggressive, less capable of maintaining, and defending, the territory."

"You are puzzled that I was not spayed?" she said.

"Yes," he said.

"But do you not think that might have made me a less heatable, less excitable, mate for you?" she asked.

Brenner licked his chops. There was no doubt that she was an eager, hot female. To be sure, she had also been such a one before, and extremely so, in her former form, at Company Station. Indeed, so hot had she been that she would have undoubtedly brought an excellent price in a market. Yes, so hot she had been that he had regarded her as fit, even, for the collar.

"Doubtless," he said. "But we are looking at this from the point of view of the Pons.

"In any event," she said, "obviously it was not done."

Brenner considered the matter. The beast at least once had to have been completely at the Pons' mercy. And surely the Pons must have realized that its fertility might jeopardize the stewardship, the guardianship, the pact! Even if they did not expect her to prey upon Pons, they surely could not guarantee that of the fruit of her body. Surely the Pons, as calculating and efficient as they were, would have protected themselves against such perilous eventualities! Doubtless, he would have supposed, that that lovely, fierce, sinuous, feline body, having fallen into the hands of Pons, would be incapable of its own replication, that that would have been surgically assured. But obviously, it had not been.

"No," said Brenner. "Obviously it was not done."

"Why?" she asked.

"Yes," said Brenner. "Why?"

"Do you think the Pons are stupid?" she asked.

"No," he said. "I do not think that they are stupid."

"I am hungry," she said.

"I will hunt," he said. "Do you wish to accompany me?"

"Certainly," she said.

"You could remain here," he said. "I could bring something back."

"I will come with you," she said.

"You are hungry?" he asked.

"Yes," she said.

"I see," he said.

"You must remember," she said, nuzzling him, pushing playfully against him, "I am now eating for several."

In a few minutes they were in the forest. They stopped near the village, but stayed back, concealed by the trees.

"Why do you think the Pons have done what they have done?" she asked.

"That they are putting themselves at risk?"

"Yes," she said.

"I think," said Brenner, "that they are willing to try. I think that they want to begin again."

Their hunt was successful. On the way back to their lair they stopped again, their jaws bloody, near the village. They listened closely.

"Do you hear it?" she asked.

"Yes," he said.

Within the village, tiny, and as though far off, they could hear the sounds of new life.

CHAPTER 42

And so, from time to time, Pons, and others, came to
gather at the platform, to gaze upward at a shaggy beast
who, at times, was silent, letting its presence be its message,
and, at other times, when so moved, would speak to them.
Beside this beast, usually recumbent, was another. And, here
and there, upon occasion, there were other beasts about,
too, sometimes on the platform, sometimes playing behind
it. Some of these beasts would accompany the Pons, and
the others, back to the village. The string remained where it
was but, after a time, the Pons, and the others, did not pay
so much attention to it. With their small weapons, made
by themselves, the string, and even the guardianship, and
the pact, was not so important. Indeed, sometimes, some
of them, over the years, left the string altogether, and went
away, to various places in the woods, to make their own
villages. Often these were accompanied by a beast or two.
These sorts of things were little noted at Company Station,
where the lighters continued to lift off from, and later return
to, their launching pads, servicing the freighters, and, later,
sometimes, the liners, paused above the station, so high as
to be invisible. A thousand years later an expedition to the
Pons was disappointed to learn that they were no longer
totemistic, but had rather, it seemed, moved to a different
cultural level, perhaps that of gods and heroes. One of these
gods, or heroes, as the case might be, had the unlikely name

'Rodriguez'. To be sure, the Pons were an interesting life form in various ways. For one thing they appeared to have become involved in an interesting symbiotic development, an unusual relationship with beasts. This was not investigated in any detail because of the dangers of doing so. It was mostly remarked upon from a distance. As it was said, the children of the Pons walked with beasts, and had become, in some ways, like unto their brothers, the lions. In another thousand years some of these unusual groupings, those of Pons and beasts, departed from Abydos, to settle upon and, some said, even to claim, far-flung worlds.

About the Author

John Norman, born in Chicago, Illinois, in 1931, is the creator of the Gorean Saga, the longest running series of adventure novels in science fiction history. Starting in December 1966 with *Tarnsman of Gor*, the series was put on hold after its twenty-fifth installment, *Magicians of Gor*, in 1988, when DAW refused to publish its successor, *Witness of Gor*. After several unsuccessful attempts to find a trade publishing outlet, the series was brought back into print in 2001. Norman has also produced a separate, three installment science fiction series, the Telnarian Histories, plus two other fiction works (*Ghost Dance* and *Time Slave*), a nonfiction paperback (*Imaginative Sex*), and a collection of thirty short stories, entitled Norman *Invasions*. The *Totems of Abydos* was published in spring 2012.

All of Norman's work is available both in print and as ebooks. The Internet has proven to be a fertile ground for the imagination of Norman's ever-growing fan base, and at Gor Chronicles (www.gorchronicles.com), a website specially created for his tremendous fan following, one may read everything there is to know about this unique fictional culture.

Norman is married and has three children.

OPEN ROAD
INTEGRATED MEDIA

Open Road Integrated Media is a digital publisher and multimedia content company. Open Road creates connections between authors and their audiences by marketing its ebooks through a new proprietary online platform, which uses premium video content and social media.

Videos, Archival Documents, and New Releases

Sign up for the Open Road Media newsletter and get news delivered straight to your inbox.

Sign up now at
www.openroadmedia.com/newsletters

www.ingramcontent.com/pod-product-compliance
Lightning Source LLC
Chambersburg PA
CBHW032254020726
47495CB00001B/103